QUANTUM MURDER

Also by Lesley L. Smith

Temporal Dreams
Neutrino Warning
Kat Cubed
Reality Alternatives
Conservation of Luck

The Quantum Cop Series:
Book 1: *The Quantum Cop*
Book 2: *Quantum Murder*
Book 3*: Quantum Mayhem*

The Space Operetta Series
Book 1*: A Jack By Any Other Name*
Book 2*: A Jack In The Dark*
Book 3*: A Jack For All Seasons*

Quantum Murder

By Lesley L. Smith

Quarky Media

Boulder Colorado

Quantum Murder

Published by Quarky Media, PO Box 3332, Boulder, CO 80307

ISBN: 978-0-9861350-5-7 (ebook)
ISBN: 978-0-9861350-4-0 (print)

QUANTUM MURDER

Chapter One

My morning was going great until I got arrested for murder.

First, at eight forty-five Saturday morning, there was no line for coffee at Boulder Brews. I swooped right up to the counter and ordered cinnamon bun coffee and a cinnamon bun to go with it. That was lucky. I couldn't believe I didn't have to wait; the place was usually a madhouse this time of day. At any rate, I was on a roll—no pun intended.

I walked across campus, sipping, nibbling, and enjoying the views of the Italianate sandstone buildings with Mediterranean red tile roofs. The sun peeked through the clouds. Sunshine illuminated the leaves in shades of yellow, brown, and orange, transforming them into brilliant stained glass. A breeze caressed my face as a few golden leaves floated down to the ground. One leaf smacked me in the face, but it didn't hit my coffee or my cinnamon roll, so no worries.

What a beautiful day.

I tromped up the many stairs to my tiny office in Gamow Tower, skirting the electron double-slit experiment I'd set up in the hall. The hallway was an unusual place to set up an experiment, but I'd discovered this floor was basically deserted—except for the physicist in the office next door, Andro, also known as my boyfriend.

Maybe today, I'd finally come up with the perfect title for the paper I'd been writing. I sat down at my desk. I'd had a scientific breakthrough in the last year when I discovered how to use quantum mechanics to shape reality. This ability was based on the von Neumann-Wigner Interpretation, which said a person observing a system changes the system. I'd discovered a unique combination of specialized knowledge combined with adrenaline enabled me to collapse the wavefunction to instantiate the reality I wanted. I called this q-lapsing.

I'd managed to explain it to some people, but, overall, hardly anyone believed me. It was a real shame because, theoretically, it might be able to solve a lot of the world's problems−like war and famine. The non-believers included the physics journals. Every time I submitted a paper, the referee said something like, "Bullshit." The last title I'd tried was *Macroscopic Proof of Schrödinger's Cat Experiment.*

I couldn't go to the public directly by calling a press conference and showing off my ability because the scientific community frowned on that type of thing. Those poor cold fusion scientists had been totally blackballed. I didn't want to be them.

"Hmm." I sipped my coffee and looked at the document on my computer. I needed to be more subtle. Sadly, subtle was not something I did well.

A knock on my open office door made me jump. "Hey, babe," Andro said.

I grinned as I took in his easy smile and mesmerizing blue eyes. I couldn't help it. "Hey, babe."

He walked toward me, and I jumped up for a kiss. As our lips met, a warm tingle spread all over my body. "Mmm." Maybe we should go over to his place and do a biology experiment.

I forced myself to quit thinking about how my body fit perfectly with his and come back to the here and now. I sat down at my desk. "What do you think of *Empirical Tests of the von Neumann-Wigner Interpretation?*"

"I think we should go out to brunch," he said. "It's nine a.m. Saturday morning. You have to take time off occasionally. You've been working too hard. I'm worried about you."

I was torn between my two favorite things: physics and food. And Andro. My three favorite things.

When I didn't answer immediately, he added, "Pancakes?" He knew I loved pancakes.

"I'm in! Just let me type something." I quickly input the new title, finished my cinnamon roll, and slurped up the last of my coffee.

He sighed. "Are you ready?"

"In a sec. I just want to read over this one thing." It was

almost perfect now.

"Why don't I go get the car, and you can keep working for a little while? I'll call when I'm by the door." Even university faculty had to park far, far away from where we wanted to be on campus.

"Sounds great," I said, still staring at the screen. I edited the paper until my cell rang.

"I'm on the street right near the south building exit," Andro said.

"Excellent! I'll be right there." With my new paper title and pancakes on the horizon, the day was looking even better. I grabbed my purse and headed for the door.

When I stepped into the dimly lit hall, I was very surprised to see a man standing there near the door to the stairs. He was balding and wore a dark suit complete with a tie. The suit and tie were odd. Few men in Boulder wore a suit. Who knew Gamow Tower was so popular early Saturday morning?

The man approached me. "Who are you?" he asked. "Do you have ID?"

I smiled. "It's okay. I work here. I'm Professor Martin."

A second man stepped out of the stairwell, this one wearing a Boulder PD uniform. I recognized him with his shaved head and firm muscles—the quintessential hot cop.

"Ben?" I asked. "What are you doing here?"

Ben didn't answer. In hindsight, that was probably not a good sign.

The first man said, "Professor Madison Martin, the Quantum Cop lady?" Only a select few people, law enforcement officers mostly, knew that. Ben was one of those officers. He must have spilled the beans to this other guy. The mystery guy must be some kind of plainclothes detective.

I nodded. "Yep. That's me." Last year, I'd been dubbed the Quantum Cop when I used quantum mechanics to help the Boulder PD and the FBI catch some nefarious criminals. I conveniently shied away from thinking those same criminals started out as my quantum mechanics students. "Is there something I can help you guys with? I'd be happy to help. Wait. Has there been a quantum crime?"

I thought I'd stamped out all the quantum crime. If it was

starting up again, that could be bad. That could be very bad. "What happened?"

"Professor Martin," the detective said, "what are you doing here in the physics building?"

"I'm working," I said.

The two men exchanged looks. "On a Saturday? First thing in the morning?" the detective said.

"Yeah," I said. I was starting to get a bad feeling about this. "I work every day. Why do you care what I'm doing?"

"Can you account for your whereabouts for the last few hours?" the detective said.

He asked that like I was some kind of suspect. "Er," I said. Apparently, I was kind of slow before my morning ration of pancakes. "What? Why? What's going on?"

"Well, Ms. Martin?" the detective asked.

"It's Dr. Martin," I said. "What was the question?" I turned my attention to Ben. "Hi, Ben." I smiled. We were sort of friends. At least I thought we were. "What's going on?"

He shook his head and wouldn't meet my eyes.

"I'll ask you again, what are you doing here?" the detective said, sizing me up.

I gulped. "What exactly are you guys doing here?"

"We had an anonymous tip that you murdered someone with quantum mechanics," he said. "Don't try any of that quantum funny business on us, Dr. Martin."

"Murder!" I said. "Oh, my God! That's horrible. Wait. Who's been murdered?" It wasn't Andro, was it? No, it couldn't be; I just talked to him on the phone.

"I didn't murder anyone," I said. Was something sucking the air out of Gamow Tower? I leaned against the wall. Breathe, Madison.

My cell rang, and everyone jumped.

I reached for it, but the detective pointed at Ben. "Officer Willis, please get it."

Ben took the phone out of my hand, answered it and said, "She can't talk right now." He turned it off.

That was rude. "Was it Andro?" Ben didn't answer. I bet it was. I wished I was with Andro now, downstairs, outside, in the fresh air. Where a person could breathe.

I was glad I was leaning against the wall because my limbs felt weak and tingly. "Who was killed?"

They didn't answer me.

"I'm not a murderer," I said. "How do you know it was murder by quantum mechanics?" It had to be some kind of mistake. I'd never fainted, but I suspected this was what it felt like. Get a grip, Mad. "I refuse to cooperate unless you tell me more." It couldn't be murder by q-lapsing. As soon as I explained that to them, they'd have to let me go, right?

"I know it's not exactly protocol, but we could show her, sir," Ben said to the detective.

"Yes," I said. "Let me see the scene. I can explain that it couldn't have been q-lapsing. I'll answer whatever questions you want if I can see the crime scene." It had to be a mistake. Maybe they were wrong, and it wasn't even murder.

The detective stared at Ben for a few moments and then turned his gaze to me. "All right."

"Where is it?" I asked. "How far away? Can I call my boyfriend while we're driving there?"

"No," the detective said. That didn't seem right. Of course, none of this seemed right.

They led me down the stairs to the first floor of the physics building. We started walking north down the hall. A bunch of uniformed cops loitered at the end of the hall near the exit.

Uh oh. "It happened here in the physics building?" I asked. "A physicist was murdered?" It made slightly more sense that they thought I'd done it. Slightly. As far as they knew, I was the only other person here on a Saturday.

"In here," the detective pointed into an office near the end of the hall.

As I peeked around the cops clustered near the door, I saw a shoe attached to a leg, attached to a torso, attached to …a mess. The poor man's torso, head, and one arm had huge chunks missing, and the edges of what was left had the most hideous texture like they had been dissolved by acid or something.

I felt hot and sweaty. My stomach roiled, and I tried to tamp it down through sheer force of will. No go. I lost my morning coffee and cinnamon roll in an explosive and embarrassing fashion, splashing all over the shoes of the uniformed officer standing next to me. "Oh, no," I moaned.

I think he moaned as well, albeit for a different reason.

I couldn't look at the victim again, but the image was seared into my brain. From about the waist down, he looked fine. But above that...

My stomach heaved again. My hands shook and got fuzzy as if I subconsciously was trying to change reality by undoing this unspeakable thing.

It was hard to even wrap my head around the state of the body. I'd never seen or even heard of anything like it.

The plainclothes detective said to one of the uniformed officers, "Take her in."

The officer got out his handcuffs. "Dr. Madison Martin, you are wanted for questioning in the murder of Dr. Barry King." Barry King? I never even heard of the guy.

"What?" I said. "No. I didn't murder anyone. I'm not a murderer." It was hard to breathe. I was definitely getting fuzzy. Calm down. Breathe. "You can't arrest me. I didn't do anything." I couldn't understand what was happening. They thought I was a murderer?

But I didn't look like a murderer. I was medium height and medium build. I was blonde. I looked like a soccer mom, for God's sake! I wasn't a mom, and I couldn't play soccer, but that was beside the point. Ugh. Focus, Mad.

The detective said. "The tipster said you murdered someone with quantum mechanics, and the body was here. We found you in the same building. You're the world expert on quantum mechanics, and the victim clearly died from something out-of-the-ordinary. You promised you'd cooperate if we showed you the body."

Wow, was that a mistake. But I was too nauseous to argue.

I sat in the empty interrogation room at the police station, still having trouble breathing. Breathe in. Breathe out. In. Out. I wasn't a murderer. How could they think I was a murderer?

Focus on something else. My day was going better than the dead man's. It was sad he was dead, and it was especially sad he'd died in such a horrible way. Who was he? Did he love someone? Did they love him? Did his loved ones know he was gone? Were they mourning him even now? My eyes filled.

Poor guy. No one deserved that. My tears escaped, running down my face. I leaned my head on my arms on the table and let my sleeves soak up my tears.

This wasn't helping. Maybe focus on something else?

When would my lawyer get here?

I lifted my head. The room had white cinder-block walls, a large two-way mirror, and a rickety table and chairs. There was a puddle of liquid under the mirror. What was that from? Tears? Pee? Ick. At least wondering made me stop crying.

I knew I didn't kill the guy. That meant there was a murderer running around in town. Were other people in danger?

Did the killer really use quantum mechanics to kill him? I didn't understand how what I saw, ugh, could be the result of q-lapsing.

Unfortunately, the best q-lapser besides me was Andro, and then probably my grad student Alyssa. Andro and Alyssa were also physicists, like me. Physicists seemed to have an easier time controlling reality, probably because they understood the concepts of quantum mechanics better.

There used to be two more good q-lapsers, my former quantum mechanics students, but they were gone now.

But before they were foiled, they made a webpage explaining how to control reality using quantum mechanics, www. controlreality.info. Who knew who might have seen that or how far it might have propagated around the internet? Potentially, there were too many suspects. I just needed to explain all this to the cops--without implicating anyone. Surely, they could see reason.

Ben stopped by the room, and I wiped my face. "Is my lawyer coming?" I asked. "This has to be some kind of mistake. And I'm worried other people might be in danger."

"The detective doesn't think it's a mistake," he said. "He thinks we've contained the danger." I couldn't tell what Ben thought. "Did you ask for a lawyer?" he said, all business. I knew from my previous dealings with him that his strictly-by-the-book behavior was sometimes at odds with his big heart.

I stood up. "You guys accused me of murder, so, yeah, I

called my lawyer."

"Then, I can't talk to you until your lawyer gets here."

"Oh." Disappointed, I looked down. "Can you tell me about the deceased? Did you guys say his name was Larry? There are hundreds of employees associated with the Physics Department. I didn't know the guy."

Ben smiled a mirthless smile. "Now that I really can't tell you about."

"Oh. I understand." But not really. I didn't understand any of this. I looked Ben in the eyes. Somehow, I didn't think he'd give me the answers I needed. "What are you doing here, anyway, if you can't talk to me?" I asked him.

"Just because I can't talk doesn't mean I don't want to." He shuffled his feet. "You're the Quantum Cop, after all. I can't believe you'd..." He trailed off. "I should go." He left me alone with my thoughts.

Dammit.

Chapter Two

After what seemed like an eternity in the interrogation room, Ben escorted my lawyer, Tom Clark, into the room. Tom was wearing a brown suit and looking rather rumpled. I guessed he wasn't expecting to do business first thing Saturday morning.

"Tom," I said. "I'm glad to see you. Are you here to get me off?"

"Get you out," he said. "Not get you off."

Ugh.

Tom nodded weakly. "Sort of. I'm going to try anyway." He sat next to me.

"Sort of? Try? What does that mean?" I asked.

Tom shut up as the balding black-suited detective entered the room and sat down at the table. "Ms. Martin, I see your lawyer finally got here." They didn't introduce themselves to each other. Had they done it outside? I really wished I knew the detective's name. It was awkward to keep thinking of him as 'the detective.'

"It's Dr. Martin," I said, but Tom poked me and shook his head.

"What were you doing in the physics building this morning?" the detective asked.

"I already answered that question," I said.

"Please just cooperate, Madison," Tom said.

What had I said before? I needed to agree with what I said earlier, right? So I wouldn't look suspicious. "Er." My mind was totally blank. I couldn't remember what I'd said before. I was just going to have to tell the truth. "I went up to my office to do some work."

"Dr. Martin," the detective said, "you expect me to believe a university professor doesn't know what day of the week it is?"

"I know what day of the week it is," I said. "It's Saturday. I basically work every day. Everyone who knows me knows that." Oh no. The mysterious tipster must know me. Was the tipster the murderer?

I still couldn't believe someone had been murdered in such a horrible way.

The detective cleared his throat. "And when did you discover the body?"

"I didn't discover the body," I said. "You guys discovered the body. I was working. Until you guys showed it to me."

Tom and the detective exchanged looks over the table.

"Didn't notice it?" the detective asked. "Didn't you smell it when you walked by?" Now that he mentioned it, I was reminded of the horrific smell when he showed me the corpse. Ugh. I definitely would have noticed that earlier if I'd been anywhere near the body.

"She's sort of hopeless," Tom said. "No powers of observation whatsoever."

The detective turned to him. "But I thought she helped solve a case last year?"

"Yeah. She helped the FBI with the physics. The agents handled the actual investigation."

"I'm not an idiot," I said. "I didn't enter the building that way. I came in from the south."

Tom poked me again, which I interpreted to mean, *Be quiet.*

"But she's the only one who can do that quantum stuff, right?" the detective asked.

I opened my mouth.

Tom said, "You plead the Fifth Amendment on that, Madison."

I do? I examined him.

"Ms. Martin?" the detective asked.

"Yeah. I plead the Fifth Amendment," I said. That's why I was paying Tom, after all, to get his advice. Oh, crap. I had to pay Tom, and I didn't have any money.

"Can I ask, do you have any physical evidence to tie Madison to the crime?" Tom asked.

The detective just looked at him. I had a feeling that was his version of pleading the Fifth.

"Any motive for Madison to do the crime?" Tom asked.

"How do you do that quantum stuff, Ms. Martin?" the detective asked.

"I plead the Fifth."

"What did you have against the deceased, Ms. Martin?" the detective asked.

I didn't even know who the poor dead guy was. My mind flashed back on his corpse, and my stomach turned. "Who was he?"

Tom raised his eyebrows at the detective. "I think we're done here, or are you charging Dr. Martin?"

The detective frowned. After a few moments, he placed his palms on the table and levered himself out of his chair. "Don't leave town." He walked out, leaving the door open.

"I don't get it," I said. "What just happened?"

"They're not charging you yet," Tom said.

"Yet?" I didn't shriek.

"You're still the prime suspect," Tom said. "They're going to try to collect evidence to build a case and prove you did it." He turned and looked at me. "You didn't do it, did you?"

"No, I didn't do it!"

"Then, you're fine," Tom said. "Probably."

"Probably!"

"Yeah. You're lucky," Tom said.

"Lucky?" I said. "I'm lucky I got arrested for murder? I don't think so." I didn't feel lucky.

"You weren't actually arrested," he said.

It sure felt like I'd been. But there was no point in feeling sorry for myself. The person we should be feeling sorry for was the victim.

I swallowed and asked, "So, what happens next?"

Tom said, "The police will investigate the murder and determine if proof is evident or presumption great that you committed the crime. In this case, the crime is murder."

This did not sound good. I felt the blood drain from my brain. "What happens if it is evident or great or whatever you said?"

Tom grimaced at me. "Then, you get arrested and charged

and go to trial."

I felt the blood drain from the rest of my head. It was hard to breathe with no blood in your head.

He shook his head. His head must have felt fine. "What are they thinking? Don't they know you help law enforcement?"

"I guess they're thinking I'm the only person they know of that could commit this crime--if it was done with quantum mechanics. And they found me in the same building as the body."

"Are you the only one who can kill with quantum mechanics, Madison?" he asked.

I shook my head. "I'm not convinced the poor victim was killed by quantum mechanics. Quantum mechanics isn't magic. There has to be a non-zero probability something will occur to make it occur with quantum mechanics."

"Let's assume for the moment it was quantum mechanics. Who else can do it?"

"There's A–" I stopped talking. There was Andro and Alyssa, but there was no way I'd implicate them. Besides, I knew they wouldn't do something like this. They were good people, not cold-blooded murderers. It had to be someone else.

"A who?" Tom asked with skeptical eyes.

"All those FBI agents I was teaching about quantum mechanics earlier last year," I said. "Like Agent Baker."

He frowned. "They can, what do you call it, q-lapse?"

My lips turned down to match his expression. "Well, technically, no. One of them, Baker, almost can. I saw her get blurry once, anyway. No one else seemed to figure it out. We stopped the q-lapsing classes when we stopped the quantum criminals last year."

"Don't worry, Madison," he said. "They didn't charge you this time. And when you're charged next time, I'll try to get you out on bail."

Wait a minute. "Next time? Try?" I said with a squeak. This whole thing was a nightmare.

He nodded.

This was really happening; I was under investigation for murder. As we walked to the front of the police station, I had to focus on breathing, so I didn't pass out. Or end up in quantum limbo. Quantum limbo was a terrifying white fog of unrealized possibilities. My hypothesis was it occurred when many possible realities competed with each other, chaotically blinking into existence. Unfortunately, I'd experienced it before. Hopefully, never again.

"So, Tom, can you give me a ride home?" I asked once we got outside.

"If you promise not to get into any more trouble," he said.

I held up my right hand and arranged my fingers. "Scout's honor. I'll be good."

"I think that's the Vulcan greeting you're making," Tom said. "Not the Boy Scout sign."

I was kind of impressed that my lawyer knew the difference between the Vulcan greeting and the Boy Scout sign. Not everyone knew that. Me, for instance. He must be a really good lawyer. Or a Boy Scout. Or a Vulcan.

He pressed his lips into a line. "Yeah. I can give you a ride home, but you're on the clock." As we went out to his car, he said, "That's me, Tom Clark, lawyer, and taxi driver."

He looked so pathetic I almost grinned, but I didn't think he'd appreciate it. Instead, I said, "Thanks, Tom. I appreciate your help."

As soon as we got in the car, I called Andro.

He answered with, "What's going on, Madison? Are you all right? Who answered your phone? What are the police doing at the physics building? They wouldn't let back me in."

"I'm okay." Sort of. "There was a murder on campus."

"Murder! Oh, no. Who was it? And what does it have to do with you?"

"I don't know who it was," I said.

In the driver's seat, Tom shook his head.

"The cops think he was killed by q-lapsing, so they sort of arrested me." I winced as I said it. Andro said I tended to get myself into too much trouble.

"Q-lapsing?" He was quiet for a few moments, which I knew probably meant he was trying to stop himself from saying something like *I told you so*. Finally, he said, "But if you're calling me, you must be out?"

"Yeah. I guess they're building their case." Don't dwell on that, Mad. I paused. "So, pancakes?"

"I'm sorry," he said. "I'm not up for it now. I have to do something. Personal."

Personal? What could he be doing of a personal nature that he couldn't tell me about? We'd been dating for almost a year. "Okay," I said slowly.

"But I'm glad you're all right," he said. "We'll get through this like we've gotten through everything else." We had gone through a lot, including fighting for our lives last year when we defeated the q-criminals. We'd both thought all that was over. "Love you, babe."

"Love you, babe," I said. But he'd already disconnected.

"Huh," I said as I hung up. "Andro was a little off." He was usually very loving and nurturing, not secretive.

Tom shrugged.

I lived with my cousin Ryan, the Chief of the University Police, and his wife and baby daughter.

When I got home, the front door was newly-bedecked with a wreath of pumpkins. It made the little brick ranch home look very festive. Inside, the living room was filled with box upon box of orange something-or-others. Ryan's wife, Sydney, a petite brunette, half-immersed in one of said boxes, seemed surprised to see me. Sydney was the Boulder version of Martha Stewart—her natural-fiber clothes always looked immaculate, and her organic vegan meals were delicious. She straightened up suddenly. "Madison! What are you doing here?"

Ugh. She probably knew I was arrested. For murder. Maybe she'd ask me to leave her home. I couldn't blame her. "Where's Emily?" I asked, cleverly changing the subject. Emily was their one-year-old daughter. She was currently nowhere in sight.

"Huh." Sydney looked back and forth. "She was right there." A large pile of stuffed orange pumpkins jiggled. "Emily!" Sydney leaned over the pile, pushing pumpkins aside to reveal her daughter wearing an all-orange ensemble featuring *Mama's ghoul* on her t-shirt. She smiled as Sydney picked her up and cradled her in her arms. "Don't do that to mama. You scared me."

Emily seemed to enjoy the attention. She seemed perfect. I was totally unbiased, too. And not just because she was totally adorable and I had helped her come into this world.

Sydney turned back to me. "Why are you home so early?"

"Why? What have you heard?" I asked.

"Is there something to hear?" She furrowed her brow. "Why are you acting so odd?"

Maybe she didn't know I'd been arrested, after all.

"Wait a minute," she said. "You aren't why Ryan had to rush out of here, are you? He was supposed to help me decorate."

I chose my words carefully. "No. I am not the reason Ryan had to rush out of here. I am very sorry to say there was a...." I gulped.

"Yes? A what?" she asked.

"A murder."

Sydney gasped, and her hand flew in front of her mouth. "Oh, no!"

"A murder on campus," I finally finished.

"How horrible. Not one of the students, I hope!" she said.

"No. It was a faculty member." I realized I didn't actually know. "Or a staff scientist in the physics department. I think he was some kind of scientist, but I'm not sure."

"Did you know him?" she asked. "Or her?"

"It was a man. I don't think I know, er, knew him." I shook my head.

Sydney started to put Emily in her bouncy chair. "Are you even sure the victim was associated with the university?"

I sat down on the couch. Was I sure? "His body was found at the university, but, no. I guess not."

She finished buckling Emily in. "I wonder if he had a family."

I had no idea. My mind flashed back to the grisly sight on the office floor. I could only pray if he had a family, they'd never see him like that. I wished I could push the image out of my mind, but I had a feeling it'd be with me for a long, long time.

"Madison? Are you all right?" She stood up. "You look sick."

"I'm okay, sort of. I saw the body. The poor man. He was killed by--"

I deliberately looked at Emily to replace the horrible image with an adorable image. I swallowed.

Sydney waited for me to get my act together.

"They think he was killed by quantum mechanics," I said.

"Oh," Sydney said. She knew none of this was good.

I looked away from her and plunged the rest of the way into the truth. "I was actually arrested for the, uh, murder. Because they had some kind of tip that I did it. But they didn't charge me." I didn't add: yet.

Sydney's forehead was all wrinkly again. "So they think you're a murderer?"

"Yeah." I looked at Emily again. I'd never ever do anything to hurt her, but was Sydney one hundred percent sure of that? "I understand if you want me to leave. I can get some things together in a couple of minutes and be out of your hair." My chest suddenly felt like the atmospheric pressure was about a million millibars.

Sydney sat down next to me on the couch and touched my arm. "No. Ryan trusts and loves you like a sister. I personally saw you save his life last year." She was referring to my quantum duel with a student where I shot him to stop him from hurting Ryan. I still felt guilty about putting Ryan and his family in danger. I still felt guilty about shooting the student even though I'd had to do it. Honestly, I also felt guilty about getting my student involved in q-lapsing. It had led to his ultimate downfall.

"And you saved Emily, too, when the umbilical cord was wrapped around her neck," she said softly. It had been one of my first successful attempts at q-lapsing. She continued, "I could never believe you'd murder someone in cold blood. You're like a sister to me, too."

I couldn't help it, my eyes filled. "Thank you," I whispered. "I appreciate that. You're like a sister to me, too."

Sydney got a little teary-eyed, as well.

There was some hugging.

After a few minutes, Sydney sniffed and said, "Well, I know just what will cheer you up—decorating for Halloween."

Turned out she was right.

Sydney and I were basking in an orange glow, literally, Saturday evening when Ryan finally got home. There were several strings of orange jack-o-lantern lights in the family room, along with various and sundry pumpkins, scary cobwebs, giant black spiders and bats and rats, and witch cut-outs. Personally, I thought Sydney had gone a little overboard, but I did feel much better.

Ryan skidded to a halt just inside the front door. "It looks like the Great Pumpkin exploded in here."

Sydney jumped off the couch. "Madison was kind enough to help me decorate, even if you weren't."

Ryan squinted in my general direction. "Madison? Sydney, did she tell you what happened today?"

I sort of ducked down on the couch, trying to look unobtrusive.

Sydney frowned. "Someone was murdered on campus? It's horrible."

Ryan nodded and rubbed his five-o'clock-shadow face. He sat down on the couch next to me. "I'm sorry I couldn't help you decorate, Sydney. It's been an awful day. I saw things."

Sadly, I knew exactly what he meant.

He turned to me. "So, Madison."

I cringed. Was this when he asked me to leave?

"Can you help me figure out who did this?" he asked.

This was not what I was expecting. "What?" Where was the yelling? Where was the ranting and raving? Where was the blaming me?

"Whose jurisdiction is the case?" Sydney asked.

Ryan said, "We've never had a murder on campus before. Boulder PD wants the case. But it was on my watch. I feel bad about it. And I'm looking pretty bad now, too. There are rumblings. My job might be on the line. If I could solve the murder, it'd do a lot for my credibility. Not to mention Madison's credibility."

My earlier heart-to-heart with Sydney was still on my mind. I appreciate Ryan looking out for me. "You're like a bro to me, bro." I punched him lightly on the arm.

He sighed. "Back at 'cha, Mad." Did he just call me a brother? "So, will you help me?"

I swallowed. "Of course, I'll help. Whatever I can do, I will. I'd do anything for you guys." Their support and belief in me was touching. It was a lifeline in the middle of all this horror.

I wouldn't let them down. I was going to find the real killer, bring him to justice, help save Ryan's job, and prove my innocence.

Chapter Three

On Sunday, I went over to The Pancake House because I was dying for pancakes, probably since I was supposed to go out with Andro on Saturday and didn't. It smelled great inside, like coffee and syrup and, well, pancakes.

I hadn't heard from Andro since our strange phone call yesterday, which was unusual. But he was the one who acted strange, so he needed to call me and not be strange. He needed to explain what his personal business was. That was my story, and I was sticking to it, for the moment anyway. Pesky details like the fact that I was the one who'd gotten into trouble again didn't enter into it.

Bottom line: my mood would improve when my stomach was full of pancake.

As I was waiting in the inevitable line to be seated, I thought I spied the familiar evil face of a (dead) quantum criminal through the crowd, namely, a handsome twenty-two-year-old man of Italian ancestry. When I looked closer, it seemed to blur and disappear. Shit. Maybe I just had low blood coffee. Yeah, that had to be it. I marched right over and procured one of those small free cups of java for wait-ers.

Then, I spotted a familiar, not-evil close-shaven head in the dining room. Casually, I rambled over through the dining room to see if it was who I thought it was, namely, Ben, aka hot cop.

It was. Out of uniform, he still looked buff. And it was a perfect opportunity for me to do some detective work to help Ryan and myself.

I smoothed my t-shirt. "Gosh, hi, Ben," I said with a big smile.

"Hey, Quantum Cop," he said, smiling and showing off his

laugh lines. Wow, I hadn't noticed before how warm his smile was. He was a good-looking man. "How's it going? Still out of jail?"

I chuckled. "Apparently."

"What are you doing here this fine morning?" he asked, rubbing his palm along his firm chest. That looked fun.

Why was I here? Oh, yeah. "I'm here for breakfast, but there's a really big line to be seated." I smiled and pointed over toward the front door. "Guess I'll be waiting for a while. Gosh, it's too bad 'cause I'm hungry." C'mon Ben, get a clue. "Yep. I'm soo hungry."

He shifted in his booth. "I haven't gotten my food yet. You could join me."

"Really?" I feigned surprise. "Gosh, that would be nice." Maybe I was overdoing the goshes. I slid onto the bench opposite him. "So, what did you order? What's good here?" As if I didn't know everything was good.

"I ordered their specialty, the giant Dutch apple pancake." He exhaled. "That's why it's taking so long."

I caught the server's eye, and she came over, all bouncy brunette-ness of her. "Oh, are you joining him?" She looked at Ben for confirmation.

He nodded. Did she look disappointed?

"Just a sec." She went off to get something or other. I hoped it was coffee. I quickly slurped down the rest of my free cup.

The waitress came back with napkin-wrapped silverware, a menu, a coffee cup, and a carafe of coffee. She was earning a giant tip so far.

"Thanks," I said as she poured. I didn't open the menu. "What can I get fast in the pancake family?" I asked.

"Dollar pancakes?" she said.

"Sounds great," I said, giving her back the menu. "Bring me a bunch of them."

"Yes, ma'am," she said, smiling brightly.

Ugh. She ma'amed me. I hated that.

"What's wrong, Madison?" Ben asked.

"I'm just so worried about my murder arrest," I said, changing gears and gazing into his eyes. I'd never noticed them before. They were surprisingly warm and kind—like a puppy. I liked puppies.

"How worried can you be if you're out eating pancakes?" he said.

"Good point." I was trying to soften him up so I could pump him for information.

My cell rang. It was Andro. I answered eagerly. I'd been waiting to hear from him since yesterday. "Hi," I said.

"Who is it, Madison?" Ben asked.

"Madison? Who are you with? Is that the same guy who answered your phone yesterday?" Andro demanded.

"Technically, yes," I said, glancing at Ben.

"What the hell is going on?" Andro said.

"Relax, Andro. It's not like I've seen him naked," I said.

Ben got an embarrassed goofy grin on his face.

Oh, yeah. I did see Ben naked at that frat party a while back, but it was a quantum mishap. "Er, I mean, yeah, I may have seen him naked, but–"

I heard a click.

"But so have you," I said. "Andro?" He'd hung up. Shit.

"Trouble?" Ben asked.

"Nothing serious." I hoped.

It wasn't like Andro to hang up on me. What was up with him? He'd been acting unusual since this whole horrible murder started. I took a sip of coffee to regroup. Just now, Andro was acting jealous. That was good, right? It meant he cared, right? I'd just have to deal with him later.

"So, anyway, I am worried about the murder charge," I said. "Have you heard anything about the case?"

Ben shifted a little. "I'm not supposed to discuss it."

"Can you tell me anything about the victim? Larry?"

Ben stared at me.

"Did he have any enemies? Are there any suspects?" I asked. "Besides me?"

Ben stared at me for a few more moments, and then took a sip of his water, and then stared at me some more. Finally, he said, "You think the guy that was murdered was named Larry?"

"Yeah. I don't really recall exactly what the police said. I was pretty upset. That whole scene was kind of a blur." Ugh. No pun intended. Q-lapsing often involved things getting blurry.

"The victim was named Barry King," Ben said slowly and carefully. "Does the name ring a bell?"

I thought for a moment and shook my head. "No. I don't think I know, er, knew him. Did he work in the physics department?"

"Yes." He paused.

"He did? What did he do?" I asked.

"I'm not supposed to discuss it," Ben said.

"What difference does it make if you tell me or if I go home and Google him?"

He shifted in the booth again. "Well, okay. Barry was a post-doc. That means he was−"

"I know what it means," I said. "He had a Ph.D. and yet worked long hours for a pittance." I used to be a post-doc.

"Okay." Ben grinned. "I was going to say that meant he was a full-time researcher at the university, but whatever."

"What group was he in?" I asked.

"Something called Bose-Einstein Condensate. I guess they do research for that music company?"

Music company? What the heck was he talking about?

The waitress arrived with our food.

She placed a behemoth monster pancake in front of Ben and a plate of cute little dollar pancakes in front of me. Yum. Quickly, I drowned my plate in maple syrup. Each pancake was like a low-lying island in a global-warming world.

"My buddy has one of those Wave Music Systems, and it's awesome," Ben said. "Hey, maybe the murder was some kind of corporate espionage−assuming you didn't do it."

"I did not do it," I said with my mouth full of fluffy dollar pancakes. "And what's a Wave Music System?" Somehow I didn't think it had anything to do with the university's physics department.

Ben poked his pancake with a fork, and it started deflating. "You know, those small stereos that have great sound."

"You think Harry was working on a stereo system?" I asked.

He shrugged. "I dunno. And it was Larry, I mean Barry."

"No. Bose-Einstein Condensate isn't a stereo; it's a phenomenon predicted by the famous physicist Albert Einstein," I said. "You've heard of him, haven't you?"

"Yeah," Ben said. "That wild-haired dude."

I missed Andro and his physics knowledge. "Yeah, that wild-haired dude."

Ben finished his syrup machinations and forked off a healthy-sized bite.

"Bose-Einstein Condensate is an unusual form of matter at really low temperatures." I attacked my pancakes again.

"So, it has nothing to do with that Bose music company?"

I shook my head, busy chewing.

"It sounds complicated," Ben said. "Boulder PD might have to ask you to be a consultant for us."

I shook my head. "I doubt they'll ask their top suspect to help them with the case." Ben sure looked f-i-n-e, but I was starting to doubt his brainpower. On the other hand, maybe I was too used to hanging out with geniuses.

Ben pointed at me with his fork. "You're right."

"And besides, aren't people usually killed by their loved ones? Like spouses?"

"Right again," he said. "Usually husbands. Of course, Harry didn't have a husband."

"Larry," I said.

Ben nodded.

"He might have a husband if he was gay," I said. "Do you know anything about his family?"

"He lived alone."

And that seemed to be about the extent of Ben's knowledge on the case.

When I got home from brunch, Andro was sitting in the family room, arms crossed, waiting for me. Were we fighting?

From his grumpy expression, I was guessing the room contained no imminent kisses. I missed his kisses. He was an excellent kisser. He looked great, though, very sexy in his worn jeans and form-fitting t-shirt and needing a shave. His slightly too-long, wavy brown hair was tousled, too. For Andro, it was uncharacteristically casual. Lucky me. I loved how he looked in jeans. Okay, if I'm being honest, I loved how he looked out of jeans, too.

"Hi, Andro," I said. "It's nice to see you. Can I help you with something?" I hoped he was here to apologize for acting so cranky lately.

"Where were you?" he asked.

"Just now, I was at The Pancake House--which I would have told you if you hadn't hung up on me. Which was rude, by the way."

"Who were you with?"

"I went by myself." Which was technically true.

Andro jumped up, blue eyes blazing, saying something. He looked delicious when he was irritated. Passionate. My mind wandered...

"Madison!"

"What?" I guessed he said something I missed. "Don't yell at me."

"I said I can't abide lying. I know you were with someone; I heard him say your name over the phone. How can we have a relationship if I can't trust you?"

I took a step toward him. "You can trust me one hundred percent. I'm not a liar. You know I don't lie. If I was a liar, would I have told you I saw Ben naked?"

Andro stabbed a finger in my direction. "Ah-ha! Ben! So you weren't alone." His face started to flush. "You did lie."

"I did not lie." Now, I was getting mad. "I went to the restaurant alone. I ran into Ben there."

"Naked?" Andro gave me an expression that suspiciously resembled a sneer.

"What's your problem?" I said. "Of course, he wasn't naked at the restaurant! You're acting like an idiot!"

Behind me, in one of the bedrooms, a crying ruckus started up.

"Don't call me an idiot!" He stomped towards the front door.

"If the lab coat fits!" I yelled after him as he stormed out, slamming the door behind him.

My adrenaline was pumping. I zapped the door with a little bolt of quantum energy in anger. I got a corresponding little bolt of pain in my head, but it was worth it. Generally, q-lapsing wasn't good for your health.

Sydney poked her head out of Emily's room, cradling her daughter in her arms. "Shh, honey, it's all right." She looked up at me. "What in the world was that?"

"I don't know." I did know something was up with Andro. He wasn't acting like his usual sweet, kind self--that was for sure.

Chapter Four

I spent the rest of Sunday trying to investigate Larry King on my computer in Ryan's and Sydney's garage, aka my bedroom, but I couldn't find anything except a bunch of stuff about someone who apparently had a show on CNN. Somehow, I didn't think it was the same guy. One of these years, I'd have to start watching TV.

I was supposed to go out with Andro Sunday night (we'd set it up earlier in the week), but I couldn't get a hold of him, so I theorized the date was off. This theory became law when he never showed up to pick me up. I was disappointed and more than a little confused.

Was he really mad at me? I'd thought our tiff would blow over, but maybe it was more serious. It wasn't like him to act so irrationally. I couldn't figure out why he'd act so out of character. Usually, he was easy to get along with. Frankly, usually, he was perfect.

What did he have to worry about? His job as a professor at the university was secure. The only relatives he had in the area were his sister Yasmin and her two daughters. Could something be wrong with them? That would be bad.

Of course, a murder had also occurred recently. And he had the skills to do it. But that train of thought should not leave the station.

With apparently nothing to do Sunday night, I offered to babysit for Sydney and Ryan, and they were thrilled. Emily and I had a great time playing and reading stories before bed.

Monday morning, I woke up at zero-dawn-thirty—maybe because I went to bed at nine o'clock p.m.—and decided to bake cookies. There was something about cookies that cheered me up. Maybe it had to do with all the Martin family celebrations featuring cookies. Or, maybe it was because they were yummy. At any rate, they were just what the doctor (me) ordered this morning after my non-date.

Sydney's Tuscan kitchen was so pretty with its cheery yellow walls and warm wooden cabinets, it almost made me want to cook more often. Almost.

Coffee was gurgling, and the oven was preheating when Sydney made an appearance in her beautifully coordinated organic cotton ginkgo p.j.'s and robe, rubbing her eyes. Even at the crack of dawn, Sydney looked perky and perfect. "Is that coffee I smell?" she asked.

"Yep. Help yourself." I pointed at the pot.

She yawned. "Thanks. Don't mind if I do." She grabbed a mug and poured. "Are you cooking?" she said, the cookie sheets on the counter registering. Why did she sound so surprised?

"Yep. I am."

"Are those bananas?" She took a sip of coffee.

"Yes, Syd," I said. "Those are bananas. I'm making my famous banana nut oatmeal cookies."

Sydney pulled out a stool at the counter. "You have a famous cookie?" She looked around. "Is Andro here? Are you trying to impress him?"

"Andro?" I asked. "Is he here?" Did he come to apologize?

Sydney raised her eyebrows. "I didn't see anyone. I'm asking you."

"Nope," I said. "No one's here. I'm not trying to impress anyone. I just felt like some yummy cookies."

"Don't you know carbs aren't good for you?" Sydney said.

"I had a tough weekend," I said. "Carbs make me feel better."

Ryan appeared, face sporting blond whiskers, hair hilariously askew. "Cookies! Awesome! I love you, Sydney!" He kissed his wife's cheek.

"You were saying, Syd?" I asked with a grin.

"Mmm, cookies." She smiled.

I spooned out the first batch and put the sheets in the oven.

"How about some eggs?" Sydney said. "Or were you two planning on having cookies for breakfast?"

"I plead the Fifth," I said.

Ryan wisely didn't say anything. I knew from experience he'd eat just about anything for breakfast—except maybe veggies.

"Thanks for babysitting last night, Mad," Sydney said as she started cooking. "How was Emily?"

"She was a delight, of course," I said. "What else could my cousin be?"

"Why didn't you go out with Andro?" Ryan helped himself to some coffee.

I shrugged. "I don't know. Something's up with him. I don't know what."

Sydney waved her spatula at me. "Open lines of communication are crucial to a successful relationship."

"Cookies don't hurt either," Ryan said.

Personally, I was with Ryan. "I know," I said. "I'll talk to Andro today. I can bring him some cookies. That should open up some lines of communication."

Ryan's cell rang. He reached into the pocket of his ratty robe and grabbed it. "Martin, here. Hey, Ben." He listened and gave me an odd look. "Just a minute. Madison, my buddy Ben here wants to know if you're available."

My mind flashed back on Ben's muscular naked bod. He must work out a lot. "Available for what?" I asked.

"You know, dating and such," Ryan said.

"She's not," Sydney said.

"Nope. I'm not," I said. "I'm with Andro." I thought I was. I hoped I was. It was amazing how much not talking to him affected me. I was used to talking to him several times a day.

"Sure," Ryan said into the phone. He listened. "Ooh, dude, she's my cousin. Not cool. What's up with the investigation? Larry King?" He looked my way. "No. The victim's name is Barry King, remember?" He smiled. "*Ciao*, dude."

Ugh! I resisted the urge to smack my forehead. The guy's name was Barry. No wonder I couldn't find anything about him on the web.

Ryan chuckled as he put his phone back in his pocket. "How did you manage to convince a cop the victim's name was Larry?" he asked me.

"You know I'm not very good with names," I said.

He grinned.

"Don't give me that look," I said. "I may not remember names, but you're just as odd as me in your own way. Why do you carry your cell phone around in the pocket of your bathrobe?"

Sydney snorted.

"What if there's an emergency, and people need to get a hold of me right away?" Ryan asked in a defensive tone.

Sydney opened her mouth and then closed it.

"Oh, and FYI, I told Ben you'd go out with him," he said.

"What!" I said.

"You and Andro are fighting. If he's going to hurt you, I withdraw my approval of him. And besides Ben's awesome," Ryan said. "We go way back. I could totally see you two together."

"Approval?" I said. "I hate to break it to you, bro, but I don't need you to approve who I date."

He shrugged.

Crying erupted from Emily's room.

"Somebody wants her breakfast." Sydney departed for Emily's room.

"Anyway, did you find anything out from Ben before you bewitched him?" Ryan asked.

"I didn't bewitch anyone," I said, keeping an eye on the eggs. "But I learned the victim was a postdoc in the Bose-Einstein Condensate group, and he lived alone."

"What's a Bose-Einstein Condensate group?" Ryan asked.

"Oh. Bose-Einstein Condensation's really interesting," I said, starting to warm to the topic. I loved to talk physics.

He held up his hand. "Wait. Am I going to understand this at all?"

Now it was my turn to shrug.

"Never mind," he said. "Check on those cookies."

Getting dressed, I checked my cell. There were no messages from Andro, but there were a bunch of urgent messages from Agent Baker. I guess Ryan had the right idea carrying his cell around with him all the time, after all. Go figure.

Agent Baker's messages all said something like, "Pick up, Madison. You better call me back, or else it's back to jail for you." How did she even know I'd been in jail?

I thought she was exaggerating, but I wasn't a hundred percent sure. FBI Agent Baker was a riddle wrapped in an enigma--with a gun.

I called her back. "Hi, Agent Baker."

"What took you so long?" she snapped. Ugh. I'd thought we were becoming friends. "I need you to come down to Denver to teach a class on q-lapsing."

"I can't right now," I said. "I have a class at nine o'clock." It was still only eight-thirty.

"Then, this afternoon."

"I'm busy," I said. The FBI seemed like a distraction I didn't have time for. I had to figure out who the murderer was. And figure out what was up with Andro. And once that was wrapped up, I had to write an irrefutable paper on q-lapsing.

"It's not a request," she said in her intimidating FBI voice. I thought of her gun again.

I sighed. "Fine."

I was raring to go, excited to teach my class at the university. Of course, it may have had something to do with the gallons of coffee I'd drunk.

This year, my quantum mechanics students were surprisingly similar to my quantum mechanics students from last year, basically an assortment of twentyish male geeks in various shades of pink and brown. The smartest kid this year was probably Juan. He was always talking back, anyway. Of course, Drew and Brandon were no slouches either, but to be honest, I had trouble telling those two apart, with their intentionally-messy hair and fraternity-worthy clothes. My bad.

I hoped my current students were not similar to last year's students in terms of morals. Last year, some of them had been bad, like, supervillain-take-over-the-world bad.

Once nine a.m. sharp arrived, I passed out the graded mid-term exams, and the students were not happy, to say the least.

Juan, of course, scowled as I gave him his test. "I still can't believe you gave us an essay question in a physics class." Juan had blindingly white teeth and perfectly coiffed dark-brown hair. He was prone to wearing the latest hippest-band t-shirt. I had a feeling he was also prone to having his way with the ladies. But I was one lady he couldn't sweet-talk.

The other students grumbled in agreement that I was unfair.

"I told you I was going to give you an essay question," I said. "Did you think I was joking? And there was an essay question on the sample exam I posted on the web." I looked around the room. "Did anyone look at the sample exam?"

No one wanted to meet my eyes.

"I can't say I was too impressed with your results on the essay question," I said from the front of the room.

Arjun held up his hand. "Professor Martin?" As usual, his clothes were neatly pressed. I'd pegged him as the class suck-up. His complaining was always very polite, which I appreciated.

"Yes?" I nodded.

"I did look at the sample exam," he said. "The essay question was on quantum mechanics, but the question you asked us on the test was about ethics. It is not fair, in my humble opinion."

If anyone needed to think about ethics, it was quantum mechanics students. Two of the young men in this class last year had turned to a life of crime after they'd learned how to control reality by q-lapsing. It took just about everything I had to stop them. One was dead now and one, the lucky one, was in an undisclosed prison under sedation. (So, not so lucky.)

This year, I was being extra careful not to teach the students how to control reality. I'd learned that lesson the very, very hard way.

I suppressed a sigh. "Do you guys understand the concept of a sample exam? It means that exam is similar to the one I would give, but not the same."

They grumbled some more. Brandon said something to Drew or the other way around.

"Ugh. I give up," I said. "You all have a new homework assignment, an essay on quantum mechanics and ethics, minimum seven hundred fifty words, due by nine a.m. Friday morning. This is in addition to the problems in the syllabus."

The grumbling started again.

"This is college, not kindergarten. Do you not understand cause and effect?" I asked. "If you keep complaining, I can make it a thousand words, or twelve hundred fifty. Is that what you want?"

They shut up.

"That's better." I smiled. "Today, we start chapter five." I uncapped a marker and turned to the whiteboard. "First, a little review. Recall, an operator is something that operates or does something. And an observable is something that one can observe, right?"

Arjun nodded and smiled. At least someone was listening to me.

I hiked up the stairs of the Gamow Tower.

Today, I was going to have a successful talk with Andro. I was going to find out what was going on with him. We were going to patch things up. Totally. Definitely.

But when I got up there, I couldn't help noticing Andro's office door was closed. Bummer. That meant he wasn't in. So, there would be no talking in the immediate future. Oh well, our talk would wait. It had waited this long.

I entered my office, dumped my stuff on the desk, and sat down at the computer. I opened up my class webpage to make sure the sample exam explained it was just a sample. It did. Good.

Then, just for the heck of it, I decided to click on over to www.controlreality.info.

The infamous webpage was back! I jumped up, knocking over my chair. Last year my villainous students had made a webpage teaching other miscreants how to use quantum mechanics to control reality. And there it was again.

Shit. I had to tell Andro. I had to tell Ryan. I had to tell Agent Baker. My hand hovered over my cell phone. I couldn't make up my mind who I had to tell first. I was shaking. Could Luke, the quantum criminal, be back from quantum-neverland? Was I in danger? Were my friends and family in danger?

And how did I know to check for the control reality webpage?

I took a breath. First things first. What would the Quantum

Cop do, or better yet, what would someone worthy of the Nobel Committee do? Probably sit down, for one. I picked my chair up off the floor and sat down.

That put my brain in gear for some reason. I needed to get rid of the page ASAP. My adrenaline was definitely pumping, so I focused on q-lapsing all the possible realities into the one I wanted.

The page blurred, ran together, and then turned gray. Good.

I sent an email to Andro, Ryan, and Agent Baker about the web page that was and now wasn't.

Maybe Andro would email me right back.

I sat in front of my computer and waited for new email.

And then there was a new email. It wasn't from Andro, though. It was from Ryan's cop friend Ben. What could Ben want?

Chapter Five

A hot cop had asked me out on a date. Twice, if Ryan had been telling the truth. Granted, it was via email--not the most romantic method--but I had to admit I was a little tempted. And then I had to admit I was confused. I was in love with Andro, wasn't I? I decided to take the multimeter by the probe and figure out what the heck was going on with Andro and me. I reached for my cell.

"Hi, Madison," Andro answered on the first ring.

"Hi, Andro," I said. I pictured his tan face smiling at me, his oh-so-kissable lips curved in a smile, his eyes twinkling. Mmm. It was a good picture. I focused on it.

And then I saw a big blur of fog in my office, which coalesced into Andro, wearing my favorite blue shirt that matched his eyes, holding his phone to his ear. He turned it off. "Was that me or you?" he asked. "I feel okay, no headache." He looked down at his chest. "Hey, wait a minute. I wasn't wearing this shirt when I left the house."

I shrugged. The pain in my head told me I'd q-lapsed to bring him here, but I didn't think he'd appreciate being summoned in such a manner. "We need to talk," I said.

He nodded. "I agree."

Did that mean he had something he needed to say? Or did he think I needed to say something? What did he think I was going to say? Did he think I was going to break up with him? Or, much worse, did he want to break up with me?

Get a grip, Mad. I made my mind stop racing.

He pulled up my ancient wooden guest chair and sat down on the other side of my desk. "First of all, I know you're not a murderer. I know you try to help people, not hurt them."

"Thank you for saying that," I said.

"But, you do owe me an explanation about the naked guy." He held his forefinger up. "What's up with that? You can't expect me, as your boyfriend, to put up with naked guys."

Boyfriend? I thought, hoped, he was my boyfriend, but I wasn't sure he still thought he was my boyfriend. I was sure, however, a goofy smile was plastered all over my face. "It was just Ben."

Andro shook his head and raised his eyebrows.

I interpreted that to mean he didn't remember. "Ben, the cop. Remember from the fraternity party a while back?"

He still looked blank.

"When we were on one of our first dates," I said, "and Ryan called us to that fraternity party where my evil student and his minions were q-lapsing." Ugh. That was the second thought about Luke I'd had recently. I paused to take a breath.

"Oh, yeah." Andro nodded and smiled. "All those girls lost their tops."

How like a man. "Sure," I said. "You remember the topless sorority girls, but not the buck-naked hot cop."

"Excuse me. Hot?" he asked in an annoyed tone. "This is the guy you went out to breakfast with Sunday morning?"

Oops. "No," I said. "I didn't go out to breakfast with him. I ran into him at breakfast. There was nothing to it. I sat with him and asked him about the murder case. But I apologize if I upset you."

"Oh." Andro looked at the floor. "Sorry. I know you're not a cheater—at least not on purpose."

I looked at him. What the heck did that mean? Is there such a thing as 'on accident' cheating? I decided to let that one go in the interests of détente.

"So, what happened to you last night?" I asked. "I thought we were supposed to go out. I couldn't even get a hold of you." I squelched the anger that had started creeping into my tone. "I was worried and disappointed." I made myself smile. "I need to be able to get a hold of you."

Andro nodded. "You're right. I'm sorry."

I looked at him.

He looked at me.

"So, what's up with you?" I asked. I had a bad thought. It

couldn't be guilt about q-lapsing Barry to death, could it? Nope. No way. Why did I even think that?

"I've just been upset about something lately," he said slowly. "It's a couple of somethings, actually. Part of it's personal, really personal."

"Well, tell me already," I said. "I'm your significant other, after all. I'm supposed to help you out with upsetting somethings. We're a team."

"Yeah. You're right." He took a breath. "I don't know why this has been bothering me so much, but Yasmin asked me to move out. She wants to get on with her life, and she says I'm getting in the way. She wants me to move out of the house away from her and the girls."

I knew Andro's widowed sister Yasmin and her two daughters were very important to him, so this must be particularly difficult. Andro would do whatever she asked, no matter how he felt about it.

I stood up and walked around the desk. "It sounds like someone needs a hug."

He looked up at me with amusement in his eyes. "I'm not a kid, you know."

"I know." I gave him a mischievous grin. I was well aware of how un-kidlike he was. I flashed back on the first time we made love, the way our bodies fit together, the smell of his skin, and how our bodies' rhythms were in perfect harmony. Whoo. I held out my arms.

He stood, and I wrapped my arms around him, resting my cheek against his warm chest. As we hugged, I hoped his worries were flying away like a data-collecting weather balloon. After a few moments, we separated.

"You were right," he said. "I did need that."

I sat on the edge of my desk. "I know the thought of moving out must be upsetting, but isn't it good that Yasmin is finally starting to move on from losing her husband?"

"Yes," he said. "Of course."

"And no matter what happens, they'll still be your sister and your nieces, right?"

"Yeah," he said.

"We'll just have to put our heads together and think of

something to make it better," I said. "In the meantime, I think someone needs another hug."

Andro grinned as he reached for me. "Yeah, and that someone is you."

I smiled into his chest. He had me so figured out.

Once we stopped, I sat down on my desk. I couldn't resist asking, "So, did you know Barry-with-a-B?"

He squinted as he took a seat. "The victim? Why is he Barry-with-a-B?"

Did I say that out loud? "No reason."

"You forgot his name earlier, didn't you?" He grinned.

Why did everyone keep thinking that about me? "Of course not. Anyway," I added quickly, "did you know him? I don't think I ever even heard of him."

Andro's face got still. "I don't know if I should say."

"Sure, you should," I said. "It's just the two of us here. And I won't say anything."

"Barry had the reputation of being kind of a jerk," he said. "I mean, I'm sure he was a good person, but he did tend to annoy people."

"Oh?" The plot thickened like cooling lava. "How so?"

"You know," he said as if he didn't want to say. "He was one of these guys who acted like an expert on everything."

I snorted. "No. A Ph.D. who acted like he was an expert. Shocking." My sarcasm was not lost Andro.

He raised an eyebrow. "No. He was really bad. Even worse than you."

What the heck was that supposed to mean?

His composure broke. "Kidding," he said and laughed.

"Hey!" I mock-glared at him and punched him lightly on the arm.

He grinned. "I'm kidding about you. But Barry was the biggest expert I've ever met on a whole campus of experts. Compared to him, all the rest of us were totally ignorant, at least that's the way he acted."

How annoying was this guy? Could it be a motive for murder?

"My mom used to say people acted badly when they felt bad about themselves," I said.

Andro was silent for a moment. "That makes sense. Do you think Barry felt stupider than the rest of us and was overcompensating?"

I nodded. "Could be."

"That's kind of sad," he said. "The whole thing is sad. No one deserves to die like that."

How did Andro know how Barry died? "Like what?"

He stood up. "You know, via quantum mechanics."

I just looked at him. I was sure he was innocent, wasn't I?

"It was in the paper, Madison," he said. "I need to go do some work today. Do you want to get together tomorrow night?"

I felt a smile break out. "You mean like a date?"

"Yes." He smiled and leaned over to peck my cheek.

I closed my eyes and got a whiff of aftershave. Making up was going to be so awesome.

Then I heard, "I'll talk to you later," from across the room.

When I opened my eyes, he was gone. I didn't even have a chance to ask, "Where exactly were you Sunday night?"

He'd made an awfully quick retreat. Why? We'd patched things up, hadn't we? Was there a chance something else was bothering him? Something more than having to move? He was probably just busy, right? Hey. Wait. What was his second upsetting something?

At any rate, I had to email Ben and tell him the date with him was a no-go, so I went back to my computer.

But first, I decided to check the newspaper stories to see if they mentioned quantum mechanics. I wasn't checking Andro's story. I'd thought Agent Baker or someone had told me they were omitting mention of that in the press, but I must have been mistaken.

I searched high and low and found several articles on the murder, but none mentioned quantum mechanics. How did Andro know about it? Had I told him? I must have. Sure, that was it. I told him. But I didn't remember telling him that.

When I finally got back to my email, I saw that both Agent Baker and Ryan had emailed me back about the Control Reality webpage. They were not pleased it had come back, to say the least. Both of them asked me if there was any chance Luke hadn't died in our quantum duel last year.

Was there?

I thought back to it. I'd found myself in a quantum fog of possibilities with my student Luke. Earlier in the semester, I'd inadvertently taught him how to q-lapse to control reality.

How was I supposed to know he was evil? He didn't look evil. He looked like a regular quantum mechanics student.

Luke and I were pretty evenly matched at quantum dueling until I'd thought of instantiating another me to help fight. Me and other-Madison had then weakened the Strong Force and made Luke's atoms disintegrate. He turned into a cloud of quarks, gluons, and electrons. I'd never forget that split-second look of surprise he gave us.

Honestly, that whole thing had been sad, too.

I didn't see how he could have survived that. But even I had to admit this new murder, and the reappearance of the webpage was all very weird. So who the hell knew what was going on at this point?

I emailed Agent Baker and Ryan that I estimated there was a ninety-nine percent probability that Luke did not survive.

What about Luke's partner in crime, Griffin? He was supposedly in custody, but how did I know for sure?

I was interrupted by a female voice saying, "Is he gone? I didn't want to see old people kissing and stuff." Alyssa Long peered in at me from my office door. She had on the grad student jeans and t-shirt uniform, and on her, it looked cute. Alyssa and I had a lot in common.

"Is who gone?" I asked.

She stepped inside. "Professor Rivas. You guys looked like you were going to go at it on the sofa again."

Again? And who was she calling old people? "I'm sure I don't know what you're talking about," I said stiffly. "I only engage in physics in this office."

"Yeah, right." She grinned and sat in the chair Andro had so recently vacated. "So Professor Rivas didn't like Dr. King, huh?"

Great. Just what we needed, rumors that Andro and Barry were enemies.

Chapter Six

My research meeting with Alyssa was interrupted by a phone call from Agent Baker. "Madison?" she asked. "Did you forget something?"

I looked at Alyssa. "I don't think so. My student and I had a meeting." I gestured at her. "I'm meeting with her."

It wouldn't hurt to stay on Agent Baker's good side, though. I smiled. "Can I help you with something?"

I heard her sigh. "You're supposed to teach us how to q-lapse, remember?"

Crap. No. "Of course," I said.

"I need you here in Denver, now. We're waiting." Then, she said only, "Jail."

"Okay. Be there in a jiff." We hung up.

"I'm sorry, Alyssa, I have to cut our meeting short."

She scowled and harrumphed out of the room.

It took about an hour to drive down to Denver, and, apparently, I didn't have time for that. There was no help for it. I would have to q-lapse.

The theory of quantum mechanics described all possible quantum states with mathematical entities called wavefunctions. A human consciousness was necessary to pick one of these, and as the theory said, q-lapse.

I chugged some more coffee and concentrated on the reality I wanted—the one where I was in Denver in the FBI field office. I thought about Agent Baker's threat to put me in jail to get my adrenaline pumping.

There was a moment of fuzziness, and then I was standing outside the conference room in the FBI field office. I'd been here several times before, which made it easy to picture and easier to transport myself here because the probability was reasonably high I would be here. But, ouch. My head hurt as it tended to do after I q-lapsed.

Agent Baker was pacing back and forth in the hall, arms crossed, mouth turned down, and usual grayish-blonde ponytail bouncing. She jumped when she saw me. "There you are! Finally. Why didn't you answer your cell?"

When I took in the lines around her eyes and mouth, I decided the stress of the FBI was aging her before her time. Of course, I didn't know how old she was—maybe it was aging her at the appropriate time.

"Sorry. I was busy," I said. "I do have a real job, you know." And it wasn't going great. "Why are you so hepped up about learning to q-lapse again, anyway?" So far, none of the agents had figured it out.

"The brass is breathing down my neck. They want quantum FBI agents like the Quantum Cop."

"Any particular reason why?" I asked, dreading the answer.

"Well, there is the little matter of a quantum corpse. Either you did it, or quantum crimes are starting up again." She peered into my eyes. "You're sure that kid Luke was neutralized?"

"Yeah." I nodded. Even though it had to be done, he had to be stopped, I didn't feel good about it. If I hadn't taught him how to q-lapse... But there was no point thinking like that. I couldn't change the past.

"And you didn't kill King?" she asked.

"Of course not!" I said. "How can you even ask that? I'm one of the good guys." Agent Baker and I had been through so much I couldn't believe she doubted me. Maybe FBI agents were extra suspicious.

She ignored my outburst and just walked into the nondescript conference room, set up like a classroom with all the chairs facing the front.

I followed. The class appeared to be made up of conservative-looking middle-aged men. It could have been the same agents that showed up in my previous class—or not. They all blended together. I guess that was sexist or some other kind of ist on my part. "So, how many of you came to my previous class?"

None of the men raised their hands.

I turned to Agent Baker, who'd taken a seat near the door. "No repeats? Why not?"

She just waved her hand, gesturing for me to continue.

"Thanks for coming. I'm Professor Madison Martin. Some people call me the Quantum Cop." I smiled and paused for laughter. There wasn't any. Tough crowd. One of the guys leaned back in his chair and crossed his arms. The rest scowled at me.

"Okay. So the idea is, there's a branch of physics called quantum mechanics that requires a conscious human mind to basically create reality."

There were some smirks. I was not feeling the love.

I continued. "The way it works is there's a bunch of math involving something called a wavefunction. The wavefunction describes all the possibilities, and the human mind collapses this wavefunction to instantiate one possibility, one reality."

It was smirk-city.

"Maybe you'd like a demonstration?" I asked.

They nodded.

I hoped I hadn't used up all my quantum mojo on my trip here. Since there were physical consequences, i.e., pain and possible aneurysm and death, I could only q-lapse a limited amount per day. I concentrated to q-lapse and create a large mug of yummy coffee. A spot on the table right in front of me started getting fuzzy. Of course, more probable things were easier to do than less probable things. It was highly probable that I'd have a large mug of yummy coffee in front of me.

Some of the feds started getting alarmed.

The fuzz coalesced into a mug of coffee. I picked it up and took a sip. Tasty. I smacked my lips. "Convinced?" I asked as I set down the cup.

The guy sitting on my right said, "Nice trick, but how does it help us catch perps?"

Agent Baker stood up. "It's not a trick. And you can do anything with it, right, Professor Martin?"

"That's right. Or, I guess not. I mean, you can't time travel or bring people back from the dead or other impossible stuff. In fact, the more improbable something is, the more difficult it is to q-lapse." While they chewed on that, I slammed the rest of the coffee to rev myself up.

From what I could tell, they needed some coffee to rev themselves up, but it wouldn't do any good if they didn't believe they could q-lapse.

Then, I concentrated on being in the back of the conference room instead of the front. And then I was.

"Hey, where'd she go?" Mr. Blabbermouth in the front said.

"I'm right here," I said.

They all jerked around to look behind them, except Agent Baker, who'd seen me materialize.

"What the hell?" one of the guys said.

I could tell already this class was going to be pointless. If none of them believed me, there was no chance they could q-lapse themselves. After a couple of hours, Agent Baker finally let us all give up, and the agents quickly made their escapes. I thought I saw Agent Baker's partner, Agent Nate Sawyer, in the crowd, but he didn't stop to say hi.

I'd been doing little q-lapses for the whole meeting, and I was exhausted. There were shooting pains behind my eyes. And my stomach growled.

Agent Baker shook her head. "I don't understand why we have so much trouble doing it when you don't."

"You, or at least they, don't believe in it," I said. "That's a crucial component. You have to believe it can happen for it to happen."

"I believe in it," she said. "I've seen you do some wild stuff."

"And it helps if you really understand physics. And you need the emotional adrenaline component," I said. "I don't think the agents had that either."

"My bosses are not going to be happy about this," she said.

My stomach growled again, and this time she heard it.

"Hungry?" she asked.

"Yeah," I said. "I missed lunch." Sadly, I hadn't even thought of bringing some banana cookies with me.

I had an unfortunate realization. I didn't have any money with me. "Shoot!" I said. "I forgot my purse."

"How did you get here then?" she started to ask. "Oh, right, you q-lapsed to get here. If I give you a ride home, can you give me some special tutoring? I have to show my bosses at least one FBI agent can do it. You owe me. I vouched for you when that homicide detective called me." She glared at me, and I tried not to think about the fact that she had a gun.

"Yes, ma'am."

Agent Baker and I went through the Taco Timbre drive-through, and she seemed to think I got a lot of food. It only ended up being one big bag worth, so I don't know what she was going on about. On the other hand, I think she got two measly tacos.

As she drove and we ate, I tried to pick her brain about the murder case. First, I tried to soften her up. "Agent Baker, it seems like I've known you for quite a while now, and we've been through a lot together. Maybe we should be on a first-name basis. What's your first name?"

She spared me a glance. "Agent."

"Oka-a-ay." I turned back to my food and then, unfortunately, dropped about four layers of my eight-layer burrito in my lap.

"You mess it, you buy it," Agent Baker said. Her tacos had disappeared with nary a crumb--an especially nice trick since she was driving.

"What?" I asked, blotting my shirt and lap with many, many paper napkins. "Buy what?"

"Nothing. I was joking. This is a government car," she said. "Just don't make a mess. Or, did you make a mess already?"

I scowled and decided her question was rhetorical. The dark, nondescript SUV we were in was obviously a government car. Even I'd figured that one out. Was that an almost-smile on her face? If so, softened agent. Check.

Once I was somewhat less burrito-y, I said, "So, Agent Baker, what do you hear about the murder case?"

"Which case would that be?" She glanced at me. "If you can tell me the vic's name, I'll tell you something." She turned her attention back to the road. How did she know I had trouble with names? I guessed FBI agents knew everything about everybody.

I definitely detected an almost-smile.

"That's easy." I'd learned this. "It's Barry–"

"Are you sure?" she asked.

"It's Lar–"

"Are you sure?"

"It's Har– wait. No. It's Larry King!"

She chuckled. "That's what I thought."

"What did I say?" I did a mental rewind. "I meant it's Barry King. I know it's Barry."

"Too late," she said.

Good grief. What was my problem with names?

She must be teasing me. A straight-arrow like her wouldn't divulge any info. "Come on, tell the truth," I said. "You wouldn't have told me anything anyway, right?"

"I guess you'll never know." Agent Baker was smiling openly now. At least I'd put her in a good mood.

For the remainder of the journey, I focused on eating.

In Boulder, we drove up to the physics building. My part of the building, Gamow Tower, had a dimly lit narrow square hallway with offices on the outside and a tiny elevator on the inside. It badly needed a remod, or at least better lighting.

When I walked by Andro's office, I was struck by a wave of sadness. What was going on with him? He wasn't acting like himself. It was almost like I didn't know him anymore, or maybe he wasn't the person I thought he was. The door was closed, so he wasn't in there.

And then I had the disturbing thought I'd been trying to avoid. Andro had the quantum skills to kill Barry-with-a-B. And he'd started acting strange and grumpy around the time of Barry's murder.

"Earth to Madison," Agent Baker said.

"Yeah. Sorry." I looked at her. "Agent Baker, are you married?"

She held up her fingers. "See any rings?"

I did not. I shook my head.

"I rest my case," she said.

"Do you know anything about men?" I asked. "My boyfriend is acting peculiar."

She focused on me. "That would be Professor Andro Rivas? Who also knows how to q-lapse? How good is he at controlling reality?" She paused. "Peculiar, how?"

Crap. I didn't want to get him in trouble. "Nothing. Never mind."

"Peculiar how?" she asked again in her no-nonsense voice.

"He can control reality, can't he? Did he know the victim?"

I didn't want to implicate him. Did he know Barry? I didn't know for sure. I never saw them together with my own eyes, after all. "Uh, no?" Think quicker, Mad. "But his peculiarity isn't quantum mechanical. He, uh, doesn't like to cuddle anymore. You know, after you-know."

"I do know." She nodded. "Men—can't live with 'em, can't disappear them without your boss getting cranky."

I froze. "What?"

"Nothing." She was smiling now, definitely smiling.

I couldn't decide if I really liked Agent Baker or was really afraid of her.

In case I was afraid of her, I wasted no more time in taking her to the double-slit experiment in the hall. It consisted of an electron gun with the condenser lens, aperture, objective lens, another aperture, intermediate lens, electron biprism, and the two-dimensional detection apparatus. Of course, the square-shaped hallway was deserted as usual. It looked like the cleaning staff had even deserted it.

"Anyway, this particular experiment taught me and Andro and my grad student Alyssa how to q-lapse, so it should work for you, too. It's a bit more methodical than what we were doing this afternoon." Did Alyssa know Barry-with-a-B?

"Alyssa?" Agent Baker said. "This woman also knows how to q-lapse? Why is this the first I'm hearing of it?"

Ugh. Agent Baker was definitely suspicious. "I misspoke. Alyssa doesn't know anything." Alyssa basically knew everything.

Agent Baker gave me the evil eye for a moment, but I didn't crack. Finally, she said, "Are you ready to do the experiment?"

"Yes, ma'am." I flipped everything on and turned to her. "You are supposed to focus on this screen here," I pointed, "and make a big blob by concentrating and q-lapsing."

She shrugged. "Okay. It sounds simple enough." She leaned over the machine and stared at the screen.

I watched her to see if she got blurry. She had on her usual black power suit, with her usual ponytail. She was totally overdressed for Gamow Tower. The dust bunnies were probably impressed. Or scared.

Wait. There! Was she getting fuzzy?

"How do you feel, Agent Baker?" I asked.

"Fine. Why?"

She stopped looking odd, and I spared a glance for the detector screen.

It was a big blob. "You did it! You q-lapsed."

She frowned. "I don't get it. What's the big deal? You said I should make a blob, and I did."

I grinned like I'd just received the phone call, "Doctor Martin, this is the grant committee. We've got a lot of money for you."

"Okay," I said. "Don't concentrate, and we'll see what we get next."

A fuzzy series of lines developed on the detection screen. "There you go," I said. "That's the standard result there. What you got before was not the standard result." My grin was back.

"Really?" Agent Baker looked unimpressed.

"Yes," I said. "Your conscious mind collapsed the wavefunction and instantiated this reality. Good job. You q-lapsed. Congratulations."

"What happens next?" she asked.

I rolled up my sleeves. "Now we get to work."

Chapter Seven

Tuesday morning, I woke at the yawn of dawn again (dammit). After stopping for appropriate caffeinated sustenance, I trudged to my office to get some more data for my new and improved paper.

Of course, Alyssa stopped by just when I was getting some good results. "When are we rescheduling my research meeting?"

I looked up from the equipment. "When do you want to reschedule your research meeting?"

She crossed her arms in front of her. "Now."

"Now, it is." I smiled. I owed her some time. "Show me what you've got."

Alyssa regaled me with her research tales until we were interrupted by Agent Baker knocking on my office door. "Madison?" she asked. "Did you forget something?" Why did she keep asking me that?

I looked at Alyssa and then back at Agent Baker.

Oh, yeah. I had promised Agent Baker I'd teach another q-lapsing class. But I'd also made a commitment to Alyssa to be her advisor.

"It's fine. We're pretty much done here, anyway," Alyssa said. "I'll read over these papers and get back to you when I finish the new calculations." She stood.

I stood. "Sounds good. Keep up the good work." I was pleased. Things were going pretty smoothly now with Alyssa after our rocky start last year.

Alyssa gathered her stuff and exited my office. I followed her and Agent Baker into the hall, where the double-slit apparatus was still set up. Several dark-suited agents meandered around the small hallway looking at the apparatus. Were these the same guys I tried to teach yesterday? I couldn't tell. I started checking to make sure all the parts of the apparatus were still aligned when Agent Baker gasped.

I looked at her. "What?"

She pointed down the hall. "That girl disappeared."

"Alyssa?" I asked, my stomach sinking. "You mean she went into the stairway?" I knew that wasn't what Agent Baker meant. Oh, Alyssa, why did you show the FBI you have the skills to q-lapse and maybe murder someone with quantum mechanics? Did any of the other agents notice?

The men were all looking that way, but I couldn't tell what they'd seen, if anything.

"No," Agent Baker said, "she got all blurry and disappeared. She's the one you mentioned before, right?" She put her hands on her hips. "I can't believe you've been holding out on me. She can q-lapse. How many more have you been protecting?"

"Uh..." For some reason, I couldn't seem to get Andro's name off the tip of my tongue. How did he know about the quantum mechanical aspects of Barry's death? But I was not going to say anything. Definitely not. No way.

Agent Baker glared at me, and I tried not to think about how she had a gun, and I was probably afraid of her. She put her phone to her ear.

What had I done? I opened my mouth to say something, anything, to make it better, but Agent Baker scowled at me. I was sure Alyssa and Andro hadn't done it, so they would be fine. Totally fine. No problem.

I went over to the five agents standing in the hall. One of them I knew. "Hi Nate. Where's the rest of the crew?" I asked. "Are more people coming?" All the agents looked generically conservative, tall, athletic, and wore dark suits. Had the FBI perfected cloning?

Nate said, "We're it."

"I couldn't get anyone else to come," Agent Baker said, joining us.

"Really?" I said. "I'm surprised since you made some progress the other day."

Agent Baker gave me a look. "You mean yesterday?"

Had it been only yesterday? "Right, yesterday," I said.

"Anyway," she gestured at the group, "here's the latest batch of recruits."

"Hey, Madison," Nate said. "What do you want us to do?"

I wasn't sure. Should we proceed like I had with Agent Baker?

"Lisa?" Nate said. I guess he got impatient.

That must be Agent Baker's first name. I'd been wondering. "Ah-ha! Your name is Lisa." I pointed at her.

"I can neither confirm nor deny that statement," she said, face expressionless.

"It is," I said. "You're Lisa."She stared at me until I got nervous about her disappear them comment the other day. That, I remembered.

I rubbed my hands together. "So, Agents, welcome to the physics building and welcome to the how-to-control-reality class. I'm happy to say Agent Baker has made some progress controlling reality by using this double-slit apparatus. Lisa," I grinned, "would you like to show everyone what you can do?" Sucking up to her couldn't hurt me or my friends.

She turned to the machine and dazzled them with her amazing feats of single and multiple blobs. At least she dazzled me.

Nate snorted and said, "That's it? One blob or a bunch of blobs? Who cares?" Ryan's friend or not, Nate was starting to annoy me. He popped a piece of candy into his mouth. Not sharing was also annoying.

"That's a lot," I said. "Lisa−"

She narrowed her eyes at me.

"Er, I mean, Agent Baker q-lapsed. She altered reality." I waved at her. "You should do as well. You're looking at the two best q-lapsers in the universe." Besides Andro and Alyssa−but they didn't need to know that.

Agent Baker's mouth thinned. "And the murderer−assuming you're not the murderer."

"Yeah." I nodded. "And that guy." Who was it? I didn't think it was dead-and-dissolved Luke, but what about Griffin? "Agent Baker, are we sure Griffin is still in custody? And he can't do any q-lapsing?"

Agent Baker looked startled for a fraction of a second. That was a first. I'd never seen her startled before. "I believe so. But I'll check and get back to you."

"Now you guys get to try q-lapsing," I said to the other agents.

Unfortunately, after three hours of trying, none of them picked it up besides Agent Baker, who kept improving.

I felt especially sorry for Nate because he really seemed to want it, staring intently at Agent Baker and me as we did it and at the other agents as they failed.

Eventually, we all packed it in. If Agent Baker had been a cheerful sort, she would have been smiling. I thought she was pleased with herself, but of course, it was hard to tell with her.

I was pleasantly surprised when Andro picked me up that evening and told me we were going to a concert at Red's rocks. "A concert sounds fun," I said. "But who's Red, and why does he or she have rocks?"

He chuckled. It was an especially nice sound considering how out-of-sorts he'd been lately. "No. Red isn't a person. Red Rocks is a place--made of rocks." He glanced at me out of the corner of his eye as we started driving south. "The rocks in question are the color red."

"A bunch of rocks sounds uncomfortable," I said.

He grinned. "You'll see."

It was an unusually warm night for October, and we opened the car windows. As the sun started to set, the views along the highway were glorious--rolling foothills covered with golden grasses swaying in the breeze and chunky red rock formations. "This land is so beautiful. It's amazing it isn't developed," I said over the noise of the wind whipping through the windows.

"It's illegal," Andro yelled back. "It's Open Space. They can't develop it."

In the distance, on a foothill, I could swear a huge mansion disappeared into thin air.

I must have made a funny face because he grinned and added, "That's Boulder for you."

"No," I said. "I thought I saw a mansion." I pointed back behind us.

"You might have. The County couldn't buy all the land

around here. There are a couple of parcels–"

"No, you don't understand," I said. "It disappeared."

"If I didn't know you, I'd think you'd been smoking something." He chuckled. "Maybe you know more about Red Rocks than you let on?"

What did these rocks and smoking have to do with each other? "Nope. Sorry, dude." I smiled. Maybe my eyes were just playing tricks on me in the fall twilight.

As we continued to drive south, the sun set on our right. One minute it was there, and then it was behind the mountains. The clouds above us glowed pink and orange as if lit by internal flames, and the sky turned the most gorgeous shade of blue.

This part of the country was stunning. I was glad I'd moved here. My old job in St. Louis and my asshole former boyfriend, Ted, were distant memories, even though it had only been a year since I'd left.

I glanced at Andro. He was pretty stunning, too. But more importantly, he was a good man with a good heart. Whatever troubles we'd been having lately, we were going to work through them. This relationship was worth fighting for.

Eventually, we pulled into what looked like a rustic park with a stone sign, *Red Rocks*. "Are you sure there's a concert here?" I asked.

He just grinned and nodded. We drove up a narrow road until it was flanked on both sides by parked cars. "End of the line, babe."

At this point, I was pretty mystified. I still hadn't seen any buildings or other significant signs of civilization besides the bunches of parked cars. He got a blanket and some other stuff out of the trunk, and we started hiking up the road.

Soon, a large shuttle van came up behind us and stopped. "Would you like a ride, folks?" the driver called out through the open door.

I was already breathing hard and had been ready to suggest Andro and I q-lapse to get to the top of the apparently-very-large hill. I said, "Definitely," and we got on board.

I'd never seen Andro look so excited. "What's up with you?" I asked.

"Just wait," he said, a grin popping onto his face.

We rode up the hill, higher and higher. I still didn't see any buildings, just a lot more parked cars and some enormous rocks that were definitely red. Finally, we got to the end of the road at the top, and the shuttle let us out in front of a dozen stretch limos. Mysteriouser and mysteriouser.

We walked down a sidewalk a little ways, and some security guys patted us down. While we were waiting, I noticed some faint music playing in the background. We walked a few more steps, and a woman scanned the tickets Andro held out, and then we were apparently in. We passed a tiny building on our right. It couldn't have been more than a couple of hundred square feet. There was no concert going on in there.

"I don't get it," I said. "Where's the theater?"

He took my hand and practically dragged me across a large patio edged with a multitude of beer booths. At the far side, he pointed down. "There."

When I looked in the direction he pointed, I gasped. Far below was a stage made of red rocks, framed by even bigger red rocks. On it, roadies arranged a variety of musical instruments. Between the stage and us were rows and rows of red stone benches, many with people sitting on them. "Wow, this is really beautiful. And unique." It was also really crowded. There must have been a few thousand people spread out below us.

Andro grinned broadly. "I know. Isn't it awesome? I think this is the best venue in the world."

"Awesome." To our east, all the lights of metro Denver sparkled like the Milky Way. "Very pretty." I was reminded of another type of Milky Way. "Can we get something to eat and drink?"

"Is the speed of light two point nine nine times ten to the eighth meters per second?" he said.

Well, duh. We got in one of the refreshments lines, and I could see people getting yummy beers and nachos and all kinds of stuff way at the front of the line. And yet we never moved any closer to it. "Speaking of special relativity, has time slowed down?" I asked.

"Yes," he said. "It's time dilation. And the distance is increasing. It's length expansion." He was such a geek. I loved it.

"Yeah," I said. "Definitely special relativity." We laughed.

"Who's playing tonight?" I asked as we continued to be taunted by successful food- and drink-procurers walking by with their spoils.

Andro shrugged. "Who cares? Everybody sounds good here." He looked at the tickets. "Hot Fusion."

"As opposed to cold fusion," I said.

"Or tabletop fusion," he added. We both guffawed as the folks around us in line gave us odd looks.

Eventually, our quest was successful, and we paid higher-than-movie-theater prices for beers and nachos and found our seats. We snuggled down under the blanket and ate and drank until the music started.

Hot Fusion was a reggae jam band with about twenty-five members. Many of the audience members did partake of a particular herb. It got so smoky, I was glad we were outside.

The food and drink, lively music, beautiful views, and most of all, being with Andro made the evening fly by.

When the concert ended, we attempted to exit. Rookie mistake. There were about infinity stairs, but there seemed to be infinity-plus people trying to use them. We were surrounded by red rocks, so there was nothing to do but wait once we got trapped in the people-jam. I briefly considered q-lapsing to get out of there, but Andro stood right behind me, pressing his body into my back, and it felt good.

"So what did you think?" he said into my hair.

"The concert was fun, and I think if you were any closer, you'd be in front of me," I said with a smile. Was he starting to get excited?

A woman screamed, and the crowd lurched.

"What the hell?"

"Shit!" The natives were very restless, shifting and muttering.

"I have a bad feeling about this," I said.

"Me, too," Andro said.

And then there was a bunch more shoving and screaming.

I was knocked into the stair railing. We were so jammed in I didn't go far. I grabbed for Andro's hand. "Let's get out of here by q-lapsing." Fear adrenaline would make it easy.

"Good idea." He clutched my hand. "Back to our seats."

I started concentrating and got that particular fuzzy feeling, and then we were back at our concert seats. They were easiest to imagine and had a high probability since we'd just been there. No one even noticed us popping out of thin air.

My head only hurt a little, but I felt shaky. I didn't know if it was an aftereffect of q-lapsing, second-hand pot smoke, or fear from almost being crushed in a riot. I sank down on the stone seat.

Andro remained standing, staring at the crowd on the stairs. "We should do something about the crowd. People could get hurt."

The crowd continued shoving and yelling.

"I agree, but what?" I said.

A calm voice came over the sound system. "Please remain calm. Please exit in an orderly fashion. Please calm down."

The calm voice had absolutely no calming effect.

Maybe they shouldn't exit in an orderly fashion. I q-lapsed to appear on the stone stage. "Hello? Is anyone here?"

The crew was packing up the instruments. A very large fellow came up to me. "How did you get here? You're not supposed to be here."

"I know." I batted my eyelashes, which didn't seem to do anything. "Do any of you guys play? If you started playing music, some of the crowd would come back to the seats and get off the stairs."Now I was surrounded by crewmembers. Some of them shrugged and grabbed instruments.

When the first notes rang out, I q-lapsed back to Andro.

Some of the people on the stairs did come back into the amphitheater as the music played.

But he was upset. "Where did you go? I was worried about you."

"Sorry." I pointed at the crowd moving off the stairs. "I popped down to the stage for a minute and asked the crew to start playing music. Look, it's working."

He smiled. "Good job, Madison. Now, let's get out of here. Do you want to q-lapse back to the car?"

My head was starting to ache from the q-lapsing I'd already done. "Let's just go back the regular way."

"Headache?" he asked.

I nodded.

We went back to the stairs, where the crowd was now much lighter. "I wonder what started all this?"

"We may never know," he said.

We continued on down the stairs until we saw nothing. Literally. That nothingness was a brand-new human-sized tunnel through several feet of red rock.

The edges looked spongy. "Wow. Look." I reached out to touch them. The surface yielded to the touch like a slightly moist sponge. It was very much like the hole in the wall Andro and I accidentally created between our offices last year. I felt shaky again.

Was what happened to these rocks what happened to Barry? I gulped. "Could this have started the riot?"

"It can't have helped," he said.

I was ninety-nine percent sure Andro wouldn't do anything wrong, but that other one percent was nagging at me. I turned to him. "You didn't do this, did you?"

He shook his head, eyes wide. "No. Did you?"

"No," I said.

We looked at each other for a moment.

"Someone here at the concert knows how to q-lapse," I said. "Someone here has the skills to kill."

"The only other person I know who can q-lapse is Alyssa. You don't think it was Alyssa, do you?" Andro asked.

"No," I said. He wasn't deflecting attention from himself, was he? "Where'd you say you got these tickets?"

"Some guys from the physics department had extras," he said.

"So, other people from the department are here? Maybe one of them can q-lapse." I gulped again. "I wonder who?"

If we knew who, we'd probably know who Barry's murderer was.

Chapter Eight

Wednesday morning after my class (which went well, thank you very much) found me in a meeting with my lawyer, Tom, at his office. His digs were located in downtown Boulder off Pearl Street in a remodeled mansion. Who knew he was doing so well? I felt like some kind of imposter, or maybe it was a pauper when I walked in and gave the receptionist my name.

Last night, Tom, Ryan, and Sydney had all felt the need to leave messages reminding me about the meeting this morning. I don't know why. Apparently, they thought I was forgetful or something.

Of course, I didn't hear the phone ring last night because I was at a concert with my boyfriend, Andro. And I didn't check my messages after the concert because creepy dissolving rock notwithstanding, Andro and I were otherwise occupied. I flashed back to our bodies fitting together perfectly, gazing into each other's eyes...

"Stop that," Tom hissed. "It's bad enough you were late."

"Stop what?" I asked.

He waved his hands at me. "That blurry thing. You should quit doing that. It makes you look suspicious."

Boy, was he a spoilsport. "Late? Who was late?" I said, "I beat you, didn't I? And I look good, too." I wore a tailored, charcoal-gray suit. My only suit. I usually called it my killer suit, but that seemed inappropriate this morning.

Come to think of it, the last time I'd worn it, I'd gotten hit by a car and narrowly avoided being killed myself. Yikes. Maybe it was my unlucky suit. Maybe I should take it off ASAP. I looked around the glass-walled meeting room and deduced people would notice if I got blurry and magically changed outfits. Plus,

Tom was right. I shouldn't q-lapse right now.

"You didn't beat me," Tom said. "I was in my office waiting for you."

"Okay, fine." I sat at the beautiful wooden table with Tom and regretted my wardrobe choice as he flipped through some papers. But I wasn't sulking.

"What are those?" I whispered.

"Police reports. They claim they had cause to question you." He shook his head. "But this is all totally circumstantial."

"Duh," I said. "I didn't kill anyone." Except my student Luke last year. Ugh. "Recently."

Tom shot me a scowl, which I knew meant *Don't mention Luke or anything related to him...*

Agent Baker walked into the room. "How's it look for our girl here?" She thought I was their girl? That was nice.

"They don't have anything," Tom said. "It just depends on how gung-ho the D.A. is."

"Or if they have any other suspects," Agent Baker said.

A young guy I'd never seen before rushed into the room and handed Tom a folder.

"What is it?" I whispered.

Tom quickly scanned the page. "Good. They got the statements from the Boulder Brews employees. They said you were in their store until almost nine o'clock Saturday morning. You're their most annoying customer." He paused. "This is good."

Most annoying was good? "Why good? What does it mean for my case?"

"Alibis are good, Madison," Agent Baker said.

Duh. I mentally slapped my forehead. Alibi. I should have thought of this before.

"Don't get too excited." Tom passed his first folder to Agent Baker.

She read, "It says the state of the body was very unique. Our experts claim it is impossible to pinpoint the time of death exactly." She continued, "Furthermore, according to FBI records, Ms. Martin is uniquely qualified−"

"Stop," Tom said. "We're all familiar with Madison's unique qualifications. There might be enough evidence for them to charge her and proceed with the case."

"Shit," Agent Baker said.

The new turn of events had my head spinning. "What does all this mean?"

"Your alibi doesn't necessarily alibi you out." He shuffled the papers on the table. "We keep going, one day at a time until they charge you. We knew this was a possibility. They questioned you, after all."

"That's it?" I asked. "There's nothing else we can do?"

"For now," Tom said, without looking at me. "I'll keep in touch with my contacts. If I hear they're going to arrest you and press charges, I'll try to let you know in advance."

Agent Baker was shaking her head. If I didn't know her, I might think she felt bad.

"All this is very confusing," I said. "What's next?"

"We need to figure out who the real killer is before they charge you and the trial starts," Agent Baker said.

"Trial?" I asked. "Do you really think it will come to that?"

They looked at each other and nodded.

How could I go to trial for murder when I didn't do anything? Don't panic, Mad. "If you say so. Thanks for your help, guys."

Tom still didn't look at me. "Tom. What else is up? Why won't you look at me?"

He straightened up. "Well, I guess you'll find out eventually." He shot a glance at Agent Baker. "There was another page in the file. Agent Baker told the cops that Andro Rivas and Alyssa Long also know how to q-lapse."

"What?" I yelled. "How could you do that? Andro and Alyssa wouldn't hurt anyone."

Agent Baker looked defiant, crossing her arms and keeping her mouth closed.

"Madison, keep it down," Tom said. "You're in a place of business. Why wouldn't Agent Baker do that? It's her job. Anyway, you should keep things in perspective. You didn't do it, right? That means someone else did. If your friends didn't do it, they'll be fine."

"Okay. Is that it?" I vowed to be mature and not pessimistic. "Is that why you called me in here?"

"No. There's the little matter of my bill."

Shit.

I trudged into my office and settled into my chair.

Andro bounded over from next door. "So? How'd it go?"

"Not good." I looked up at him. Did he have any idea the cops might be looking at him for the murder? I should warn him. That would be the mature, responsible thing to do.

"Aw," he said quietly. "Somebody needs a hug. Come here, *mi amor*. Tell me about it. What happened?" I liked it when he called me *mi amor*.

As I collapsed into his arms, I figured I could warn him the cops knew about his q-lapsing ability a little later. In a couple of minutes.

"It'll be all right, Mad," he said to the top of my head.

Being in his arms felt so good. A few tears may have escaped as I rested my cheek against his warm, firm chest. Okay, I full-on cried. I felt bad for Barry and scared for myself and Andro and Alyssa. And a teeny-tiny part of me might have been scared Andro had done it.

Afterward, looking at all the dark blotches on his silk shirt, I said, "I guess I better have this dry-cleaned."

"Washable silk," he whispered.

"Really?" I asked. "Wow, you're smart. How do you know so much?"

"Just lucky, I guess." He smiled. "And here's something else I know. Things could be worse. Being a murderer would be worse."

"That's true." I gathered my courage. "Andro, I have to tell you something."

"They didn't charge you. And you have an awesome boyfriend. And−"

"All right, already. I give. Things could be a lot worse."

He smiled. "Do you want to come over tonight? I'll cook some dinner, and we could watch a movie."

"That sounds perfect." He was perfect. "Andro, will you move in with me?" I asked.

At the exact same time, he grinned and said, "I'm thinking Shawshank Redemption." He paused. "Wait. What did you say?"

"Nothing." So much for being mature. That lasted, like, a minute.

"I think you said something, Madison."

My heart felt like a tectonic plate being crushed in a subduction zone. "All right. I said, Andro, will you move in with me?"

He was quiet for a moment. Finally, he said. "Wow. I didn't see that coming. I had no idea you felt—"

I interrupted him. "Forget it. I don't know why I said it. I know you have to move, and it just came out. It's too soon. I didn't mean it." Did I?

"Andro Rivas?" a voice from the hall said. The voice came from a man in a Boulder PD uniform. Shit.

"Andro," I said, "I need to tell you something."

Two cops came into my office.

He said, "I'm Andro Rivas. What can I do for you?"

The one in front said, "Andro Rivas, we have some questions about the murder of Barry King."

His face froze. Then, he said, "Am I under arrest?"

The cop frowned. "Not yet."

Yet? I couldn't believe they were moving so fast with him.

"What's going on?" Andro stammered. "I don't understand."

"Agent Baker may have mentioned to the cops that you know how to q-lapse," I said. "They're doing an investigation. I was about to tell you."

"Well, why didn't you?" he asked.

"I thought we had more time," I said.

"You're making it very hard for me to trust you, Madison," he said.

He was right. Crap.

The cops led him out into the hall. I followed them.

"Andro, I'll call Tom, my lawyer, for you. Okay?"

He just looked dazed.

"Tom'll help you," I called after him.

In the meantime, I was going to find the killer. It wasn't me, and it couldn't be Andro. It just couldn't be.

I went back to my desk and sat down. I was shaking. Tom and I had a brief conversation in which he agreed to meet Andro and warned me not to come over. As we hung up, I could swear he said something like, "Who knew physicists were so good for business?"

66

Tom might not be far off the mark. After the concert last night, I knew the killer might well be here in the physics building. Unfortunately, I didn't know exactly where Andro had got the concert tickets, and I couldn't ask him right now.

But I knew exactly who to ask, Nancy the administrative assistant, who ran the physics department. The department chair thought he ran things, but he was wrong. Nancy was the real power behind the ergonomic chair.

I went downstairs, pasted a smile on my face, and strode into the office around the front counter. "Hi, Nancy. How are you? It's so nice to see you. Have I said recently what a great job I think you're doing?"

Sitting at her desk in the back of the room, she narrowed her eyes. "What's this?" She pointed her pen at me. "What do you want? You want something."

"What, I have to want something to talk to you?" was on the tip of my tongue, but she may have had a point.

"And what are you wearing?" she asked. "Why aren't you wearing one of your geeky Einstein t-shirts?"

She was dressed beautifully as usual in a wrap dress that clung to her curves. But she wasn't usually quite so grumpy. What was up with her? Maybe bad moods were contagious.

I took a breath. "I'm sorry to say I had a meeting about the murder with my lawyer this morning."

She flinched.

"I didn't do anything. I swear. I would never hurt anyone."

I didn't want to meet her eyes, afraid I might blurt out they suspected Andro now. Thank goodness Andro had tenure, and they couldn't suspend him easily. There was something worrisome attached to that thought, but I put a pin in it.

"I do think you're doing a great job, and I apologize if I haven't mentioned it much lately," I said.

She frowned.

"Or ever."

She relaxed a bit, taking a sip of coffee from the mug on her desk.

"And you're right. I do want something," I said. "But just a little information."

She relaxed some more.

"I was wondering if you heard about anybody making plans to go to a concert at Red Rocks last night. That's all. No biggie."

She considered me. "If I tell you something, what's in it for me?"

"What do you want?"

"You can do that weird quantum stuff, right?"

I nodded.

"I want you to owe me a favor, anything I want. No questions asked."

"Okay." How tough could that be? She was an administrative assistant, after all.

She considered me some more. Finally, she said, "There was a big group of the low-temperature guys going."

"Low-temperature?" I prompted.

She curled her lip as if to say I was unbelievably ignorant. "Ultracold Atoms and BEC."

"BEC? As in Bose-Einstein Condensate?" I asked.

She nodded. "Yeah. Of course. Doesn't everyone know that?" She glanced at her mug and turned it, so the picture faced away from me. "Is that all? I have work to do, you know." She shuffled papers on her desk.

"Yes," I said. "Thanks, Nancy. You rock."

Ultracold Atoms and BEC, huh? Barry had been in BEC. Did this mean that one or more of Barry's colleagues knew how to q-lapse?

Did that mean one of my colleagues in the physics department had committed cold-blooded murder?

And, if so, would they do it again?

I shivered, and it didn't have anything to do with low temperatures.

Chapter Nine

I was on a quest for a murderer and had a feeling it had something to do with that weird tunnel at Red Rocks. Thanks to Nancy, I knew some of the low-temperature guys were at the concert. I was determined to interrogate them. One of those low-temperature guys was going to crack like, well, something at a really low temperature.

I sauntered to the cinder-block-walled, tile-floored hall containing the low-temperature labs. They were all surprisingly small rooms chock-full of wires, pieces of metal, computers, equipment manuals, and empty soda cans and chip bags.

At the first lab, I knocked on the open door. "Hello? Low-temp guys? Are you here?" The room was only about twenty feet by twenty feet. Surely, only a couple of people could even work in here at one time with all the equipment.

No one answered, so I assumed no one was around, and thus they wouldn't mind if I went in. Maybe I could find a ticket stub from the concert or a printout of the Control Reality webpage.

The polite thing, maybe the mature thing, would have been to come back when someone was there, but this one time, I did not do the polite thing. I crept through the lab door, trying to tiptoe in my pointy going-to-lawyer-meeting shoes. I passed several tables piled high with electronic machines but no signs of quantum mischief. There were also several metal boxes on the floor with lots of wires going into them, but not quantum clues.

"What do you think you're doing in here?" a nerd on the floor demanded, popping his greasy head up from behind some equipment.

I was so startled my mind shrieked danger. I q-lapsed and

ended up back on the couch in my office in the Gamow Tower. Collapsing the wavefunction was related to probabilities, and it was very probable I'd be on my couch, so it wasn't surprising I'd ended up there.

Unfortunately, my couch wasn't going to solve any mysteries, so I forced myself to get up and trudge back down the stairs the old-fashioned way.

Greasy-head had stood up, and his mouth was hanging open. His t-shirt had a guy cleaning a window, and the quote *I do do windows if they've got Bose-Einstein condensation.*

I had been planning to ask him if he was a low-temperature guy, but his shirt gave him away. His shock also gave him away as not the murderer. "Hi, there, Bose-Einstein guy," I said.

He just stood there and stared.

Based on his shirt, I decided a bad joke might work to get him talking. "What did the thermometer say to the graduated cylinder?"

The guy took a breath and mumbled, "You may have graduated, but I've got a bunch of degrees?"

"Nice. Yes." I smiled. "Hi. I'm Professor Martin. Nice to meet you."

"Hi. I'm Chris. I'm a grad student. What the hell just happened? It seemed like you disappeared into thin air. But that's crazy."

Considering Chris's reaction, it was likely no one in this lab was q-lapsing. I stalked for the door. "Thanks."

Chris followed me. "Seriously. What did you just do?"

Crap. I didn't need to teach more students to q-lapse. "I'm not at liberty to say," I whispered. "You know, national security. Forget you saw anything unusual."

Before I stepped into the hall, I added, "Oh, yeah, did anyone in this lab go to a concert the other night?"

"Like with music?" He frowned. "No. I don't think so."

In the next lab down the hall, also a small equipment-filled space, a young woman answered when I knocked on the partially opened door. Her t-shirt said *Absolute zero is cool.* She took one look at me and said, "Whatever you're selling, we're not buying," and started to close the door.

"I'm not a salesman. I'm a physics professor." I smiled. "Hi.

I'm Professor Madison Martin. I don't think we've met. Who are you?"

Her eyes narrowed suspiciously. "Do you work here? I thought I knew all the female physics professors." Sadly, very few women worked in the physics building even in this day and age, so she probably did know them all. Except for me, of course.

"I promise," I said. "I started last year. Maybe you know my grad student Alyssa Long?"

She relaxed. "Oh, you're Alyssa's advisor? She said you were really nice." Was *really nice* too nice? I made a mental note to be meaner to Alyssa.

"And you are?" I asked again.

Her smile accentuated the points of her nose and chin and made her look a little like an elf. "Oh, sorry. I'm Isabella Rodriguez, a grad student. Nice to meet you. Come on in. What can I do for you?"

I debated what to tell her about my troubles and landed on nothing. I didn't have a lot of experience being considered a murderer, but I was guessing they weren't too popular. "I was at Red Rocks at the Hot Fusion concert the other night, and I just wanted to thank whoever got the tickets. I heard it was this group?"

"Hot Fusion?" she said. "It sounds like the bomb!"

I laughed. "Good one. Did you hear anything about it?"

Isabella wrinkled her nose and her forehead. "I did hear something about some people going to a concert, but I didn't go. Do you want me to ask around?"

"That would be awesome. Thank you." I felt like I should reciprocate somehow. "Your t-shirt is cute. Funny. Actually, the guy next door had on a cute one, too."

"Oh, yeah, Chris." She smiled. "We have kind of a pun competition going between the low temp labs. I've got a million of them. You know, like *Gravity brings me down*. Or *If sound doesn't travel in a vacuum, why are vacuum cleaners so noisy?*"

Those were pretty funny.

"Ooh, here's one. *What's a tachyon?*" she asked.

"A particle with imaginary mass that travels faster than the speed of light?" I said.

"Yes." She giggled. "But no. *A tachy-on is a particle with bad taste.*"

I snorted. "That's a good one." I liked her. "Hey, we should do lunch or something sometime."

"It's a plan," she said, smiling.

I felt a lot better after talking to Isabella. I liked her, and she was on the case. I had a feeling she'd figure something out.

Back in my office, I decided to look over Alyssa's latest batch of calculations and look up some more papers for her. Then I realized I needed to grade papers for my next quantum mechanics class, so I got into that.

Luckily at about six p.m. I noticed what time it was, so I just had time to rush home to change my clothes for my date at Andro's house.

At home, Sydney was bouncing Emily in her arms on the family room couch. "What happened at your meeting this morning? I've been on pins and needles waiting to hear. Does your lawyer think you're in the clear?" Oops. I should have texted or called her earlier.

"No. I'm still the primary suspect."

"I'm sorry, honey." Syd shifted Emily and patted me on the arm.

I exhaled. "Tom thinks they're going forward with the case."

"Oh, dear." Sydney's mouth turned down. "I must admit I thought they might find someone else."

"Me, too. Another bad development is the police questioned Andro," I said.

"Andro? I can't believe it," Sydney said. "He's such a sweetheart. You don't think he actually knows anything about the murder, do you?"

Except for the quantum mechanics connection? "No way." My heart went out to him, sitting there being interrogated, worrying what would happen next.

But there was also the little matter of what I blurted out to Andro earlier. I paused. "Actually, I need some advice. I may have committed a bit of a faux pas earlier today."

"You? Commit a faux pas?" Syd smiled. Emily smiled too, but that might have been a coincidence.

"I sort of asked Andro to move in with me," I said.

72

A booming voice from the doorway said, "You what?" It was Ryan.

Sydney shook her head. "Oh, honey."

"It just slipped out," I said. "I didn't mean it." I pretty much did mean it. "I took it back. I was freaked out from the murder and everything, and he was sweet about comforting me. It's no big deal, right?"

Ryan put his bag down on the couch. "I don't know, Mad. Of all the things you've done, and you've done a lot, this might be the most boneheaded. Where would you guys even live? Not here."

I started to get an icky feeling in the pit of my stomach. "No. You're wrong. This isn't totally boneheaded, is it?" I turned to Sydney. "He's wrong, right?"

Sydney shrugged. "If Andro's thinking along the same lines, he might like it. Of course, guys tend to want to ask those big questions. Right, Ryan?"

He didn't answer.

I turned back to him. He was now on the couch with his head in his hands. "What's wrong, Ryan?"

He lifted his head. "I'm getting a lot of heat about the murder investigation. My bosses aren't happy that the prime suspect is related to me."

Prime suspect. He meant me. I gulped.

I tried calling Andro's cell, office, and home phone, and they all went straight to voicemail, so I decided to meet him at his house. I could take him out to dinner when he got home. But when I got to his house, I saw his car in the driveway.

I marched right up and knocked on the door, looking forward to our date.

He immediately yelled, "Come in." Had he been there all along, not answering his phones? That wasn't like him.

Andro sat alone at the kitchen table, still dressed in his work clothes. His house was very similar to Sydney and Ryan's, a small ranch built right after World War Two with an open floor plan. I could see him in the kitchen from the front door. There was no sign of his sister or nieces.

"Hello, Madison," he said, his face very still. "I was

wondering if you'd show up."

Wondering? Didn't we make plans?

He didn't seem happy to see me. I knew him, and that expression--or more accurately, lack thereof--was not a good sign.

"So, hey there, Andro. How's it going?" I walked towards him nonchalantly, playing it cool.

His unmoving face beheld me. Unfortunately, he only looked like that when he was really upset.

"Did the thing with the police go okay?" I knew it couldn't have gone totally wrong because he was home. He hadn't been charged. But it couldn't have gone totally right, or he wouldn't be so upset.

He didn't answer me.

"Is it something else?" I paused. "Whatever it is, I apologize."

Silence.

What if Ryan was right and Andro was freaked out about the moving-in proposal? "If you're concerned about that thing I said earlier, I was just joking. I don't want to move in together. Not that I'm saying I never want to move in together or that I wouldn't want to move in if you want to," I said. "Or that I do want to move in together." I was blithering. "You talk now."

"Not everything is about you, Madison," he said, the skin around his mouth tightening. "They questioned me about a murder. Legal trouble is the last thing I need right now. Did you even stop to consider that showing up here might get me in more trouble? Trouble I don't need?"

"I guess not," I said.

"And gee, maybe you should have mentioned earlier that the cops wanted to question me about the murder."

Who was this guy? I'd never seen Andro act like this. "I apologize about that. I'm sorry. I meant to tell you. But you didn't do it, so it should all work out, right? In the meantime, I'd like to help you if I can. What happened with Tom?"

He frowned. "He met with me a couple of minutes. He left."

What was going on? Tom came through for me. Was I going to have to give him a talking to? "Why not?"

"Not all of us are rich or have rich relatives and can afford to pay for expensive lawyers," he said.

"I don't get it. You have a house in the same neighborhood as me. Couldn't you put that up as some kind of collateral?"

"I shouldn't even have to deal with this." Andro gritted his teeth. "It's Yasmin's house, and they already had a second mortgage for their business."

"Oh." I wasn't sure what to say. "Do you want me to see if I can raise some money?"

"No." He appeared to be glaring at me.

"Are you mad at me or your situation?" I waved my hands around the room. "It's not my fault someone was murdered. And I don't think the cops truly suspect you. I know you are a good person and this is all a mistake. I know I should have told you about the cops, and I'm sincerely sorry. Or are you mad about my suggestion to move in together?"

Andro sighed and leaned against the back of his chair. "You did surprise me with that, Mad. I can't help thinking that you do want to move in together."

"I don't," I said. "I like things the way they are. I mean besides the whole murder thing."

He raised his eyebrows like he didn't believe me. "At any rate, it raises the issue of where this relationship is going."

Didn't the woman usually raise that issue? "No, it doesn't." I was getting a very bad feeling. My hands started looking blurry.

"I had no idea you were even considering getting serious. I think you're a good person, besides the whole murder thing, as you say."

That was kind of a low blow.

"And we've had fun together, but I'm not sure we're right for each other vis à vis marriage."

Vis à vis? Who talked like that? And marriage? "Who said anything about marriage? I thought we both liked each other. We both like physics. We both live in Boulder. We both like beer. We have great sex." I forced a grin. "You can't deny that. And most importantly, we love each other--at least I thought we did. Have you changed your mind?"

"So, you do want to get serious," Andro said. "It's hard for me to admit this, but I'm not sure..."

"What?" If I felt any worse, I was afraid I might end up in

quantum limbo. It had happened once before when I was really worked up, like now. "If you have something to say, just say it."

"I'm not sure we're compatible long term," he said. "I mean, I'm Catholic, and you're... I'm not even sure what you are. Catholicism and family are important to me."

I was stunned. He hadn't gone to mass once since I'd known him. "What are you saying?"

He gazed at the refrigerator like it was suddenly fascinating. "There's a lot going on with me right now. I'm saying we're in different places. Maybe we should take a break."

"A break?" I was shaking, and my hands looked like they were made of white quantum mist. "Family is very important to me. And if Catholicism is important to you, I totally support that."

My shaking arms look misty. "I don't think we need to take a break. I love you. I want to help you through this. I know I've made mistakes, and I'm sorry if you've been dragged into them. I thought we were partners. Aren't we?"

"I want to take a break," Andro said. "Frankly, I've got more important things to worry about than our relationship and your feelings."

I moved away from him. "I understand you are in a bad situation." Did he say he didn't care about my feelings? He didn't care that my heart felt like it was being crushed to smithereens? It was hard to breathe.

"Please leave," he said.

I couldn't believe this was happening. I couldn't get air into my lungs.

He stood up. "I asked you to leave my house." He pointed at the front door.

If I had enough oxygen, I would have said, *How can you say that?* But I just stared at him. Who was this man? Where was my boyfriend? Where was the love of my life?

"Fine. I'll leave." He moved around the table.

I stepped between him and the door, but he easily moved around me, strode to the front door, and opened it. "You better be gone when I get back."

He slammed the door behind him.

Chapter Ten

I had to get away from Andro's house. In a panic, I q-lapsed and ended up back in my office and not in quantum limbo. Yeah, for no limbo, at least. I sprawled on the couch and thought about going home but decided against it. I mean, what was there to do at home, cry? Of course, Ryan or Sydney would probably give me a hug. I wavered for a second.

But, no. I couldn't deal with my Andro situation right now, and they would want to talk about it. I should try to get some work done with all this unexpected free time. It had been too long since I looked at my own research. I took four aspirin, went to the computer, and soon was lost in the data.

Some time later, I was disturbed by something, and the hairs on the back of my neck and arms (and, to be honest, legs) went up. I glanced at the tiny atomic clock icon on my computer, and I'd been working for three hours straight. One of the reasons I loved research was it took my whole mind, absolutely all of my concentration.

But something was off, now. It felt like someone was watching me.

I stood up and stretched, looking around the small room. I couldn't see anything wrong, and there definitely wasn't anyone else in my office, so what was with this feeling?

I sat back down at my desk and picked up a paper. I couldn't focus on the words, though. They were blurry. What was up with that? I was too young to need bifocals.

A noise made me look at the door. The door and the wall immediately around it had gotten sort of blurry. It appeared to be made of fog, like the ghost of a regular door.

And then the door and adjacent portions of the wall

disappeared entirely, leaving a gaping hole in the wall. Someone q-lapsed my door away!

"Leave my door alone," I stood and yelled. Why would someone get rid of my door?

Then I felt a strange pressure surrounding me, pressing in on my skin. I held up my hand, and something pressed in on it from all sides, but I couldn't see anything.

"Shit!" Was someone trying to attack me with quantum mechanics? Was it Barry's killer? I tried to concentrate to counterattack, but I'd already q-lapsed too much today and was worn out.

Who could assail me like this with quantum mechanics? And then my breath caught in my throat. Andro could do this.

"Who's there?" I ran through my office to the giant new hole in the wall and peered into the hall. The light was off out there.

I heard a strange *ulp* sort of a noise. The pressure let up, and then footsteps ran down the corridor. Whatever had been happening, I'd thwarted it.

I ran after said footsteps. The hallway was too dark to make out the person.

Mystery-attacker, who had Andro's build and coloring, opened the stairwell door and pounded down the stairs.

I started running down the stairs. I had to find out if it was Andro or not. I pounded down the stairs but wasn't catching up to the mystery attacker.

I had to slow him down or distract him somehow. Maybe some verbal intimidation was called for? "I'm gonna get you! You're dead meat!" I had to stop yelling for a moment to gasp some air. "You shouldn't have messed with the Quantum Cop!"

The footsteps stopped, and I heard a *thwack.* "Ouch! Shit!" a voice said.

I kept running and soon came across a man lying on the stair landing. He had brown hair and wore a black sweatsuit. When he looked up at me, I saw Andro's blue eyes, Andro's sculpted cheekbones, and all the rest of him.

"Oh, God," I whispered, my eyes filling. I couldn't believe it. Andro tried to hurt me?

His eyes widened as he looked up at me. "You bitch!" he yelled, his face bright red. He clutched his ankle and got to his feet. He took a menacing limp towards me. "You fucking bitch!" He shook his fist. "The next time I see you, you're dead!" He bolted for the door of the stairwell.

I'd never seen Andro act like that. When he was upset, he shut down. He didn't yell. I didn't even know he had a temper. It didn't seem like him at all. After a couple of seconds, I shook off my shock and followed him out of the stairwell onto the main floor.

A few students were standing around, pointing at livid Andro limping quickly across the lobby towards the doors.

Alyssa glided up to me. "Was that Professor Rivas? What's wrong with him? He looks hurt."

"He fell on the stairs." I was very confused. Should I call the cops to report the incident or call an ambulance to help him? "I don't know for sure who it was."

"What do you mean, you don't know who it was?" Alyssa put her hands on her hips. "It was Professor Rivas. Didn't you see him?"

I just looked at her. I couldn't admit it was Andro to myself, much less to anyone else.

She scrunched up her nose. "What? Do you think someone's impersonating him? With quantum mechanics? Is that even possible?"

I hadn't thought of that, but it sounded way better than Andro trying to hurt me. Or acting so out of character.

When someone q-lapsed, they used a human mind to select among the myriad of possibilities. Theoretically, if there was a nonzero possibility the q-lapser resembled Andro, he could q-lapse to resemble him. But it seemed like a circular argument. "I don't know." I sighed. "It's been a long day. I'm going home." I called Ryan. He agreed to pick me up.

When his car pulled up, I barely had the energy to open the door. Fighting with your boyfriend, q-lapsing, being attacked, and running through the physics building really took it out of you.

"Madison, what's wrong?" Ryan asked.

I got in. "Somebody just tried to do something to me. It was some kind of quantum attack."

Ryan shook his head as we pulled out. "What happened?"

I shrugged. "Honestly, I'm not sure what happened." As I

looked at my cousin, I could feel my chin quiver. "All I know is someone who looked like Andro tried to hurt me."

"But you're okay?"

"Yeah."

Ryan clenched the steering wheel until his fingers were white and pressed his mouth in a tight line the rest of the way home.

Sydney met us at the door. "What's happening?"

"I have to make some calls." Ryan stalked to the kitchen, pressed a button on his cell, and then proceeded to pace back and forth around the kitchen.

I sank down on the couch and watched him. "Things did not go well with Andro." I paused. "We're on a break." I slid sideways, laying my head on the arm of the couch. Something was wrong with Andro. I wished I knew what it was.

Sydney leaned over to try to give me a hug. "Oh, honey. I'm so sorry."

"That's not even the worst of it," I said. "He, or someone who looked just like him, attacked me in the physics building."

"No. I can't believe it," Sydney said. "Andro wouldn't hurt you."

"I can't believe it either," I said.

"Oh, honey." Sydney rubbed my back.

Ryan stomped back into the family room. "I checked in with my officers. Nobody's seen Andro. Sorry, Mad, I couldn't find out anything else."

I just lay there. Why would Andro attack me? He wouldn't, would he? Alyssa must be right. Someone had to have been impersonating him.

But that was a new quantum mechanical ability. How would that even work? It seemed too improbable. We'd never seen quantum impersonation before. Did that mean we had a new quantum criminal?

"Madison?" Sydney asked.

Why would anyone attack me? And why would they do such a bad job of it?

Ryan frowned. "I don't get it. Why aren't you more freaked out?"

I shrugged—not easy to do when you're lying down. "I'm

freaked. I'm just very tired. It's been a long bad day." I stopped for a moment to gather my thoughts.

"Alyssa suggested someone might be impersonating Andro with quantum mechanics," I said.

"I never heard of that," Sydney said. "Has anyone ever done that before?"

"Not that I know of," I said slowly. But how would I know?

"And why do it?" Ryan asked. "To frame Andro?"

"That almost makes sense." I sat up. "Maybe the murderer did try to frame Andro." But, if so, why? What did they have against Andro? That led me right back to the question of what was going on with him.

Ryan and Sydney exchanged one of their secret-marriage-language glances. I was guessing it was their *Madison's acting kooky again* glance.

"Don't worry," I said. "I'm freaked out on the inside. Despite what happened last year, I'm not used to being attacked." I shrugged successfully. "It must have been the murderer who tried to hurt me. But if it was, why didn't he finish me off?"

Ryan exhaled. "Start at the beginning and tell us what happened."

I did not sleep well. I kept turning my argument with Andro over in my mind. Should I have said or done something differently? I also couldn't stop thinking about the attack. What was the point? To hurt me? If so, why? And if so, why didn't he? And why did he look like Andro? Could it have been Andro?

Additionally, Ryan and Sydney had some kind of loud whisper argument late into the night. All I could hear was "*Ssss*" and "*Zzzz*" at various decibels.

By the time I dragged myself into their Tuscan kitchen seeking the elixir of life, aka coffee, Emily and Sydney wore adorable matching outfits with pink and orange flowers and stripes. Ryan had on his ratty bathrobe with his cell making that bulge in his pocket. Someone less mature, or at least less tired than me, might have made a joke about said bulge.

"Wow, Sydney," I said. "You and Emily look really cute. What's the occasion?"

Sydney stopped washing dishes. "Emily and I are going to

visit my mom."

This was a surprise. "When did you decide this?" I asked.

"Last night," Sydney said.

Ryan gave me a sheepish look.

What was that about? "Call me crazy, but this all seems kind of sudden. What's up?"

They didn't answer me. They wouldn't even meet my eyes, and then it hit me. They thought I was dangerous, or at least someone dangerous was after me. They wanted to get Emily away from me.

"I would never do anything to hurt you guys. And I'd die before I'd let Emily get hurt."

Emily gurgled in her high chair, in agreement, no doubt.

Ryan shot Sydney a look. "It's not you," he said.

"After last night, we're just a little worried Barry's murderer might come after you," Sydney said. "Or maybe even after us. Like that Luke kid did last year." The flying lawnmower incident had been bad. Very bad. Very very bad.

Who was the attacker? My chest felt like carbon being crushed into diamond. Who knew what the murderer would do? "Please don't leave your home on my account. I'll leave. I'm leaving. I'm moving out right now." I stood up.

Ryan held up his hands. "We don't want you to feel obligated to leave. We promised you could stay here."

"I sincerely appreciate everything you've done for me. But I need to leave now." I stalked to the doorway and turned. "Maybe I can buy a house in the neighborhood."

Ryan snorted. "Yeah, right."

"What?" I asked.

"Are you forgetting our house cost half a million?" he said.

Yikes. I had forgotten. "Maybe I can rent a room in the neighborhood. But don't worry. I'll make it very clear that we don't have anything to do with each other anymore. I will get you guys out of danger."

Leaving my family would break my heart, and here I thought my heart broke last night when Andro and I broke up. But no, apparently, there was room for more breakage.

On top of that, the person I wanted to talk to about all this was Andro. But I couldn't.

82

QUANTUM MURDER

My chest felt like I was being crushed inside a black hole.

Part of my get-Ryan's-family-out-of-danger plan was to go talk to the woman who knew everything and wasn't afraid to share it, i.e., Nancy. I pasted a smile on my face and strode into the physics department office. "Hi, Nancy. How are you? It's so nice to see you. Have I said recently what a great job I think you're doing?"

Sitting at her desk in the back of the room, she said, "Yes. The last time you were in here. Yesterday. When you wanted something."

Oh, that's right. It seemed like a lot had happened since then. Focus, Mad. "Good. So how are you? How's it going? What's new?"

She gave me a sympathetic look. "I was sorry to hear about you and Andro breaking up."

She did know everything. I didn't have to act to muster up some moist eyes. "Thanks. Yes. It's pretty rough."

"Maybe you'll get back together at some point?" she said.

Implement plan now. "No. I doubt it," I said. "In fact, I don't care about him at all anymore, and I don't care who knows it." Part of my sleepless night had resulted in the hypothesis that the killer was trying to frame Andro for attacking me and presumably for Barry's murder as well. Maybe it would be best to go along with the nefarious plan for the time being to lull him into a false sense of security.

Nancy's perfectly shaped eyebrows went up, and she squinted slightly as she pursed her lips. Okay, she was skeptical.

I needed to sell it more. "He's not the man I thought he was. He's evil. You know he was questioned by the police about the murder, right? He's a..." I forced myself to say it even though every atom of my being didn't want to. "Murder suspect."

Nancy had a look on her face I couldn't interpret, like her skeptical look but with eyes more narrowed and her chin tucked towards her chest. Maybe it was her super-skeptical look?

I barreled on. "But anyway, I came in to tell you I need to change my address with the university. I'm moving." I gathered my resolve. "I'm finally getting away from that horrible Ryan Martin and his family. I hope to have nothing to do with them ever again." I hoped to keep them safe.

Nancy's eyebrows had risen much higher. "Really? I thought you were close."

I shook my head vigorously. "Oh, no. They're terrible. They're nothing to me. Nothing. They kicked me out after all I've done for them. I've done hours and hours of free babysitting. Good grief. I even saved their lives. I wash my hands of the ingrates."

She shrugged. "Okay. Whatever." She typed some stuff on her keyboard. "So, what's your new address?"

"Ah." Dammit. I needed an actual address. "I'll have to get back to you." Action item: get an address.

I whirled around, and who did I almost crash into? Andro, of course, as handsome and professorial as ever—not at all like a murderer, or even like an ex-boyfriend.

He did, however, look horrified. I'd never seen that expression on him before—as if I was the devil's excrement or something equally disgusting. I cringed.

"Andro?" My voice squeaked. "What are you doing here?" I wanted to ask him where he'd been last night, but I was afraid to. "How long have you been standing there?"

"What the hell?" he said, shaking his head.

My chest started imploding. What must he think of me for saying all that? Would he understand I was trying to protect Ryan's family? "How much of that did you hear?"

Andro continued to shake his head and look at me like he was in shock. Finally, he said, "I cannot believe what I just heard."

"Can we talk? In private?" I asked. If we could get in private, I could tell him what was really going on, that I was trying to protect Ryan and his family.

"No." His expression was stony.

"Maybe you could call me, or email me, or text me, then," I said.

He didn't answer.

Okay. Turning and walking away, letting Andro think I meant all that stupid stuff I said was one of the hardest things I ever did. But I had to do it to protect Ryan and his family.

I could barely walk, as now, the entire universe was

crushing all of me inside that black hole.

Chapter Eleven

In the hall, outside the physics department office, since I was being crushed by the weight of the universe, I was shaking. Okay, Mad, take a breath. What were you going to do? I was going to go up to my office.

As I focused on breathing and not being crushed to death, I walked to the stairs and overheard some students chatting.

"Do you know of anyone who needs a roommate, man?" one guy said. "Mine is driving me *loco*. I have to get out of there."

"No," another guy said. "But you should check the bulletin board over there. They have a bunch of notices and stuff."

What a good idea. It could solve my current housing dilemma. And why didn't I know about this neat old-school bulletin board?

I checked the board and saw a flier saying, *Mature female roommate wanted. Scientist a plus!* That sounded great to me. It must be fate. I tore off one of the little strips of paper. When I realized the address was in my current neighborhood, I was so excited I decided to go over there immediately. I definitely needed a change of scenery to get my mind off things.

When the young woman opened the door, I got a déjà vu feeling. She reminded me of an elf, and her t-shirt said, *I wear this shirt periodically* and displayed a periodic table of the elements. I knew this woman.

"Madison, er, Professor Martin," she said. "Are you here for that info? How did you know where I live?"

"Hi, Isabella," I said. "This is a coincidence. I actually wasn't looking for you. I'm looking for a place to live." I held out the little strip of paper.

"Oh, wow." She took a step back. "You're looking for a place to live?" She quickly glanced into the house and bit her lip. "I do need a roommate. I guess that would be okay. Come on in." She stepped out of the doorway and beckoned me inside. "It's kind of messy. I wish you would have called first."

"I don't care about how messy it is." The layout of the house seemed to be a clone of Ryan and Sydney's place, but this place was furnished in early graduate student. An eclectic mix of furniture greeted me, including a pea-green couch, two rickety wooden chairs, a World War Two-era gray desk, and a variety of large colorful throw pillows on the floor. But there was no empty-beer-can pyramid, no video game paraphernalia, no high-tech stereo, and no flat-screen TV. In fact, the ancient TV on the rickety stand appeared to have a cathode-ray tube. "So no guys live here, huh?" I asked, smiling.

"No," she said. "It's just me right now, and I cannot afford the rent. Did you want to live with a guy? Not me." She shook her head. "Never again. They're too much trouble. I used to room with my best friend until this guy moved in. The next thing I knew, they fell in love and got married and moved out."

It looked like I'd never get married. "Well, you'll probably never have to worry about that with me." I forced a laugh.

She just looked at me.

Focus, Mad. This young woman was obviously sad about her best friend moving out. "That's too bad, your best friend moving out. That's the kind of thing that can really bring you down." Before I could stop it, my brain skittered to like breaking up with the love of your life can bring you down.

She tried to laugh. "Nah. Only gravity brings me down."

I smiled. "Gravity brings me down, too."

"So, what do you think?" she said. "Are you interested? Or is it too weird? To live with a grad student? Does it seem weird?"

I'd lived with many grad students in the recent past. Of course, that was when I was a grad student. Isabella and I had hit it off right away, though, and I needed some more female friends. "I wasn't a grad student so long ago." I paused. Was it weird? "It might be weird if you were my grad student, but you're not." I needed a new place. "When is it available? What's the rent?"

"It's available immediately. The lease is in my name. You'd be subletting. And the rent is seven hundred dollars a month, including utilities, which is very reasonable for Boulder. Usually, I ask for first month and last month's rent as a deposit."

I gulped. I'd already borrowed money from Ryan and Sydney to pay lawyer Tom. And when, er, if I was put on trial for murder, I'd have to borrow a lot more. I needed another source of income. Maybe the FBI could pay me? I'd probably have to teach some of them to be good q-lapsers for that to happen...

"Professor Martin?"

"What?"

"I said, since you're a professor, I guess you're trustworthy. We can forget the deposit."

I really liked this woman. "I'm in!"

I gave Isabella a check for the first month's rent, and she gave me a key. We agreed I'd move my stuff in that night.

I was headed back to work on the bus when my cell rang. My heart beat like someone having, well, heart palpitations. Please be Andro. But caller ID said it was Ryan.

"Where are you?" he asked.

"Hi to you, too," I said.

"I'm at your office, and you're not here. You're always here if you're not with Andro, and I know you're not with Andro."

Way to rub it in, dude. It felt like I was having more palpitations. "Ooh." I rubbed my chest. I didn't know if my heart was palpitating because I was afraid Andro might have attacked me or because I was afraid he'd believe the stupid lies he'd overheard this morning, or because I missed him or all of the above.

Ryan continued, oblivious to the pain he was causing me. "Syd just called and said the police were at the house, looking for you. They want to question you about the attack last night."

"Ugh, not the police again." Was the attack only last night? It seemed like a long time ago, so much had happened. This week was lasting for-ever.

"Madison!"

"I'm on the bus. I rented a new place. I'm on my way back to work."

"How could you rent a new place already?"

"It's a college town, dude. People are moving in and out and here and there, all the time."

"I guess. But I thought you didn't have any money."

"It's a sublet. I didn't have to pay a deposit. Is my living situation really what you wanted to talk about?"

"No. You're right. I called to tell you Sydney told the cops you were at your office. They're coming here to question you."

I blew out a huge gust of air. "Stall the cops until I get there."

"Okay. But hurry up." He paused. "You don't really think Andro attacked you, do you?"

Ah, Andro. My heart palpitated again. "I don't know. I don't think so. I'll be back soon." To be interrogated by the cops. Again.

I hated my life.

Back in my office, my least favorite detective, Baldy, sat in my desk chair in front of my computer. Ryan lounged on my couch but jumped up when he saw me. "Madison! There you are!"

You could cut the tension in the room with an industrial diamond. "Hi, Ryan. Yep. Here I am." I turned to the cop. "Don't you need a warrant to be in here?" Of course, my lack of an actual door made physically keeping people out tricky.

He eyeballed Ryan.

Ryan said, "I told him it would be okay. The Martin family cooperates with law enforcement."

Did the cop look nervous? Angry? I had trouble reading him. "I'm sorry, I've forgotten your name. What was it?" In fact, in all our dealings, I knew he'd never deigned to give me his name.

He pursed his lips, and I knew he knew that I knew he'd never told me his name. Finally, he said, "It's Detective Davis. Where have you been this afternoon, Dr. Martin?"

So we were back to Dr. Martin? Was that a good sign? "I had to do an errand." I hoped it was a good sign anyway.

"Must be nice gallivanting around and doing whatever you want in the middle of the workday."

I didn't take his bait. I was going to stay cool and calm and collected and some other good word that started with c. Cute? "Yes. It's nice. I try to gallivant every chance I get."

"I understand you were attacked last night here in your

89

office in the physics building," he said.

How did he know that? "Yes." I walked towards my desk. Get out of my chair, dude.

"Why didn't you report it to the police?"

"Uh." That was a good question. Why hadn't I? At first, I couldn't really believe I was being attacked. And then I couldn't face being attacked by Andro. And then I wasn't sure the miscreant was Andro despite looking exactly like him. How was I supposed to explain all that in some police report?

And then this morning was a fiasco. And then, that was too many 'and thens.' "I reported it to Ryan." I pointed at him. "He's police."

Baldy gave me a look that said, *Not regular police.*

"Anyway, I've been busy," I said. "I was just about to." Come to think of it, how did he know about it? I spared a glare for Ryan. Did he tell him?

A hot uniformed cop skidded into my office. "Sorry, that took so long. You wouldn't believe how far away I had to park." A hot cop I knew.

"Ben," Ryan said and smiled. It was the first time I'd seen him smile in a while.

"Officer Willis," Detective Davis said. "I was starting to think something had happened to you. You're a cop. You can park wherever you like."

Ben shrugged. He looked good. He looked like someone who wouldn't dump me or attack me. "We're in an unmarked car. You know the Chief says we should do things by the book."

"I thought I told you to stay with the car, anyway, Willis."

"I thought I could help," Ben said.

Then, Ryan blurted out, "They're dating." Why would he say that?

Ben gazed at me, and a slow smile spread over his face.

My own face grew hot.

"Is this true, Officer Willis?" Detective Davis asked.

"I asked her out, sir. More than once," Ben said.

He asked me out more than once? I checked my memories of the last few days. Oh, yeah, he asked Ryan when I was making my famous banana nut oatmeal cookies. Mmm, cookies. I wondered if there were any left. And he'd emailed me, too.

Ryan said, "Madison told me you guys were going out."

I didn't recall telling him that. Granted, my memory was bad for non-science stuff, but it wasn't that bad. I knew we hadn't gone out yet. Good grief, Ryan, you're going to get your buddy in trouble for dating a murder suspect.

"Generally, I don't recommend dating murder suspects, Officer Willis," Davis said. "And you should have mentioned this before we came over here."

"Yes, sir," Ben said.

"He probably just wanted to see his sweetie," Ryan said.

More blood rushed to my face. I probably glowed like Chernobyl's neutron moderator. I wasn't sure what to say. I didn't want to contradict Ryan and make him look like a liar in front of the Boulder cops. What was with him?

I glanced at Ben. He was mighty attractive. Did I want to go out with him, my Andro mess notwithstanding? Among other attributes, Ben looked like he could protect me if I got attacked again.

Detective Davis scanned the room from one to the other of us. I'm sure we made an awkward tableau. "The two of you," he pointed at Ryan and Ben, "should leave and let me talk to Dr. Martin alone."

Great. Just want I wanted, to be alone with this jerk. Not.

I wanted to call my lawyer, but I didn't want to pay him more money.

"Officer Willis, wait for me in the lobby," Davis said.

Ryan and Ben sauntered into the hall and presumably down to the lobby.

"So, Dr. Martin." Detective Davis pointed at my guest chair.

Gee, how nice. Offering to let me sit in my own guest chair. This guy was an asshole. Stay calm, Mad. I sat. "I should call my lawyer."

"Do you have something to hide?"

Just my immense and growing dislike of him. "No."

"You were attacked?" he asked.

"Yes, sir."

"Can you tell me about it?" He swiveled to face the big hole in my office wall. "And what happened to your door?"

Despite everything, I didn't want to say anything that would implicate Andro. I was sure he wasn't a murderer or an attacker. Pretty sure. Sort of sure. Maybe sure. Ugh.

"Dr. Martin?"

"Sorry," I said. "I was here working last night at about nine p.m."

"Nine o'clock at night?" He looked surprised.

Gee, maybe I'm not a total slacker after all, huh? "Yes. Nine p.m. I felt something bizarre. Then my door disappeared." I pointed at the large hole in the wall. I really should report that to maintenance or something. "I felt a bizarre pressure on my skin. I jumped up from my desk and ran out into the hall to try to stop whoever it was. I saw a man in a dark tracksuit. I chased him into the stairwell. He tripped and fell down some stairs and cussed me out. Finally, he limped out of the stairwell, through the lobby, and out of the building."

"What did he look like?" He looked skeptical.

Andro! "I'm sorry. I didn't get a good look at him. It was too dark."

"Does this building have surveillance cameras?"

He must know that from his murder investigation. Was he testing me? "No."

"Are there any surveillance cameras on campus?"

More tests? I shrugged. "You'd have to ask Ryan about that."

"You said he cussed you out. What did he say? What did he sound like?"

"He said something like, *You bitch. I'm gonna kill you.*" Come to think of it, his voice was nothing like Andro's voice. In the excitement of the moment, it hadn't registered. Hurray. It definitely wasn't Andro.

"Dr. Martin?"

"Sorry. What?"

"You didn't think it was worth reporting?" the detective asked.

That the voice wasn't Andro's? How did he know I was thinking that?

"You didn't think it was worth reporting someone threatened your life?" he said.

"Oh, that. Come to think of it, I should have."

"So why didn't you?"

I thought the attacker was my boyfriend, and I couldn't wrap my head around it. "I've been busy." Losing my boyfriend. Losing my home. Finding a new place to live. "And it's not the first time I've been threatened. Irate freshmen say stuff like that all the time when you give them a bad grade. And pre-med students, forget about it."

"Freshmen, no matter how irate, are not the same thing as murderers."

He was probably right about freshmen, but, as I'd found out the hard way last year, seniors were another matter. "We don't know if the person who attacked me is the murderer."

"Did anyone else see this attacker?"

Alyssa and the other students she was with. What were they doing there in the lobby at nine p.m. anyway? "Not that I recall."

Baldy gave me the evil eye for a few moments. Finally, he said, "To summarize, a mysterious bad guy you didn't see and can't describe, attacked you, threatened you, and ran off? Is that it?"

That didn't sound too plausible. "Yes. But there's proof." I jumped up. "My door is proof." I strode over to the doorway. The doorframe was gone. I touched the remnants, spongy concrete. It was all too similar to what happened to poor Barry. I couldn't help it; I shuddered. So much for calm and cool and cucumber-y.

Detective Davis levered his considerable bulk up and over to the door and touched the concrete. "It's strange. I'll give you that. But how do I know you didn't do this?"

"Why would I get rid of my own door? I like doors!" You can slam them in detective's faces, among other things.

I had a brainstorm. "Maybe if you check the local hospitals, you'll find someone who came in with injuries consistent with falling down the stairs."

"Not a bad idea, Dr. Martin. Maybe you aren't totally incompetent at law enforcement."

Maybe you are totally incompetent at being a decent human being. But I wisely kept that thought to myself. My act was a little bit together. "Since I had to go out earlier and gallivant about, I actually have a lot of work to do now. Do you think I could get to it?"

Detective Davis cast his grumpy gaze upon me. "All right." He stepped to the hall. "I'll be in touch."

As soon as he left, my cell rang. It was Ben.

"Ryan texted me that Detective Davis left your office," Ben said.

He did? How did he know? I poked my head into the hall but didn't see Ryan.

"I only have a few minutes. Was what Ryan said true? Will you go out with me?"

"I don't want to get you into any trouble, Ben." I paced around my office. "I am a murder suspect after all."

"Oh, come on, Madison. I know you didn't murder anyone."

"You do?" My throat felt tight with gratitude. I liked this guy.

"Of course. You're one of the good guys, er, girls."

"I am?" It felt good to be appreciated, even by a relative stranger.

"Sure. I'm a cop. I know these things. I know people. I don't share pancakes with just anyone, you know."

The more I knew Ben, the more I liked him. And I needed a friend right now. The pancake reference tipped the balance. "Okay. What were you thinking?"

"How about this? We could hang out."

That did sound nice. "When were you thinking of?"

"Tonight?"

"Actually, that's a no-go. I have to move tonight."

"Perfect! I'm an awesome mover. You may not have noticed, but I work out."

Oh, I noticed. Boy, did I notice. "Are you sure? Moving isn't any fun."

"I'm sure. Here comes Davis. Gotta go."

"Okay," I said quickly. "That sounds nice. Meet me at Ryan's house at about seven o'clock?"

"Yes, sir. I'll definitely do that, Detective Smith." He hung up.

I went over to my desk and sat down. A date, no a hang-out, with Ben Willis. Cool. Then my eye hit the coffee mug Andro had given me, *World's Best Coffee Drinker*. I was so confused.

"So?" a loud male voice said from the hall.

I jumped to the tropopause.

It was Ryan. "Don't sneak up on me like that!"

"I wasn't sneaking. It's not my fault you don't have a door. What happened with Ben?"

"We're going to hang out tonight."

"Cool." He smiled. "I'll get some beer. We can order a pizza." You'd think he was the one with a hang-out date tonight.

"I think you're forgetting I'm moving out of your house tonight. Any beer-drinking or pizza-eating will happen at my new place."

"Oh, yeah. Darn." He deflated.

"It's for your own safety, bro. And Sydney and Emily."

"Yeah, I know. I'll buy you guys some beer anyway and put it in the fridge. I know what Ben likes." He rubbed his hands together and strolled into the hall.

And maybe you can drink some, too? "Thanks, Ryan," I called after him.

After I was alone for a few moments, I realized I had no idea what hanging out consisted of on the dating spectrum. Was it a date or not?

Maybe an even bigger question was: what was with Ryan's cupid act?

Chapter Twelve

After my grilling by Detective Davis, I realized I had to put my murder investigation into high gear. I hadn't been working on it hard enough. My physics research had been distracting me. That ended now.

I reviewed what I knew so far. A man was killed. The cops thought the victim was Barry King. How did they even know it was Barry King?

The cops thought the murder had been done via q-lapsing. How did they know it was q-lapsing? When exactly did the guy die? How come they couldn't tell? What was the official cause of death?

Was my attack related to the murder? Had it been a diversion, or had he been trying to kill me? How did he impersonate Andro?

Well, crap. What I knew so far was a bunch of questions.

After working a little with law enforcement over the last year, I also knew of one place I might find some answers: the medical examiner's office. I grabbed my eco-pass and headed for the bus stop.

The entire bus ride, I wracked my brain, trying to deduce a way to get the info I wanted out of the ME. I couldn't figure out a way to get it legitimately, so illegitimately, it would have to be. My tentative plan was to q-lapse the door open, find the report on Barry King, take a photo, and q-lapse out if need be.

When I got off the bus, I stopped and got a coffee because it helped with q-lapsing. Plus, I figured a coffee would make me look like I fit in at the Justice Center. Lawyers liked coffee. And who ever heard of criminals trying to commit crimes while holding an enorme paper cup?

QUANTUM MURDER

Thus, I walked right into the Justice Center (no problem with security at the front), to the area where the ME's office was. Of course, I hit a locked door pretty soon, but I'd been expecting it.

What was the probability that this door would be unlocked? It was non-zero. In fact, I bet it was unlocked a lot. I gulped some coffee, concentrated on the possibility that the door was unlocked, and focused on q-lapsing.

The lock clicked. I opened the door. The whole thing had only taken a few seconds.

Down the hall was the ME's office, and by looking through the window, I deduced no one was home. Excellent. I did the door-unlocking thing again. I opened the door and strolled in like I owned the joint. Confidence was key in a successful investigation, or at least in a successful breaking and entering.

Barry King's file was open on the desk.

I quickly paged through it. ID: Tentative. Barry King via Driver's License. No fingerprint match in database. No dental match possible. Time of Death: Inconclusive. Cause of Death: Inconclusive. Next of kin: Unknown. This was followed by a bunch of grisly pictures I tried not to look at and some incomprehensible medical data.

"Dammit!" I didn't know any more now than I knew this morning.

"Who are you?" a young woman asked me. Where'd she come from?

"Me? I'm a new intern," I said, pulse rising.

"*I'm* the new intern," she said. "Where's your ID? How did you get in here?"

"Uh..." I concentrated on the probability that I was sitting in my office.

And then I was. That so-called fact-finding mission was a bust. All I'd discovered was the ME didn't have any facts yet. And I forgot to take any pictures of the report.

I had a totally uneventful afternoon stewing. I still couldn't believe I'd been so unlucky this morning, saying all that negative stuff when Andro was right there. Why didn't he call me? Why wasn't he in his office?

I went home, looking forward to seeing Ben. At least one

human liked me.

Ryan was true to his word and stocked the fridge with beer, aka bribery, for his buddy Ben. I didn't know if I should feel flattered Ryan wanted me to date his friend or worried he thought Ben needed to be plied with beers for it to happen.

Ryan, Sydney, and Emily went out to a Halloween party for Emily's playgroup. They were all dressed in homemade *Curcurbitas* costumes. It turned out *Curcurbitas* is the genus of pumpkins—as Sydney informed me. Emily was a *Baby Boo*, Syd was a *Lumina,* and Ryan was a *Big Max*. It was amazing what stay-at-home moms could accomplish. And they weren't near me, so they were safe from any impending attacks.

I was feeling sad about having to move out as I packed up my pitiful collection of stuff. Ryan and his family were the only relatives I had in town, or in the state, for that matter. I was there when Emily was born. I saved her life. I wasn't sure I could live without my daily ration of baby-Emily-adorableness, but I was about to find out.

That's what I got for pissing off murderers, apparently.

At seven o'clock on the dot, a friendly knock rapped at the front door.

So far, Ben was making a great impression.

I rushed to the door and swung it open. It wasn't Ben. It was Andro. I jerked back. Or was it Andro? Maybe it was the imposter? Was he here to attack me? My heart was sprinting like I was scared. "Andro?"

"Madison?" he asked. "What's wrong?"

It looked like Andro, from his wavy brown hair to the tips of his slightly pointy leather shoes. And it sounded like Andro. That was good. I sniffed. It smelled like Andro. That was good, too. "You're not here to attack me, are you?"

"Attack you?" His volume increased. "What are you talking about?"

Okay, that was a stupid question. If he had been here to attack me, it's not like he would announce it. And I didn't really think he was here to attack me. That clumsy, villain-y guy the other night didn't sound like Andro. This guy did sound like Andro.

"What's going on with you? Is this why you were acting so

bizarre in the physics department office?"

I nodded.

"You were attacked? That's horrible. I'm sorry." His voice quieted. "How? With quantum mechanics?"

I nodded.

"Like Barry? Are you okay?" Wow. He looked worried about me.

"Yeah. I'm okay," I said. "But the attacker looked exactly like you."

He seemed stunned. Finally, he said, "I would never hurt you."

"I know that. What are you doing here?"

"You were so weird this morning, weirder than usual, I was concerned," he said. "After I calmed down, I couldn't believe you meant the things you said." Concerned sounded good, but what exactly did he mean by *weirder than usual*? I felt a frown coming on.

"Madison?" Andro asked. "Why did you say those things?"

"I'm trying to publicly distance myself from you and from Ryan and his family to keep you safe from Barry's murderer."

"You have to know I still care about you," he said.

If he cared about me, why did he want to take a break? Ugh. I appreciated his concern, but why did he have to be here now? Even I knew Andro and Ben meeting on my front stoop was not going to be a good thing.

I peered at the street, willing Ben to be late.

"Madison?"

"Yeah. I'm just surprised to see you. I wish you would have called first." I couldn't stop myself from grimacing at him and adding in a snarky tone, "Since we're on a break and my feelings are so unimportant and all."

"Can I come in?"

I needed him to leave before Ben got here. My palms started sweating.

"Madison? We need to talk."

Be late, Ben. Be late. "I know we need to talk. I want to talk."

And there's Ben if the hot guy parking the vintage Mustang in front of my house meant anything. Of course. My luck was impeccable, as usual.

Andro would not understand this at all despite the fact that he was the one who said we should take a break, and there was nothing going on between me and Ben.

"I'm sorry," I said, "but this isn't a good time for me."

Ben got out of his car and grinned at me across the lawn. Damn, he had a nice grin.

"Hey, Madison," Ben called out. "Hey, Andro. How's it going?"

Andro froze for a moment and then slowly pivoted.

"Hey, Ben," I said. "Andro, you recall Ryan's ho–." Ack. Not Ryan's hot cop friend. Why did I get so stupid when I was nervous? I wiped my sweaty palms on my pants. "Ryan's home-boy, right?"

"The naked cop," he said. "Now, it all comes back to me." He pivoted back my way, face still.

I hated that damn still-face look he had. I knew he was suppressing his emotions, trying not to yell or jump up and down or look angry.

I sighed. "Ben's here to help me move."

Ben had joined us on the front stoop.

"You're moving?" Andro asked, face still still.

"Since I was attacked, it's not safe for Ryan's family for me to be here. Anyway, Andro, I need you to leave now. Sorry. I'm busy."

He just stood there for a second, staring at me. Still. Did I detect a speck of surprise?

"Madison?" Ben asked. "Is he bothering you? Do you want me to get rid of him?"

Like that would ever be a good idea. Andro would never forgive that scenario. But I knew Ben was just trying to be cop-helpful. I flashed him a smile. "No, thanks. Andro was just leaving."

"I think Ben here is forgetting that I can q-lapse," Andro said.

Ben took a step back.

He was acting like taking a break wasn't his idea, but it was, and now he had to live with the consequences. Was I pleased he was struggling a little? I had to say yes.

He stared at me for a moment and then walked away. It felt

like he took all the oxygen with him.

"What was that about?" Ben asked as we went into the house.

I sighed again. Agent Baker's wise words came back to me. *Men, you can't live with 'em, you can't disappear 'em without getting into trouble.* "I don't know."

I closed the door behind us. "Thanks for helping me move. I appreciate it." I walked to the refrigerator. "Ryan bought us some beer." I smiled. "I'm not sure if he's paying you to be my friend, or what."

Ben snickered.

Well, that was a stupid thing to say, Mad. I got out two *Negra Modelos* and handed him one. Wait. *Negra Modelo*? That was Andro's favorite beer.

"Nice." Ben took a swig.

What were the odds Andro and Ben would like the same beer? "You like *Negra Modelo*?"

"Yep." He took another swig. "It's my favorite. Ryan and I discovered it years ago on a spring break trip to Mexico." He stopped. "Actually, Ryan probably wouldn't want me to tell that story."

Nothing makes a person want to hear a story like, *I can't tell the story.* "Oh, come on."

He smiled. "Sorry." He drank his beer.

Okay. We couldn't talk about that even though I was dying to. "Did you hear anything more about the murder investigation?"

"Yes."

"Well?"

"I can't say." He grinned like the cat that knew the canary very, very well.

Hmm. A person who could keep a secret. I wasn't sure how I felt about that. "You're an unusual person, Ben."

"Oh? How so?"

Now, it was my turn to grin. He deserved some of his own medicine. "I can't say."

He smiled. "Good one."

I smiled back.

"So, what are we moving? I hope it's not a bunch of furniture because I didn't bring a truck."

I pointed to the open door of my room, the former garage, gesturing for him to follow. "I saw your car. Nice. How long have you had it?"

"Original owner."

I felt my forehead crinkle. "Isn't it from the 1960s? You can't tell me you were driving in the 1960s."

He chuckled. "No. I wasn't even born in the sixties. That would be a good trick. My pop was the original owner. I bought it from him."

"I remember riding to Little League games in it, going for ice cream, and driving it to high school."

"Wow. Such a nice car must have made you popular." We entered my boudoir, aka the garage.

"I was popular. But it wasn't because of my car." He took a swig of beer and grinned at me over the bottle. "In fact, my first time was in that car."

I felt my face get hot. This did not feel like a platonic hang-out. "Well, I'm not touching that."

"That's what she said." Grin.

I had to stop myself from grinning back. Such jokes didn't deserve encouragement, right? "I mean, I'm staying away from that."

"That's what she said." He held up a finger. "But only at first."

Good grief, don't laugh, Mad. "I meant, I'm staying away from that topic." I took a sip of beer to foil the giggles. "Anyway! Boxes. Here they are."

He looked around the room at the few packed suitcases and boxes. "For a girl, you don't have very much stuff."

I glanced around, too. "Yeah, you're right." I had bought some furniture and other household stuff a few years ago with my former boyfriend Ted, but when I moved out, I didn't take any of it with me. I heard through the grapevine he was engaged to the little tramp he cheated on me with, so I wasn't about to ask for it back now.

"We might be able to do this in one trip," Ben said.

I stuck my key in the front door at Isabella's place while trying to balance a box on my hip.

Isabella called out, "It's open."

I tried the knob, and, sure enough, it was open. I pushed open the door and almost dropped the box.

Ben was right behind me with a box under his arm. "Whoa, there." He reached around me, one arm grabbing my box, the other still holding his.

It felt like a hug. It felt very good, and also very bad. What about Andro? "Thanks. I got it." I lurched into the family room and proceeded to drop the box. Toiletries, condoms, and feminine hygiene products spilled out all over the floor. When I turned back to Ben, he looked exceptionally amused. If I hadn't been blushing from the pseudo-hug, I was definitely blushing now. Good grief. I was supposed to be an adult. Why did I have so much trouble acting like one?

"Should a' let me help you," was all he said, smiling and shaking his head slightly.

Isabella rushed up, wearing a *Talk nerdy to me* t-shirt, glanced at me crouched over my spilled items, and then back to Ben. "Let me help with that, Dr. Martin." Then, leaning down, she mouthed, "OMG. He is so hot." She helped me refill the box.

"Thanks, Isabella." Thanks a lot. Like he didn't notice when you said he was hot. "And I thought we agreed you would call me Madison." I straightened up.

"Right. Thanks, Dr. Madison, er, Madison." She went back to the family room.

The tiny bedroom down the hall had white walls, hardwood floors, and a bed presumably belonging to Isabella's previous roommate. I guessed beggars like me couldn't be choosers when it came to free furniture.

"I think it's a step up from your previous accommodations, a bedroom that's actually a bedroom rather than a place to park a car." Ben placed his box on the bed. "And a double bed, huh?"

My face heated up again like molten magma. What was wrong with me?

Ben's phone chirped, and he checked a text. "Huh."

"What?"

"I'm hoping to make detective someday, and I asked the guys at the station to keep me posted if anything strange happened. There was a weird crime. I'm thinking it might be a

quantum crime. You know I had that weird experience last year."
Oh, boy, I knew.

What he said finally registered, and my heart leapt into my throat. More q-crimes? I had to grab the wall to hold myself up. "What's the crime?" Please don't say murder.

"The Apple Store at the mall was robbed," Ben said.

I straightened. "How is that weird?"

"None of the alarms or anything went off."

It didn't sound quantum to me. "Can you say inside job?"

He shrugged. "The guys at the station said it was weird. I'll check it out tomorrow."

We managed to bring in the rest of my stuff, including some more cold beers, without any further embarrassing incidents.

Ben and I walked into the family room where Isabella and a familiar-looking greasy-headed young man were sitting on the couch watching TV.

"Were you here before?" I asked him.

"Just got here," he said. His t-shirt with a guy cleaning a window and the quote *I do do windows if they've got Bose-Einstein condensation* also looked familiar. I thought his name was Chris.

I handed Ben a beer and held out the remnants of the six-pack to Isabella and her friend. "Beer?"

Chris's eyes lit up, and he reached for one. "Awesome!"

Isabella looked at him with amusement as she took one.

"Did you hear anything about the concert yet?" I asked her.

"Nope." She opened her beer.

I took one and opened it. "I was thinking we'd order a pizza. Anyone interested?"

"I'm in," Ben said. "I assume I'm not paying."

"No," I said. "You're not paying."

"I'm in if I don't have to pay!" Chris said.

"Fine," I said. "It's my treat. It's a special occasion. How often does a person move, after all?"

"Pineapple!" Chris said.

"I vote for tofu," Isabella said.

I felt my bottom lip tug down. I turned to Ben. "As my special super-helpful guest, please veto pineapple and tofu."

"Yeah." He tucked his thumbs into his jeans pockets. "Cops

don't eat tofu or pineapple. We like meat."

"Cop?" Isabella asked.

"You're a cop?" Chris said.

"Yeah, he's a cop," I said. "This is Officer Ben Willis. Did I not introduce him?"

Isabella and Chris glanced at each other.

"Nah, you didn't." Ben grinned and shook his head.

"I just remembered I have a bunch of work to do at the lab," Isabella said.

"I just remembered I have a bunch of work to do at the lab," Chris said.

Then, like a flash, they both stood up and sped out the door.

"Was it something I said?" Ben said.

"Maybe they don't like cops?" I said. But, why would that be? Guilty conscience?

Guilty of what?

Chapter Thirteen

When I woke up early Friday morning in an actual bedroom, in a double bed (on twin bed sheets), I was very disoriented. For a second, I almost panicked and q-lapsed myself to my office. But all the boxes around the bed saying *Madison's winter clothes* and the like clued me in. I was at my new place.

I got up to take a shower, and there was no sign of Isabella. I looked in her bedroom and the kitchen and the family room, but nope, no sign. It occurred to me I had no idea where she was, and then it occurred to me I didn't know her at all.

I missed people I did know, even though it had only been a day. I missed waking up with Andro. I missed Ryan in his ratty pocket-bulging bathrobe, Sydney in her coordinated ginkgo p.j.'s and robe, and Emily gurgling and grinning in whatever cute outfit she happened to be wearing. I guessed it was the beginning of a new, independent, mature period of my life.

To begin my new beginning, I stopped on my way to work at my usual place, Boulder Brews, and ordered some cinnamon-bun coffee and two cinnamon buns. As usual, it was very crowded. Waiting in line to pay, my phone rang. Caller ID said Ben Willis. A morning-after call and we hadn't even hooked up. Very classy. "Hi, Ben. How's it hanging?"

He laughed. "What?"

So much for mature or at least polite. "I mean, good morning, Officer Willis. How are you?"

"I am fine, Dr. Martin." He played along. "How are you?"

"Fine. Thanks for asking." The line inched towards the cash register. I wondered if the cashier was one of the people who'd told the cops I was annoying. "And thanks again for helping me move last night."

"I wanted to apologize for going into cop mode last night after those kids ran out," he said. He had questioned me about Isabella and her friend. I hadn't been able to tell him much.

"Oh?" I said. "I do like apologies."

"Yeah. Sorry. I was off the clock and shouldn't have acted like I wasn't."

I decided to try to give him a little grief. "You were on a clock? Like a grandfather clock? I must admit I didn't see any clocks."

"Ha, ha." But he didn't sound amused. I guessed he didn't appreciate my unique sense of humor. No one's perfect. "Anyway, I read the report on that robbery at the Apple Store, and it does seem weird. There was also a panty raid at the tri-delt sorority house last night."

I couldn't help it, an incredulous laugh escaped my mouth. "Panty raid? Did it also involve a time-machine trip back to 1950?" The line for coffee centimetered forward.

Ben snickered a little as well. So, he did have a sense of humor. Good. "I'm telling you it was strange. It's like the panty-raiders got in and out of the sorority house via magic, or..."

I filled in the blank. "Quantum mechanics?"

"Yeah. So will you help me with the cases?" His voice took on a hopeful lilt there at the end.

I briefly thought about the nefarious webpage. Could it be back again? Plus, these quantum crimes might lead us to Barry's murderer. Maybe. "Yeah. I'm in. Email me the reports."

"Consider it done." He was quiet for a few moments. Finally, he said, "So, I was also wondering..."

In my peripheral vision, I spied a familiar evil face through the crowd, which gave me a strong feeling of déjà vu. Who the hell was that? I elbowed my way through the crowd.

"Hey!"

"Ow!"

"Watch it!"

The mystery man possessed a perfect white smile, symmetrical Italian features, short dark hair, and was about six feet tall. To summarize, he was very handsome and looked a lot like the most nefarious quantum criminal of all time, my former student, Luke Bacalli. I wanted to run away, but I had to know if it was him. I started to call out. "Lu–"

"Madison?" Ben said in my ear.

At the same time, someone touched my shoulder from behind, and I jumped to the stratopause.

"Madison?" Andro said. Seeing him wasn't a big coincidence since this was the only coffee shop between our neighborhood and campus.

"Are you still there?" Ben asked.

"Sorry, B–oy. I gotta go." I quickly hung up and scanned the room for Luke. Was it really him? How could it be? I killed him, didn't I? We battled for reality itself, and only one of us walked away. I prevailed, but it had been close. I couldn't see the mystery man anymore.

"I think your order is up, Madison," Andro said.

I turned my attention back to the cash register, and the young woman there yelled, "Last call for a large cinnamon coffee and two cinnamon buns! Come get your food, dammit!"

"Oops. You're right, Andro. Just a sec." How did he know that was my order? I darted to the register. "Sorry. I'm here," I said to the woman. "The cinnamon stuff is mine." I reached into my bag for my wallet.

"Dr. Martin." She frowned. "I should have known."

Annoying, check. "Sorry." I handed over the money. Where had Andro gotten to? "Andro?" I called out.

He appeared behind me again, and I jumped again. "What?" he asked.

"Where'd you come from?"

"I was right here." He frowned. "What's going on with you this morning?"

"Sorry." Word of the day, apparently. "I can't believe I'm about to say this, but I think I may have just seen Luke Bacalli." I had a hard time wrapping my mind around it. Or, wait. Could someone be impersonating him?

"What!" Andro's head whipped around the jammed restaurant. "Where? How?"

I pointed over to where I thought I'd seen him. What was more probable, Luke somehow reassembling his quarks and gluons and electrons or someone impersonating him? Or maybe I was mistaken, and the guy didn't look like him. Maybe I was just seeing things. I hoped so.

Andro tried to run over there, but the crowd was uncooperative. It was more like a brisk walk trying to squeeze between people packed like atoms in a solid. I followed in his wake, sipping my coffee.

"Where?" he asked. "Where is he?"

"I thought I saw him here." I shrugged. "Maybe I was wrong." I prayed I was wrong. What he put me through scarred me for life. He threatened the lives of everyone I loved most, Andro, Ryan, Emily, Sydney. I couldn't go through that again.

"Did you see him or not?"

"I'm not sure. Sorry." And if I killed him, he made me a killer. Killing him might have killed a piece of my soul.

"How would that even be possible?" Andro asked. "How could Luke be alive?"

"I'm not sure." The sorry was implied.

"I thought you said you destroyed him?" Andro held his face very still. Neither one of us had forgotten Luke had almost killed him last year.

I knew Andro well enough to know he was very upset. But what were we going to do if Luke was back? Curl up into a little ball? We had to continue on with our lives as best we could. "Do you want a cinnamon roll? I have an extra." I held up my paper bag. It had felt like a two-cinnamon-roll day, but I knew how to share.

He shook his head.

"In our quantum duel, I definitely made his atoms fly apart," I said. "No question whatsoever." I was sure about that.

"So? Doesn't that mean he's dead?"

"I don't know. What is mind or soul or consciousness? Could they linger long enough for Luke to q-lapse and reassemble himself?" I shrugged. "I don't have to tell you how bizarre all this is. Sorry."

Andro stared at me.

We stood there in silence for a few moments, surrounded by coffee-seeking college students. Neither one of us knew how to deal with the possibility Luke was back.

"You stopped by last night to talk. I'm sorry I was busy." Ugh. Quit saying sorry, Mad. "Do you want to come over for

109

dinner tonight, see my new place? I'll cook."

All this Luke business reminded me how I almost lost Andro for good last year. And how much I loved Andro even when he was going through whatever-he-was-going-through. And he had made an effort to talk to me last night. That was something, right?

That got his face moving. "Cook? You?"

I smiled. "I made some cookies the other day." Whatever happened to those cookies? Were there any left? "I can cook."

His face relaxed. "Since when?"

"I'll have you know I have a Ph.D., mister. I can do anything."

He snorted. "I'll believe you can cook when I see it."

"Hey. It's simple chemistry." I smiled again. "We've cooked together before."

"As I recall, our culinary forays tend to end with us making out like teenagers and eventually having something delivered." He smiled.

Ah. That's what I recalled, too. It fit my definition of 'cooking.' I was guessing that scenario wasn't in our near future. "I promise I can cook an actual meal." Assuming Isabella had some pots and pans and plates and other cooking paraphernalia.

His smile faded. "What about that Ben guy?"

"What about him?" I said. "We're just friends." Did Andro know that was him on the phone just now? "That wasn't him on the phone just now. It wasn't. Absolutely hot, I mean, not."

"Madison, I can tell when you're lying." He stared at me for a moment longer and then pivoted and walked away without saying anything more. He was a good pivoter.

I said, "Sorry," but he was already out of earshot.

When I got to my office, I heard a noise from next door, i.e., Andro's office. If we broke up, or rather if we stayed broken up, it was going to get very awkward. Especially since I didn't even have a door. Ugh. Maybe ugh was the word of the day.

I debated getting up and going to ask him about coming over for dinner again. Or making other plans to talk.

I looked at the hole in the wall where my door used to be.

I debated getting up and going to ask him if he'd help me fix

110

my wall using quantum mechanics.

But we were getting into a bad dynamic where I kept apologizing, and he kept walking off. That wasn't going to work long-term.

And I'd thought we had potential long-term. I sighed. I'd thought he might be The One.

In a colossal failure of nerve, rather than talking in person, I decided to email him. So, I did. The ball was now in his court. He needed to contact me.

Then I stared at my computer, willing for him to email me back.

Email me back, dammit.

I double-checked the control reality webpage, and it was still gone.

I waited a few minutes more, but it appeared that a watched email account was similar to a watched pot. Namely, no phase change occurred in the dihydrogen-oxide.

Just when I'd quit focusing on email and started focusing on my research, Alyssa walked into my office because, of course, I didn't have a door. "Hi, there, Alyssa. Did we have an appointment? Or did you have some fabulous new results to show me?"

She glowered at me. It was going to be one of those days. Fortuitously, I had an extra cinnamon bun to console me.

"I can't believe you sicced the cops on me," she said. "How could you do that?"

"I'm sorry," ugh, "you were questioned by the police, but it wasn't my fault."

"No?" She put her hands on her hips. "Then, whose fault was it?"

"It was your fault. You q-lapsed right in front of a bunch of FBI agents Monday afternoon. I've been trying to keep you out of it."

"Well..." She looked at me. "Then..."

"Are you all right? They didn't arrest you or charge you or anything, did they?"

She dropped her arms. "No."

"Maybe you owe me an apology for barging in here."

"Maybe so." But she said in an unapologetic manner.

I raised my eyebrows at her.

"Sorry," she said more softly.

Sorry was nice when you were on the receiving end of it. "Thank you. I appreciate that." I leaned back in my chair. "So, do you want to talk physics? You know I love to do that." I grinned.

"I'm not prepared. I was kind of worked up about the cops." She dipped her chin.

Just as well. I still needed to solve Barry's murder. "Did you tell them anything?"

"No. Like what?"

"Do you know anyone else who can q-lapse?"

"Just you and Professor Rivas. And Griffin and Luke, and they're out of commission, right?"

"Yes." I hoped so, anyway. I needed to figure out a way to be sure about that.

"I'll try to get some work done to show you by tomorrow afternoon, okay?"

"Sounds good." She was friends with my new roommate. "Hey, what can you tell me about Isabella Rodriguez?" Avoiding Ben was pretty suspicious. Who would want to avoid him?

Alyssa shrugged. "She's nice. She's a grad student in the low-T group."

"Is she dating that grad student, Chris?"

"I don't think so. At least if she is, it's not serious." She pursed her lips. "Actually, Isabella's very popular with all the guys down on that floor. I'm not exactly sure what's going on there."

"Aren't you and Isabella friends? She mentioned she knew you."

"Just to smile and say hi. You know there aren't that many women in the department. I wouldn't say we hang out."

"What do you mean by very popular?"

"I don't know. I shouldn't have said anything. It's probably nothing."

And after that Alyssa clammed up. She wouldn't say anything further.

Just who was I rooming with?

Chapter Fourteen

I couldn't parse what Alyssa had been trying to say, or not say, about Isabella. Was Isabella polyamorous? What if it was relevant to the murder? If so, should I investigate?

But I needed to stay in my office in case Andro wanted to talk. I glanced at my computer and then at the wall between our offices.

He did not seem to be rushing to write me back or come over to talk. I decided to give it a rest and go downstairs and ask my go-to gal, Nancy, what she knew about Isabella.

I smiled brightly as I strode into the office. "Hi Nancy. How are you? It's so nice to see you. Have I said recently what a great job I think you're doing?"

Sitting at her desk in the back of the room, the corners of her full red lips descended. "What do you want?"

"Nancy, I'm crushed." I perched on the corner of her desk. "I don't want anything. I just wanted to say hi."

"You only say hi when you want something." She pointed her pen at me. "Get off my desk."

I stood up. "That's not true. I appreciate all your hard work."

"Prove it."

I thought quickly. "I came down here to ask if you wanted to go out to lunch with me." Yes. Now that I'd said it, it sounded like a great idea. I liked Nancy. She didn't take crap from anyone. This would give us an opportunity to get to know each other better. And maybe I could also ask her about Isabella.

"Really?"

I nodded. "Yes, really. I'm just sorry I haven't asked before."

"Are you buying?"

"Sure," I said. "When is good for you?"

"How about today at noon? You can meet me here."

"Sounds great."

Nancy glanced at the chairman's office. "Since you're being so nice, I'll tell you Professor Chen wants to know how many grants you've applied for and what your chances are."

Grants? Shit. I hadn't applied for any yet.

She leaned closer. "Between you and me, if you got a grant or two or three, he'd be a lot more likely to overlook your current legal troubles."

"Thanks for the tip, Nancy. I appreciate it. I look forward to lunch." I did look forward to it. I smiled at her.

She actually smiled back, and it lit up her whole face. She was a beautiful woman. With her hourglass figure, I was surprised the nerds around here weren't lining up to date her. On second thought, maybe she intimidated them. "What's that look?" she asked.

"Your outfit is pretty, as usual."

She smiled again. "I could give you some fashion tips if you wanted."

Why did she think I needed fashion tips? "Uh, thanks."

Chen's door creaked open, and his eyes lit up when he saw me. "Oh, Professor Martin. I've been meaning to make an appointment with you." Chen was very tall and slender, with a head of straight grayish-white chin-length hair. Somehow, he always made me think of The Beatles (from the early days).

"To talk about my grant applications?" I smiled. "I've been meaning to make an appointment with you, too."

"Yes, and to talk about your undergrad advisees."

Shit. I hadn't done anything with them yet, either. "I'm ready whenever you are, sir." Hopefully, he wasn't ready.

"Good." He nodded. "Sometimes new faculty take a while to get into the swing of things, but I can see you're right on top of it."

Forget one lunch, I owed Nancy a month of lunches. When I glanced at her, she was scrutinizing me.

"How does my calendar look, Nancy?" Chen asked.

She typed some keys on her computer, and a calendar popped up. She glanced at me again. "You're pretty booked up this week. I think you're going to have to wait until next week to meet with Professor Martin."

"I'll leave it in your capable hands." He turned to the coffee maker. "I'll see you then, Madison."

"Yes, sir," I said.

While he was pouring some coffee, Nancy said quietly to me, "So, I'll assume the end of next week is better than the beginning?"

"You read my mind. Thanks." Maybe I owed Nancy a car. Too bad I didn't have the cash to give her a car. "I'll see you at noon."

Chen went into his office and closed the door behind him.

She nodded as she started typing. "Why aren't you in class?"

Shit. It was after nine o'clock. Why wasn't I in class? The last thing I needed was to give Chen a reason to fire me. He'd almost let me go last year. I didn't want to go through that again.

I was late. There was no time to waste. I wasn't sure how long my students would hang around waiting for me. But I needed my notes and stuff. I pulled myself together, concentrated, and q-lapsed to my office, grabbed my stuff, and q-lapsed down to my class.

When I appeared in the basement classroom, the students gasped. They seemed surprised. Duh. I should have seen that coming. They'd never seen q-lapsing before—assuming they weren't involved in the new quantum crime wave.

Q-lapsing in front of them was a huge mistake on my part. Ugh. I should have known better. Students could go off the deep end with this kind of information. I should probably quit q-lapsing altogether, except for emergencies. Or FBI classes.

Crap. Crap. Crap. I was discombobulated by everything that had been going on. And now I had a headache, too. But I needed to focus on my class.

Juan was the first to regain the ability to speak. Figured. He wasn't the alpha-male in the class for nothing. "Where did you come from?"

"I'm thinking this is the controlling reality we've heard about," Arjun said with his hand raised like he wanted me to call on him. They heard about controlling reality?

Some of the students were nodding, and some still just

115

looked confused.

I grabbed a pen and tried to write down who was nodding.

Unfortunately, then they stopped nodding and started staring at me.

"What are you doing?" Juan asked.

Crap. That was the word of the day, apparently. They must not like me staring at them. So much for figuring out if any of my students might know how to q-lapse by staring at them. "I'm taking attendance, of course," I said.

"Can we start class now?" Arjun asked, but his tone meant *start class already*.

I resisted the urge to say something snarky. I forced a smile. "Sure. Of course. Today we're going to start by," I glanced at my notes, "reviewing uncertainty relationships. Who remembers what those are?" The uncertainty relationships were related to the fact that everything in quantum mechanics had to be couched as possibilities.

Instead of answering my question about uncertainty relationships, they looked at me like it was 9:08 a.m.–sleepy, the same way they looked every morning.

"Remember?" I said. "For example, the formula is delta-e times delta-t is equal to what?"

Arjun raised his hand.

I nodded at him.

"Greater than Planck's constant over two times pi," he said.

I nodded. "Good. Now, recall Planck's constant is the physical constant used to describe the sizes of quanta, also called the quantum of action."

They nodded like they remembered this. Yay.

"We talked about what delta-t meant in this case," I said.

"The change in time," somebody in the back yelled out.

I smiled. "Close. Let's discuss it some more."

The students all started talking at once, and we were off.

The hour flew by, and before I knew it, they started acting antsy and putting their stuff into their bookbags. "Good class, guys," I said, signaling they could go. They all seemed to grasp that a state that only exists for a short time cannot have a definite energy. And I'd successfully taken q-lapsing off their minds.

After class, I hot-footed it back to my office and started investigating grant opportunities and emailing my undergrad advisees.

I did notice Ben sent me an email with some attachments, but I wisely stayed on task for a while, at least.

Eventually, I couldn't resist reading the police reports. At the Apple Store, all the doors were supposedly locked and the security system armed. The security system showed none of the doors had been opened, but several machines were missing when they opened up the next morning. All the employees swore up and down they hadn't been involved. Among other things, it was odd that only some of the stuff was stolen. Why not clear the place out if they'd somehow hacked the security system?

It also turned out there'd been two panty raids last at two different sororities. Both of them had M.O.s similar to the Apple Store theft: all the doors locked, the security systems armed, no record of any doors or windows being opened, but items stolen, specifically, panties, rather than Apples. I could hardly believe it. Weird. The girls were understandably freaked out. I was a little freaked out.

The thefts did all seem like they could be the result of something like quantum tunneling. Which meant they might be a result of q-lapsing.

At noon I raced down to the physics department to meet up with Nancy.

She jumped up from her desk. "Where should we go?"

"Have you been to Burritos and Beers on The Hill?"

She narrowed her eyes at me. It seemed like she did that a lot. "Are you asking me that because I'm a Latina?"

"No. I'm asking you that because they have yummy burritos and beer. But it's totally up to you. We can go wherever you like."

"I do like burritos." She glanced at Chen's door. "Do you think I could have a beer at lunch?"

"Definitely." I put my arm around her shoulder and steered her towards the door. "Nancy, I think this is the beginning of a beautiful friendship."

We had a lovely walk across campus. It was one of those glorious Indian summer days, all golden sunlight, colorful leaves, and ornamental grasses swaying in the wind.

At Burritos and Beers, I got my usuals: the Poblano Pesto Mole Burrito and a Lemon Hefeweisen beer. It sounded like an odd flavor combination, but the spices and tastes melded together beautifully.

After some hesitation, Nancy got the same combo. The male employees seemed eager to help her, rushing her food out and thanking her profusely.

As we headed for one of the graffiti-covered tables surrounded by mismatched chairs, my mouth started watering. I should come here every day. As soon as I sat down, I took a big burrito bite.

Nancy took a tentative sip of beer. "Wow. This is lemony. It's different." She put down her mug. "It reminds me of lemonade."

As I chewed and surveyed the industrial-chic decor, I realized Andro and I had had our first meal together here about a year ago. Suddenly my eyes felt heavy with moisture. Would we ever have another meal together? The way things were going, it didn't seem likely. I blinked back the tears.

"Madison?"

"Yes." I looked at Nancy and made myself smile. "So, how do you like it? Did you try the burrito yet?"

She pointed at her giant burrito with a big chunk missing. "Yeah. It's good but totally inauthentic. It's nothing like real Mexican food."

I grinned. "I never said it was authentic. But how can you go wrong with mole?"

Nancy took another bite. "Yeah. You can't."

I debated pumping her about Isabella but decided there was no diplomatic or decent way to do so. "So tell me about your family, Nancy. I saw you had a lot of pictures on your desk."

She regaled me with cute stories about her cute nieces and nephews and cousins and even showed me some more pictures on her phone. As she was flipping through the pictures, I saw one of her and a vaguely familiar-looking man with his arm around her, both of them smiling at the camera.

"Wait. Go back. Who's that you're with? You guys look happy."

"Oh. It's not important." She blushed. "An old boyfriend from a long time ago. We broke up last year."

"Show me."

She shook her head. "No. It's history."

I didn't pry. But why did the guy look familiar?

After lunch, back at the physics building, I decided to give my Isabella fact-finding mission one more try. She'd acted odd last night when she found out Ben was a cop, and Alyssa's comments about her were pretty odd, too. Her friend Chris must know something about her. The only question was would he be willing to tell me anything, and if so, could we avoid being spotted by Isabella?

As I walked down the cinder-block-walled, tile-floored low-T hall, I got a powerful sense of déjà vu.

At the first lab, I knocked on the open door. "Hello? Chris, are you in here?"

He stood up from where he'd been apparently sitting behind some equipment. "Madison? Er, Professor Martin? What are you doing here?" He was wearing an *I know I lost an electron around here ...I'm positive* t-shirt and jeans, but he'd seemed to have washed his hair. He looked good, at least compared to when I'd seen him before.

"Professor Martin?"

"Sorry. Yeah. You look nice. Clean."

He grinned. "Thanks."

"I know you're friends with Isabella. Now that I'm rooming with her, I wondered if there was anything you could tell me about her."

"Why?"

Good question. That was the trouble with grad students, they were too smart. Because I'm suspicious she's involved in a murder. I couldn't say that. "In case her birthday or anything is coming up, and I need to get her a present. Or if she has any pet peeves I should avoid. Generally, anything I would need to know to be a good roommate."

He nodded like this was perfectly rational. "That makes sense." It did? Maybe grad students weren't too smart. "She's really nice and really beautiful, as you know." Poor guy. He was a goner. "Her birthday isn't coming up, but I think she'd enjoy presents whenever. And if you wanted to buy her food or beer, she'd be happy with that."

Gee, a poor grad student that wanted free food and beer. What a shock. One of the reasons I was so poor now is I racked up huge credit card debts when I was in grad school. This was getting me nowhere. "Is she dating anyone?"

"Why?" He put his hands on his hips. "Are you interested?"

Down, boy. I'm not the competition. "No. I guess I wondered if we should implement a sock-on-the-door policy or anything."

"As far as I know, she's not dating anyone seriously."

"And humorously?"

"Huh?"

"Is she dating anyone not seriously?"

He shook his head.

"Why didn't you guys like my cop friend, Ben?"

Chris gaped like a fish out of water.

"Never mind." He was no help. "Thanks." I took a step back. "I'll probably be seeing you around, then, right?" He clearly had a thing for Isabella. For his sake, I hoped I'd see him around her.

"Maybe not, er, yes, sure." Poor kid, I'd rattled him.

"Okay, then. Thanks." I wheeled around and walked back down the hall.

As I started up the stairs, I couldn't help thinking it was odd that Chris had said he might not be spending time with Isabella. Why was he so rattled? After I climbed a floor, still pondering, I turned around and went back to the low-T hall.

Back in Chris's lab, I didn't see him. "Chris?" I stepped inside. I passed several crammed-in tables covered with jumbles of electronics and several metal boxes on the floor with lots of wires going into them. "Chris?"

He wasn't there.

I stepped into the hall. "Chris?" He hadn't passed me on the stairs; I knew that. "Chris?"

The door to the men's room opened, and Chris stumbled out. "What? Professor Martin? What are you doing here?"

But I couldn't process his questions because my brain was stuck on his hair. It was back to all its greasy glory. How could that be?

Chapter Fifteen

When I finally got back to my office Friday afternoon, Andro still hadn't emailed me back, and he wasn't in his office. But all Nancy's talk of nieces and nephews had made me think of Andro's nieces, which made me think of his sister, Yasmin. I decided to call her. We got along well, ever since I'd helped the police figure out who killed her husband.

She answered right away. "Oh, Madison, I'm so sorry about this whole thing with Andro."

What was the whole thing? Our breakup? "Me, too."

"He's so broken up about it."

"He's upset about our breakup?" That was a relief, at least.

She gasped. "You guys broke up? Oh, no!"

"Technically, it's a break, not a breakup. But you didn't know? Then why is he upset? What's *this whole thing*? What's going on with him? I know you asked him to move out. Is that it? Or is there something else?"

She was silent for a few moments. "You have to talk to him about it."

"So there's something to talk about?" I knew it!

"You have to talk to him about it."

"Come on, Yasmin. Is there something, or isn't there?"

"Okay," she said. "There is. And it's big. Huge."

"He's not sick or anything, is he? You're not sick? Or your girls?" Please no.

"No. It's nothing like that."

"You can't give me a hint?" I asked.

"No. You need to talk to him about it."

"Well, pinning him down to talk is turning out to be easier said than done. I even offered to cook."

"You cook?" I could hear the smile in her voice. "Wow. You're pulling out all the stops. Yeah. He can be hard to pin down when he's upset." And that's where we left it. Dammit.

I tried to work on solving the murder, but I didn't have any leads. The crime itself was totally unhelpful. Other mysteries related to the murder included my attempted attack, the new tunnel at Red Rocks, and maybe Andro and Isabella acting odd—but I didn't know what any of that proved. Additionally, I may or may not have seen Luke or someone who resembled him. Maybe Ben's weird crimes would lead somewhere.

I got back to physics work. First, I got ready for my class Monday. Then, I finished emailing each of my advisees a *what's up?* Finally, I went back to looking up grant opportunities.

My cell rang. Finally. Andro must be calling about dinner.

"Madison?" It was Ryan.

"Hi." I may have grumbled.

"Hi to you, too. Ms. grumpy-pants."

A burst of laughter escaped. "What? Ms. grumpy-pants? That sounds like something I'd say."

"Yeah, okay. You're a bad influence on me."

I grinned. "Are you calling for a reason? Or just to insult me?"

"Brace yourself. I heard through the grapevine that there was a bank robbery."

Oh, no. Don't say it, Ryan. Not quantum mechanics.

"A bank robbery via quantum mechanics."

He said it. "Oh, no." I groaned. "Well, I told you the webpage was back. I got rid of it, but who knows how long it was up before I discovered it? Are there any leads about who did it?" Like Luke back from the dead-and-dispersed?

"Supposedly, they're posting an article about the bank robbery in the paper this afternoon."

I was already clicking over to the paper. "Thanks."

"I'll see you at home later."

"No, you won't, dude."

"Oh, yeah. Right." He paused. "Well, take care."

"You, too." We hung up.

I clicked around the paper but didn't see an article about a quantum bank robbery. I did see the article about Barry's murder.

I skimmed it, scrolling down. Towards the bottom was a picture of Barry King, smiling, looking happy. "Wow!" I jumped up. It was the guy from Nancy's phone. Nancy used to date Barry! Why didn't she mention it? And why hadn't I thought of asking her about him? She knew everyone, after all.

The two of them dating had to be a coincidence, right? I waffled back and forth about if I should tell the cops about Nancy and Barry, but I didn't have that many friends and wasn't eager to sacrifice one. Alyssa certainly hadn't taken being questioned very well. I doubted my brand-new friendship with Nancy could withstand a police interrogation.

While I was still waffling, Ben, the cop, walked right into my office. I really needed to fix that giant hole in the wall.

"Hey, Ben." He did look good in his form-fitting uniform.

"Hey, Madison," he said. "You didn't call me back."

Was I supposed to call him back? I didn't recall that.

"You hung up suddenly this morning. And you called me *boy*. I gotta say that was a bit strange, girl." He smiled and parked his fine tush on my desk.

"Oh! This is about our phone call this morning!" Why was my memory so flaky? I guess I had a lot, like quantum criminals, on my mind.

"Yeah. What other strange thing would I be talking about?"

"I don't know, the quantum murder, the possibly-quantum robberies, the new quantum bank robbery, little things like that."

"There was a quantum bank robbery?" he asked. "Recently?"

"Yeah. That's what Ryan said anyway, but I haven't been able to find out anything about it. Have you heard anything?"

"No, but I've been out on patrol. I only got off now."

"Got off?" I grinned.

He grinned back. "So, do you have a little while to go check out the Apple Store with me?"

Did I? I did promise I'd help him. Now was as good a time as any. "Sure. While we're at it, can you give me any tips on how to investigate stuff? It seems like all I have are questions and disparate facts. How do you put them together to solve the crime?"

He rubbed the sides of his chin. "At the academy, they

taught us to chase down all the possible leads and to talk to all the people involved in person. A lot of times, you get ideas for new questions or leads when you're talking to witnesses or possible suspects. When you catch someone in a lie, that's usually significant, so you always have to check their stories."

It sounded like wandering around and asking questions, which was basically what I'd been doing. "Okay. Thanks. Do you want to take the Hop?" The Hop was the bus that ran between the university and the mall.

"I have my motorcycle," he said.

"That sounds like much more fun." I grabbed my purse.

In no time (darn), we were at the Apple Store. It had been fun sitting behind Ben, hugging him as we zoomed through town in the sunshine.

Inside the store, he asked for the manager.

A middle-aged geek approached us. "Did you have some new info about the robbery?"

"No, sir," Ben said. "I brought an expert on this type of crime." He pointed at me. "We were hoping you could go through what happened again."

"I already went over it with the other cops, but okay." He gestured to the glass storefront, and we walked that way. "The front doors were locked. The security system was armed."

I noticed the whole front of the store was see-through. I knew it was easier to q-lapse to a place you could picture or were familiar with. "Do you have any kind of gate or anything here at night?" To obstruct the view.

"For additional security?" the manager asked. I let him think what he wanted. "No. This glass is bullet-proof."

"And you're sure the security system was on?" I asked.

He nodded. "I can show you the records on the computer."

"I assume there's a back door," Ben said. "Can we see that, too?"

The manager agreed. We wended our way through the geniuses and the customers to the back of the store and went into the *Employees Only* area. The manager showed us some security records that seemed to prove the system had been armed and nothing had been opened. I had no idea if they could have been faked. He showed us the back door, which had no window and was totally nondescript.

"So?" he finally asked. "Does all this tell you something? Can you get the guys that robbed me? Can we get the stuff back?"

"Thank you, sir," I said. "This has been very helpful. We will get back to you."

The manager looked at us a few moments as if he wanted more but finally said, "All right. Thanks."

As Ben and I exited the shop, he asked, "So what did you figure out?"

"*Figure out* may be strong words. The windows at the front make it easier to q-lapse into the store. But other than that…." I shrugged.

"Why do the windows make it easier?"

"Q-lapsing is all based on quantum possibilities. So, if the q-lapser can picture themselves someplace, make it more probable, then it actually becomes more probable they're there."

"Huh," Ben said, shaking his head. "This stuff is weird."

Then, I wondered if the thieves had actually been in the store posing as, or being, actual customers. That might make it more probable still. "They might have been customers."

"Do you know when?"

I shrugged. "It could have been any time."

"I'm not sure how helpful that is," he said.

I shrugged again.

When we got back to the university, he offered to walk me back up to my office. Was he worried I might be attacked again? I decided not to question it, not to look a gift-cop in the mouth.

When we arrived at my office, he seemed to be in a good mood. I decided to take advantage of him, er, it. "Is there any chance you could find out about the quantum bank robbery and let me know what happened?"

"Maybe." He leaned in. "If I do you a favor, would you do me a favor?"

"A new favor? I already said I'd help you with the Apple Store and the panty raids. What about the sororities, by the way? Do you want me to go over to them with you?"

He nodded. "Yeah. But it turns out it's not so easy to get permission. I'll have to let you know."

I licked my lips and leaned in. "So, what kind of favor were you thinking of?" Was he going to ask me out on a date-date rather than a hangout-date? What would I say?

Someone in the hall cleared his or her throat very loudly. With my luck, it would be Andro. I jerked backward away from Ben at the speed of light.

It was Ryan. Geez, my office was as busy as the Moscone Center during the annual American Geophysics Union's Fall Meeting.

"Sorry. I didn't mean to interrupt," Ryan said, grinning.

Ben stood up. "You weren't interrupting."

Aw. He wasn't?

"Ryan. Nice to see you." Ben clapped Ryan on the shoulder. "Thanks for the beer the other night. What's up?"

"Yeah, Ryan." I resisted the urge to grump it up. "What are you doing here?"

"I'm on my way home from work," Ryan said. "I just thought I'd stop by and say hi to Madison."

"That's nice," I said. "Hi."

"Hi," he said. "So, did you hear anything about the quantum bank robbery? Maybe Agent Baker called?"

"No," I said. "Nothing more. And it wasn't in the paper. It would be nice to know what we're dealing with. In fact, I just asked Ben, my friend on the force here, to find out about it." I turned to Ben. "What was your favor?"

He just smiled.

Ryan said, "Quantum bank robbery?"

Ben shrugged. "Okay. I'll see what I can do." He faced Ryan and the gaping hole leading into the hallway. "Ryan, we should get together some time, play basketball or something."

"Yeah. That sounds great," Ryan said. "I'll text you."

Ben walked towards the location of the former door. "I'll be in touch with you, too, Madison."

"Okay. Thanks, Ben."

Once he'd left, Ryan came over to my desk and sat down in the rickety visitor's chair. "You two looked cozy. Is something going on there? I think something's going on there." He grinned.

I shook my head. "What is up with you? Why do you want me to be with Ben so much? I thought you liked Andro."

Ryan glanced at the door-shaped hole in the wall.

"Ryan. Come on. Give. What's up?" He was acting the way he did when he was a little boy and didn't want to admit he'd done something wrong.

He glanced at me. "I shouldn't say anything. It's a rumor. It could be wrong."

"Fripping say it already."

"Sydney heard a rumor..."

"What did she hear? Spill it already!"

"She heard that Andro got someone pregnant."

"What?" I jumped up, knocking over my chair. "No. That's impossible. We're exclusive. No way would he cheat. No way."

"It's not you, is it?" Ryan asked. "You're not pregnant, are you?"

For a second, my brain froze, picturing me and Andro smiling and bouncing a baby. Andro would have his arm around me. We'd all be amazingly happy together in our own cute little home.

"Madison?"

"No, it's not me. I'm definitely not pregnant." I started to sit back down.

"Mad! Your chair!"

"Right." I turned around and righted my chair, and then sank down. "I don't believe it."

"I'm sorry, Mad." He shook his head.

"It's not true," I said. "It cannot be true. But whatever is going on with him, I'm going to find out."

I shoved Ryan out of my office and rushed over to Andro and Yasmin's house.

When I got there, I pounded on the door.

Yasmin answered. Even after a long day of work, she looked beautiful. "Andro's not here."

"Then, I'll wait!" I stomped inside and promptly saw Yasmin's daughters Maria and Theresa staring at me from the couch, mouths hanging open. I deflated. "Hi, girls. I didn't use my inside voice there, just now. That was wrong. I'm sorry."

Yasmin closed the door behind me. "I guess you can wait for him."

"Come sit by us, Auntie Madison," Maria, Yasmin's

youngest, said. I'd spent a lot of time here over the last year.

"Yeah, Auntie Maddie," Theresa said.

They were so cute. If Andro did have a child, I bet they would look just like them. Adorable.

"What's wrong, Auntie Maddie?" Theresa asked.

"It's just grown-up stuff," I said. "Nothing you need to worry about."

"I'm going to go finish making dinner." Yasmin stepped back into the kitchen area.

"You should be happy like us," Maria said. "We have a new cousin."

"Yeah," Theresa said, "She's super-cute."

I bolted up from the couch. "I think I should go help your mom with dinner, after all." I rushed into the kitchen area. "Yasmin," I whispered. "Maria and Theresa just told me they had a new cousin. You have to tell me what's going on. Now."

She glanced at her daughters. "Oh, dear." She looked at me. "You really need to talk to Andro."

"Someone else already told me he cheated on me and got somebody pregnant," I said.

"That's not true! Andro wouldn't cheat," Yasmin said. "He's a good man."

"I know he's a good man. But I need to know what's going on." I paused. "Someone else told me he might be involved in Barry King's murder."

Yasmin covered her mouth with her hand. "That's not true. Andro wouldn't hurt anyone." She paused. "At least not intentionally."

"Unintentionally?" I stood right in front of her. "Did he unintentionally hurt someone, Yasmin?"

Her eyes filled. "You really need to talk to him yourself."

I grabbed her hands. "I'm talking to you. I love you guys. Please tell me what's going on. Maybe I can help."

She slowly nodded. "Andro found out recently he has a daughter."

I had to grab the counter to keep from falling over. "That's a surprise, all right. How old is she?"

"What the hell is going on here?" someone said from the front door.

QUANTUM MURDER

It was Andro.

Chapter Sixteen

To protect Andro's nieces from any possible fireworks, I convinced Andro to come over to my new place to continue our discussion about his newly-discovered daughter. I was still reeling from the news, so I could only imagine what it was like for him.

My new place was only a few blocks away, but I didn't rent it because it was close to Andro's house. It was because it was close to where I worked. And Ryan's house. Andro's house had nothing to do with it.

Anyway, when I got home, Isabella was parked on what I was quickly discovering was her favorite place on the couch in front of the TV. She had on one of her cute science t-shirts. She smiled broadly when she saw Andro. "Professor Rivas! Welcome to our home."

He glanced at her. "Okay."

"It's an honor to have you here," Isabella said.

"Okay," he said.

"Do you want a beer?" I asked him, already headed into the kitchen area.

"Yeah." He looked at the floor.

"I would have gotten you a beer, Professor Rivas," Isabella said. "In fact, I'll get you anything you want–"

"Who are you?" Andro finally really looked at her.

I quickly grabbed the bottle opener along with the two beers and rushed back into the family room. "Here we go." I handed one to him.

"I'm Isabella."

He didn't reply.

"I'm a grad student," she said. "In the physics department."

He looked at me.

"Let's go to my room," I said, "where we can talk in private."

He nodded.

I led him down the hall to my room. We went in, and I closed the door behind us. Unfortunately, there was no place to sit besides the bed. And Andro and I had spent a lot of time in bed in the last year. It brought up a lot of memories, nice memories, loving memories, hot memories. I felt my face flush.

He awkwardly perched on the edge of the bed.

I opened my beer and passed him the opener, loitering by the door.

He opened his beer and took a swig.

"So, I guess congratulations are in order?" I said. "I imagine whatever the circumstances, being a dad is pretty great, right?"

His face froze for a moment. Then it relaxed, and he said, "I am so mad at Angie, Angela. That's the mother. She didn't tell me about Sophia. Not a word, not a fucking word." He scooted back and leaned against the wall at the head of the bed.

"How old is Sophia?"

"She's three!"

Phew. That was long before I met him. But, poor Andro. Family was everything to him. This must have been a shock. I couldn't imagine having a child and not knowing about her. It must be torture for him.

"I missed the whole first three years of her life! Everything! I missed her crawling and learning to walk and learning to talk and everything! All of it!"

I sat down next to him, leaning back against the wall, too. "That's horrible. I'm sorry you missed all that."

"Family is very important to me. When I think about that poor little girl thinking she didn't have a father, or that her father didn't want her or love her..." His voice grew hoarse and trailed off.

"I'm so sorry, Andro." My eyes grew heavy. "Do you need a hug?"

He blew a burst of air out of his nose then took a swig of beer. When he lowered the bottle, he flashed a grin at me for a split second. "You mean you need a hug."

I held up my hands. "I'm just saying I'm here for you." I

paused. "Is that why you've been so strange lately? Or is there something else?"

"Isn't that enough?"

I nodded. "Yes."

"In addition to not telling me about Sophia, Angie told all her friends and relatives that I refused to help her out. And we know a lot of the same people. I met her through Yasmin's husband, Armando. Angie's brother Fernando worked with him. So, a bunch of Armando's old crew, including Fernando, confronted me one night, accusing me of all kinds of shit. They said I should go to jail, or worse, for not paying child support." He shook his head. "I haven't seen much of them since Armando died, but I thought we were friends. They all actually thought I would abandon Angie and Sophia. They thought I would abandon my own flesh and blood." He looked at me with bewilderment in his eyes. "How could they think that?" My heart went out to him.

"Angie told them." This Angie woman sounded like trouble. In fact, she sounded like a grade-A bitch. What was her problem? "Have you talked to her?"

"Briefly. I asked her if Sophia was mine, and she said yes. And, then, I was so mad, I got off the phone before I said something I'd regret." He scowled. "I want to sue for partial custody, but I don't have any money for a lawyer. And when I discussed it briefly with Tom, he said my current legal troubles would make getting custody very difficult."

Oh, shit. I cringed. I was the reason he currently had legal troubles. Or, wait. No, I wasn't. Barry's murderer was the reason we were both having legal troubles. "If there's anything I can do to help, please let me know. Surely, you have a chance at custody? You have a Ph.D. You're a respected university professor. You helped the FBI last year." I took a breath. "You're her dad!"

He shook his head, looking down at the bed. If I didn't know better, I'd guess he was trying not to cry. But he was a rock. Rocks don't cry.

"Why did you want to take a break from our relationship?" I asked. "You aren't blaming me for the police questioning you, are you?"

"Yes."

Stay calm, Mad. I took a sip of beer. "It's not my fault you were questioned. It's the murderer's fault." I paused. "You don't think I'm a murderer, do you?"

He pierced me with his blue eyes.

Take your fripping time answering me, why don't you?

"No," he said. "I don't think you're a murderer. But—" Now it was his turn to take a sip of beer. "But it's because of you that I learned how to q-lapse. If I'd never met you, I wouldn't be involved at all. Plus, Tom said you'd probably be considered a bad influence by family court."

Bad influence? I was a great influence. I was the Quantum Cop. "Oh, Tom said that, did he?" My lawyer Tom and I were going to have a chat. Calm down, Mad. I took another sip. But then I couldn't help it, I turned to face him. "You're not saying you wish you'd never met me, are you?" He'd better not be saying that.

He started to say something but stopped.

"Maybe you should leave," I said. "Now. Before one of us says something we regret."

He gave me his still-face look, and then he got off the bed and walked to the door. He opened the door and turned back to me. "To be clear, I'm not sorry I met you, Madison," he said quietly. "You're a remarkable person." He closed the door behind him.

"Ugh!" I threw my almost-empty beer against the wall, and it bounced off, landing on the floor and dribbling a little beer out. How could he act like such a jerk and then say something so nice? I was all set to be angry at him, and then he reminded me he's really sweet.

Why is it the people we care about the most can aggravate us the most?

After I calmed down a bit, cleaned up the beer, and got another *Negra Modelo*, I tried to make a plan. Obviously, it would simplify Andro's life as well as my life if Barry's murderer was caught. Not to mention little Sophia's life. And Ryan and his family's life.

I got out my laptop and started making a list. Why was Barry killed with quantum mechanics? Was he killed with quantum mechanics? Why did someone make a hole in a giant rock at

Red Rocks? Why did someone impersonate Andro? Why attack me, and why did they do such a poor job? Were those weird crimes Ben flagged quantum crimes?

Since so much different stuff had been occurring, I couldn't help thinking that more than one person might be involved, and they had differing q-lapsing abilities. Barry's murderer, for example, was very good at it. Unless it had been an accident? Or maybe it wasn't due to q-lapsing at all?

On the other hand, whoever attacked me was not very good at q-lapsing.

Why did Isabella and Chris rush out of here the other night when Ben was here? Why did Nancy lie about knowing Barry? Why did Chris act like he hadn't just seen me when I was outside his lab?

And, finally, there was the new quantum bank robber. Who was it? At least the why was obvious here: money.

That reminded me. I clicked over to the paper to see if the bank robbery article had been posted yet. It was, although it didn't say anything about quantum mechanics. Reading between the lines, with the huge opening in the cinderblock wall and in the metal reinforcing, it sounded very similar to the quantum bank robbery Griffin and Luke had pulled off last year. But, then, there'd been a witness, a guard. There wasn't a witness this time. When I finished the article, I couldn't help thinking this quantum criminal was very effective. Again, it seemed as if different quantum criminals were at work.

As the FBI's foremost expert on quantum mechanics (thanks to me), Agent Baker had to be working the bank robbery. It wasn't too late at night, so I decided to call her.

"Martin," she said. "Are you staying out of trouble?" So, now we were on a last name basis? Was that a step up or down?

Was I? "Yes, Baker," I said.

She made a noise that sounded a lot like a growl.

"Yes, ma'am? Anyway, I was wondering if you caught the recent bank robbery case. It sounds like that bank robbery last year."

"Yeah. I caught the case. It does resemble Griffin and Luke's bank robbery last year. You should come down to the scene and see if you can glean anything."

I nodded. Doh. She couldn't hear that. "Okay."

She paused.

"Agent Baker?"

"Yeah." She paused again. "Madison, I have something to tell you, and I don't want you to get alarmed."

Okay, now I was alarmed.

"I double-checked on the status of the Griffin kid, and he's gone."

"He died?" Poor Griffin. "How could that happen?"

"No." She cleared her throat. "He escaped."

"What?" I jumped off the bed. He tried to kill me. And Andro. And Ryan and his family. My heart started beating so fast it was like it was trying to make a break for it.

"He disappeared. It was reported immediately. But I wasn't in the loop."

"I thought he was in custody! Sedated!"

"I know I told you I'd check on him, but I didn't get around to it until this latest bank robbery. And he's gone."

"We have to warn Andro and Ryan ASAP! What happened?"

"We're not sure," she said. "We're still investigating. The security system at the prison was fubarred."

"I can't believe this." How could Griffin get out? Did that mean Luke was back? He was evil. We were all in trouble if he was back. Reality itself was in trouble if he was back.

There was a knock at my bedroom door.

Absentmindedly, I said, "Come in."

Andro sauntered in. He smiled warmly.

But I didn't smile back. My eyes were riveted on the silver can of Coors Light in his hand. Andro'd told me he drank so much Coors Light freshman year of college and got hungover so many times, he'd never touch the stuff again. He'd definitely never pick it up with his favorite right there in the refrigerator next to it.

"Hey, babe." His voice sounded strange.

"Madison?" Agent Baker asked.

I dropped my phone.

"Madison, are you...?" Agent Baker's tinny voice trailed off.

Chapter Seventeen

I didn't know who the Andro-looking person was in front of me, but I knew it wasn't Andro. "Uh, hey, babe," I said to the Andro-imposter. "I'm surprised to see you again." I scrutinized him. He did look surprisingly like Andro. For someone to impersonate him so well, they must already resemble him or be unusually good at selecting improbable quantum possibilities. Or, something else was going on here. Who was this person really? Whoever he was, I was impressed by his quantum capabilities.

I faintly heard Agent Baker's voice coming from my phone on the bed. It sounded tiny and far away.

"I'm sorry I rushed out of here just now," fake-Andro said. "We need to talk." Interesting. He must have been spying on me. Creepy. Was he waiting outside the house for the real Andro to come out?

"Okay." I turned away from fake-Andro for a second and scooped up my phone. "Uh, sorry about that, Lisa." Oops, I wasn't supposed to call her Lisa. I must have been more nervous than I thought. I fake-smiled at fake-Andro. "I gotta go, Lis. Bye." Oops, I did it again. I hung up.

Fake-Andro took a step towards me. Was this the guy who attacked me in my office Sunday night? It had to be. It was unlikely many people could impersonate Andro so well.

Was he here to attack me now? Probably. I mentally surveyed my skin. Nothing was pressing in on it, so no quantum attacks. Yet.

I quickly shoved my phone in my pocket.

"Gosh, Andro," I said. "It's nice to see you again. So soon." Hey, I was pretty good at fake sincerity, even when nervousness was morphing into fear. I wanted to run away, but I had to find out what fake-Andro knew, what he wanted, and who he was, if possible.

Most of all, I had to find out if he was the murderer.

As I stepped towards him and the open bedroom door, I heard the television set on in the family room. Oh, no. I had to protect Isabella, too.

"Yes. I was just here," he said woodenly, watching me.

"Yeah. I know. I was here, too." Fake-Andro seemed a bit stupid. I quickly walked past fake-Andro into the hall. "Isabella?" I glanced back at him. "Andro took one of your beers. I hope that's okay."

Isabella didn't answer from the family room. Did fake-Andro do something to her already? Did he hurt her?

I quickly walked down the hall to the room in question. "Isabella? Where are you?" She wasn't in the family room or the kitchen area. And all the doors in the hall had been open, so I didn't think she was in one of those rooms. Could she have left abruptly for her lab like she did the other night?

Sadly, I had no idea. For her sake, I hoped she'd left. I didn't want her to get hurt via a quantum attack, or a regular attack, for that matter.

Fake-Andro followed me down the hall to the family room. "What are you doing?" He seemed particularly interested. Why?

"I'm just looking for my new roommate. You haven't really had a chance to talk to her yet. She's awesome. Isabella!"

She didn't answer. She must have left. It was probably just as well. I didn't want to put her in danger.

"So, Andro, what did you want to talk about?" I indicated the couch. I tried to study him for clues without him catching on as we sat down.

"Madison?" fake-Andro asked over the blare of the television. Why would Isabella leave the house without turning off the TV?

"Sorry, what?" I was having trouble concentrating. It turns out danger does that to me. I looked down at my hands. Still no bizarre pressure.

Fake-Andro grabbed the remote, pointed it at the TV, and stabbed one of the buttons without looking at it.

I'd seen Isabella do the exact same thing. Crap. Those

beers I'd had must be slowing down my brain. Isabella hadn't left the house to go to her lab or anywhere else. Isabella was right here. She was fake-Andro. She had to be. No one else could use her remote like that. Shit!

Some other things were falling into place. What if she could impersonate other people, too? Was that her impersonating Chris the other day in the low-temperature lab? That would explain why 'Chris' wasn't sure he'd see Isabella again and why the real Chris was so confused afterward.

But why was she going around impersonating people? And how?

Did she attack me in the physics building?

Did she murder Barry?

And, first and foremost, what was she trying to accomplish right now? Attack me? If not, I should try to lull her into a sense of security so she'd tell me what she was up to.

"Yes, Andro," I said, hopefully convincingly. "I'm just a little worried about my roommate, Isabella. It's not like her to just leave the house with no word and with the TV set on." Clearly, I had no idea what she was like. "She's a good egg."

"Good egg?" Fake-Andro gave me a sickly smile. "Okay. I can tell you know it's me," she said in Isabella's voice. "What gave me away?"

It was bizarre hearing Isabella's voice come out of Andro's face. "The remote—you know it too well. And the beer." I pointed and then put my hand in my pocket, touching my phone, trying to call 911 without her noticing.

She nodded and then closed her eyes, seeming to concentrate. Slowly, she became blurry and turned back into herself, complete with *I read quantum physics magazines for the particles* t-shirt. That was also a clue she was familiar with quantum mechanics. I should have figured this out earlier. I resisted the urge to smack myself in the head. Plus, the way things had been going, she might cover smacking me anyway.

"Isabella, what are you doing?" I asked. "You're a promising graduate student. Why impersonate Andro?" Did I want to confront her about attacking me at my office? What if that set her off? I had mixed feelings about this young woman. She had everything going for her, but she probably tried to hurt me.

I needed to know if she was involved in Barry's murder, and I really needed to know how big a threat she was to me and the people I cared about.

"I was trying to find out what the cops knew about Barry's murder and about the quantum bank robbery," she said.

"Quantum bank robbery?" I shook my head. "Oh, Isabella. Were you involved in a bank robbery?" Sympathy and support seemed like a better approach on my part than accusations.

"Of course not," she said. I didn't believe her.

"Do you know who the other quantum criminals are?" I said. "If you help the authorities, they'll go easier on you."

She scowled at me. "What makes you think there are other quantum criminals? Maybe it's all me." Somehow, I'd insulted her.

"Did you attack me the other night?" Did I manage to call 911? Did I dare pull my phone out to check?

"Ding, ding, ding." There was that sickly smile again. "Yeah, that was me. Pretty good, huh? You didn't know I could q-lapse, did you?"

She actually expected to be praised for attacking me? What was wrong with this girl? "You're right, Isabella," I said loudly, hoping the call had connected. "I did not know you could q-lapse."

"Why are you talking so loud?"

"I did not know you could q-lapse, Isabella." She wasn't attacking me now, and frankly, if that was her earlier, the attack was pretty half-assed. "Did you kill Barry?"

Her fake smile faltered. "Yeah." She shifted her weight. "I killed Barry. Yep. It was me." She seemed nervous suddenly.

Staring at her, I didn't think she had the mojo to kill Barry. I thought she was lying. But in her current mood, if I implied she wasn't powerful enough, she'd probably try to prove me wrong.

"You know the police think I did it," I said instead. "You wouldn't want to confess to them, would you?" I smiled, much more convincingly than her, I hoped.

She started trembling and reached up and rubbed her forehead.

"How are you feeling there, Isabella? Starting to get a headache?"

"No!" That was a yes. Q-lapsing was tough on the brain. How had she done it without a lot of coffee or some adrenaline? Last year Luke and Griffin had injected themselves with adrenaline. Maybe there was an empty syringe hidden around here somewhere?

Then, I felt a pressure surrounding me, pressing in on my skin. I held up my hand. Something pressed in on it from all sides, but I couldn't see anything. She was attacking me again! "Hey! Stop it!"

But when I looked at her, she just looked like she was in pain, her face all scrunched up, her body shaking. She dropped her beer, and it glugged out on the throw rug.

The pressure on my skin increased. My pulse raced. I closed my eyes, concentrating, trying to q-lapse to make the bizarre pressure go away.

I focused. *Everything was normal here, totally normal.* There was no bizarre high-pressure system in my living room. That was by far the most probable scenario. Slowly, the pressure lifted.

When I opened my eyes again, my head hurting, Isabella was in a heap on the floor next to the couch.

She lifted her head and opened her eyes wide. "How did you stop me? You didn't do that before. He said–"

So, she did attack me before. But she seemed like she was in bad shape now. "Does your head hurt?" This girl had me very confused.

But *he said* meant there was someone else involved. I knew it! I leaned towards her. "Who said what?"

She let her head fall back on the floor, closing her eyes.

"Was it Griffin?" I asked.

She opened her eyes and threw me a worried glance.

"It was Griffin!"

She said, "No."

I leaned over her. "Tell me who it was!" I had a horrible thought. "It wasn't Luke, too, was it?" I thought I foiled him last year.

The front door burst open. Finally, the cavalry had arrived. My pocket call must have worked.

But when I straightened up and looked, it was Ryan and Sydney, not the cops. I stepped towards them, putting my body between them and Isabella to protect them.

"Agent Baker said you were acting oddly," Ryan said. "You called her Lis? She did not like that."

I didn't even remember that. I stared down at Isabella. Something was wrong—even more wrong than a moment ago.

Sydney said, "What's wrong with that poor girl?"

"Poor girl?" I said. "She attacked me! She confessed to killing Barry. Where's Agent Baker? Where are the cops?" There was no sign of the cops. "And Ryan, why did you bring Sydney?" I pointed at her. "It's dangerous! Isabella's a quantum criminal."

"I'm not delicate, Madison." Sydney put her hands on her hips. "I've been doing yoga for years. I'm in better shape than either of you are." She pointed at me and Ryan.

Ryan held up his hands. "Let's calm down. Focus on the girl. What's wrong with her?"

"I'm fripping calm," I said. "Where are the cops? Where's Ben? I thought I called them." I yanked my phone out of my pocket. Apparently, I'd accessed my calendar instead of calling 911. Shit.

Sydney walked over to Isabella. "She doesn't look so good." She leaned over. "She's really pale."

I knelt down next to the girl on the floor and touched her shoulder gently. "Isabella. Stop whatever you're doing." What was she doing?

She looked at me with pleading in her eyes and opened her mouth as if to say something.

Then, I realized her partner in crime must be doing it to her.

"I'm calling 911!" Ryan whipped out his phone.

No sounds came out of Isabella's mouth. Watching her try to talk made my heart ache.

"Stay with me, Isabella." I tried to focus on q-lapsing to stop whatever was happening with her. But I didn't know what was happening to her.

"Madison!" Ryan said. "That's your q-lapsing face."

I couldn't spare him the concentration to say I was trying to help her. Her chest stopped rising and falling. What was wrong with her? Concentrate, Mad! *She's okay. She's okay.*

Sydney knelt down next to us. "What should I do?" When she touched Isabella, she winced as Isabella's skin caved in a bit. "Oh, no." She drew her hand back quickly. "That is not right."

"Isabella!" I tried to get her attention, but she was still, too still.

I was getting too freaked out to q-lapse. I didn't know what was happening to her. "Hang on, Isabella! Fight it!"

She blinked her eyes and opened her lips. She looked so sad and confused and afraid.

"Isabella? I'm so sorry. I don't know what to do." I was full-on panicking. Her face didn't look like a person's face anymore. It was too still, and the color was off. Her eyes were the last to go. I could swear she was aware all the way to the end.

My heart ached. I failed her.

Gazing into her empty eyes, there was nothing left.

Isabella was gone.

My eyes filled. "Oh, Isabella. What did you get yourself into?"

Sydney squeaked and fell backward onto the floor.

Ryan strode across the room, leaned down, and scooped Sydney up in his arms. She buried her face in his chest. "Don't look, hon. No one can help her now."

Poor Isabella. She didn't deserve to die. She was still a young woman, with her whole life ahead of her.

Sydney started crying, muffled by Ryan's chest.

A siren approached the house.

Ryan looked at me with an odd expression and said, "Who killed her?"

Chapter Eighteen

Unfortunately, when the cops arrived, it wasn't Ben. And even more unfortunately, when they saw the body lying in my family room, they called in reinforcements.

And they wouldn't let me or Ryan and Sydney leave.

I'd sunk down on the floor and was having trouble focusing. What just happened? Isabella, poor Isabella, had mentioned a *he*, right? She didn't deserve death. I couldn't look at her. Poor Isabella.

Was this whole thing my fault? I should have never figured out how to q-lapse. I should have never moved in with Isabella.

A man yelled at me. "Madison!"

When I focused, I realized the yeller was Detective Davis, and he was standing right by my cousin Ryan. Oh, no. "What?"

"Did you kill this woman, Dr. Martin?" Detective Davis asked.

Ryan inserted himself between me and the detective. "You need to call Tom, Madison."

I just looked at him. Tom? Tom who?

"You need to call your lawyer, Tom Clark," Ryan said. "Davis, she confessed to killing Barry King."

Detective Davis scowled at him. "I'm taking all of you down to the station for questioning."

Someone led me to the back of a police car.

The next thing I knew, someone had hauled off and slapped me in the face. Hard. "Madison!" a woman said. It was Agent Baker, and she looked mad.

My cheek stung. "What?"

"What's wrong with you?" Agent Baker said. "You haven't

answered any of my questions."

"What questions?" I hadn't heard any questions. "And who says there's something wrong with me?" I looked around. I was in an interview room at the Boulder police station. When did I get here?

"Tom thinks you're in shock," she said. "He said you didn't answer any of his questions, either."

"Tom was here? When?"

"Honestly, Madison! I passed him in the doorway of this very room. Get it together, girl. What's wrong?"

Isabella collapsing and the life leaving her eyes was wrong. I shuddered. "What's not wrong? A girl is dead!"

"I'm well aware," she said. "But this wasn't your first dead body. I don't understand why you're so upset."

"This was a girl, a student! She was a friend of mine." Sort of. "She died right in front of me. She didn't do anything to deserve that." She'd said she killed Barry, but I didn't believe her.

Even if she did attack me, which it looked like she did, she deserved jail but not death.

"With all due respect, I don't think we know what she deserved at this point." Agent Baker paused. "All I know is I don't know much. Can you tell me what happened?"

I told her today's whole sordid tale from fake-Andro's arrival to the light draining from Isabella's eyes.

When I finished up, I emphasized, "Right before Isabella died, she said, *He said*. Whatever she was up to, she wasn't working alone."

"He said?" Agent Baker scowled. "Who's *he*? And what did the mysterious *he* say?"

I shrugged. "I don't know. What about Griffin? Is he still missing? All I know is someone else, a man, must have been involved."

Agent Baker looked grim. "I don't know what happened with Griffin. How could he escape? And how could he remain at large? We've been looking for him." She sighed. "So, you think this mysterious *he*–possibly Griffin–was using her as his puppet?"

"Yeah. Probably. That's what I think. To take the fall for him for the murder. She also mentioned the quantum bank robbery."

She grimaced. "So, who's *he*?"

"That's the question."

"Do you think *he* killed Barry?"

"I guess," I said. I hadn't seen any actual evidence that Isabella was a killer. She wasn't a very good q-lapser.

"So based on your story, the killer could be this dead Isabella or might be some mystery man and might have the ability to impersonate someone else?"

I nodded.

She frowned. "This shit makes my head hurt."

"Yeah," I said.

"The problem with your theory, Madison, is we have absolutely no evidence about any mysterious *he*. Now the cops think Isabella killed Barry. You said she confessed, right?"

"Yeah, but I didn't believe her."

"And she was involved with the bank robbery?"

I hung my head. "Yeah. That's what she said." I didn't know what to believe on that front.

"Case closed, as far as the cops are concerned," Agent Baker said.

"Come on, Lisa."

She glared at me.

"I mean, Agent Baker. You don't think that one young woman could have caused all this trouble, do you?"

"What? Women can't be master criminals? You aren't being sexist, are you, Madison?"

I was shocked. How could she accuse me, of all people, of being sexist? I was the opposite of sexist. "No. I'm not sexist. I knew Isabella, at least a little. She wasn't believable when she confessed to killing Barry. And who would, or could, commit suicide via quantum mechanics? Someone else must have been involved."

"I don't think you know what this Isabella would have done. Let's face it, Madison, your people skills are not the best."

It wasn't the first time someone had told me that. Could I be wrong about Isabella? Could she have done it?

I don't know what behind-the-scenes wrangling went on, but the cops let me go. I guessed they thought they got their man, i.e., Isabella.

When I got my personal effects back, including my phone, there was a voice message from Ryan. "They let us go. I have to get Sydney home. She's not doing well. And we need to pick up Emily from the neighbors. We rushed out of the house pretty quickly when Agent Baker called. Call me when you can."

I wasted no time in calling him.

He answered before the first ring tone finished. "Mad?" he whispered.

"Yeah. Why are you whispering?"

"Sydney and Emily are here sleeping."

Emily usually slept in her own room; how could Sydney and Emily be asleep in the same room? Focus, Mad. "Are you guys all right?"

"We'll survive."

"Is Emily okay, too?"

"Yeah." I imagined him nodding in his ratty plaid bathrobe. "How about you? They didn't charge you or anything, did they? I'm sorry I blurted out stuff to the cops. I was freaking out a little. I've never had anyone die right in front of me like that." He paused. "Are we okay?"

My brain wasn't firing on all cylinders today either. I couldn't really blame him when he knew considerably less than me about q-lapsing. "Yeah, I guess so."

Frankly, I was surprised we weren't more upset after what we'd seen today.

I wanted to ask him if I could come stay in my old room, but I wasn't convinced they'd caught Barry's murderer. I didn't want to put Ryan and his family in danger. "I don't want to go back to Isabella's place."

"I'm sure they've taken the body by now."

"Yeah, but I can't go back there, Ry. I definitely can't sleep there."

He didn't say anything in return.

I knew he thought I was angling for an invite. I hoped I'd have the fortitude to turn him down if he did. I wasn't going to put them in danger. Again.

He didn't invite. I couldn't blame him. He needed to take care of Sydney and Emily. "I think I might go sleep in my office."

QUANTUM MURDER

"Not Andro's house?"

"No." Ryan knew better than to pry.

"You know, they have these things called hotels, Madison, where there are beds right there just waiting for you."

"I know." I didn't want to spend the money. I didn't have the money. I had to pay Tom. And besides, with everything that had happened, I felt safe in my office surrounded by my familiar computer and books and papers and diplomas.

"Take care, Madison. You know I love you."

My throat felt tight. "Me too. Be careful."

There was also a voice message from Ben. "I heard through the grapevine that they caught Barry's murderer. Congratulations! You're off the hook."

There was no message from Andro.

He probably didn't know the news yet. This was good for him, too, as far as his custody situation went. I could tell him the good news. My finger hovered over the key that would call him. I didn't press it down.

I gave Ben a call. "Hey, Ben. Thanks for the congrats message."

"No problem. Conga-rats." Did he giggle then? Could he be drinking?

"Ben, have you been celebrating?"

He giggled again. "You know it, girl. Plus, I needed a drink. I got called to the scene. It was bad. I don't like it when young people die. That girl was practically a kid." I'd thought cops were immune to such thoughts. Apparently not.

But he didn't have to tell me it was bad. I knew it was bad. "I hear you."

"Do you want to come celebrate with me, Madison? I'd like to celebrate with you. I'd like to do all kinds of stuff with you." Wow. No filter at all. He must be drunk.

"Thanks, I guess," I said. "I'm not up for celebrating tonight. It's been a rough day."

"I hear that. Let me know if you change your mind; I'll probably be up late." He hung up abruptly.

In my office, I kept tossing and turning on the couch. I couldn't get comfortable.

In what felt like the middle of the night, I bolted up. Isabella's family. Did they tell Isabella's family what happened? That she was dead? How much did they tell them? Did they tell them she was a murderer? What must they be thinking now?

When I checked my phone, it wasn't even ten o'clock. Could they even reach her family? What if they didn't know about her death yet?

I knew the physics office had emergency contact information for everyone, including students. I got up and went down to the office. Unfortunately, I couldn't find Isabella's emergency contact.

I did find Nancy's home address and let's face it, Nancy knew everything. Plus, this was an emergency. Isabella's family had to know what had happened to her.

So, I q-lapsed to Nancy's condo. It was about two miles south of campus with ten units per building and had nice stonework along the bottom half.

When I knocked on the front door, I heard giggling. I didn't know she had a daughter. I could have sworn when we went to lunch, she just talked about her nieces.

The door swung open, and it was Nancy, smiling, tying the sash on a red silk robe. With her happy expression and smooth skin, she looked more beautiful than ever. "Madison, what do you want?" She glanced over her shoulder. "Now is not a good time."

A man emerged from the shadows of her front hallway. "Who is it?"

I hadn't actually met the man before, but I was pretty sure it was Barry-with-a-B King, aka the dead man.

My blood thundered in my ears, and a wave of moist heat washed over my body. "What. The. Hell?"

Nancy slammed the door in my face.

Chapter Nineteen

I teetered on Nancy's front stoop, grabbing hold of the exterior wall to keep from falling over. And my head hurt from q-lapsing over here.

I thought I'd seen Barry. But that couldn't be true, could it?

Once I quit feeling like I was going to faint, I turned back to the front door and started pounding on it. "Nancy! Open up! I know you're in there! And who's that with you? Is that Barry? If he's not dead, you need to tell the cops! Nancy!"

I paused for a moment, resting my throbbing head on the front door. If Barry wasn't dead, it would solve all my problems and all Andro's problems. And all our Andro-and-me problems. Okay, maybe not all of those.

Nancy did not come back and open the door. I may have heard some yelling through the closed door, but if so, it was very faint.

"Nancy!" I needed help, but I was afraid to call the cops. What if they didn't believe me about Barry? I'd just seen Barry with my own two eyes, and I wasn't sure I believed me.

Could it be someone impersonating Barry? It looked like they'd been having sex. Why would an impersonator have sex with Nancy? And why would she have sex with him? Surely, she could tell if her lover was an imposter or not.

I definitely needed help. Ben had said he'd be up late, and I could call, and he was a cop, right? I called him.

It took him several rings to answer. "Hey, there, Maddie," he said, slurring his speech. "I knew you'd call me back."

He sounded like he'd been drinking more. Well, he'd said he was going to. "Hey, there, Ben. Are you all right?"

"Me? Right? I'm as right as rain. I'm as right as ...something that's really right." He giggled. I guessed giggling was the activity of the day. "Is this a booty call? 'Cuz I'd be right with that, too."

Well, crap. He was too drunk. He couldn't help me. "Never mind, Ben. I'm over at my friend Nancy's house, and I needed a ride home."

"I'll come to get you!"

"No! Ben, that's a bad idea. You shouldn't drive."

"I'll call my buddy, Ryan. He'll drive."

"No, Ben!" I didn't want Ben to wake up Ryan and his family after the bad evening they'd all had. "Don't call them!"

But Ben had hung up already. Shoot.

I turned and pounded on the door again. "Nancy!"

I heard a bang that sounded like a car door slam. Then the garage door started to open next to me. I took a step that way.

But before I could get very far, a brand-new red mini-cooper zoomed out. It looked like there were two people inside, but I could only see the driver, and it was definitely Nancy. The car backed out of the driveway at warp speed.

I made a half-hearted attempt to run after it. "Nancy! Come back! What's going on?"

The car zoomed away.

My head hurt. Probably from q-lapsing, but being betrayed by a friend didn't feel good either. I walked back to the front stoop and sat on the concrete pad under the tiny overhang. I leaned back against the front door.

If Ryan and Ben didn't show up by.... I looked at my phone; it was only ten o'clock. It seemed later. If Ryan and Ben didn't show up by ten thirty, I was going to call a cab.

But, soon, Ryan's Subie showed up, and he jumped out. Ben sort of fell out. "Madison?" Ryan yelled across the tiny lawn as he approached. "Are you okay?"

"I'm okay," I said. "I'm sorry we bothered you." Actually, it had been Ben who bothered him.

Ryan rushed up to the little porch and helped me get up. "Why are you on the ground? Were you attacked?"

"I wasn't attacked. Did Ben say I was attacked?" I felt my face flush and glanced at Ben. "This is Nancy Hernandez's condo. She's the physics department secretary."

"You're supposed to call them administrative assistants

now." Ben had finally caught up to us.

Ryan shot him a dirty look. "Why are you sitting on the ground outside Nancy's condo?"

Ben reached for the front door and started knocking.

I touched his arm. "Chill, dude. She left."

I turned back to Ryan. "I saw Barry King or at least someone who looked just like him, with Nancy." I pointed at the front door. "It looked like they'd been having sex."

Ryan looked surprised. "You watched them have sex?"

What? Why did his brain go there? "No."

"The dead guy?" Ben wrinkled his nose. "Was it some kind of necro-whatever thing?"

"Ben! How much did you have to drink?" Ryan asked him.

Ben shrugged. "After that Isabella thing, maybe I needed a drink. And, I'm off duty."

I had forgotten about Isabella for a few minutes. Those were nice minutes, but they were over now. I shuddered. If Barry was still alive, it could clear her name. Her family deserved at least that. But if Barry was still alive, who was that body in the physics department office?

Ryan said, "Did they verify Barry's identity?"

Ben held up his finger with elaborate care. "No. There weren't enough teeth left to compare, and his fingerprints weren't on file. But we have his ID from his wallet, and he hasn't been seen since the incident."

Until now. Maybe. The ME's report had said all that, but I thought they would have gotten more info by now. "So, we're not sure the corpse was Barry?" Could the corpse not be Barry?

"Technically, we're still waiting on DNA, but we're pretty sure it was Barry," Ben said.

"So, what? We're thinking quantum imposter here?" Ryan asked. He pointed towards the condo.

"I guess," I said. "But it'd have to be someone who wanted to have sex with Nancy."

"That would be everyone," Ryan said.

I gave him a look.

"Yeah," Ben said.

I gave him a look.

"Everyone single," Ryan added. "She's hot."

"Yep." Ben thoroughly nodded. "Maybe she's in on it."

I couldn't believe that. "Anyway, why are we standing around outside in the middle of the night talking?" My head hurt. I should really stop q-lapsing. "Ryan, please go home to your family."

"You're my family, too," he said.

"I feel bad that I keep putting you through this stuff."

"It's not your fault. It's the quantum criminals."

"I'm worried about Nancy," I said. "I don't think she knows what's she's getting herself into."

"I'm worried about you," Ryan said.

"Yeah," Ben said. "You don't look so good."

"Gee, thanks," I said. Women love being told they don't look good. Ben was kind of annoying when he was drunk.

"Let's go," Ryan said.

"What about Nancy?" I asked.

"What about her?" Ryan said. "You said she left."

"But what if Barry's holding her hostage or something?" I said.

"I'm pretty sure a dead guy isn't holding her hostage," Ryan said. "You saw her leave, right? Did she look like she was being held hostage?"

"Well, no," I said. "But whoever she's with is tricking her." I paused. "Do you think we should call it in to the police?"

"And tell them what? A dead guy kidnapped her? Or maybe a zombie got her?" Ryan asked. "Come on. I'm taking you two home."

"I know dead guys don't do anything," I said. "And there's no such thing as zombies."

Ben made a sound that suspiciously resembled a giggle.

Ryan gave him another dirty look.

"Man, this quantum stuff is weird," Ben said.

We started walking towards the car. "Where are you taking me?" I asked.

"To your house, Isabella's house?" Ryan said.

"No." I shivered a little. "I can't go back there, not tonight. What if they haven't finished cleaning up?"

"Who's they?" Ben said. "The police don't clean anything up. You're gonna have to clean up any mess left behind."

That settled it. "No. I'm not going back there."

"I guess you're coming to my house, then." Ryan unlocked his car.

"No." I got in the back seat. "I don't want to put you and your family in danger. Please take me back to my office."

"You were already attacked there, Madison," Ryan said. "And you don't have a door. I'm not taking you back there."

Ugh. I hated stalemates. And my head hurt too much to think straight.

Ryan and Ben put on their seat belts in the front seats.

"She can come to my apartment," Ben said and made that giggly sound again.

"Madison?" Ryan asked. "What do you think?"

Ben was a cop. And he didn't have a family for me to worry about. And he could defend me if worst came to worst. Did he have a gun? Probably. If he wasn't too drunk. Speaking of drunk... "Ben, do you have any painkillers? My head hurts."

"Oh, yeah. I got some good drugs from when I got injured on the job." He twisted around in the front seat to examine me.

"Ben, I'm sure you're joking about handing out prescription meds," Ryan said. "Madison, what do you want to do?"

"I'm happy to take Ben up on his kind offer." I was hoping he hadn't been joking about the meds.

"Cool." Ben definitely giggled then.

"Madison?" a soft male voice said.

I didn't recognize it. The bed jiggled. I smelled coffee. I opened my eyes.

Ben sat on the bed in his form-fitting cop uniform, waving a cup of coffee under my nose.

I grabbed it. "I have to warn you, if you ply me with coffee, I may never leave."

He grinned. "That's fine with me."

I lifted up the covers and peeked underneath. I was just wearing a too-big Boulder PD t-shirt. "Nothing went on last night, did it?" I didn't remember anything happening. I sipped the elixir of life. Ah.

"Would it be so bad if it did?" Ben said.

"It wouldn't be bad." I grinned. "But it would be complicated."

Andro would never understand. Ack. Andro. He'd probably never understand as it was. Maybe this, here, now, was the final nail in the coffin of our relationship.

I'd thought Andro was The One. My eyes felt heavy.

"Are you okay?" Ben asked.

I blinked rapidly, driving tears away. "Yeah." I took inventory. My headache from q-lapsing was gone.

The coffee was quickly waking me up. "Are you okay?" I asked. "You seemed pretty drunk last night."

"Drunk? Nah. I can hold my liquor. I can't even remember the last time I was drunk."

So you regularly giggle? But I didn't say that. "Thanks for letting me stay here." I glanced around the room. It was very plain, no pictures on the walls, no clothes strewn anywhere. "Is this your guest room?"

"Yeah." He smiled. "Disappointed?"

Yes. No. I was confused. "Nice bed. It's comfortable."

Ben got a text. He took his phone off his belt and glanced at the display. "Crap. I'm late for my shift. My partner's outside waiting. I have to get going." He stood up. "I left a spare key to the apartment on the kitchen table. And the business card for a cleaning crew."

Cleaning crew? Why did he think I needed a cleaning crew? I didn't look that bad, did I? Oh, yeah. Isabella. Ugh.

"Help yourself to more coffee." He strode to the doorway. "We'll talk later. Maybe go to the sororities?"

Sororities? I nodded vaguely.

And with that, he was gone. I heard the front door open and close.

I wanted to lay back in bed and pull the covers over my head, but I knew I couldn't do that. Whatever the quantum criminals were up to, they were getting more bold and more reckless.

Except, of course, for Isabella, who wasn't getting up to anything.

I just had to take my day one step at a time. That was it. I leaned against the headboard and drank the rest of my cup of coffee. And then I got up and took a shower, only scaring myself slightly with my own crazy-haired reflection.

After I got dressed in mostly yesterday's clothes (I borrowed a t-shirt from Ben), I got some more coffee, sat down at Ben's kitchen table, and checked my phone. His apartment was small but neat. Everything seemed to have a place.

Of new messages, there were many. Crap. There were several from Agent Baker, several from Ryan, two from Sydney, one from Tom, one from Boulder PD, and a few from unknown numbers.

I started in on them.

When I got down to the blocked numbers, one of the messages made my blood run cold. "You bitch! The next time I see you, you're dead!" And it was in the freaky not-Andro Andro voice.

It had been left after Isabella had died.

Chapter Twenty

I felt like I didn't understand what was going on. I needed some kind of help investigating these quantum crimes. But the only people with law enforcement expertise who might help me were Ben, who was busy, and Ryan.

I got on my cell. "Hi, Ryan. How's it going, bro?"

"Fine," he said slowly. "What do you want?"

He knew me too well. "Is there any chance I could talk to you about Isabella and everything that's been happening?"

His muffled voice said, "It's Madison. She wants to talk about Isabella." He must have been talking to Sydney. "Are you sure?" he said to her. "You've been having a tough time, Syd, too. Okay."

"Sounds good, Madison," he said at a normal volume. "When and where?"

At Boulder Brews, the coffee and cinnamon buns were delicious as usual, but the shop was almost empty—not as usual.

"Hey, Mad." Ryan appeared at my table with a big cup of coffee.

"Aw. I was going to treat you." I'd been pondering what to say to him. I still wasn't sure if I should play him the threatening message.

"It's fine." He paused to take a sip. "What's up?"

"First of all, I want to apologize for putting you and your family in danger again."

"You already apologized. And it's not your fault. It's the criminals' faults."

"Thanks. I appreciate that."

"So, what's up? I want to get home to Sydney and Emily—they say hi, by the way."

"Hi, back at them." I took a sip and gathered my thoughts. "I guess I wanted to talk things out and get your advice about what to do next."

"With the investigation?" He rocked back in his chair. "Isabella killed Barry. That's the main thing. And she did the quantum bank robbery, too, right?"

"Just bear with me, okay?"

He nodded and drank some coffee.

"A man with Barry King's ID was killed, and his body was found in the physics building."

He nodded again.

"A positive ID hasn't been made yet. No face. No teeth. No fingerprints on file. I guess they're working on DNA. How does that work?" I looked at him.

"Oh, I can talk now?" he said. "I assume a scientist like you knows what DNA is."

"I know what it is, deoxyribonucleic acid, but how do they do IDs with it?"

"Ah. Yeah. Regular people don't have DNA on file. The police have to get DNA from a blood relative of Barry and then compare it to the DNA of the corpse."

"Okay. That makes sense. So, at this point, it might not be Barry's body."

"I guess," he said grudgingly. "But who else would it be? Are there any other thirty-ish Caucasian men missing from the physics department?"

"Did they even check?" I started typing some notes on my phone.

"It's got to be Barry. Isabella confessed, right?"

"Yes," I said. "But I didn't believe her. I don't believe her."

"No offense, Mad, but you're not exactly the best judge of character."

Why do people always follow 'no offense' with something offensive? "I may not be a good judge of character in general, but I think I do have a pretty good handle on twenty-something female physicists at the University of Colorado."

He shrugged.

"She mentioned a *he*. She was working with someone." Ryan frowned.

"And Griffin escaped from custody." Darn, I forgot to tell him last night with everything that had happened. Darn, I needed to tell Andro, too. I wasn't sure that was appropriate for a text message, though. And I couldn't call him right this second.

"What!" Ryan slammed down his cup, and some coffee slopped out. "Why didn't someone tell me?" Griffin had played a big part in threatening Ryan's family last year.

He reached for his phone and made a call. "Sydney, I think you and Emily do need to go visit your mom. I don't know if Isabella was the murderer." He glanced at me. "But Griffin's out of prison." He paused. "I don't know. I don't know. Yes, I can go with you guys, at least for the weekend. Start packing. I'll be home within the hour."

He hung up and stared at me. "I can tell you don't think all this is over, and I hope you're wrong." He waved his hand around to indicate, *continue*.

"Another wrinkle is that I thought I saw Barry at Nancy's house. As you know."

"I don't know if you saw Barry or only someone who looked like Barry," he said. "But, thinking like a cop, it would tend to indicate Nancy's involved."

I made some more notes.

"And then there's the quantum bank robbery," I said. "Isabella was involved somehow. She knew q-lapsing was involved at the least."

"Quantum bank robbery is more Griffin's style," Ryan said. I had to agree. "Did you go to the scene?"

"No."

"You could," he said. "Banks are usually open Saturday mornings these days. You could go snoop around."

"I was talking to Ben, and it seemed like investigating crimes basically involves wandering around, asking questions, generally snooping, and trying to find things that don't fit."

"That's it in a nutshell. Ben's a good guy. Do you like him?" Ryan looked hopeful.

"You've been pushing Ben," I said. "You must have heard Andro got someone pregnant?"

"I may have heard something about something," he said slowly. "What did you hear?"

"Sophia is three years old," I said. "He didn't cheat on me. He's a good guy."

"Not taking care of your daughter is not good-guy behavior."

I had a feeling I was getting a small taste of what Andro'd been going through lately. "He didn't know about her. The mom lied to him."

"Oh." Ryan examined the table like it was suddenly fascinating.

"And now that he knows, he's all in for his daughter. Count on it," I said. "But I don't want to talk about Andro. As for fake-Andro, I do think that was Isabella. She was the one who attacked me in my office."

"I'm glad something about this case is resolved," he said.

"Yeah, me too," I said. "What I don't get is how do you impersonate someone?"

He raised his eyebrows. "You're asking me? I don't know."

"Me, neither," I said. "There's also the possible quantum crimes at the Apple Store and at the sororities."

"I didn't hear anything about those." I filled him in, and he said, "Eh. Those might not be anything. Is that it?"

"There's the weird tunnel at Red Rocks."

"Could have been Isabella."

"Yeah." She did work with the low-temperature guys. She definitely could have been at the concert. That would mean she lied to my face though. But I guessed I'd already discovered she was a good liar. "And when that Chris guy acted oddly, it could have been Isabella."

"Chris? Acted odd how?" He glanced at his phone.

"Never mind." I should go talk to Chris, though. He might know something more about Isabella.

"Is that it?" he asked.

I scrutinized him. He clearly wanted to get going. "Sure, Ryan. I appreciate you talking to me."

He stood up. "I know you feel bad about that girl's death. I'm sorry."

"Me, too." I felt bad for her family. What did the police tell them? That she was a criminal? A murderer? They must have told them something by now. "Be safe," I said.

"You, too." He left.

I took a few more notes and finished off my coffee. Was that it?

I wracked my brain. I'd also thought I'd seen a mansion disappear off highway 93. That was weird. But I didn't see how that could be involved.

And actually, I'd also thought I'd seen Luke a couple of times in the crowd. Could that have been impersonation?

I flicked through my notes. Any other missing Caucasian men? I could ask Ben to investigate. Ask Agent Baker for an update on Griffin. Question Nancy if I could find her. Check out the bank. Question Chris. Try to figure out impersonation. And, if I got really desperate, I could drive up and down highway 93.

I sent Ben and Agent Baker each a text with their asks.

I stared at my phone. I needed to call Andro. I womanned up and did it. I got his voicemail. "I didn't want to leave this in a message, but you need to know Griffin Yin escaped from custody. Sorry." Dammit, I didn't mean to say sorry. "It's Madison." Awkward. Like he didn't know that. I hung up before I could do any more damage.

If I was going to get down to Denver to the bank before it closed, I needed to go now.

Agent Baker texted me back saying there was no new info on Griffin, but she'd keep me posted.

I texted her back, asking for the address of the quantum-bank-robbed bank.

She called me. "Why do you want the address of the bank?"

"I thought I'd go check it out," I said.

"I don't have time to go over there with you."

"I just wanted to look around. It's basically what you law enforcement types do, right?"

"Yeah. I can text you the address," she said. "But if you get in trouble, I disavow you." Gee, melodramatic, much? She texted me the address.

I had a traffic-free (yay, Saturday) drive down to Denver and pulled into a nondescript bank parking lot with almost an hour to spare before noon. The parking lot was almost empty. I hoped that didn't mean they were closed.

But, nope, when I strolled up to the front door, a skinny male employee popped outside and opened the door for me.

"Welcome to Front Range Bank. How may I help you today? Are you a current customer? Or would you care to open a new free checking account?"

I forced a smile. "First, I'd like to look around." Free did sound good. "But do you have any literature on these free checking accounts?"

"Yes, ma'am. Right this way." He led me to a pile of pamphlets on a desk near the front door. "Here you go. I'd be happy to answer any questions. Do you have any questions?"

"Not yet." I smiled again. "Can I catch my breath?"

"Yes, of course, ma'am. You're welcome to utilize our seating area here." He walked over to some plush chairs in front of a flat-screen TV on the wall. Can I turn on the TV for you, ma'am?"

Quit ma'aming me, dude. "No, thanks," I said. "I want to study your pamphlet." And check out the bank.

"Can I interest you in a free cup of coffee?"

"Sure." I nodded. Free coffee? If I had any money to deposit, this would be the place.

"I'll be right back." He rushed off somewhere.

I sat down and checked out the bank. The lobby was a relatively small area, maybe fifty feet by fifty feet divided up with some cubicles and the front counter where three very bored-looking young women stood slouching. Behind the counter was a hallway that must go back to the vault area and maybe some other offices?

Mr. Manager emerged from the back, carefully carrying a paper cup of something. He speed-walked to me, saying something over his shoulder to the other employees as he passed them. It must have been along the lines of *get ready* because they all straightened their posture and smiled over at me.

He handed me the coffee.

It was surprisingly tasty. "Thanks." I smiled at him.

He smiled back.

"I have to say the customer service here seems very good, maybe a little too good?" I said. "Why are you trying so hard? Where are the other customers?"

"You didn't hear?" he asked.

Hear you were quantum-bank-robbed? "Hear what?"

"I'm sorry to say the vault was robbed the other day, but it's the one and only time we've been robbed. We have an excellent record. Your money is super-safe with us."

"Oh, wow," I said. "That sounds horrible. Was it like in the movies with a mask-wearing gun-toting crew and *hit the floor* and all that?"

He sort of laughed. "No, it was at night. No one was here. No one was hurt. Thank goodness." He twirled the wedding ring on his finger.

"That's good, at least. So, did the police catch the guys?"

He shook his head. "No. But the FBI's on it. Agent Sawyer's been super helpful."

That was a familiar name. "Agent Nate Sawyer?"

"Yes. Do you know him?"

Would a random customer know Agent Nate Sawyer? Probably not. "I must have read something in the paper, after all." I didn't think I had Nate's number, so I'd have to ask him about the robbery the next time I saw him.

He looked at me eagerly. "So?"

I shook the pamphlet. "Thanks." I leaned down as if scrutinizing it.

"Okay." He walked over towards the front door.

I sipped the free coffee.

Some more customers trickled in.

I did read the pamphlet. They had a nice deal on checking. I debated going over to the counter and asking the other workers if they knew anything about the robbery, but I was guessing they didn't.

I checked out the main area again. Quite a few other customers had amassed by now. I guessed it was the rush right before they closed for the day. I wanted to see the vault, but I didn't see any sign of it. It had to be in the back. Presumably, the restrooms were back there, too? There was one way to find out.

I strolled up to the counter, surreptitiously snapping a few photos with my phone along the way.

Mr. Manager said, "Yes? Can I help you?"

"Can I use your restroom?"

His overly-friendly demeanor slipped. "The restroom is for

customers only."

"Of course, it is," I said. "I meant can I use the restroom after I sign up for my free checking account?"

"Yes! And today, you get a free fifty dollars just for signing up." Free fifty dollars sounded good.

I didn't need a new checking account, but if this was the kind of thing detectives had to do, I guessed I would. "Sounds great."

Filling out all the paperwork took longer than I thought, and by the time we were done, I really did need to use the restroom.

The manager gave me the key and escorted me down the back hall. Further down, I could see a huge hole in the wall.

After I did my business, he was waiting there for me. I handed him the key.

"Hey, is that where the robbery took place?" I pointed. "Do you think I could see it?"

He stared at me for a few moments. "Yeah. What the hell." He led me down the hall to the back and pointed at a six-foot hole in the wall. Inside you could see the safety deposit boxes.

That seemed like it was asking for trouble. "I can see the safety deposit boxes."

"Yeah, we moved all the contents to another branch for safekeeping until the repairs are done."

The hole was definitely weird. "Can I touch it?"

He shrugged. "Whatever."

I did, and it seemed as if the cinder blocks had dissolved. It was very similar to what'd happened at my office. I guess the cement in cinder blocks was susceptible to q-lapsing. It made sense. If the ratio of ingredients was off, the cement would crumble.

A shiver went up my back. This robbery did resemble the quantum bank robbery my former students had done. It resembled it a lot.

I snapped some more pics on my way out. The manager didn't seem pleased when he figured out what I was doing. But I held up my checking account paperwork and smiled.

After lunch, when I went to Nancy's place, she didn't answer the door when I knocked. I walked around the outside and peered in the windows but couldn't see anything.

I went to the physics building. I figured I could snoop around Nancy's desk and also talk to Chris. Or, if he wasn't there, get his home address.

Immediately my desk-snooping resulted in a discovery. Nancy's mug said, *Schrödinger's Cat Wanted Dead or Alive*, and had a picture of a dead cartoon cat superimposed on a live cartoon cat. She knew about quantum mechanics. She probably was involved in all this. Unfortunately, I didn't find any other helpful tidbits like a folder labeled *Master Plan* or *Nefarious Quantum Criminal Phone Directory*.

Oh, well, off to find Chris. I found him right away in his lab. "Hi, Chris. I wasn't sure you'd be here."

He looked horrible. His hair was even more askew and greasy than normal. His eyes and his nose were red-rimmed. "You mean because of Isabella? Yeah, I can't believe she's gone." His chin trembled.

"Me, neither," I said softly.

"And I can't believe she did all that stuff they said she did, either. She was a good person. She's not a murderer. Well, you knew her. You were her roommate."

Sadly, I didn't know her very well. And now I never would. Chris was in no shape to be cross-examined. "You look like you need a hug."

His chin quivered some more, and his eyes overflowed.

"Come here." I enfolded him in my arms.

"What am I going to do without her?" He started sobbing.

"You're going to remember the good in her, and you're going to keep going, day by day. Minute by minute, if you need to."

He finally stopped crying, and we separated.

"Are you feeling any better?"

"I guess." He wiped his face.

"When's the last time you ate?"

He shrugged. "I don't know."

"Let's go over to Burritos and Beers on The Hill. I'll buy you dinner." It was getting close to dinnertime.

He scrunched up his nose. "I don't like burritos. Besides, I'm a gluten-free vegan."

Wasn't this the same guy that was going to let me buy him

164

pizza the other day? "Okay. We can go wherever you want."

We ended up at a little dive called Vegan World, basically in the alley behind Burritos and Beers. The employees knew Chris by name, yelling, "Chris!" when he entered. We had to wait at the counter to place our orders.

"I haven't been here before," I said. "What's good?"

"You haven't been here?" Chris opened his eyes wide. "It's one of the best gluten-free, vegan places in town."

There were more? After living in Boulder for over a year, clearly, I still hadn't explored all its many facets.

I was just glad he didn't seem like he was about to veer into tears again. "What do you recommend?" I asked.

"Ah." He bobbed his head. "Vegan Surprise. Definitely."

"What's in that?"

"It's a surprise." I must have been giving him an odd look because he said, "I don't know. It's like the Special of the Day. Whatever's the freshest and most delicious."

Well, that sounded pretty good--if anything was good here. I glanced around the hippie-filled room. Did I smell incense or pot?

We both ordered Vegan Surprise, and I paid.

"So." I examined him as we stepped to the other end of the counter. He still seemed sad. Did I have the guts to grill him about Isabella? No.

I needed to change gears. "I've got a mystery on my hands, Chris, maybe you could help me with."

"Oh?"

"What would you do if you wanted to impersonate someone else?"

"What?"

"If you wanted to look like someone else, what would you do?"

"Huh." He gazed off into the distance. "You mean like in a play or something?"

"Maybe." He might be onto something. "Yes."

"Easy," he said. "I'd use makeup and stuff. I had a roommate who was a theater major. They have all kinds of makeup and stuff. He could make himself look like an old man or a lady or a giraffe or anything."

Why hadn't I thought of that?

Chapter Twenty-One

Saturday night, I never did have the heart to grill Chris about Isabella. He started crying again. I ended up staying up late, hanging out with him, trying to make him feel better. It may be that I'm not totally cut out to be a detective.

I did get some texts. Agent Baker said there was no new news about Griffin. Ryan said he and his family made it to Sydney's parents' house safe and sound. Andro said he was busy. Ben said I could stay with him tonight.

When I got in Saturday night, Ben was already in his bedroom, presumably asleep.

When I got up Sunday, he'd already left for work. He didn't bring me coffee in bed first, either. Bummer. He did leave me a note to help myself to food and drink in the kitchen. I was starving after my vegan dinner, so I made myself a big plate of cheesy eggs and toast.

I sat at the kitchen table and ate and pondered. I had two very scanty leads, makeup, and the disappearing mansion. But I was determined to clear Isabella's name (of murder at least) and figure out who the mastermind was.

Chris had told me the theater majors were rehearsing some big play all day in the theater building on campus, and I could probably stop by if I wanted to. I didn't have a parking permit for campus, but there actually was some free parking on Sundays if you knew where to look. I successfully found a free spot and walked over to the theater building. The weather was still warm and sunny. I loved Indian summer.

When I entered the theater, I couldn't see a thing. It was dark in comparison to the October day outside. Gradually, my eyes acclimated, and I could see several people on the stage. I sauntered down there.

"Hi, there," I said.

They froze. One of the young men said, "Rehearsals are closed."

"That's okay. I just had a couple of questions. I heard you guys might be able to help me."

"Why should we help you?" one of the men said.

"I'm faculty. Do you want to see my ID?" Had I brought my faculty ID with me?

"No," the first man, the director maybe, said. "That's okay. What's your question?"

"I need to do an experiment in which I look like someone else. What should I do?"

The questions came too quickly to see who was talking.

"Who do you want to look like?"

"Why do you want to look like someone else?"

"What kind of experiment?"

"What department are you from?" the director asked.

"Physics," I said slowly.

They all gaped at me.

"What kind of experiment?" the director asked.

I gathered my thoughts. "I don't want to take a lot of your time. I know you're busy. I just want to know if it's possible for one human being to make themselves look just like another human being."

"Yeah."

"Yes."

"Sure." The director started pulling things off his face, revealing he was a she. She turned off some kind of little machine, too.

I stepped closer to her. "Wow. What are all those little bits of rubber?"

"Essentially little bits of rubber," she said, her voice totally different.

"What happened to your voice?"

She held out a tiny machine. "It's tech."

Wow. I hadn't known it was so easy to change your appearance and your voice.

How did this fit in with q-lapsing?

It turns out it's impossible to study the landscape while you are actually driving on the highway. I drove up and down the stretch of highway 93 twice before I finally deciphered that. I parked and tried walking the stretch, but it turns out that takes a long time.

I didn't learn anything from my highway lead–if it even was a lead.

Back at Ben's, unfortunately, he texted that he was pulling a double shift that night, so I was on my own. I was disappointed because I'd wanted someone to bounce ideas off.

Ryan was out of town with Sydney and Emily.

Agent Butler was busy.

Andro was still busy.

I went to bed early.

The alarm went off on my phone. It was ten minutes before my quantum mechanics class. Oh, yeah, my job. Unfortunately, I was still in Ben's apartment, miles from campus.

I threw on my clothes, stumbled to the kitchen, and chugged a mug of cold coffee.

I thought about how probable it would be that I'd be in my office in the Gamow Tower a few minutes before class. In point of fact, it would be very probable. I concentrated, visualizing the different possibilities and picking one of the most likely ones. I q-lapsed to appear at my desk in my office.

My head only hurt a little. I was getting pretty good at this.

With everything that had been going on, I'm sorry to say I hadn't looked over my lecture notes for today's class. Since I couldn't go back in time, there was no help for it. I grabbed my notes and the textbook and started jogging down the hall for the stairs.

As I reached the door for the stairwell, I heard, "Madison!" from behind me. When I turned around, I saw what appeared to be Andro standing in the doorway of his office. "When did you get into the office?" he asked.

I skidded to a stop. Was it really him? "Andro?"

"Yeah." He grinned. "Who else would it be?"

I walked in his direction. "Nobody. Never mind."

"Did you hear?" He actually smiled. I loved his smile.

Hear what? That I spent the weekend at Ben's apartment? I swallowed. "Uh..."

"Did you hear they caught Barry's killer? We're off the hook." He reached out his arms to hug me.

Never one to turn down a hug, I stepped into his arms, mind racing. But what if Isabella wasn't the killer? What if Barry wasn't dead? Who was that body? And who killed Isabella?

When I stepped back and looked into his eyes, he looked so calm and collected (and handsome). He was back to the old Andro I knew.

Did he get my message about Griffin? He wasn't acting like it.

"I talked to Tom, and he said this changes everything," he said. "I'll have no problem getting at least shared custody of Sophia. I'm sorry I've been so busy and so grumpy lately." I hadn't seen him looking so relaxed in weeks.

I was happy for him. "That's great news." I didn't have the heart to tell him I didn't think Isabella had done it. My phone alarm went off. Saved by the bell. One minute until my class.

He smiled again. "Class? I won't keep you." He took a step back into his office. "Maybe we can go out to dinner tonight to celebrate?"

Could I last a whole dinner without revealing my reservations about Isabella's guilt? And what would he think when he found out I spent the weekend at Ben's apartment? "Let me check my schedule." I turned back to the stairwell.

I ran down the stairs. As I approached the ground floor and the physics department office, I wanted to see if Nancy was at her desk, but I didn't have time. Instead, I jogged down to my basement classroom.

When I finally got to class, a few minutes late, the students were definitely getting restless.

Juan said, "Nice of you to stop by."

Enrico said, "Is that what you were wearing yesterday?" How would he know? We didn't have class yesterday, and he definitely didn't stop by my office.

All the guys snickered.

I resisted the urge to give them a pop quiz. My bad mood

wasn't their problem. And they were paying a lot of money for this class. I did owe it to them to be here on time.

"Can we start class now?" Arjun asked, but he used a tone that meant *start class already*. At least he was consistent. He was even well-dressed as usual. Did he iron that crease in his pants, or did he have a wife who did it?

"Yes. We can start class," I said. "I'm sorry I'm late." I put my stuff down on the table in the front of the room. I glanced at my notes. "So, last time, we covered the uncertainty relationships. Now we're going to use them to look at one-electron, one-dimensional energy eigenvalue problems. We're going to solve the time-independent, uh, equation."

In fact, the name of the equation was the Schrödinger equation and last semester it brought up the famous Schrödinger's cat thought experiment. And that led, in turn, to discussions of different interpretations of quantum mechanics, which led to property damage, felonies, murder, and reality itself being endangered. Yikes. I didn't want to go back down that road.

"Professor Martin?" Arjun asked. "Is there something wrong?"

One of the guys in the class snickered and said, "Senior moment."

Haha. They couldn't get my goat. Minor disrespect was child's play compared to quantum duels. I forced a smile. "I'm well past being a junior or a senior. I've been out of school a while now." I paused. "But you aren't. Who knows what an eigenvalue is?"

Arjun raised his hand. Of course.

"Yes, Arjun?"

"Yes, ma'am. An eigenvalue is a number, basically a solution, associated with an operator and a boundary condition."

"Good," I said. "We've been studying eigenvalues which are vectors with real, discrete components." I examined the students. They mostly seemed bored. "And when I say real, I mean real in the mathematical sense. Not imaginary, not involving the square root of minus one." Still bored. I knew an easy way to fix that. "Everyone get up. We're all going to solve the equation at the board." I gestured to the ring of whiteboards on three walls of the classroom. "Grab a marker and go up to a board. You can ask your neighbor for help if you get stuck."

Reluctantly, the young men all lumbered up.

"Here's the equation." I wrote on the board at the front. "What is the solution?"

When I walked around to see how the guys were doing, I was very surprised that Brandon and Drew had already written the answer down. They were smart, like the other guys in the class, but they weren't that smart.

"Nice job, Brandon," I said to Brandon.

"Nice job, Drew," I said to Drew.

"I'm Drew," the one I'd thought was Brandon said.

"I'm Brandon," the other one said.

"Sorry." Yikes. That sort of was a senior moment. "Anyway, nice job. Did you read ahead?" That wasn't unheard of. It wasn't often heard of, but it had happened.

Next to us, Arjun said, "Don't make fun of the teacher. She can't help it if she's not as smart as--" He stopped himself from insulting me, which I appreciated. "Don't make fun of the teacher." What fun were they making?

I turned to him, raising my eyebrows to ask what he meant.

He pointed at the first guy, "That is Brandon." He pointed at the second guy. "That one is Drew." I was right, after all.

I turned back to the two fraternity guys, dressed alike, coiffed alike, as usual. "Give me a break, guys."

But they didn't look smirky and proud of themselves as I expected. They looked worried. "Guys? What's going on?"

Did they look a little blurry? Shit. I leaned closer. I couldn't handle it if another person died in front of me. I reached for the closest one, whoever he was. "Are you all right? Hang on!"

But the two young men blurred out and disappeared.

"Chod!" Arjun said.

I was left reaching for air. This was not good. Had Drew and Brandon learned how to q-lapse, or had the men in here been imposters? But who would spend their time coming to my quantum mechanics class if they could do anything? I had a sneaking suspicion. Luke and Griffin might spend their time coming to my class. But if it was them, what were they up to?

But somebody had said something. I faced Arjun. "What?"

"Oh, excuse me, Professor Martin," he said. "But they just disappeared. That was unusual."

The rest of the students were attracted to Arjun's outburst. "What?"

"What's going on?"

Arjun pointed at the empty space, arm shaking a bit. "Drew and Brandon just disappeared."

I was shaking a bit, too. Could they have been hurt? "Can somebody please call Drew or Brandon and find out if they're okay?"

Juan and Enrico whipped out their cells, pressed screens, and chatted briefly.

"Huh," Juan said, hanging up first. "Drew said he and Brandon were still at the fraternity house, and they'd been there all morning."

"Yeah," Enrico said. "Apparently, there was a killer party last night."

Thank goodness they weren't hurt. I held up my hand. "Never mind the details."

"But if they were at home, who was here?" Arjun asked.

"Good question." I needed to sit down. Should I continue this class? I couldn't in good conscience endanger these men. But, presumably, the imposters wouldn't come back this morning. I forced a smile. "But I do know this time-independent equation is going to be on the next exam. Back to work!"

With much grumbling and grouching, the young men went back to the whiteboards.

How, in God's name, did the imposters look so much like Brandon and Drew? I didn't understand this quantum impersonation at all. It didn't make any sense. It didn't seem probable that someone could look exactly like someone else, even with makeup.

After class, I trudged up the stairs, stewing. How could I continue to teach my class if it put the students in danger? The imposters hadn't hurt anyone this time, but that didn't mean they wouldn't.

I gulped. Could these be the people that killed Isabella? I should have canceled class as soon as they q-lapsed.

The physics department already had two bodies on its hands, Isabella and Barry/fake-Barry. Didn't the university owe its students and employees safety and security? And as part of the university, wasn't I responsible, too? I bet the parents of my students would think I was.

Instead of going back to my office, I made a detour to the first floor and went into the physics department office, seeking Nancy.

Professor Chen darted out of his office as soon as he heard me enter. "Nancy?" When he saw me, he frowned. "Oh, it's you."

"So, she's not in yet?"

"No," he said. "And she didn't call or email."

"I know that's not like her," I said. "I'm concerned about her. Let's go in your office and talk."

Chen nodded and gestured towards his office.

I walked in, and he closed the door after us. He waved his hand at his guest chair, and I sat. His office was so crammed with papers we were in danger of being buried in a paper avalanche.

"So, this is hard to say," I said. "But." Wow. It was really hard to say. I saw Nancy with a dead guy the other night. It sounded crazy.

"What's hard to say, Madison?"

I just had to say it. "I stopped by Nancy's house the other night, and she was with a man who looked very much like Barry King."

Professor Chen crinkled up his eyes. "Was she in trouble?" His voice rose. "Why didn't you call the police?"

I flashed back to my memory of Nancy belting her silk robe, hair tousled, skin flushed, as she answered the door. She looked happy. "I'm not a hundred percent sure she was in trouble. She didn't seem to think she was in trouble."

"What do you mean the man looked like Barry? How much did he look like Barry?"

"I don't think I ever met Barry, so I don't know who the guy was. But he did strongly resemble pictures of Barry I've seen. And I did call the police." Professor Chen didn't need to know the police, namely Ben, was tipsy at the time. "And I called the university's Chief of Police. They came right over, but Nancy drove away with the man, seemingly of her own volition."

"I don't understand." Professor Chen shook his head. "What are you saying?"

What the heck was I saying? "I guess what I'm saying is Nancy did not think she was in danger, but I do. There have been some new quantum crimes, and I'm worried this is related. If you want to file a missing persons report on Nancy with the police, I'll help."

He looked at his watch. "I don't think we can yet. How long has she been missing?"

Good question. "I'm not sure."

"Not enough time has elapsed," he said. "Doesn't it have to be twenty-four hours?"

"Yeah." Stupid police rules. I suppressed a sigh.

"I'll keep trying her cell phone," he said.

"Sounds good." It sounded like crap. "Actually, I have a meeting with FBI Agent Baker later. I'll ask her to investigate, too, okay?" That was one of my many phone messages this morning. She wanted to meet. With all that had happened lately, it was our first chance.

He let out a breath. "That sounds like a good idea. Thanks, Madison." He gave me a look like he expected me to get up and leave. "Is there something else?"

It was also hard to say I might have endangered some students. "So, there were just some intruders in my quantum mechanics class downstairs."

"Intruders!" He stood up. "Why didn't you tell me?"

"I'm telling you now. Two young men apparently impersonated two of my students using quantum mechanics. I'm concerned my students might be put in danger in the future. I think we need to suspend my class meetings."

He sat back down. "I don't understand. How can people impersonate other people with quantum mechanics?" Then he quieted, and his eyes went somewhere else. He seemed to be recalling something. There had been a lot of quantum crimes last year to recall.

Personally, I recalled last year when the walls and floor and ceiling of rooms in the physics building got all fuzzy and changed, morphing into something else, becoming fluid. I shuddered.

"I trust your judgment on this, Madison," Professor Chen said. "If you think we should cancel your class, we should. The last thing we want is to put students in danger." He leaned over his desk and looked at me as if he wanted to say something else like, *If you hadn't figured out how to q-lapse, none of this would have happened*, but maybe that was just my guilty conscience.

I walked right into Andro when I got to our floor. And it wasn't even on purpose.

"Whoa, Madison," he said, grinning. "You should watch where you're going."

Why was he so happy? Oh yeah, he thought the quantum crime spree was over. He thought the murderer had been caught.

My expression must have given me away because he asked, "What's wrong?"

I said, "Let's go in your office." I stalked in and closed the door after he followed. "I have to tell you something you're not going to like. I don't think Isabella killed Barry, or if she did, she didn't work alone." I decided to leave the identity of the first corpse alone for now. "There are at least two more quantum criminals in town."

Andro's face got still, and he settled on one of his guest chairs. "How do you know?"

"For one thing, what looked like two of my quantum mechanics students just disappeared in the middle of class."

"That doesn't mean they're killers," he said. "It doesn't even make them criminals."

"I know, but whatever they were, they impersonated students and q-lapsed away," I said. "It definitely means they can q-lapse."

Andro looked at the floor.

"I guess the bottom line is if you can get a custody hearing about Sophia, sooner would be better than later."

"The police think this whole thing is over," he said. "But you don't?"

"I'm sorry, but I don't think it is." I didn't want to stress him out again, but if this information could help him and his daughter, it was worth it.

Chapter Twenty-Two

Andro and I had agreed to finish our discussion later tonight at Boulder Brews. He was going to try to get a custody hearing today, and I had an appointment in my office with Agent Baker. After lunch, she texted me that *They were on their way up*. Who were they?

I found out soon enough as Agent Lisa Baker and Agent Nate Sawyer appeared. Yay, me. "Hey, Agent Baker, Agent Sawyer." If they were impressed I recalled both of their names, they didn't show it.

Agent Baker crossed her arms and frowned as she stepped into the room.

Agent Sawyer didn't look much happier.

"What's this about?" I asked.

Agent Baker looked at Agent Sawyer.

"I had a very interesting discussion with the manager of Front Range Bank," Nate said.

"Oh?" I was so cool, I was absolute zero.

"Yes." Nate continued, "He said a suspicious middle-aged woman named Madison Martin came to the bank Saturday and snooped around the crime scene." Middle-aged? That was harsh. I was only a couple of years older than the guy, if that. "He thinks she might be the robber."

I expelled a bunch of air. In hindsight, I probably shouldn't have given them my name. "That's just stupid. Why would the robber come back days later? To admire their work?"

"Yeah," he said.

"That's ridiculous." I glanced at Agent Baker. "Right? And besides, Agent Baker told me which bank it was."

She said, "Dis. Avow."

Nate sat in one of my visitor chairs.

Agent Baker sat in my other rickety chair. Was that her almost-about-to-smile expression? "How did he get your name?"

"I may have opened a checking account," I said stiffly.

Agent Sawyer snickered. Agent Baker appeared to be trying not to laugh.

Was it possible they'd just been yanking my chain?

"So, did you learn anything?" Nate asked.

"It seemed similar to the quantum bank robbery last year. The hole was about the same size and everything. I'd say q-lapsing was involved."

"Anything else?" Agent Sawyer said.

"I have some pictures," I said. "Would you like to see them?"

"We have plenty of pictures," Agent Sawyer said.

"Can you tell us something about the mechanism of how they might have gotten into the vault?" Agent Baker said.

I leaned back in my own rickety chair. "They probably altered the chemical composition of the wall."

Agent Baker said, "Explain."

"Matter is made of molecules. I'm not an expert, but the wall was probably made of molecules of oxides of calcium, silicon, and aluminum. Each of these molecules, in turn, is made of atoms composed of protons, neutrons, and electrons. Changing the numbers of the particles in an atom changes what the chemical is and, thus, its physical properties. Cement is strong but whatever they turned it into was weak."

Agent Sawyer was smiling. "It sounds complicated."

"Are you saying the thieves are chemists?" Agent Baker said. "That would be something at least."

"Yeah," Agent Sawyer said. "They must be chemists."

I did something like this to my office wall last year, and I didn't know much chemistry. "No. Unfortunately, I think the person or persons involved just wanted the wall gone and q-lapsed to make it happen."

"So, bottom line, not chemists," she said.

I resisted my first impulse to snap at her. "What about the security tapes?"

"Static," Agent Sawyer said.

"Basically, the exact same M.O. as the bank robbery last

year," I said. Committed by Luke and Griffin. That was not good. My conviction that Luke was dead or dispersed was itself dying or dispersing.

"Could that Luke kid be back?" Agent Sawyer asked.

"I don't know," I said. It was starting to look more likely.

"Any leads on Griffin?" I asked.

The agents glanced at each other. "No," Agent Baker said.

The three of us sat there unhappily. "Is this really the reason you guys are here?"

"No," Agent Baker said. "We want another q-lapsing lesson. I think I'm on the verge of getting good. And I have a good feeling about Nate here, too."

At five-thirty at Boulder Brews, I had just taken my first sip of their Oktoberfest seasonal ale when Andro strode in the door.

He smiled and waved. That was a good sign, right?

I held up my frosty mug and pointed at the counter.

He detoured over there and ordered a drink. By the time he joined me at the small table, most of my ale was gone. How had that happened? I may have been a tad nervous. We'd left things a little unresolved. Did he believe that the quantum baddies were back or not? Did he get a custody hearing?

As he sat down, he said, "What happened to your beer?"

I shrugged. "It was yummy."

"Do you want me to get you another one?"

"No, thanks." I had to at least try to keep my wits about me. I needed to know if Andro and I were over or not as a couple. I also needed to know if he had my back if we had to duel quantum criminals.

"It's nice to see you," I said carefully. I had no idea how things stood between us. Of course, staying at Ben's probably wouldn't help when he found out.

"It's nice to see you, too." He smiled faintly.

I bit the lead projectile. "I must admit I'm confused about us," I said. "Thank you for stopping by my new place to talk the other night. Thanks for telling me what was going on with you, finding out about your daughter and everything." And thank you for saying I was a remarkable person but was that some kind of goodbye?

Andro reached across the table, grabbing my hand and squeezing it gently. "I'm sorry about how I've been behaving lately, Madison. I shut you out, and I know that isn't how a couple is supposed to act."

I nodded but didn't say anything, afraid to interrupt him when he was on a roll.

"I do love you," he said. "Very much"

Wow. My eyes felt heavy. I nodded and surreptitiously (I hoped) wiped a tear away. "I love you, too," I whispered, voice husky.

"I know I said we should take a break. And I'm sorry for that, too."

I nodded again. Good grief, he was going to think I was a bobblehead. "So." I had to clear my throat. "You don't want to take a break? You want to get back together?" Surprisingly, I wasn't totally overjoyed. He'd hurt me. I didn't understand how he could shut me out of his life so easily.

He released my hand and glanced down at the table. "My life has changed a lot. And the things I said... I said them in the wrong way, but in some ways, we are very different."

My heart felt like it was in the vacuum of outer space. "So, you do want to break up?"

"No." He looked up at me. "Definitely not. I need you in my life."

"What does that mean then? Dating?" I could live with dating. Dating was good. Dating could let us regroup.

"I guess." He held up his hands. "If you still want to. But, my daughter needs to be my number one priority right now."

"I understand that." I leaned over the table. "Does that mean you got a hearing about your daughter? What happened?"

He beamed at me. I'd never seen that smile. "I got joint custody of Sophia!"

Wow. My eyes suddenly felt hot and heavy for another reason. "Oh, Andro. That's wonderful. I'm so happy for you." Reluctant to steer us away from the happy moment, I picked up my beer and took another sip.

"I've got to hand it to Tom, he was helpful," Andro said.

"But I thought you said you couldn't afford Tom." I had called and begged Tom to help when I was waiting for Agent Baker this afternoon. Yeah, Tom. He came through.

"He said we could work something out." He smiled some more.

"Have you met Sophia yet? What's she like?" I had a horrible thought. If Luke was back, he might hurt Sophia if he found out about her. Maybe Andro and I shouldn't get back together even for dating. And I couldn't ask him to help me fight. He needed to be there for Sophia. And protect her.

"Madison?" He was looking at me, and he didn't look happy at all anymore. "What's wrong?"

"I'm really happy for you and Sophia."

"Yes," he said. "You already said that."

"It's just that I, uh." Stall, Mad. He doesn't want to hear he might put his daughter in danger. He didn't want to hear Luke might be back. I was more chicken than that. I was a pterosaur. "I went to the bank robbery scene, and it was similar to last year." I paused. "Wait. I have some pictures."

I pulled out my phone and scrolled to the first picture I took when we got to the bank. But as I scrolled through the pictures, one of the customers in the background looked a lot like Luke.

"Madison?" he said. "What is it?"

I was probably imagining it, right? "Does this guy in the background look familiar at all?" I passed him the phone.

He stared at the little screen, face stilling. "Shit." That didn't sound good. Andro rarely cussed. Nervously, I finished off my beer as he stared at my phone.

Finally, he said, "I thought you said Luke was gone, dead. You said that. You were sure."

"I was sure last year." I paused. "I've been getting less sure. And now that I've seen the picture, I'm even less sure."

He shook the phone. "But it could be an impersonator, right? It might not be him."

I opened my mouth, but I didn't know what to say.

And then a white mist appeared next to our table.

Chapter Twenty-Three

In Boulder Brews, Andro and I stared at the white quantum mist developing next to our teeny-tiny cafe table.

"Should we get out of here?" Andro asked.

The mist got bigger.

He had a daughter to take care of now. "Yes." I nodded. "You, go. I'll handle it." Whatever it was. My heart beat as rapidly as the microwave frequency in the official U.S. cesium fountain atomic clock.

He hesitated. "No. I can stay and fight. I don't want anything to happen to you."

"Go, Andro! I'm sure. Sophia needs you." I pointed to my phone on the table. "I'll call for help if I need it." But who would I call if not Andro?

The mist was almost six feet tall.

He still hesitated. I could tell he was torn between protecting me and protecting his daughter. Finally, he nodded and said, "Call me when you find out what it is." He jogged for the door, glancing back often.

I braced myself for fight or flight.

And Agent Baker coalesced out of the mist. "I did it!" She grabbed her forehead. "Ow, my head."

I grabbed my cell and texted Andro. "It was Agent Baker. Come on back."

I turned my attention to Agent Baker. "Sit down. Let me get you a coffee. It'll help with the headache."

She sat.

I got up and took a step to the barista counter. "And, by the way, congratulations. Awesome job with the q-lapsing. I'm proud of you." I was glad another one of the good guys had finally figured it out.

She grinned weakly.

The place was getting more crowded as students came in for their Friday night beers. By the time I got back to the table with Agent Baker's coffee and my new beer, Andro was there showing Agent Baker the picture on my phone.

She looked grim, and I didn't think it was all about her headache.

I handed her a coffee.

She gratefully took a sip. "How can you guys keep q-lapsing if it hurts this much?"

"Actually," Andro said, "I try to avoid it."

I shrugged. "You get used to it."

"So, what's the scoop with this picture?" she asked. "You think Luke was really at the scene?"

"It might be an imposter," Andro said.

I glanced at him. "And it might be Luke." I sipped my new beer. Mmm. "I hate to say it, but too much has happened. I think Luke's back."

Andro frowned and looked down at the table.

Agent Baker sipped her coffee. "Like what?"

"Well, first of all," I ticked off my finger, "someone released Griffin from custody."

"What!" Andro said.

Agent Baker and I looked at each other, and for once, we were in sync. Oops. We should have told Andro about Griffin. In my defense, every time I'd tried to talk to him over the weekend, he'd texted he was busy.

"Sorry," I said to Andro. "I did leave you a voicemail. I'm guessing you didn't hear it?"

He shook his head.

"Griffin and Luke were pretty tight," Agent Baker said.

"Very tight," I said. "Best friends. Second of all, the new bank robbery's M.O. was exactly like the job Luke and Griffin pulled off before. Third of all, someone threatened me multiple times."

Agent Baker interrupted. "I thought it was that girl Isabella?"

"She did confess to the first attack," I said. "But someone else, a man, put her up to it."

Andro groaned.

Agent Baker looked skeptical. "How do you know?"

"For one thing, I got another threat from the same voice after she was already dead."

"You didn't tell me that," Agent Baker said.

"You didn't tell me that," Andro said.

"We haven't been communicating very well lately, Andro."

Agent Baker held up a hand. "Can we focus on the matter at hand, please?"

"And, this morning, I think there were two imposters in my quantum mechanics class."

"You didn't tell me that," Andro and Agent Baker said at the same time. Now they were in sync.

"Who was it?" he asked.

"I don't know," I said. "They impersonated two students of mine, Drew and Brandon."

Agent Baker frowned. "The quantum criminals do seem to be obsessed with you, whoever they are. That fits with Luke and Griffin being involved."

Andro leaned back. "But how does this fit in with Barry's murder? And the hole at Red Rocks?"

"I don't know." But I recalled Nancy in her red silk robe. "Maybe it has something to do with Nancy." I hoped she was okay.

"Who?" Agent Baker asked.

"Nancy, the physics department secretary, Nancy?" Andro asked.

"Administrative assistant. Yeah," I said. "I saw her with dead-Barry or with someone who was impersonating dead-Barry, and I think they'd just had sex."

"Ick," Agent Baker said.

"Well, he wasn't dead at the time," I said. "Whoever it was, he was definitely alive."

"This is one of our stranger conversations, Madison," she said. "And we've had some strange ones, so that's saying something."

Someone jostled our little table, putting my beer at risk. Egad. I grabbed my precious frosty mug before it spilled.

"So, what's our plan of attack?" Agent Baker asked.

"Find out what's going on?" Andro said.

Someone bumped my chair. It was really getting crowded in here. I started getting a weird feeling of déjà vu. The last time I'd been in here and it had been so crowded, Andro was here and I was talking on the phone to Ben, and something had happened.

"Mad?" he asked.

"What's wrong?" Agent Baker asked.

But I lost the thought. I couldn't remember what had been on the tip of my brain. "Nothing's wrong." I shook my head. "I just had a weird feeling. I don't know what the next step is. Do you guys have any ideas?"

"Honestly, I can't think with this headache," Agent Baker said. "And all these people and all this noise isn't helping."

"Well, it wasn't this noisy earlier," Andro said. "Maybe it's time to call it a night?"

Andro and I certainly weren't going to figure anything else out here tonight about us. "Can I give you a ride home, Agent Baker?"

"I'm fine," she said. "Oh, wait. I don't have a car. Yes, please."

The three of us stood up. "Andro, do you want to try to get together sometime?"

He gave me a look I couldn't interpret, and I thought I knew all his looks. "Actually, I'm not sure I can."

"Okay," I said. I slammed the rest of my beer and turned to Agent Baker. "Come on, let's go."

We elbowed our way through the crowd. My déjà vu feeling came back. But I didn't remember anything more.

It turned out Agent Baker lived in Golden, south of Boulder. As we drove south on Highway 93, I got another déjà vu feeling. The views along the highway as the sun started to set were glorious− rolling foothills covered with golden grasses swaying in the breeze and chunky rock formations. "Pretty drive," I said.

"Yeah," Agent Baker said. "It's Open Space. They can't develop it."

"They can if it disappears when you look at it," I muttered.

"What?" she asked.

"The other day, I thought I saw a mansion disappear

somewhere along here."

"What? Stop the car."

I pulled into a gravel driveway on the side of the road.

"What is going on with you?" she asked.

"I saw a mansion along here before, and then it disappeared." My earlier déjà vu resolved itself. I remembered something else. "And I think I saw Luke at Boulder Brews."

"You might have mentioned these things before," she said drily.

"A lot has been going on," I said. "What with people being murdered and impersonated and such."

"You have a point. But what do you mean a mansion *disappeared*?"

"I mean one minute it was there, and another minute it wasn't," I said.

"Are you sure it didn't just slip out of view behind a hill or something?"

I considered her statement. Was I sure? "I'm not sure. But isn't that the kind of thing you can check? Don't you guys have spy satellites watching us all the time?"

The look on her face was priceless. "I can neither confirm nor deny such a thing." She got out her phone. "But let me make a call." She punched the screen and then waved at me. "Go away."

"Go where? We're parked in the middle of nowhere in my car."

"Just get out and walk around or something." She turned her attention to her phone. "Yeah, hi. It's Lisa. Just a sec." She gave me one of her patented evil-eye stares.

"Fine." I carefully checked to make sure no cars were about to come whizzing by on the highway and run me down, opened my door and got out.

Outside, it wasn't quite full dark yet, and the first stars were emerging. Right above me, three bright stars in a line shone brightly. "Hello, Mr. Orion. Nice belt you have there."

The evening breeze was cool, and I shivered. Come on already, Lisa.

After a few more minutes of shivering and looking up at the stars, Lisa, I mean Agent Baker, flipped on the overhead light in the car and waved me back.

As I got in, she said, "We have a lead. There does appear to be an intermittent building near here."

"Intermittent building?" I gave her my skeptical look.

"You're skeptical?" she said like I wasn't allowed to be skeptical. "It was your idea in the first place. I want to go check it out."

"Are you sure about going on a mission now?" I asked. "How's your head?"

"I'm okay. The coffee helped." She peered at her phone. "It's just recon. I'll give you directions."

"Turn off your lights," Agent Baker said.

The gravel road we were on was barely a road, so if I turned off the headlights, we were gonna be doing some off-roading real soon, and my old Prius wasn't up for it. "Are you sure?"

In the dark, I imagined her eyes boring into me and her hand reaching for her gun and tried not to sound nervous.

"Maybe we should go on foot," I said. "I thought this was just supposed to be recon."

"All right," she said. "Park."

I parked, and we got out and started walking down the path.

Agent Baker's phone illuminated her face as she stared at it.

I couldn't help thinking that made her kind of an obvious target. I shivered and it wasn't entirely because of the cold. "Maybe you should turn that off," I whispered.

"The phone? Why?" But she soon corrected herself, seeing the light on her hand and arm. "Thanks." She shut it off and put it back in her pocket. "It's probably at the end of this road, anyway." Calling this stretch of dirt a road was generous.

I nodded. Of course, in the dark, she probably couldn't see it.

We crept along the so-called road as it climbed a hill. As we crested the rise, we saw a huge glass and concrete mansion, complete with a wall of windows looking out on a pool and the mountains. It was all lit up as if for a party. "Frip." I crouched down.

"What?" Agent Baker sidled over to me. "How do you know

this is it?"

"It looks like Luke's mansion from last year," I whispered. "On the tropical island."

And then a man walked out the open sliding glass door toward the pool.

I froze.

Chapter Twenty-Four

Agent Baker and I were crouched in the tall grass and brush behind the crest of a hill in the middle of nowhere on a cool October evening.

A man, dressed only in board shorts, walked across the pool deck towards the steaming pool.

"What's he wearing?" Agent Baker whispered. "It's practically winter."

The man in question was around six feet tall, well-built, with dark brown hair. I let out a breath. It wasn't Luke. Luke was thinner and younger and had less body hair—and don't ask me how I knew that.

A gorgeous Latina, dressed only in a teeny-weeny red bikini, emerged from the house. "Shoot," I whispered. "It's Nancy."

"Well, she doesn't look like she's being held against her will."

The couple kissed enthusiastically next to the pool.

"No, she doesn't."

"Who's the guy?" Agent Baker asked. "He looks familiar."

He did look familiar. I squinted, trying to place him. He was with Nancy, so it stood to reason it was her ex, aka Barry-with-a-B King, aka the dead guy. I didn't think I'd ever officially met him when he was alive, but the guy did look like his pictures. "It looks like Barry King."

The couple got in the pool with much giggling and splashing.

"What? The body we recovered at the physics building?" Agent Baker turned to look at me. "Come on, Madison."

I shrugged. "Either the dead guy was impersonating Barry, or this guy is."

"But that doesn't make any sense," she said. "What was special about this Barry character?"

And then another man sauntered out on the pool deck. He was shorter, chubby, Asian, in his early twenties, and starting to lose his hair. I knew him well. Too well. And it didn't bode well for the other guy's real identity. Griffin had been Luke's sidekick, and I had a sneaking suspicion he still was.

"Shit," Agent Baker said. "It's Griffin. What's he doing here? There's an APB out for him." She stood up. "I should take him in."

I grabbed her arm and pulled her back down. "I don't think that other guy is Barry. I think it's Luke.

"Shit!" She glared at me. "You said you killed him."

"I thought I did."

She glared some more. Finally, she said, "I don't get it. How can he look like this other guy?"

Griffin took a running jump and cannon-balled into the pool, splashing water everywhere.

Nancy and Barry/fake-Barry didn't seem happy with him.

"I don't get it either," I said. "It doesn't make sense, but there it is. Luke and this Barry guy do look somewhat alike: six feet tall, dark hair, attractive. Maybe Luke picks a reality where he looks like Barry and instantiates it. Maybe he's picking a reality where he had cosmetic surgery. Maybe he's altering our perception of him, and he doesn't truly look any different. Or maybe he's wearing makeup."

"My head hurts," Agent Baker said.

"Join the club." My legs also hurt from all the crouching. I sat down in the dirt. "What are you going to do?"

Agent Baker grabbed her phone from her pocket. "Call for backup and take the bastards down."

I knew she was going to say that. "How? We tried to take them down last year, and that didn't work out so well. And what about my friend, Nancy? She hasn't done anything wrong. Probably. They might hurt her. Or she might get caught in the crossfire."

Agent Baker pointed at the couple frolicking in the pool. "She's aiding and abetting fugitives." She dialed and the screen illuminated her face.

"The phone is shining on your face. Move back." I pointed

down the hill.

She crab-walked a little ways down the hill.

I followed her. "What about keeping them under surveillance for a while?"

She ignored me, whispering into her phone.

I was cold. I lay down. The dry grass was prickly and poked into my back. I looked up at Orion, the hunter. Stars were pretty. I did not think about the horrible quantum duel I fought with Luke last year. I didn't think about how Luke attacked my family. I didn't think about Andro almost dying.

I didn't think about a young man and a young woman with their whole lives ahead of them, both dead within the last few days.

And most of all, I didn't think about a promising young student disintegrating into a swirl of invisible quarks, gluons, and electrons at my hands. If he was back, how?

I was the one who'd taught everyone about q-lapsing. Was this whole thing my fault? People died because of me? As I lay there, water started leaking out of the corners of my eyes and down the sides of my face.

Eventually, Agent Baker poked me and whispered, "We're meeting them by the car."

I sat up.

"You seem odd," she said. "What's wrong?"

I wiped my face. "Nothing. Let's go." We crouched down and jogged towards the road.

At my car, we had to wait a bit for backup to arrive. I couldn't resist raising my objection to barging in, guns blazing. "We had a heck of a time capturing these guys before. What makes you think anything will be different now?"

"It'll be different because we need it to be different. You should call Andro." Andro's helped me take down Luke last year. She faced me. "If you have another plan, I'm all ears."

Unfortunately, I didn't have another plan.

While we were waiting, Agent Baker said, "Aren't you going to call Andro?"

"No," I said, still feeling sad and sort of numb.

"What do you mean, no?" she said. "We need him."

"Other people need him more." I forced myself out of

zombie mode. "Besides, now you can q-lapse. And you're trained in apprehending criminals and stuff. You're going to be way better at fighting bad guys than Andro ever was. He's an academic, after all. Plus, he was a distraction to me when he got hurt."

"Aren't you an academic?" she asked with raised eyebrows. I could see them in the headlights of the cars that approached us.

I didn't answer her.

Soon after, some nondescript black SUVs drove up, parking behind my battered Prius. A bunch of nondescript people, dressed in black, including black bulletproof vests, jumped out. One of them handed Agent Baker a vest, and she shrugged off her standard blazer and put it on.

The agent got another vest out of the SUV and held it out to me. "Dr. Martin," he said. "Madison?"

I finally focused on his face. I didn't recognize him.

"Do you want a vest?"

"No." I shook my head. Get in the game, Mad. "Guns aren't their M.O. Those vests aren't going to do anything for you."

The agent looked alarmed for a second and then shrugged and dropped the extra vest back in the vehicle. "Suit yourself."

In the meantime, the agents were crowded around Agent Baker as she talked to them in a low voice.

She stopped talking, and there was a bunch of nodding, and they all unholstered their weapons and checked them.

Agent Baker came over to me. "Are you ready?"

"What's the plan?" I asked.

I saw her visibly suppress a sigh. "We're going to advance on the house on foot, and when we get in range, we'll take them into custody."

"So, no quantum mumbo jumbo?"

She glanced at her team. "It's too unreliable." How many of these guys had tried, and failed, to learn to q-lapse?

"Why do you need me then?"

"In case of quantum mumbo jumbo."

"Fair enough." No one offered me a gun, and I didn't ask for one.

The whole group of us crept along the path to the mansion.

In the moonlight, it looked like some kind of surreal trick-or-treat expedition. Give us some candy, or we'll shoot you.

Somehow Agent Baker and I ended up at the rear of the team. When we crested the hill, several agents were lying in the scrub, guns focused on the pool area.

"Let's go," she said to me and started jogging up to the house, gun pointed in front of her.

I followed.

"FBI!" she yelled as she stepped onto the concrete. "You're under arrest. Let me see your hands."

The three people in the pool froze for a second, eyes drawn to her voice.

The taller brown-haired man in the pool looked right at me and smiled. As he did so, his face morphed into the symmetrical Italian features I remembered so well. Luke.

"FBI!" Agent Baker yelled again.

Luke glanced at Griffin, and they both smiled.

And then, they both disappeared.

A moment later, the house, the pool, and almost everything else disappeared as well.

Nancy was left, wet, lying on the ground in a little red bikini on a cold October evening. "What?" She started shivering. "Wh-What just happened?"

I successfully resisted the very strong urge to tell Agent Baker *I told you so.*

Behind me, various agents cursed.

"What the fuck?"

"Shit."

Agent Baker ran to me. "What are you standing there for? Follow them."

"What happened?" one of the agents said.

"Where'd they go?" another of the agents said.

I held up my hands. "Fine. I'll try." I was regretting those beers now.

I tried to concentrate. *I am where Luke and Griffin are. I am where Luke and Griffin are.* I screwed my eyes shut, willing myself to be elsewhere.

"Why isn't it working?" Agent Baker said.

"I'm not sure." Once I opened my eyes again, I spied Nancy

shaking.

"Explain what happened to the house." Agent Baker scowled.

"I don't know," I said. "Maybe it was likely there wasn't a house here."

Nancy looked like she was literally freezing to death. The agents weren't helping her. They were just peppering her with questions.

I q-lapsed so I was holding the blanket from my office. Yay. I could still q-lapse.

Nancy was shaking and starting to look a little blue.

I wrapped the blanket around her.

"Nancy Hernandez?" Agent Baker said.

She nodded.

"You're coming with us."

Agent Baker started leading her back to the SUVs.

I really didn't want to go with them. I wanted this whole day to be over.

I q-lapsed so I was back at my car, quickly got in, turned around, and drove back to Boulder. I stopped at an ATM and got the maximum cash out, which was close to my maximum cash. Then I went to a hotel, Boulder Bed and Breakfast, and checked in for the night, paying cash.

Hopefully, neither Luke nor the FBI could find me.

And hopefully, I hadn't put my friends and family in more danger.

Chapter Twenty-Five

I was lying in the flowery bed of the flowery bedroom at the bed and breakfast and, of course, I couldn't get to sleep. Wasn't that always the way when you were exhausted, and the only thing you wanted was sleep? Maybe it was too many flowers. Or, maybe it was the fact that I was totally stressed out, and my brain wouldn't shut off.

I punched my pillow again and rolled around, trying to get comfortable.

And then, there was a knock at the door.

I bolted upright. The bad guys found me! Were they here to kill me? I tried to focus my mind to q-lapse and rabbit out of there.

"Madison?" a man whispered on the other side of the door. "It's Andro." The whisperer did sound a lot like Andro. "Are you there? Come on. Open the door." But how did I know it was truly Andro?

And how did he know I was here?

"Madison, if you're in there, say something. Please. I've been looking all over town for you." He sounded worried.

"If I was Madison," I said, getting up and moving over to the door, "which I'm not saying I am, how do I know you're you?"

"Madison!" he said. "Thank God! I've been worried sick. Ryan called me and told me what happened."

"I say again, how do I know you're Andro and not some impostor?"

"Would an impostor know the first time we had sex it was here?" he asked.

I felt blood rush to my face. Andro and I had had sex here, in this very room, for the first time, and it was as hot as the core of a high-luminosity main-sequence star. I unlocked the door and opened it.

On the other side stood my on-again-off-again Andro, and he looked great, hair tousled, cheeks flushed, eyes flashing.

"How did you find me?" I asked, waving him into the room. "I didn't register under my name."

He stepped inside, and I closed the door behind him. "Maybe Alberta Einstein wasn't the most covert name you could have chosen. And this is the only hotel you've stayed at in town, isn't it?" He stopped and smiled at me.

"We should really come up with some kind of password in case of impostors," I said.

"Okay. What?" He held up a finger. "And don't say, Alberta Einstein."

Darn. He read my mind. "How about *Three quarks for Muster Mark*?"

He said, "Say what?"

"You know, from *Finnegan's Wake* by James Joyce."

"No." He shook his head. "What are you talking about?"

"It's where the physicist Murray Gell-Mann got the term 'quark.'"

"Okay," he said. "That's definitely obscure enough. No one is going to stumble on that."

"Good." I grinned.

He grinned back. "Speaking of okay, I'm glad you're okay," he said. "Are you okay? You look okay."

"Yeah, I'm okay."

"I'm so relieved." He held out his arms. "I know things have been unsettled between us lately, but how about a hug?" He knew me so well.

He enveloped me in his arms. Suddenly, I felt much better. I didn't feel so alone. I didn't feel so much like everything was my fault. "Mmm." He felt great, firm and warm. He smelled great, with his special Andro smell—which I hadn't been getting enough of lately. He was pretty great, in general.

"What's the noise you're making? That's your cinnamon roll noise. I'm not a cinnamon roll," he said, starting to pull away.

"I'm upset, so you're a cinnamon roll if I say you're a cinnamon roll." I held him close. "Mmm."

After a few more moments, we separated. I sat down at the top of the bed and leaned back on the headboard. "You used to like me to lick your frosting."

He laughed, sitting down on the bottom of the bed. "Fair enough. I stipulate we've both enjoyed plenty of, ah, frosting-licking."

He didn't seem overly inclined to pursue any more frosting at the moment. Darn. "So why are you here?" I said. "As you can see, I'm fine."

He grabbed my foot and squeezed it. "I was worried about you, Mad. Ryan called and said there'd been an FBI raid on Luke's mansion? Was it really Luke? Was Griffin really with him? And they got away?"

"The news ticker version is: I was driving Lisa home from Boulder Brews, and we found probably-Luke's mansion, called for FBI backup, and stormed the castle, but probably-Luke and probably-Griffin got away. And the mansion disappeared, leaving Nancy lying in the dirt in a teeny-weeny wet bikini in October. The FBI got bupkis. They can't even look for clues."

"Probably-Luke? Meaning you think it was Luke, but you're not sure?"

"Yeah." It was nice how Andro understood me.

His foot squeezing was turning into foot caressing. "Why didn't you call me? I could have helped."

"I thought you wanted to protect yourself for Sophia?" Was I a bad person if I was jealous of a little kid? Yep, little bit. Get over it, Mad.

"I want to protect you, too, babe." His hand ascended my leg like a NASA Earth-Observing-System satellite flying for the North Pole.

I reached for his hand. "What are you doing?"

"What?" He grinned. "I can't caress the woman I'm dating?"

That was right. We were dating. I couldn't help grinning back. "You can caress. Caressing is good." I caressed his hand in my hand.

"And this room is bringing back memories." His grin took on an X-rated attitude. "Some very good memories. We had a good time here. Didn't we?"

"We definitely had a good time." I scooched down the bed

towards him. "And what's this *the* woman I'm dating business? Am I the only woman you're dating?" Was he the only man I was dating? What about Ben? Yikes. Why was I thinking about Ben?

"Of course, babe." He leaned down and planted a quick kiss on my lips. "You rock. How could anyone else compare to you?"

I felt my lips curve into a smile. That was more like it. "When do you have to leave?"

"Oh, not for hours and hours."

"Gosh, whatever will we do with all that time?"

"I predict we'll think of something." He touched my cheek with his hand, tilted his head, and touched his lips to mine. Mmm.

We stopped and gazed into each other's eyes for a moment. It felt like coming home.

I put my arms around him and pulled him to me, smoldering, as his chest pressed against mine. Our lips touched, and tongues explored...

"Babe, I have to go," Andro said.

When I opened my eyes, the sun was shining through the B & B's thin curtains onto Andro's handsome face. I could get used to this dating thing. "What time is it?" He was fully dressed.

"It's six o'clock." He leaned down and kissed me thoroughly on the lips.

"In the morning? Wait. I can't process this without caffeine. People get up this early? What's up with that?"

He jumped up and took a step for the door. "Today, I'm a dad." He said it in such an awe-inspired way, my eyes filled.

"I know you'll do great," I said, my voice husky. "Have fun."

"Thanks." He opened the door and bounced out.

As soon as he closed the door behind him, all my worries rushed back. Probably-Luke and probably-Griffin were still on the loose, and who knew what they'd do next? And were they really Luke and Griffin? I had to admit, I didn't understand this impersonation stuff. I didn't think I could impersonate anyone.

And my friend--or former friend--Nancy, was in custody for doing nothing much. She didn't deserve that. And worst of all, two people were dead.

I rolled over and tried to go back to sleep.

At ten o'clock, I reluctantly got up and stopped hiding from my life. Among my many missed messages, Agent Baker had called multiple times. Apparently, Nancy was in custody, but she refused to talk to anyone but me. I got my butt in gear and drove down to the Denver FBI field office. Luckily I didn't have class on Tuesdays.

Agent Baker let me in the FBI interrogation room where Nancy, still wearing her teeny-weeny red bikini, huddled, looking miserable. I glared at the guy sitting in there with her. "Seriously?"

He shrugged.

I glanced back at Agent Baker. "Surely, you guys could at least find some sweats or something for her."

Agent Baker's eyebrows creased her forehead. "Yes." She gave the departing agent her deadeye stare, which was more baleful than her evil-eye stare.

The agent gulped and said, "Right away, ma'am."

I sat down at the table. Why did interrogation rooms look so nondescript? Did they think boredom would make you more likely to confess? "I'm sorry I didn't come sooner, Nancy."

She dipped her head. "I haven't said anything yet. I don't have a lawyer. Can you help me get a lawyer?"

Agent Baker sat down next to me.

"Yes, I can help you get a lawyer, but are you sure you need a lawyer? You didn't do anything wrong, did you? They just want to ask you some questions." I turned to Agent Baker. "However, I must admit I assumed they'd at least treat you decently. Isn't this against the Geneva convention or something?"

She aimed her deadeye stare my way.

When I couldn't take it anymore, I said, "What?"

"USA Patriot Act." She leaned back and crossed her arms. "Or, if you'd rather, USA Freedom Act."

"What about it? You can't tell me the FBI thinks Nancy here is a terrorist."

"We don't know. Maybe she's a terrorist." Agent Baker faced Nancy. "She won't talk to us."

Nancy looked even more miserable than before.

"Nancy's not a terrorist. She's a secretary." I reached for her hand and squeezed it. "I'm sorry you got caught up in all this."

Nancy's eyes filled, and she looked down at the table. She said something, but I couldn't make it out.

"What?"

She lifted her head. "I'm an administrative assistant, not a secretary."

"Yes." I glanced over at Agent Baker. She almost smiled. "You definitely are. You are an administrative assistant. I apologize."

Nancy nodded and seemed a little less dejected.

"Can you tell us what happened, Ms. Hernandez?" Agent Baker said.

Nancy surveyed me.

"Go ahead," I said. "It's okay."

"The other night, I got a call from a blocked number, and when I answered, the man said he was Barry." Her face brightened. "I couldn't believe it. It was so wonderful. I mean, the police and everyone said Barry was dead. It was a miracle."

"You had a social relationship with Barry King?" Agent Baker asked.

"Yes," Nancy said. "We dated for about six months, but it was over about six months ago. He broke up with me. It wasn't my idea."

"What happened after he called?" I asked.

"Then he came over, and I was happy to see him again, considering he was supposed to be dead. He said the police made a mistake."

"Did you ask him where he'd been the last few days?" Agent Baker asked.

"No. I was just glad he wasn't dead. He said I was beautiful and breaking up with me had been a mistake. I guess one thing led to another and, you know..."

I did know. My mind started going back to last night. I understood one thing leading to another. One thing leading to another could be very, very good. Focus, Mad.

"Oh! That's when you stopped by, Madison," she said.

"Madison?" Agent Baker asked. "Are you flushed?"

"No," I said and gestured for Nancy to continue.

"Barry invited me to his new house, and we drove over

there," Nancy said. "It was gorgeous. And huge. And his bedroom was beautiful. We stayed in bed yesterday, doing you-know."

I wondered when Andro and I might be doing you-know again.

"And then we went swimming−I still don't get how the patio was so warm−and then you all showed up." She frowned. "And then I'm not sure what happened. Did you all drug me?"

"What do you think happened?" Agent Baker asked.

"The house disappeared?" Nancy said. "But that doesn't make any sense."

I agreed. It didn't make sense. "See, Agent Baker, Nancy was just an innocent bystander. She's not a terrorist. She just made out with her ex-boyfriend. If that was a crime, we'd all be in jail." Especially me, apparently.

"Are you sure the man was Barry?" Agent Baker asked.

"Of course, it was Barry," Nancy said. "Who else would it be? It looked like Barry."

I had a brainstorm. "Did all of him look like Barry−if you know what I mean?" I may have been referring to his private parts, but that didn't mean I was obsessed with private parts. My question was totally reasonable.

"What?" Nancy asked. "What do you mean?"

When I glanced at Agent Baker, she was definitely wearing a small smile.

Good grief. I was going to have to be the one to spell it out. "Nancy, did his penis look like Barry's penis?"

Chapter Twenty-Six

I couldn't believe I'd just asked about a penis in an FBI interrogation.

"Excuse me?" a man asked at the doorway. "I'm supposed to drop off these sweats." It was some younger agent I'd never seen before, and he looked scared. What must he think was going on in here?

"It's fine." Agent Baker stood up, got the sweats, and handed them to Nancy, who promptly put them on. The agent ducked out as soon as humanly possible.

Nancy sat back down. "I don't understand. You're asking me about his penis?"

"If it was Barry, he would have all of Barry's parts," I said. "If it was an impostor, presumably he wouldn't know what Barry's parts looked like, so he wouldn't be able to impersonate them. So, was it Barry's junk or not?"

Nancy looked thoughtful. "I guess..."

"Yes?" Agent Baker and I leaned forward.

"His, uh, parts did look different. They–"

"Whoa. Stop right there." Agent Baker interrupted. "I don't want to know."

I wanted to know a little.

Agent Baker shook her head. "Actually, strike that. I don't want to know, but I guess I need to know." She gestured at the big mirror. "Get a sketch artist in here."

A sketch artist! What would they even do with a sketch of someone's privates? It wasn't like they could put it up on the most-wanted list at the post office, right? Or out on an APB? They couldn't use it in a lineup. Nonetheless, I had a feeling I was going to know entirely too much about the suspect in a few minutes.

In the meantime, Nancy had a very strange look on her face.

"What's wrong?" I asked her.

"Does this mean Barry is dead?"

I glanced at Agent Baker. She wasn't talking. "We don't know for sure."

"I wasn't having sex with Barry?"

I scrunched up my face. "Probably not."

"Then who the hell was I having sex with?"

I shrugged.

"Oh, no. I think I'm going to be sick." Nancy leaned over, and Agent Baker managed to slide a trashcan under her stream of vomit.

Poor Nancy. This was the worst interrogation I'd ever been to. And I'd been to far too many interrogations, so that was saying something.

The young, nervous agent brought Nancy some water and paper towels and left again.

"What's taking the sketch artist so long?" Agent Baker asked.

A tinny voice replied through the intercom system. "The regular guy is on a case. But we've got another guy on the way."

"Are you all right, Nancy?" I asked.

"I don't know," she said in a small voice.

"Can we ask you some more questions?" Agent Baker asked.

Nancy sighed and nodded.

"Did your lover mention any future plans?" Agent Baker asked.

"Please don't call him that," Nancy said.

"Did the suspect mention any future plans?" Agent Baker asked.

Nancy grimaced. "Just future plans for what we were going to do in bed. Oh, Jesus."

"Did he say anything about why he was with you?" I asked. "Did you get the sense that he knew you?"

"Yes. I do think he knew me. He mentioned the physics department where I work and something about my office. That's one of the reasons I thought he was Barry. That, and he looked exactly like Barry." Nancy nodded. "But, yeah. He wanted to know my work schedule, supposedly so he'd be able to spend the maximum amount of time with me, he said. And he kept saying I was so beautiful, the most beautiful woman he'd ever met."

The fact that the mystery man had complimented her didn't seem very helpful. Nancy was very attractive, sort of a cross between Sofia Vergara and Penelope Cruz, and quite tall for a woman. Hell, I was on the verge of complimenting her.

"Was that kind of complimenting typical for Barry?" Agent Baker asked.

"No, I guess not," Nancy said.

"Anything else you talked about?" Agent Baker asked.

"He was very interested in my life. He asked about my birthday and my family's birthdays and about my pets' names, stuff like that."

Uh oh. Stuff one might use for a computer password? "You have keys to the physics building and the main office, don't you?" I asked. "And you have access to all the department accounts, don't you?"

"Uh oh," she said.

Agent Baker frowned.

The door opened, and a man in a form-fitting Boulder PD uniform bustled in. "I hear you need a sketch artist?"

"Yes," Agent Baker said. "Please take a seat. I hope you're good with penises." From the other side of the door, raucous laughter broke out, only to be cut off when the door closed.

"Thanks, guys," the man muttered, coming around the table with his large sketch pad. He sat down at the only empty chair at the table. "I can do penises. Er, I mean..." Our eyes met.

It was Ben.

"Madison," he said in surprise. "Hi."

"Hi, Ben." I felt warmth spread over my face like the uncontrolled oxidation of combustible vegetation.

"Are you the one with the penis?" he asked.

If it was possible, my face felt even hotter.

Agent Baker may have snickered. But when I looked at her, her smile was ghosting away.

"No." I pointed at Nancy. "Her. She's going to describe it, the junk, er, the stuff, you're going to draw."

An oh-so-faint snickering noise erupted from next to me again. Was I imagining it?

Ben glanced at Agent Baker. "Ma'am?"

"Yes. Please just draw what Ms. Hernandez describes to you."

Ben dutifully got out his pencil and drew.

The image on the pad was a lot like a car wreck--I didn't want to look, but I couldn't help myself.

When he was finished, we had a very thorough picture of our suspect. Ben tore the picture off the pad and handed it to Agent Baker.

Agent Baker thanked him.

After looking at me but not saying anything further, he got up to leave. I didn't know how to interpret that. Did he think I was part of the penis police? Did I make him nervous now? And here I'd thought we'd chemistry.

But I was with Andro, wasn't I? Bad, Madison.

I stood up, too. "Ben, can I talk to you outside?"

"Sure."

We stepped out into the hall.

He grinned, but it seemed forced. "So, that happened."

"What? You don't usually sit around sketching penises?"

He gave me an alarmed look.

What the hell was I saying? "Scratch that. Never mind," I said. "How's it going? Are you okay?"

"I should be asking you that," he said. "Ryan actually called my apartment looking for you last night. How odd is that?"

Why was it odd? "It's not that odd. I did spend the weekend at your apartment, and Ryan knew. He drove us there, right?" I smiled. "Thanks for that again." Ben was nice. And he did flirt with me the other morning when he brought me coffee in bed. I didn't imagine that. I resisted the urge to caress his firm chest, which looked awesome in his uniform. And come to think of it, his chest looked awesome out of his uniform. Bad, Madison.

"Yeah," he said. "But don't spread it around."

He didn't want people to know I was at his apartment? Was he ashamed of me? "Uh?"

He leaned in and grinned. "It'd ruin my rep if people found out I had such a hottie stay over in my apartment and I didn't make a move."

I felt my face stretch into a smile. He thought I was a hottie. "Your rep is safe with me." I liked this guy.

The door to the interrogation room opened. Agent Baker said, "What are you doing out here? We're not finished."

"Bye, Madison," Ben said. "Bye, Agent Baker. Thank you for this opportunity." He held up his sketch pad.

She just stared at him until he left.

I went back into the interrogation room.

"Are you charging me with something?" Nancy asked.

What would that be? Ill-advised sex? Back-sliding with an ex? Speaking of which, what was going on with me and Andro? Was last night a one-time thing, or was it going to become a regular thing again?

Could something go on with Ben?

"Madison?" Agent Baker asked. "What's wrong with you today?"

What was wrong with me? Why was I so boy crazy all of a sudden? Physics, I needed to focus on physics. That was nice and logical. "Nothing's wrong with me. I'm a physicist."

"Whatever," Agent Baker said. "As I was saying, you know what this means, don't you?" She pointed at the sketch.

We all needed to take a cold shower? Or we were the penis police? That probably wasn't what she was getting at. I sighed. "Yeah. A skilled quantum criminal pulled all that q-lapsing off. Probably, Luke's back." Not that I'd had any idea what his junk looked like. Until now. Ugh.

"Can I go?" Nancy asked. "I cooperated."

"Come on, Lisa," I said. "Let the poor woman go. She's suffered enough."

She gave me the evil eye.

I said, "Come on, Agent Baker."

She put both hands on the table, braced herself, and looked at Nancy. "I guess so. Nancy, please don't leave town."

"Leave town? What are you talking about?" Nancy looked from me to Agent Baker and back again. "I'm not leaving town. After all this, I'll barely be able to leave my house. You are going to catch these guys, aren't you? I really need you to catch them. I feel so violated. Please catch them."

Agent Baker looked grim. "I will."

Nancy turned to me.

I said, "We'll get them. I promise." I hoped it was sooner rather than later.

Nancy gave a little nod.

We all stood up.

Agent Baker said, "Madison, we need you back here tomorrow for the task force meeting. We have to get a handle on all this quantum stuff."

"You're putting the quantum task force back together?" Last year it had been convened to catch the nefarious quantum criminals, aka my seemingly run-of-the-mill quantum mechanics students, Luke and Griffin.

She nodded. "And this time, we will get some more agents to q-lapse." Right now, she was the only one that could do it. "We have to catch these guys. Once and for all."

I could tell when I was being drafted. "Yeah. Okay."

"I don't understand what's going on," Nancy said.

"Don't worry," I said. "I'll explain it to you."

As we went out the door, Agent Baker shook her head and rattled the large piece of sketch paper. "I don't know how we're going to handle this BOLO."

Who cared about those stringy ties?

Agent Baker must have read my expression because she said, "That's a *be on the lookout*, Madison."

Oh, right. That made more sense.

Chapter Twenty-Seven

Wednesday, I wanted to stay in bed all day with the flowery covers up over my head. Even better would have been to get Andro to join me in bed all day. But that wasn't going to happen.

I had responsibilities. I had to deal with my class, and I was supposed to drive down to the Denver FBI field office and help Agent Baker with the quantum task force.

When I passed through the B & B's dining room, it was deserted. Hurray. More coffee for me. I filled two big paper cups with coffee from the insulated dispenser before the proprietor noticed. Coffee helped with q-lapsing, so I had to take a lot. It was practically a matter of national security. Yeah.

I sat down at the table for a second to check my messages and texts and caffeinate. Agent Baker had left me one last night at about ten p.m., saying she was going to go back to the site of the mansion and take another look around. Nancy's plea must have gotten to her. If I got the message in time, I was supposed to meet her there. Oops.

I called her, but it went straight to voicemail. Oh well, I'd see her soon.

I stopped at the physics department office on my way down to Denver. Nancy was not in. I knocked on Professor Chen's door.

"Nancy?" he opened the door.

"No, sorry, sir. It's just me. I wanted to double-check that you're okay with me canceling my quantum mechanics class today."

"What?"

"We talked about it Monday. I'm worried the kids are in danger."

"Do it. We can't endanger the kids."

I sent a quick email to the students canceling class and reminding them of their reading and homework assignments. I also said we'd play Friday's class by ear, i.e., I'd send out another email before then.

Down in Denver at the FBI, Agent Sawyer paced back and forth just inside the front doors like he was impatient or something. "There you are."

"Hi, Nate," I said. Ha. We were on a first-name basis. He glared at me.

Maybe we weren't on a first-name basis. "Hi, Agent Sawyer?"

"Why do you insist on being late for everything?"

"Chill. I'm, like, five minutes late. You're lucky I'm here at all. I had to cancel my class."

"Lisa's missing," he said. "And her last call was to you. Please tell me you know where she is."

Now I felt even more guilty about missing her message. I shook my head. "Sorry. She said she was going back to the site of the disappearing mansion last night at about ten o'clock, but that was the last I heard from her." Could something have happened to her? Oh no…

"You have to tell the group that." He grabbed my arm and practically dragged me to the meeting room.

The meeting room was more like a meeting auditorium. There must have been two hundred people in there. Of course, two hundred FBI agents were nothing compared to four hundred hostile freshmen in Physics 101, so I wasn't worried. Not super worried, anyway. My adrenaline level was on the rise, though.

I glanced over at Nate. He looked nervous. Wow. I'd never seen him look nervous before. "Are you all right?"

"Of course, I'm all right. I'm always all right. Why wouldn't I be all right?" So, not all right. Check. I guessed he and Agent Baker were closer than I'd realized.

He pointed at the podium.

I slowly walked up to it and tapped the microphone. The taps boomed in the large room. "So, I'm Dr. Martin," I said. "I'm supposed to tell you Agent Baker left me a voicemail last night at ten p.m. stating she was going back over to the site of the disappearing mansion."

The agents that had been at the raid the other night looked grim. The agents that hadn't been there looked skeptical.

An older man in a charcoal gray suit stood up from the front row and walked to the podium.

I stepped away from the microphone.

He leaned toward it. "I'm Director Lopez. Finding Agent Baker is our number one priority." He turned to another one of the agents in the front row. "Gonzales, put together a SWAT team and get over to that mansion site ASAP."

Agent Gonzales did everything but salute. "Yes, sir." He turned to the crowd.

"I can go look at the mansion site right now, if you want," I said to Director Lopez.

"What?" he said.

"I can q-lapse and pop over there and pop right back."

"What?" He furrowed his brow.

I realized by the time he and I were on the same page, I could have been there and back again.

I concentrated and q-lapsed and found myself standing in the middle of grass-covered foothills where there had been a mansion for at least long enough for us to raid it. Just as I appeared, I thought I saw something flicker in my peripheral vision, but when I tried to focus on it, it was gone.

I studied the ground. There were a lot of footprints and scuffed and disturbed dirt. Had we left it this way the other night?

As I walked toward the mountains, there was no sign of flattened grasses or swimming pool-shaped holes. I paused to think about the mysterious case of the appearing and disappearing mansion. I didn't think it was possible to move a mansion from one place to another. But, this was prime real estate. There was a slim chance a mansion would be built here. Was that what happened? Someone took advantage of that small but non-zero possibility? This quantum stuff was all very confusing.

Anyway, if Agent Baker had come here, there was no sign of her now.

I yelled, "Agent Baker, Lisa, are you here?" just to be sure.

Nothing but the October wind answered me.

But as I turned to go, something glinted in the sun. I leaned down. It was a phone, a very fancy phone, and it looked a heck of a lot like Agent Baker's phone. I pulled out my phone and dialed her.

The phone lying on the ground started ringing.

Ugh. She would never have left her phone behind. I was getting a bad feeling. I wished I'd gotten her message in time to meet her. I really hoped she was okay.

I shoved both phones in my pocket, concentrated, and q-lapsed to the FBI auditorium. Ow.

When I popped back, the auditorium was totally silent. Then, it erupted into chaos.

"What the hell?"

"How'd she do that?"

Director Lopez was talking into the mic at the podium. "Order, please. Gentlemen, ladies, please." He turned and looked at me. "Dr. Martin, get over here."

I stepped up to him, and he patted my shoulder. I guess he had to check for himself that I was truly here. My head hurt.

I held out her phone. "She must have been there last night. But she's not there now."

Lopez frowned as he took Lisa's phone. I seemed to derail what he'd been about to say.

"I'm sorry to say, there might have been signs of a struggle there," I said.

Lopez turned to Agent Gonzales, who was still in the auditorium. "Get going."

Gonzales and some other agents jogged out.

The agents still in the auditorium were getting restless.

"Maybe you should give Agent Baker's presentation," I said.

Lopez didn't seem to know what I was talking about.

"Agent Baker was going to give a presentation to the quantum task force about everything that had been going on. I think Agent Sawyer was working with her. He probably has it."

"Our first priority is finding Lisa," Director Lopez said.

"I understand that," I said. "That's my priority, as well. But how can they help," I pointed at the crowd, "if they don't know what's been going on?" I hoped Agent Gonzales's team had at least some idea of what they were getting into.

"Sawyer!" Lopez said.

Nate jumped up and approached us. "Yes, sir?"

"Do you have Lisa's presentation about the quantum crimes?" Lopez asked.

"Yes, sir." He looked more nervous than ever, if that was possible. "It's all loaded up and ready to go." He indicated the large screen behind us. Why didn't Nate give it already?

"Make it quick," Lopez said.

"Yes, sir." Nate approached the podium and woke up the laptop sitting there. "Agent Baker and I put together this summary of the quantum crimes. I suspect something in here is related to why she's missing. I'm sending you the presentation and supporting documents now." He pressed a key. I heard a bunch of pings from the audience.

He said, "Last year, there was an act of minor robbery and vandalism at the University of Colorado student union, followed by a full-fledged bank robbery..." He clicked through pictures of the crime scenes.

"This fall, there was another bank robbery. More significantly, a researcher at CU, Barry King, and a graduate student, Isabella Rodriguez, were murdered by quantum mechanics." He showed Barry's picture on the large screen in the front of the room. Before. And after. Ugh. "And here's Miss Rodriguez." I quickly looked away. Poor Isabella.

Some of the tough-as-nails agents looked nauseated. Some looked scared. All of them looked mad.

"We thought she was responsible for the death of researcher Barry King."

"We thought the case was closed. Until Monday night. Monday night Agent Baker and Dr. Martin were driving south on Highway 93 when they saw a mansion that shouldn't have been there." He clicked something, and I turned around to look at the screen. "Here's the satellite view of the location as of two weeks ago." We saw an aerial view of rolling foothills covered with dried grasses and the occasional scrubby tree or bush. "This shot is twenty-four hours later." Click. Bam! A mansion appeared, complete with a huge patio, in-ground pool, and Jacuzzi.

One of the agents in the audience said, "How many days

between this picture and the last one?"

"As I said, twenty-four hours, one day." He clicked back. "Nothing there." He clicked forward. "Mansion there."

The audience members shifted in their seats and muttered amongst themselves.

"We staged a raid of the mansion Monday night." He showed some close-up pictures of the mansion, taken at night. "Now, I'm going to show a movie we took during the raid."

Someone took a movie?

He messed around on the computer, and a low-resolution movie appeared on the screen. At night, a bunch of bullet-proof-vested FBI agents crept towards a large house as three people (two men and a woman) cavorted on the patio.

"I thought that guy was dead," someone in the audience said.

In the movie, I spied myself wearing the same outfit I had on right now. And it didn't look great, even two days fresher. When all this was over, I should really consider a makeover.

As the team approached the mansion, one of the men in the video finally saw us, smiled, and his face morphed into someone else's face.

The crowd muttered.

I heard someone ask, "How the hell does that work?"

"I thought *that* guy was dead," someone in the audience said.

"I'll come back to this," Nate said. The two men disappeared, followed closely by the house. The woman stumbled onto the dirt and immediately started shaking.

The audience talked and exclaimed.

"That's Nancy Hernandez. We took her into custody and questioned her extensively. She cooperated fully and is no longer considered a person of interest. You have her statements and info in the files I just sent."

"Here are close-ups of the suspects," Nate said. He showed a still-frame of the taller man in the video. "For a while, we thought this man, Barry King, might have faked his death somehow and was involved in quantum crimes. But now we think this man is Luke Bacalli." In slow-mo, Barry's smiling face morphed into Luke's smiling face. "And this is his partner, Griffin

213

Jin." He showed Griffin's face. "Griffin escaped from a maximum security facility a few weeks ago even though he was sedated at the time."

Someone in the audience asked, "How could he escape while sedated?"

"We think he had help."

"I thought Bacalli was declared dead," someone else asked.

"He was." Nate threw me a glance. "Clearly, we're revisiting that theory. You also have information on the suspects in your packets. That's where we are. We believe Bacalli and Jin are responsible for bank robberies and at least two murders."

"If they can make mansions and bank vault walls disappear, and they can escape from maximum security, how the hell are we supposed to get these guys?" somebody in the audience called out.

Everyone looked at me. It was a very good question.

I didn't have an answer.

Chapter Twenty-Eight

The FBI was freaking out because one of their own was missing and presumed something. I didn't know what they presumed, but it wasn't good. I couldn't really blame them for freaking out. I was worried about Lisa, too.

Virtually all the agents stood and started muttering and milling around and giving me evil *maybe we should shoot her* looks. At least, that was how I interpreted their looks. This quantum stuff must be too weird for this straight-arrow group.

Director Lopez loomed over me. "Are you sure you've told us everything you know, Martin? Where's Lisa Baker?"

"I'm sorry, but I don't know where she is," I said. "I want to find her as much as you do. I understand you're concerned about her. I am too. But, I didn't do anything to her."

At some point, while Lopez was intimidating me, Nate joined us. "I don't think Dr. Martin did anything to her, sir."

Phew. At least one person was on my side. I didn't hug Nate (officially my new favorite person), but I wanted to.

"Where the hell is she, then?" Lopez scowled.

The crowd of agents was closing in on us. Was it getting harder to breathe?

"Collapsing the wavefunction is based on probabilities," I said. "It's easier to be in a place where you're more likely to be."

"Huh?" Nate said.

From their expressions, I could tell Director Lopez, and a lot of the other agents were thinking the same thing. They didn't understand what the heck I was talking about, and they were seconds away from blaming me and taking me into custody. Of course, with my q-lapsing skills they couldn't keep me in custody, but I didn't want to go down that road.

LESLEY L. SMITH

"If she had to q-lapse to save herself from something," I said, "she's more likely to be somewhere right now where she usually is, for example, her home or her office. If I had to guess, I'd say she was there." Of course, if she was kidnapped, none of that was relevant, and we basically knew nothing. I was going to assume she q-lapsed.

"And you're sure she figured out this q-lapsing, as you call it?" Lopez asked.

"Yes. I taught her." I was getting claustrophobic at the press of agents surrounding us. And it wasn't helping my headache any.

Calm down, Mad. If I got nervous or scared enough, I might q-lapse away by accident, and I didn't want that. I tried to concentrate on my breathing.

Lopez started pointing at agents. "You, go to her office. You and you, go over to her apartment."

"I'd be happy to help. I can look for her, too," I said.

"Oh, no, you don't. I don't want you leaving the building again until we find Lisa. In fact, I'm assigning an agent to watch you."

I glanced at Nate. Was he still on my side? "Can he watch me?" He seemed to be the only person not showing me outright hostility.

"Is that okay with you, Sawyer?" Director Lopez asked.

"Yes, sir." Nate gave a curt nod. "Madison might have a unique perspective that could help."

"To be clear, if Lisa doesn't show up, you are in some serious shit, Martin," Director Lopez said. "Take her to the second-floor interrogation room, Sawyer."

If she didn't show up? If she was injured, or worse, I'd never forgive myself.

Director Lopez went over to the microphone on the podium. "The number one priority is finding Agent Lisa Baker."

Nate directed me out the door. "You look like someone just kicked your puppy."

"I've been hoping she just q-lapsed and reappeared somewhere else, and we haven't found her yet. What if she doesn't come back? What if she can't come back?" What if she was prevented from coming back? Now I was a nervous wreck.

"Uh." I wasn't sure what to say. If she was attacked, I might be the only one who could help her, and I couldn't do anything in custody. I glanced at him as we walked down the hall. "Am I in custody?"

"Why?" He stopped walking and looked at me. "Should you be in custody?"

"If I'm in custody, I can't help Agent Baker if she needs it."

"Do you think she needs your help, your unique type of help?"

"I don't know. If she just popped into her office or apartment, wouldn't she have called someone by now?"

"Yeah." He took his phone out of his pocket. "But my phone's off for the meeting." He looked at it.

Crap. My phone was probably off, too. What if Agent Baker had been calling, and no one answered their phone? I patted my pockets. Where was my phone? Unfortunately, when I found it there were no new messages. I shook my head.

"She didn't call me either." Agent Sawyer put his phone away.

I was starting to feel stupid about standing in the hall talking. "We should call everywhere she's spent a lot of time." A thought struck me. "Are her parents still alive? Past residences are a good bet, especially if she lived there awhile."

"Right." He seemed pleased with my idea. "Her file should have info on past addresses." He pressed a button on his phone. "I need all the phone numbers of past residences of Agent Lisa Baker."

"Yeah." He nodded. "Good point." He glanced at me. "I hadn't thought of that. The addresses would have new phone numbers now. Yes. Please do what you can. They're looking them up."

The more I thought about it, the more I thought Agent Baker's childhood home would be the place she'd go, assuming she'd had a primary home. That would be where she felt safe. "Get the current phone number for the place where she grew up. She'd especially go there if she was attacked. It would be instinctual."

"I'm working on it." Nate frowned. "Do you think she was attacked?"

I didn't think she'd just leave her phone lying around if she'd had a choice, but I only shrugged.

We waited, standing in the hall.

Finally, he said into the phone, "Lay 'em on me." He started inputting numbers into his cell. "Thanks, man." He hung up and placed a new call. "I'm calling the house where she grew up in Chicago. It's ringing."

"Good." I was shaking.

"Hello? It's her! Lisa? It's Nate Sawyer. Are you okay?" He paused. "I'm sorry to hear that. Do you need an ambulance?" He paled. "Shit. I'm sending an ambulance."

"Let me talk to her." I grabbed the phone. "It's Madison. What's wrong?"

Nate dashed back to the auditorium.

"My head's throbbing," Agent Baker said. "It feels like it's going to explode." Her voice was faint. Poor thing. She sounded horrible. I hoped she was okay.

"Hang in there, Lisa." Manipulating reality taxes your brain. No one had died as a direct result of q-lapsing too much. Yet. I didn't want her to be the first. "We're sending help."

A hoard of agents ran out of the auditorium, led by Director Lopez. "Agent Sawyer says you've got Lisa on the phone." He grabbed the phone from me.

"She's at her childhood home in Chicago," I said. "She needs an ambulance."

"Lisa, it's Jesus Lopez. Please answer me. We're worried about you. Lisa?" He stared at me. "She's not answering."

"She's at the house where she grew up. Send an ambulance, already." I briefly considered trying to q-lapse to go to Chicago, but I didn't know Chicago, and it wasn't probable I'd be there.

"What did you do to her?" Director Lopez advanced on me.

"Me?" I said. "I didn't do anything to her. Except find her. Just now."

"Sir, maybe you should calm down," Nate said.

"This isn't about me," I said. "Call her an ambulance." I very carefully did not consider why she'd needed to go to her safe place. Quantum duel? With who? Correction: I unsuccessfully tried not to consider why she'd needed to go to her safe place.

"We already called." Nate grabbed the phone from Lopez. "Lisa?"

That was a relief. If Agent Baker could be helped, she would be.

"You." Lopez pointed at me. "We're going to keep an eye on you until we're sure Lisa's okay and you're not responsible."

I sighed. This was getting to be a theme. I could leave; they couldn't keep me here, but I didn't want to be on the FBI's shit-list. "Yes, sir. Whatever you need."

My sucking-up seemed to mollify him a bit. His expression calmed anyway. "Sawyer, keep an eye on her."

"Yes, sir." Nate gestured down the hall, back in the direction we'd been headed.

The interrogation room was just like every other interrogation room I'd been in lately. A battered table, four rickety chairs, bad lighting, no air movement, and a big mirror on one wall.

As I sat down in one of the chairs, my stomach rumbled. I checked my phone. It was long past lunchtime. "Is there any chance we could get some food in here?"

Nate sat down in one of the chairs. "Lunch? You're lucky you're not on your way to Guantanamo already."

"Yeah, I know." Q-lapsing was nothing but trouble. I wished I'd never discovered it. And I really wished my students had never figured it out. "What do you think is going to happen with the Quantum Task Force?"

"It's probably toast."

Mmm. Toast.

"Are you thinking about eating toast?" Nate grinned slightly.

Yes. "No. Why would you say that?"

"I am. I missed lunch, too."

I grinned back at him. "Well, good, sir, what would you like? I'm in the mood for a toasted Asiago cheese bagel with cream cheese and some cinnamon bun coffee, ooh, and a cinnamon bun with cream cheese icing."

"Why are you torturing yourself like that?" Nate leaned back in his chair. "No one's going to bring you any food."

Oh, ye of little faith. "I could get some food by q-lapsing."

"Seriously? If that's true, what can't you do with your

q-power?"

That was a good question. "That's a good question. I know it's easier to do stuff that's more likely, and it's harder to do stuff that's less likely."

He snorted. "If q-lapsing is so great, why don't you go check on Lisa?"

I'd already considered that. It wouldn't work because I didn't know Chicago. I didn't think I'd ever been to Chicago. I couldn't picture any place in Chicago, and most of all, it was very improbable I would be in Chicago. But. "Hmm."

"What?" Nate asked. "You're going to Chicago to check on Lisa?"

I couldn't go to Chicago, but I could go to St. Louis, where I used to live, and I could drive to Chicago. What was that, a four-hour drive? "What hospital is she going to?"

"I don't know that." Nate's cell beeped, and he looked down at it. "Yes, I do. Saint Anthony's on West Nineteenth Street." He looked up at me. "Are you thinking of going to Chicago? You promised Lopez you'd stay here. You can't leave."

"I need to know what happened to Agent Baker," I said. "What if she was attacked? What if she's still in danger?"

He opened his eyes wide. "You think she might still be in danger?"

I didn't know, but if she was in a quantum duel, all bets were off. "Maybe."

He shook his head. "I promised Lopez I'd keep an eye on you. No."

I smiled at him in what I hoped was a forgive-me-for-what-I'm-about-to-do way. "Sorry, Nate."

I concentrated and q-lapsed to appear in the living room of my former St. Louis condo where I lived with my former boyfriend, Ted. *I'm in Ted's condo in St. Louis.*

And then I was in Ted's condo in St. Louis. It only made my head hurt a little more. Of course, I'd spent a lot of time in this living room, so it was pretty probable that I'd be here. Judging by the exact same furniture, Ted still lived here alone. I'd hate to run into him.

The key turned in the front door lock. Crap. I looked left. I looked right. Should I hide? What should I do? Unfortunately, I hesitated too long. The Skank Jessica walked through the tile foyer right into the living room.

When she saw me, she screamed and dropped her keys and backpack on the floor.

Awkward.

"Hey, Jessica," I said, waving. Jessica was the reason Ted was my former boyfriend. I'd walked in on them having sex on that very couch, there. Ick.

"Madison! This is a surprise! Wow, I haven't seen you since... I, um, am so sorry about what happened. Really sorry. I know we were friends, and I..."

I wasn't about to give her the satisfaction of being nice to her, even though she looked guilty and miserable. I just glared at her.

"Hey, how did you get in here?" she said.

"I have a key." I did. Somewhere. Speaking of keys and looking at her car keys on the floor gave me a great idea. If Jessica let me borrow her car, I wouldn't have to take the time to borrow one from someone else. "Sorry if I startled you. A friend of mine is in the hospital in Chicago. I'm trying to get there ASAP." That was even true. "I came here to ask Ted if I could borrow his car, but maybe I can borrow yours instead. Is there any chance?"

"In the hospital?" Jessica frowned. "What happened?"

"She was mugged." Sort-of true. "We don't know if she's going to make it. I need to get there." True.

"Oh." Her hand covered her mouth. "I'm sorry to hear that. But Chicago? That's pretty far away."

"Yes. That's why I need to leave ASAP. Please. Can I borrow your car? I wouldn't ask if it wasn't an emergency."

"I'm not sure," she said slowly.

"You owe me." She owed me for stealing my boyfriend right out from under me, practically literally.

"I guess if it's an emergency." She retrieved her keys and held the car keys out to me.

I quickly grabbed them before she changed her mind.

"You'll bring it back, right?"

I was already in the kitchen. I needed some food. "I'll try." I opened the cabinet where Ted used to keep the cookies and

221

chips. Score. I grabbed them.

"What do you mean, you'll try?" she asked.

I opened the fridge and got out some sodas.

"I mean, I'll try."

"But," she said. "Wait. How did you even get here?"

I was out the door.

Chicago, here I come!

Chapter Twenty-Nine

As I suspected, the drive from St. Louis to Chicago was super boring.

After approximately four hours, I pulled into the parking lot of Saint Anthony Hospital. I may have exceeded the speed limit a bit. *Mea culpa.*

I'd had plenty of time to think about how to get in to see Agent Baker and decided my best bet would be to pose as her sister. Did she have a sister? I had no idea. But we looked a little bit alike, so who knew, the nurses might buy it.

I walked right up to the admissions desk. "I'm here to see my sister, Lisa Baker. She was admitted approximately four hours ago."

"Who are you?" the admitting nurse asked.

"Her sister. Madison Baker."

She typed some stuff on the computer in front of her and then narrowed her eyes at me. "Her record doesn't say anything about a sister."

I leaned over the desk. "I'm her sister, and I know she's an FBI agent, and there's probably an FBI agent guarding her right now. Please just let me see her." And if she was my sister, we were definitely on a first-name basis.

"I don't know." The nurse shook her head. "Let me call someone." She grabbed the phone on the desk and dialed.

I could clearly see the empty hallway behind her, which presumably led to Lisa's room. When I glanced at the nurse, she was still waiting on her phone call, which I was guessing was not going to go my way.

"Never mind," I said. Then, I pointed to my right. "Oh, my gosh, what's that!" As she jerked and looked that way, I q-lapsed and popped up behind her in the hallway. I quickly started walking away.

A dark-suit-clad man loitered outside one of the rooms down the hall. It must be Lisa's room. As I sauntered by, the door was open, and I could see her lying on the bed. I focused on the scene, searing the room into my mind. At least she had a private room.

As soon as I was out of sight of the agent, I q-lapsed into her room. I quickly closed the door most of the way.

I approached the bed, dreading the worst (seriously hurt), hoping for the best (not seriously hurt). "Lisa?" She looked different without her signature ponytail and dark blazer, more vulnerable, more human.

"Madison?" she said, voice weak. "What took you so long?"

I pulled up a chair. "Sorry. I had to drive from St. Louis."

She frowned. Was she in pain? "Why didn't you just take an airplane?" Duh. I should have taken a plane.

Her brain was clearly working (better than mine). She looked okay. There were no visible injuries. She just seemed tired. I asked, "How are you? Are you okay?"

"I think so," she said. "The doctors didn't know what to make of my condition, but they say I'm getting better."

I'll admit it, I was afraid to ask about her condition. I felt responsible. "Can you tell me what happened?" I asked gently.

"I had a gut instinct that we'd missed something at the mansion site, so I went back. Was it only last night? I texted you."

"I know. I'm sorry I didn't meet you." I felt super-duper responsible. "Did something happen? Was someone there?"

"I thought I saw someone, a man, in my peripheral vision."

Crap. That was probably important. "Can you describe him?"

"No, it was dark, so I'm not sure. The next thing I knew, I was surrounded by fog."

Double-crap. I squeezed her hand. That was not good. That meant several different possibilities were competing with each other. "Sounds scary."

"It was. Then, I'm not sure what happened. I panicked or something. That's the last thing I remember before waking up this morning with a huge headache at my folks' old place. They don't live there anymore, so it was pretty awkward."

"Well, we're all glad you're okay, Director Lopez and Nate, and everyone else in Denver."

"I had no idea q-lapsing could be so scary," she said. "Is it like that a lot?"

"Sometimes." When quantum criminals are attacking, that is. "You should probably avoid it, at least until you make a full recovery."

She shook her head slowly. "Yeah. I'm not doing that again if I can help it."

I hoped she could help it.

In the room's doorway, a man cleared his throat. "How the hell did you get in here?"

"It's okay, agent," Lisa said. "Madison's a friend of mine."

Friend? Yay. Maybe she'd let me call her Lisa now.

"Like hell it's okay," the agent said. "I'm calling Lopez." He activated his phone.

"Sorry, Lisa, I have to go," I said. "Feel better soon."

The agent was staring at me and nodding. "Yes," he said into the phone. Then, he said to me, "Lopez is pissed at you, lady. He says you need to leave here and report to him in Denver immediately."

Lopez was intimidating enough when he wasn't pissed. I didn't think I'd be paying him a visit in the near future.

"Doesn't even make any sense," the agent said. "You're in Chicago. How could you report to him in Denver immediately?"

I squeezed Lisa's hand one last time. "Take care of yourself. I expect to see you back in Denver ship-shape in no time." I stood up and walked toward the door. "I'm going," I said to the agent. "You take care of our girl."

"I will," he said.

I walked down the hall to the ladies' room and once inside, scrutinized the place in case I needed to come back to the hospital. I even took some pictures with my phone. There was a sketchy moment when another woman came in and asked me why I was taking pictures in the ladies' room, but I toughed it out.

When she finally left, I q-lapsed and appeared in my office in the physics building. Ow. It was the only place I felt safe anymore. Even with the hole in the wall. I collapsed on my couch and gazed around the tiny room, taking in my books, papers, and posters. My office was messy. Now, my head really hurt. Too much q-lapsing today. I took a bunch of painkillers.

I was relieved Lisa was on the mend. But I was alarmed at her description of the mystery man and quantum limbo. I'd only ended up in quantum limbo in the direst of circumstances. She must have been in some kind of quantum duel? I needed to go back to the mansion site and check it out again.

I lay down on my couch, clutching one of my pillows to my chest.

I wasn't entirely sure why I felt safe here since I'd been attacked and didn't even have a door. I really needed to get myself a new office door by hook or by q-lapsing soon.

My stomach rumbled. All I'd eaten was junk food in the car. I checked the time on my computer. It was dinnertime. I wished I had someone to eat dinner with.

I decided to call Andro. His cell went to voicemail. When I called his house, his sister Yasmin said he was with Sophia. Yay for him. I bet he was having an awesome time.

I could call Ryan, but he had his own family to worry about, and I was clearly a trouble magnet.

A cop could probably take care of himself, though, right? Maybe he could even come with me to the mansion site after we ate. That settled it. I called Ben. "Hey, Ben. How's it going?" When he didn't answer right away, I added, "It's me, Madison."

"Hey, Madison." He paused and then said in an odd voice. "You're welcome."

"Thank you?" I had no idea why I was supposed to thank him, but with my flaky memory, anything was possible. I had a sudden bad thought. Could q-lapsing hurt my memory? Was that why my memory was so bad?

On the other hand, my memory (for non-physics things) had never been great.

"You sound like you're not really thanking me," he said.

"Oh, I'm really thanking you," I said. "I'm thanking you so much I'm taking you to dinner. What do you say to Boulder Brews?"

"Great. When are you picking me up?"

Shoot. My car was down in Denver in the FBI parking lot. "You're picking me up outside the physics building in ten minutes." Oh, crap. I still needed to deal with Jessica's car.

"Can do," Ben said. "See you then." He hung up.

I texted Ted and told him I'd left Jessica's car in the west parking lot of Saint Anthony's Hospital, at West 19th Street and Sacramento Boulevard in Chicago. Yeah, it was a wimpy move. I'm not proud of it, but I had bigger problems than Jessica's car.

I hung up and raced down the stairs to meet Ben.

At Boulder Brews, they were still serving their Oktoberfest seasonal ale. I ordered two frosty mugs at the counter and brought them back to the tiny table where Ben sat.

The restaurant wasn't nearly as crowded as it had been the last time I was here, Monday night. Was that right? I was just here a couple of days ago?

As I set them down, he grinned and reached for both of them. "Thanks. What are you drinking?"

I sat down. "Ha. Ha." I reached for one, and he relinquished it with another grin. The first sip was delish, with hints of pumpkin, nutmeg, cinnamon, and clove. "Mmm."

Ben laughed. "I've never met a girl who liked beer as much as you."

I might as well take that as a compliment. "Thanks." I took another sip and leaned back in my chair. He was really very handsome. Muscular. He looked sort of Australian. I wondered if I could get him to talk with an Australian accent. I did have the sense not to suggest it. "So, what are you in the mood for?"

"What are you offering?" Was he flirting? Did I want him to be?

"I'm having a burger with all the fixings. You can have anything you want."

He smiled, and it had definite sexual overtones. "Anything?"

That smile promised a lot. I felt very confused. "Yep. Anything that's on the menu. My treat."

He grabbed one of the menus from the middle of the table and scanned it. He dropped it on the table. "Burger sounds good."

I glanced at the counter. "Supposedly, they have waitresses

here. But I've been here many times and haven't ever seen any evidence of it."

A waitress glided up to our table. She looked about eighteen years old. "Can I help you?" She gazed at Ben, obviously liking what she saw.

"We'll take two burgers with all the fixings." He glanced at me with the hint of a smile.

"I'll put that order in for you right away, sir. I'm Lily."

"Hi, Lily. I'm Ben." He leaned towards her, smiling. "It's real nice to meet you."

She blushed. "It'll be right up."

Apparently, the only thing you needed for good service here was a hot cop. I grabbed my mug for another sip and looked at Ben over the top of the mug.

He did look good. Even out of his uniform, he had a very fit athletic cop-y vibe.

"Madison?"

How could Ben look so good when I was in love with Andro? But was Andro in love with me? He had said he was, but he wasn't acting like it.

In fairness, I thought I loved Andro, but was I acting like it? No.

What did that mean?

I put my beer down. "So, what's new with the Boulder PD? Any parties with underage drinking? Any brawls? Couch fires? How about underage pot smoking?"

He laughed. "All of the above."

"What's the quantum panty-raid situation?" I asked.

"So far, it's just the two sororities, or at least that's all that's been reported."

"Did you want me to go investigate with you?"

"No. I stopped by the two sororities this afternoon with one of my colleagues." He grinned. "It turned out all the guys wanted to help me investigate."

"No surprise there. Did you guys figure anything out?"

He shook his head. "No. The external security cameras didn't show anything, and they didn't have any cameras inside. It remains a mystery."

"The most mysterious thing about it is why would anyone

bother?"

"Yeah." Ben chuckled. "But on the bright side, the young ladies invited us back any time."

"I bet they did, two handsome young cops."

"You think I'm handsome?"

Shoot. I just smiled mysteriously.

Later, when we were finishing up our burgers (I only spilled BBQ sauce on myself once), talk turned to the FBI.

"So, that was interesting yesterday," he said.

"The you-know-what sketch?"

"Yeah, the sketch," he glanced around. No one was sitting particularly close to us. "What do you think they're going to do with it? It's not like they can put out an APB."

"I know. Right?" I snickered. It felt good to relax. "But once they catch him, he'll have to do time in the penal system."

"Hard time, no doubt." He smiled. "So, what's going on with the quantum task force?"

My shoulders tensed up. I had a bad thought. Was I sure this was, in fact, Ben Willis, Boulder PD officer? We didn't have a password. What if the man sitting across from me was an imposter, a nefarious quantum criminal? "Why do you ask?" I asked slowly. Ben and I really needed to set up a password.

"I just hoped my work helped out in some way. I wouldn't mind getting a job at the Bureau someday."

Would a nefarious quantum criminal know about the sketch and the task force? If so, we were doomed. I decided to trust Ben. "The task force is in a shambles. Agent Baker got hurt in some kind of quantum altercation. She's in the hospital in Chicago."

"She was there at the sketch, right? Is she going to be okay?"

"Yes. She's going to be okay." I nodded. "But it's a big mess. Nate, Agent Sawyer, says the task force is toast, whatever that means."

Ben whistled. "How can they just stop investigating quantum crimes, especially after an agent got hurt?"

"Actually, I'm glad you mentioned that," I said. "Is there any chance you'd go with me tonight to check out the place where Agent Baker got hurt?"

"Aren't there actual FBI agents who can do that?"

"Not that actually know anything about q-lapsing."

"I don't know anything about it other than it exists." He looked at me steadily for a moment. "You're going to go out there by yourself if I say no, aren't you?"

"Yeah."

He sighed. "Okay. Count me in."

A little later, after we finished dinner, we drove south on Highway 93 until we arrived at the nondescript turnoff, full of new tire tracks and footprints. "Here. Turn in here."

Ben parked, and we got out. The October breeze ruffled my hair. It was much colder than it had been this morning. There was no sign of Gonzales' team. If they'd been here earlier, they must have left.

"Flashlight?" he asked.

"You want one, or you've got one?"

"I've got one in the trunk. Should I get it out?"

I felt a grin stretch my face. "You must have been a boy scout!"

"I plead the Fifth on that."

"You were!" My grin got bigger. "I bet you were. You must have been super cute in your little uniform."

He walked around to the trunk. "Let's just say, I've always looked good in uniform."

No doubt. I walked back next to him and put my hand on his arm. "It's almost a full moon. I don't think we need it. Besides, our night vision will be better without it."

He shrugged. "Which way?"

I pointed down the dirt path.

Every time I'd been here, something strange had happened. The breeze kicked up again, and I shivered.

Chapter Thirty

Ben and I were trekking through dried two-foot-tall grass in the middle of nowhere at zero-dark-chilly.

He sped up next to me and touched my arm. "What do you expect to find out here?" He looked into my face in the moonlight.

"I'm not sure what I expect to find." I looked into his face. He seemed like someone you could rely on. "Agent Baker met up with foul play here. I'm just trying to get more information." I didn't mention that both Lisa and I had seen something in our peripheral vision the last time we were here.

"You know I'm not on duty, right?" he said. "If we run into any trouble, I don't have my gun. I don't take it when I'm going drinking."

"I know you don't have a gun." There was no place to hide any kind of gun in his outfit. "And good. You had beer. Drinking and shooting sounds like a bad combination." Drinking and q-lapsing was an impossible combination, as far as I could tell. I'd been good and only had one beer.

We continued walking through the scrub until we reached the spot where some of the vegetation was smashed down—presumably by FBI agents, or maybe quantum duels.

I leaned down, peering at the ground. "I think I found Lisa's phone here earlier. Look around for any clues."

He did some peering down of his own.

Out of the corner of my eye, I thought I saw something too big to be grass. I whirled around to face it.

In the moonlight, it was hard to make out, but it appeared to be fog in the shape and size of a person. "Hey! Hey, you!" I took a step closer. "Freeze!"

LESLEY L. SMITH

"What the?" Ben said.

As I stepped closer, the fog solidified into a man, a man I knew only too well: Luke Bacalli. At least the man looked like Luke Bacalli. I was starting to regret all the one beer.

Luke seemed surprised to see me.

"You're under arrest, Mr. Bacalli," I said. "Come with us quietly."

Ben came up next to me and crouched in some fighter's stance.

Luke laughed. "Yeah, right, Maddie."

A peaceful citizen's arrest was worth a try. Suddenly, drinking and shooting didn't sound so bad. It had to be better than drinking and confronting quantum criminals without any weapons.

"Do you know this guy?" Ben asked. He did not look happy.

When I glanced back at Luke, two more foggy figures stood next to him. One of them resolved into his long-time sidekick, Griffin Jin.

Griffin looked at me and smiled. "Hi, Maddie. Long time, no see." Griffin was very annoying.

I couldn't make out the third figure in the moonlight. He or she didn't solidify enough.

"What's with this Maddie crap?" I said. "You guys call me Professor Martin."

"Seriously?" Ben asked.

"Who's this loser?" Luke asked. "Did you dump Andro? Oh, wait. I bet he dumped you."

Griffin snickered.

The shadowy figure laughed. Who was he or she? Something about him or her sounded familiar.

Geez, these guys were annoying. "No! There was no dumpage!"

Ben readied to attack.

I knew that wouldn't do any good. I needed to unleash a quantum firestorm of whup-ass, but what exactly would that firestorm consist of? Unfortunately, what with the beer and all the annoyingness, I was having trouble concentrating.

I concentrated to q-lapse and hit them with static electricity lightning bolts. *Zoom. The lightning bolts were hitting them.*

Nothing happened.

Screw it. I let out a blood-curdling attack scream and rushed Luke.

Next to me, Ben rushed Griffin.

We both landed smack in the dirt, not on any quantum criminals.

Luke and Griffin had q-lapsed themselves away to parts unknown.

The third foggy figure said something that sounded like "Ack" and disappeared, too.

Ben sat up, brushing dirt from his chest. "What the hell was that? Why did they call you Maddie? Everyone calls you Madison, don't they? Exactly how well do you know those criminals?"

My mouth was full of dirt. Blech. I spit it out as I sat up. "Well, on the bright side, we know for sure Luke and Griffin are involved."

"That doesn't seem too bright from where I'm sitting," he said. "Why didn't they do a better job of attacking?"

"I think we startled them," I said. "Plus, if they've been q-lapsing a lot lately, they may not have been able to do much more." Damn, if that was true, we should have tried harder to arrest them.

"How can we catch them if they just pop away?"

I cleverly ignored his very good question. "And now we know they have at least one other collaborator," I said. "Who seemed familiar to me." I brushed the dirt off my top. Oops. I looked down my shirt. Some of it went down there.

"What?" He paused, staring at me or maybe my top. "And what are you doing there with your shirt?"

Why was he so interested in my top? "Why?"

He didn't answer.

"I not doing anything with my shirt." Did he want me to do something with it? "I think there must be something special about this location. The quantum criminals have been seen here multiple times."

"The FBI should set up surveillance here," he said.

"Yes. Good point." Didn't someone suggest that earlier? I pulled out my phone and called Nate.

Thursday morning, I stopped in the physics department office for some coffee on my way in.

I was very pleasantly surprised to see Nancy sitting right there, nice and normal, at her desk. I was guessing she'd gotten over her ordeal, at least mostly. "Hi, Nancy," I said. "How's it going?"

She jerked back, looking up from her computer. "Okay, I guess." She curled her lip. "I still can't believe I was having sex with someone I didn't know."

"I'm sorry that happened to you." It was creepy. "I'm available if you ever want to talk about it."

"So, did you find the penis yet?" she asked.

I couldn't change gears that quickly. "What?"

"Did you find the penis you were looking for?" she said loudly.

"Shh!" I glanced around the office, but we appeared to be the only ones there. "No. As far as I know, they didn't find the mystery penis. Of course, there's the issue of how would they look for it?"

Professor Chen poked his head out of his office. Shoot.

"Did I hear the word penis out here?" he asked. "That is not workplace appropriate."

"No, sir," Nancy and I said at the same time.

"I'm glad you're here," Professor Chen said. "We need to talk, Madison."

Had any good conversation ever followed *we need to talk*? I trudged after him into his office.

He closed the door after me. Another bad sign. He sat down and gestured at his guest chair.

"I got an odd call yesterday from a Director Lopez of the FBI, saying you were involved in an agent going missing."

"Oh?" I asked neutrally. Last year when I'd run into trouble, Chen had suspended me. How many chances would I get?

"Director Lopez thinks one or more of your quantum mechanics students is a criminal. Based on my conversation with Lopez and the conversation you and I had the other day, I contacted your quantum mechanics students and told them your class was canceled until further notice.

"Oh?" My heart sunk like mercury in a thermometer at the North Pole.

He leaned forward. "We need to investigate your students and get to the bottom of this. I told them all to schedule a makeup meeting with you today." He narrowed his eyes. "Do you want help interrogating them?"

And then, like that, my heart rose. Apparently, I wasn't out on the street yet. I did not say, *You're not suspending me?* or *You're not firing me?* I didn't want to give him any ideas.

"Madison?"

"What was that?"

"Do you want help interrogating your students?" He was sixty if he was a day and had spent his whole life in academia, a lot of it sitting in that very chair. He stared at me.

"Thank you, sir, but I think I'll ask a member of law enforcement." I stood up. "Was that it?"

"Yes. We need to get these criminals. Bring them to justice."

"Okay." Was he actually being supportive of me? I turned and started walking for the door.

"The university and this department don't need any more bad publicity after last year."

Ah ha. I reached the door.

"Madison."

I turned to face him. "Yes, sir."

"I don't need to make you take more sexual harassment training, do I?"

"What? Oh, the thing with Nancy. No, sir. It's related to her case, her disappearance." I opened the door.

The corners of his eyes drooped. "Nancy's case? That doesn't sound good. Is she all right?"

"I'm not sure, sir." We both looked at her sitting at her desk but didn't discern anything. At least I didn't.

As I lumbered up to my office, I considered various law enforcement officers I could get to help me. Lisa would be my first choice, but she was still in Chicago, maybe still in the hospital. Nate would no doubt be busy with his new surveillance detail and Lisa's case. And I didn't want to wear out my welcome with Ben, so I probably shouldn't call him since I just saw him a few hours ago.

LESLEY L. SMITH

Andro, while not exactly a law enforcement professional, did know how to q-lapse. That's who I should ask: Andro. Unfortunately, when I got up to our floor, there was no sign of him in his office.

There were plenty of signs of my students, however. They sat or stood in the hall outside my office. And since the Gamow Tower was so small, and since the experiment was still set up, they pretty much took up what remained of the space.

"Finally!" one of them said.

Arjun was right in front of my office. "Why did you cancel class?" Since I didn't have a door, I appreciated them waiting in the hall.

"Uh." Somehow I didn't think they'd appreciate that I'd been dragooned to help the FBI.

Juan thrust his phone in my face. "Professor Chen had someone send us texts, saying class was canceled- not that we're complaining."

"It's because of the trouble we had last time, Monday," I said.

"What's going on?" someone asked.

They all crowded around me. One or more of these kids might be the mysterious third quantum criminal I encountered last night with Luke and Griffin. Was I in danger? Was I putting the other kids in danger?

"Take a step back. You're squishing me," I said. "I just need to meet with you individually to make up for the canceled class yesterday and probably, tomorrow." I walked into my office and grabbed a blank piece of notebook paper off my desk. I handed it to Arjun. "Please sign up for a fifteen-minute interval. The first available interval starts at ten o'clock."

Arjun started writing on the piece of paper, and the others crowded around him instead of me. Phew.

Gradually, they all signed up and walked away.

When I was finally alone, I breathed a sigh of relief. Sadly, it occurred at nine-forty.

The crowd of students had brought home the point that I was sick of having no office door. The university would probably fix that right after hell reached absolute zero.

I concentrated on the probabilities and q-lapsed to pick the likely possibility in which I did have an office door that locked. *I have a door.* It worked, and I only got a little headache as a result.

Then, I took some aspirin and relaxed a little behind my desk, which was behind my locked brand-new door.

I did need someone to help me question the students.

I called Andro's cell, but it went straight to voicemail. Ugh.

Who did that leave? University Chief of Police Ryan Martin was a definite possibility. I didn't want to put him in danger, but he did have a Master's in Criminology. He'd be helpful. And he could get here in twenty minutes, especially if he was in his office across the street.

I called his cell.

"Madison!" he said. "Long time, no see. I miss you."

Suddenly, my eyes felt heavy. Ryan and Sydney, and Emily were my only family. I cleared my throat. "I miss you guys, too. But I need your help in a professional capacity. I need to interrogate my quantum mechanics students and try to find out which one, or ones, of them, is a criminal. Are you available?"

"When?"

I glanced at the clock on my computer. "In about fifteen minutes."

"Where?"

"Here, at my office."

He chuckled. "You're stuck, huh? I guess so. I'll be right over."

I made a list of questions, including the times and dates of all the recent quantum crimes, including Barry's death, Isabella's death, Lisa's attack, the Apple Store theft, the panty raids, and even the pathetic fisticuffs last night. I also wrote down a joke, so I could get them to laugh to compare to the laugh I heard last night.

Ryan arrived right before my first student, Arjun, of course.

"Where'd this door come from?" Arjun asked.

Ryan glanced at me. "The university installed it, of course. What else?"

"Who's this?" Arjun pointed at Ryan.

"This is Mr. Martin," I said. "He's helping me out today, Arjun."

Arjun shook his head. "There's no way this door was just installed. We were here less than an hour ago, and the wall was damaged, too. Now, everything looks fine."

"Can we get down to business?" I asked.

"Martin?" Arjun asked. "Who is this man? I know you're not married."

"How do you know I'm not married?" I asked. "I could be married." He better not be implying no one would want to marry me because I was marriable. I was very marriable. People would be lucky to marry me.

"Are you married?" he asked.

Ryan put his hand over mine. "Maybe you want to focus on the questions, Madison?"

He had a good point. "Good point." I turned back to Arjun. "Please turn in your homework from Wednesday." The syllabus had homework due every day we had class scheduled.

He frowned, dug around in his bag, and handed me some papers.

"Do you have any questions about the reading for this week?"

"No."

"Do you have any other questions?" I asked.

"What's he doing here?" Arjun asked.

"Do you have any other questions about the class?" I said.

"When will we have our regular class again?" he asked.

"I'm not sure," I said.

"Monday?"

"Yes," I said. It was a whole weekend away. Who knew what would happen by then?

Ryan gave me a questioning look.

I shrugged. We might as well assume so until it was proven otherwise.

Now for the tricky part: interrogate the student about quantum crimes without giving him any hints about how to commit quantum crimes. "It appeared that we had two impersonators in our Monday class. Do you know anything about that?"

"No." Arjun shrugged.

"Do you know how it was accomplished?" Ryan asked.

"No."

Ryan looked at me as if to say, *Now what?*

I asked Arjun for his alibis during all the recent quantum crimes. His answer every time was *At the library studying*. I didn't know whether to believe him or not, but when I asked if anyone could confirm that he was at the library studying, he said, "I was studying, not socializing." After more prompting, he gave us some names of library employees who could vouch for him.

Ryan took notes on his phone.

"What do you do with dead elements?" I asked.

Arjun looked blank.

Ryan looked blank.

"Barium," I said.

Arjun did not laugh or make any other noise. Neither did Ryan.

"Okay, Arjun," I said. "Thanks for your help. Please send the next guy in."

That's about how the entire day went and what a long day it turned out to be.

Drew and Brandon stuck to their story that they just skipped class Monday and didn't know anything about any imposters. Of course, it could have been them in class, and they just q-lapsed out. We didn't call them until after they'd disappeared.

After the last student, well into the cocktail hour, Ryan stood up. "You owe me for that, Mad."

"Do you think any of them are quantum criminals?"

He shook his head. "I have no idea, but most of them don't have alibis." He pointed at his notes.

I had no idea, either. "I'll email the notes to Agent Nate after you send them to me, and we'll see if he can figure anything out."

Ryan snickered. "Agent Nate?"

"Nate. Agent Sawyer. Whatever. Thanks for your help, Ryan," I said. "I do owe you. Did you have anything specific in mind in terms of payback?"

He grinned. I knew he liked having me owe him. I was guessing I was in for a marathon babysitting session at some point in the future once all this was resolved—assuming all this was resolved. "I'll let you know," he said.

From the hall came the sound of a door opening. It sounded like it came from the office next door, i.e., Andro's office.

"Later, Madison." Ryan quickly strode out.

I followed him out into the hall to say hi to Andro. "Hey," I said, just as Andro swung open his door. I smiled.

Andro startled. "Hey." He didn't smile.

This is the guy I had hot steamy sex with earlier this week? This is the guy I wasn't hooking up with Ben for? I felt myself frown. "So, how's it going?"

"Fine." He just stood there like a handsome log.

I started to get a bad feeling. "What's the password?"

"What password?"

Chapter Thirty-One

In Gamow Tower, I froze. Fake-Andro stood in front of me again. I'd thought Isabella was fake-Andro, and she was history. How many damn fake-Andros were there? How did they impersonate him, anyway? I didn't know how to impersonate anyone.

"Earth to Madison."

Uh, oh. Fake-Andro was talking to me. I should try to humor him/her until I could figure out what his/her game was. "What?"

"I said if you forgot your computer password, the system administrators can probably tell you what it is or reset it."

Huh. What was he talking about? I shook my head. Oh, yeah, password.

That was good to know about the computer password–but off the point. Focus, Mad. The point was to act totally normal, to lull him/her into a false sense of security so he/she would let something slip. "Thank you, Professor Rivas. Yes, indeedy, my week's progressing all too speedy. And you yourself are looking tweedy, not at all seedy."

"What? Are you on drugs?"

Well, that clinched it. Real-Andro knew I didn't do drugs. And, apparently, I rhymed when I tried to act totally normal. "Drugs? Ughs." Stop talking, Mad. Words flashed through my mind: bugs, hugs, jugs, mugs. But I didn't say them. Quite possibly, all this q-lapsing was doing something detrimental to my brain.

Or I was panicking.

Then, I felt a pressure surrounding me, pressing in on my skin. I held up my hand, and something squeezed in on it from all sides, but I couldn't see anything. Fake-Andro was attacking me! Again. Why did fake-Andro always have to attack me? "Hey!

Stop it!" I said brilliantly.

I reached out and concentrated on selecting the possibility in which fake-Andro slipped and fell on the floor. That could happen, right?

The next thing I knew, fake-Andro was flying through the air. Smack. Yep, there was the wall. Ouch. That looked like it hurt. I guess that was the possibility in which fake-Andro had been running down the hall and tripped into the wall.

The pressure on my skin had stopped.

I raced down the hall and stood over fake-Andro, crumpled in a pile. He/she still looked like Andro. I was a little impressed. I also had a headache.

Fake-Andro opened his eyes. "Ack."

I heard that last night when I was with Ben. This must be the mysterious third figure. While I was pondering that, fake-Andro got to his feet and lurched for the stairway door.

I lurched after him. As I ran down the stairs after fake-Andro, I started to get a huge case of déjà vu. Oh, yeah, I'd been in this situation before. Maybe some verbal intimidation was called for again? "I'm gonna get you! You're dead meat!" I had to stop yelling to gasp some air from all the running and chasing. "You shouldn't have messed with the Quantum Cop." I had to keep chasing him because I didn't know where he was going. Why didn't he just q-lapse away? Maybe he couldn't.

This time fake-Andro didn't trip on the stairs like he did last time. Was this the same fake-Andro as before? Sadly, I had no idea.

He did exit on the first floor.

I gained on fake-Andro as we ran down the first-floor hallway.

He grabbed the door handle for the physics department office and threw open the door, and I was right behind him as he entered.

"Nancy? Is that you?" Professor Chen darted out of his office as soon as he heard us enter.

Fake-Andro, heading for Nancy's desk, looked directly at Chen and hesitated.

Oh, no! Was this Nancy? It was, wasn't it? My heart sank.

When Chen saw us, he frowned in disappointment. "Oh,

Andro, Madison, it's you. Why are you panting? Have you seen Nancy? I'm worried about her. She rushed out of here a little while ago."

I turned back to fake-Andro, who was now picking Nancy's cell phone off her desk. "You should be worried about Nancy, Professor Chen." I approached fake-Andro. "I'm very sorry to say, she's been up to no good."

Fake-Andro called someone.

"She's been up to shenanigans, illegal, possibly murderous, shenanigans." I pointed at Nancy, aka fake-Andro. "Nancy, how could you? I thought we were friends." I was very disappointed in Nancy. Why had she turned to a life of crime?

And how the hell had she impersonated Andro? They were both of Chicano ancestry, but he was a man, and she was a woman.

She said something into the phone.

"Put down the phone."

"What the hell are you talking about, Madison?" Professor Chen came closer to us. "This isn't Nancy. This is Andro Rivas. What's wrong with you?"

Nancy put down the phone and said in her own voice, "Now you're going to get it." It was bizarre hearing Nancy's voice coming out of Andro's mouth.

"What's happening?" Professor Chen asked.

Nancy morphed back into herself.

Chen gasped.

"If you turn yourself in, the authorities will go easier on you, Nancy," I said in what I hoped was a soothing voice. I didn't want to have to fight her. We were friends.

A foggy figure started forming next to Nancy.

Shit. That's all we needed: reinforcements.

I glanced at Chen, and he was just standing there in the middle of the physics office, gaping. This was not going to be pretty.

"Please, Nancy. I know you're a good person." I really hoped she was a good person. I wasn't sure at this point. "Do the right thing. Turn yourself in. We don't want anyone else to get hurt."

The foggy figure looked pretty rotund. So, Griffin, then. Shit.

LESLEY L. SMITH

But, better than Luke.

"Chen, go back in your office and lock the door." I gently pushed him in the direction of his office.

"Hey, there, Maddie," Griffin said, now totally solidified.

Shit.

Chen gasped again. "How? Where? What?"

I pushed him towards his office again, and he scrambled over there and slammed the door behind him.

"Hi, Griffin," I said. "I was just telling Nancy here the authorities might go easy on you guys if you turn yourselves in."

"Yeah, right." He sneered.

Okay. In his case, that was unlikely since he'd escaped from maximum security and all. "I don't want to hurt you guys. I like you guys. Please surrender." I did like them--except for the criminal stuff.

"She is pretty powerful," Nancy said, rubbing her arm. "She threw me into the wall."

Griffin just glared at her.

Nancy shut up.

The floor started waving like it was an earthquake. They must be q-lapsing to cause an earthquake. I struggled to keep my balance.

The walls and ceiling got blurry. What now?

Distracted, I fell on the floor and started getting thrown around by the waves. Bizarre tile waves hurt when they smacked into you. "Ouch." I'd had enough of this. I concentrated on steadying the floor.

It stopped roiling and changed to more of an undulation.

"I need your help, Nancy!" Griffin said. "Concentrate!"

She stared at the floor, narrowing her eyes.

I managed to stand up again. I stared at the walls, willing them to solidify. *The walls are normal.* They stabilized. My headache increased. I stared at the ceiling. *The ceiling is normal.*

"I called the police!" Chen called out from his office, door slightly ajar. "They're on their way!" He slammed the door closed, hiding, apparently.

Crap. Just what we needed: more potential victims. Or bullets flying. I did have to fight these two.

"Stop it!" I pointed at Griffin, willing him to slam into the floor.

Stop.

His powers of concentration were much better than they'd been last year. He held out against me.

We stared at each other. I could see a vein pulsing in his forehead.

I tried to make him hit the floor hard. *Hit the floor.* I don't know what he was trying to do to me.

I felt his mind waver a smidge and slammed him into the floor. He hit it at a high rate of speed, higher than I'd planned. He didn't move. The ceiling went back to normal, and the floor quieted.

Now, my head really hurt.

When I turned my attention back to Nancy, she looked scared.

"I don't want to hurt you," I said. "Surrender."

We heard sirens approach.

"I can't." Her eyes filled. She held up her forefinger. "Favor! You owe me a favor!"

I did vaguely remember something after the Red Rocks concert and me agreeing to do her some undisclosed favor at some time in the future.

"Let me go," she said softly.

The sirens got closer. They were almost right on top of us.

I didn't welch on promises. I sighed. "All right."

She took a step away from me but then looked surprised as her body fuzzed out. She was gone.

I collapsed in the one chair that wasn't lying on its side. Oh, my head hurt.

I woke up in a toothpaste-green room on a rolling metal bed. Ugly. On the bright side, my head hurt a lot less.

"Mad?" a familiar male voice asked. Ryan's voice.

"Hey, Ryan." I tried to smile. I don't know how successful it was since Ryan drew back.

"Hey. How are you feeling?" He reached for my hand and gave it a little squeeze.

"I feel okay, considering," I said. "How did I get here?"

"As far as I can tell, there was some kind of quantum fight in the physics department office. Professor Chen wasn't all that coherent. He called the police, and when they got there, the office was wrecked, and you were passed out. An ambulance brought you here to the hospital."

"What about Griffin? Did they take him here, too? Or take him into custody?" I hoped the quantum fight hadn't been for nothing.

"Griffin Jin?" Ryan asked. "He was there?"

Crap. He got away. Double-crap. Infinity-crap.

"There was no mention of him by the cops or anyone." He paused. "You fought Griffin? By yourself? So, he's definitely out of prison?" His lips drew down. I knew he was worried about his family.

"Yes, he's out. I'm sorry." I squeezed his hand back.

"Where's the Quantum Cop?" Lisa's voice boomed down the hall.

Ryan stood up and stepped to the doorway. "Here, Agent Baker."

Lisa came in, pulled up a chair and sat down. "I brought your car back from Denver. Why do we always seem to be meeting in hospitals these days?" She had dark circles under her eyes, and her ponytail was coming undone. It was great to see her.

"I guess that's what happens to real-life kick-ass heroines." I grinned.

She grinned back, so my grin must have looked like a grin. "Guess so."

"Are you sure you're okay?" I asked. "Should you be in the hospital recuperating?"

"I'm okay," she said. "Besides, kick-ass heroines don't lollygag around the hospital. So." She paused. "What happened?"

"I was just trying to find out," Ryan said. They both stared at me expectantly. "Madison?"

I'd sort of screwed up, and apparently, I couldn't weasel out of it. "Ryan and I interviewed my students today, checking alibis for the crimes."

They nodded.

"Ryan had just left when Andro showed up at his office. But it wasn't Andro."

"How did you know?" Lisa asked.

"He didn't know..." I had a bad thought, a very bad thought. How did I know these people were truly Lisa and Ryan?

"Didn't know what?" Ryan asked.

I stared at them. They looked like Lisa and Ryan. But shouldn't Lisa still be in Chicago in the hospital? Shouldn't Ryan be protecting his family? "Where's my phone?"

"Is this about the case?" Lisa stood up, went over to the cabinet, and started ruffling through the drawers. "Here." She handed me my phone.

I punched the contact for FBI Agent Lisa Baker.

Lisa's pocket started ringing. She took it out and looked at it. When she saw my name, she raised her eyebrows and turned it off.

I hung up and punched the number for Ryan Martin.

Ryan's pocket sang, "I was working in the lab late one night when my eyes beheld an eerie sight for my monster from his slab began to rise and suddenly to my surprise–" Flushing, he took out his cell and pressed the screen.

Lisa and I both looked at him.

I said, "Seriously? The Monster Mash?"

"Sydney changed my ringtone for Halloween. It's a joke."

"Why did you just call us?" Lisa asked.

"Andro and I set up a password since someone was impersonating him. The guy today didn't know it. I was just checking that you guys were you since we don't have passwords."

"We could have stolen their phones," Lisa said.

Ack. "Did you steal their phones?" I asked.

Lisa gave me her baleful stare. Okay, real Lisa. Check.

"Are you saying you don't know your own cousin?" Ryan asked.

No faker would put up with the Monster Mash, that was for sure. "Of course, I know you, Ry."

"Anyway, now that we've settled who we are, what happened today?" Lisa asked.

"How do we know you're you?" Ryan said to me.

I gave him my own version of the baleful stare. I'd been practicing.

247

"You were saying?" Lisa said.

What had I been saying? "Uh."

Lisa and Ryan exchanged a look that I hoped didn't mean, *Uh oh, she's got brain damage.*

"Andro impersonator," she said.

"Oh, right. Today I knew the Andro wasn't the real Andro because he didn't know the password we'd set up." Where was the real Andro? Was he okay? What about his family?

"Madison!" Lisa said.

"We had a quantum duel," I said. "She wasn't a very good fighter. I chased her down the stairs."

"Wait. She?" Lisa asked. "Who was it?"

I exhaled. "I chased her to the physics department office, where I found out it was Nancy."

"Nancy!" both Lisa and Ryan yelled.

"Way to bury the lead, Mad," Ryan said. "I thought she was a victim in all this. I thought she was your friend."

Lisa was nodding. "It all makes sense. She's been entirely too involved. We should have figured it out earlier."

"Yeah," I said. "Forget secretary, er, administrative assistant, she should have been an actress."

"Continue," Lisa said.

"So, we were sort of fighting in the office, and Chen came out and distracted me, and Nancy called for reinforcements, and Griffin showed up."

Lisa raised her eyebrows again. Her eyebrows were getting quite a workout.

"Griffin and I fought, and I sort of accidentally slammed him into the floor."

"How do you sort of accidentally slam someone—" Ryan said.

"Continue," Lisa said.

"I thought I'd bested him," I said. And then I let Nancy go. I didn't want to say that. "I got distracted, er, I mean, my head was hurting, and..."

"Which was it?" Lisa asked. "Distracted? Or in pain?"

"Uh, I guess my head was really hurting, and Nancy got away," I said. "She q-lapsed and popped away." She did technically q-lapse away, but I wasn't entirely sure it was her own doing.

Lisa looked suspicious, or maybe it was my guilty conscience. "If you beat Griffin, why wasn't he there when the unis got there?"

I shook my head. Ow. "I don't know. I guess I passed out at that point. Maybe Chen knows."

Ryan spoke up. "Chen's a basket case. I think they had to sedate him."

Lisa frowned. "So, to summarize: we have three confirmed quantum criminals. I caught sight of them and ended up in the hospital. You had some kind of throw-down with two of them, and you ended up in the hospital. And to top it off, they all got away scot-free, and their crimes have been escalating."

I pursed my lips and nodded. "Pretty much."

"How are we going to catch them?" she asked.

"Beats me," I said.

We needed to figure it out ASAP.

Chapter Thirty-Two

It turns out almost having a brain aneurysm doesn't rate an overnight hospital stay, at least with my insurance.

Ryan very kindly offered to let me stay in my old room at his house. I said no to protect him and his family, but he wouldn't take no for an answer. Possibly, I didn't try too hard to get him to take no for an answer.

When I entered Ryan's family room still decked out with strings of orange jack-o-lantern lights along with various and sundry pumpkins, scary cobwebs, giant black spiders and bats and rats, and witch cut-outs, my heart hurt. I missed living with Ryan and Sydney, and Emily. "Wow. It's so festive and spooky here. I miss living here with you guys."

Judging by the way Ryan was hugging his computer, he missed living with Sydney and Emily, too. They were Skyping. Sydney must still be at her parents'. Good for her. "Madison was in the hospital, so I said she could stay here tonight," he said to the screen.

I peered into the laptop. Sydney cradled *Mama's Ghoul* in her lap. "Welcome, Madison." Emily babbled in agreement.

I teared up a bit. It felt like home here. I cleared my throat. "Thanks. I hope I'm not putting you guys in danger. I can go. I know the quantum criminals are dangerous."

"By that reasoning, you're practically the only one who can protect us," Ryan said. "The Quantum Cop."

That was true.

"Besides, Madison, you are our family," Ryan said. "We love you."

"Yes," Sydney said. "Emily wouldn't have survived if you hadn't saved her. We owe you everything."

Emily agreed.

My eyes felt heavy. They thought I was family.

We all cleared our throats.

"So, what's this I hear about the FBI quantum task force being disbanded?" Sydney asked.

I nodded. "Yeah. The FBI freaked out when Agent Baker got hurt." I resolved if the FBI wouldn't, or couldn't, keep people like Sydney and Emily safe, someone else would have to step up. "I guess we'll have to start our own quantum task force."

I glimpsed Ryan beholding his wife and daughter, his eyes full of love. He held up his hand. "I'm in." I knew he would be. He was like a dog with a bone when it came to protecting his family.

"So, it's me and you, and we need Andro and Alyssa because they can q-lapse," I said. "And Agent Baker, Lisa." I still wasn't sure what to call her.

"We should include Ben and Nate, too," Ryan said. "They've been pretty involved in the investigation."

I nodded. "Good point." I glanced at my phone. "I'll set up the meeting for tomorrow night." It was too late tonight.

"Did you get some dinner?" Sydney asked me.

My stomach growled in reply. "I could eat."

"I left Ryan a bunch of meals in the freezer. Offer her dinner, Ry."

"Would you like some dinner, Madison?" he said.

"Why, yes, Ryan. That would be delightful," I said.

Mama's ghoul started fussing. "That's my cue to log off," Sydney said. "Catch these guys. Emily and I really want to come home."

"And I really want you to come home," Ryan said.

I wandered off to check my bed in the garage, but actually to give them some privacy.

After they signed off, Ryan came into the garage with a beer. "Want one?"

I did want one. "Better not. They gave me pain meds at the hospital."

"I never thought I'd see the day Madison turned down beer." He glanced at me. "How badly are you hurt?"

The doctors didn't seem to know what to make of my condition. I shrugged. "The docs ended up deciding it must have

251

been some kind of bad migraine." I smiled weakly. "Whatever they gave me seemed to help."

"Come on," he said. "Let's see what Sydney left us."

I followed him into the kitchen and sat at the breakfast bar.

He opened the freezer and examined the well-labeled plastic containers. "We have lentil loaf, spicy tahini, vegan shepherd's pie, tofu, and veggies in peanut sauce." He turned around and looked at me. I must have been frowning because he laughed.

"How many meals did Sydney leave anyway?" I said. "Hasn't she already been gone for several days?"

"Yeah. She's trying to help me eat healthier."

"What about those banana cookies I made? Any of those left?"

"You're kidding, right? That was over a week ago. I scarfed them up right away. I mean, look at the competition."

I frowned. "Is there any chance we could order a pizza?"

He slammed the freezer closed. "Yes. Something meat-y."

We ordered the carnivores special.

A little later found us eating pizza and discussing the quantum crime situation.

As we were wrapping it up, I said, "So, the most important thing is we have two bodies, Isabella and maybe-Barry. Everything else is minor."

"The bank robbery wasn't exactly minor," he said.

I nodded. "True."

"The body was definitely Barry King," Ryan said. "You didn't hear? The DNA results came back. You probably didn't hear the cause of death, either."

"No. What was it?" Please don't say quantum mechanics.

"It was a heart attack."

Whoa. That was a huge surprise. "Say what? Since when do heart attacks cause...what we saw?"

"Afterwards, his body was dissolved with acid."

"What!" My mind reeled. "Heart attack and acid? Q-lapsing might not even be involved!"

"I know. And that's not all. Isabella also died from a heart attack."

"Poor girl." I took another big bite of pizza. "And poor Barry.

This whole thing has been a nightmare—but not necessarily a quantum nightmare."

By the time we went to bed early, I felt a million times better.

First thing in the morning, I went over to Isabella's place. I needed to take a shower and change clothes, and all my stuff was there. But I was dreading seeing whatever mess Isabella's body had left behind.

When I unlocked the door, I got a surprise: no mess. When I started down the hall, I got another surprise; an older woman appeared in front of me from one of the bedrooms.

I jumped to the thermopause.

She shrieked.

I shrieked.

When we both finally caught our breaths, she said, "Who are you?"

I said, "Who are you?"

"I'm the owner."

"Oh, nice to meet you." I calmed my heart and held my hand out for a shake. "I'm Madison Martin, Isabella's roommate."

"Roommate?" She did not shake my hand. "I don't know anything about any roommate."

Oh, shit. "I'm Professor Martin," I said quickly. "I was subletting. I'm a responsible adult. I work at the university. I have a Ph.D."

She frowned, eyeing me. "You don't look like a responsible adult. That t-shirt looks filthy, and what's a clone?"

My shirt said, *Clones are people two...(or three or four...).* It was an old one I'd left behind at Ryan's house. "It's a science joke." But she had me on the filthy part. Who knew when it'd last seen the inside of a clothes washer?

She didn't even slow down. "And who sneaks home, if this is your home, so early in the morning? Is this some kind of walk-of-shame thing?"

"No, it's not a walk-of-shame thing." I struggled not to get irritated.

"Is that a pissy tone?" she said. "Don't take a pissy tone with me."

So, not totally successful in not getting irritated. I focused on my breathing for a moment. "I apologize, ma'am. I'm just here to take a shower and change clothes. I need to get to work. At the university."

"How do I know you live here? Maybe you're here to rob the place. I don't know you."

With a key? I held out my key to show her. "I promise I live here. I signed a lease with Isabella."

"The dead girl?" The owner frowned, the wrinkles around her mouth deepening. "Yeah, that was sad."

"Yeah." I nodded solemnly.

"If you signed a lease, where is it? Are you sure you knew Isabella? What's her last name?"

My brain froze. What was Isabella's last name?

"Ah-ha!" She jabbed her index finger in my direction. "You are a thief."

"No, I'm not." I took a step towards my room. "Look, I just moved in. This is my room. See how all the boxes say, *Madison's clothes*, and stuff like that?" I pointed. "I'm Madison."

She glanced in the room. "I don't care. Even if you did sign a lease, it wasn't with me. I'm selling. I'm sick of dealing with renters. They're always sneaking out without paying."

Geez, this lady was a real peach. Isabella did not sneak out. I very deliberately did not think about her gruesome murder.

She advanced on me. "It's time for you to go. Or I'm calling the cops."

"I'm not afraid of the cops," I said. "I help the cops. And the FBI."

"Yeah, right." She pulled the latest cutting-edge iPhone out of the front pocket of her voluminous cardigan. "I'm calling."

"Call away." I dodged her, marched into my room, and slammed the door behind me. There was a chance I was seriously screwed here. I'd given Isabella almost everything in my bank account. I needed to find that lease. Now.

I hadn't unpacked any of my boxes or suitcases yet, so I knew it wasn't in any of them. That didn't leave much. I inspected the room, and I didn't see it. Could it be in my office at work? Did Isabella actually give me a copy? I couldn't remember. I got down on the floor and looked under the bed. Nothing.

"I called," the old woman said on the other side of my closed door.

"Great," I said back through the door.

"What?"

"Great!"

I got out my phone and called my old buddy Lawyer-Tom.

"Madison?" he said. "What is it? You didn't murder someone else, did you?"

"Tom! I didn't murder anyone!"

From the hallway, I heard, "Did you say murder?"

"Okay, technically," he said. "What do you want? It's too early for a social call. I'm billing you for this."

"Fine. I'll make it quick." I'd make it really quick since I was broke. "I rented a room in a house from Isabella, and now the owner is here, and she wants me to leave. Do I have to?"

"Isabella Rodriguez, one of the people who was quantum-murdered?" he asked.

Rodriguez, that was it. I yelled, "Rodriguez!" Poor Isabella.

"Yeah," I said to Tom. "So, legally, what kind of shape am I in?"

"You're screwed," he said.

"Is that a legal term?"

"Okay, screwus maximus, if you prefer," he said. "In this case, yes, you're screwed unless you signed a lease with the owner. Did you?"

"No. It was a sublet with Isabella."

"Yeah, you're screwed. I know this kind of thing happens all over town, but a sublease document that you sign with some random girl isn't legally binding. If you're physically on the premises, you can force them to legally evict you, and that can take time through the court system, but then you can't leave the premises, and it's a big mess."

"Fine," I said. "I've heard enough. Thanks, Tom."

"I'll put your new bill in the mail," he said. "Where?"

That was a very good question. "I guess, my office." We hung up.

It had been a long time since I heard anything from owner-lady in the hall. I knew enough about my life to know that probably wasn't a good sign. "Owner-lady? Are you out there?" I shuffled over to the door and opened it a crack.

Two uniformed police officers were creeping down the hall, guns drawn, pointing my way.

"Shit!" I slammed and locked the door. Why did this kind of stuff always seem to happen to me? There's nothing like guns pointed at you to make your adrenaline pump.

"Come out with your hands up!" one of the cops said.

Yeah, like that was going to happen. They'd take me down to the station, and I'd probably have to call Tom again and get another bill again.

"If you just come out, you won't get hurt." one of the cops in the hall said.

I sat down on the floor behind the bed, as far from the door as possible. Clearly, I was going to have to q-lapse and go to my office. The only question was if I was going to be able to pop my boxes of stuff there first or not.

And then, I heard a loud pounding sound, and my door crashed open.

Okay, so no boxes.

I concentrated, focusing on q-lapsing so I was in my safe little office in the Gamow Tower. *I'm in my office.*

"Put up your–"

Chapter Thirty-Three

I landed in my office fine, with no trouble. My head barely hurt at all. But it probably would if I tried to move all my boxes here. I needed some coffee ASAP to rev up my quantum engine. I could pop some coffee here, but that seemed like a waste of quantum mojo. I could go down to the physics department office and get some, but that coffee usually wasn't very good. The Boulder Brews coffee was good.

Maybe Andro would bring me some coffee? I pulled out my phone.

"Babe," he said. That was a promising opening, wasn't it?

"Babe, yourself," I said. "Where are you?"

"I'm about to leave the house for work," he said. "Where are you?"

"I'm in my office already."

"So early? Did you sleep there?" His volume rose. "Did something happen?"

I briefly thought about the quantum throw-down yesterday resulting in the hospital visit and two armed cops breaking into my bedroom just now. Define trouble. "No, no trouble. I'm an early bird. I'm a go-getter." I needed to protect him so he could protect his daughter. I missed him, though.

He sighed. "Fine. Don't tell me. Why did you call?"

"I was wondering if you could maybe stop at Boulder Brews and get me a coffee?" It was right on his way to work.

"Sure, I can do that," he said. "Is that it?"

"Cinnamon roll?" I said hopefully.

He laughed. "Fine. See you soon." We hung up.

I went over to my computer to check my bank balance and figure out when my next payday was.

Soon Andro showed up with a ginormous coffee for me and a paper bag that smelled heavenly. We kissed. He passed over the goodies, and I took them gratefully.

"Thanks, I owe you." I owed him all kinds of stuff, including an honest conversation about what had been going on.

"You're welcome." He smiled and crossed his arms. "And, hey, nice door."

I nodded and opened the bag to spy two cinnamon rolls. Yay. I took one out and took a big bite. Mmm. Creamy cream cheese icing. Cinnamon. Mmm. I was reminded of a recent conversation with Andro about icing.

I looked at him. What was he wearing? Was that a suit? Wait a minute. He rarely wore an actual suit to work.

How did I know this was Andro?

"What's the password?"

"What? I'm sorry I don't speak cinnamon-bun." He grinned. Well, at least he was in a good mood.

I swallowed. "I said, what's the password?"

"Oh, yeah." He raised his eyebrows. "Musty quarks? Misty squarks? Something with quarks. Why?"

He hadn't heard about the throw-down yesterday. He didn't know I was in the hospital. Gosh, he just brought me coffee and cinnamon buns for no reason. "I was just wondering why you were wearing a suit. You look awesome, by the way. Very handsome. And professional." He did look awesome. I wanted to tear the suit right off of him. What was it about dressing up that inspired undressing?

"Quit looking at me like I'm a breakfast pastry." He grinned again. "I'm meeting with my new landlord today and signing a lease for my new two-bedroom apartment."

I could live with Andro! That would solve all my problems. In emergencies, we could fight quantum criminals together. And he'd probably spot me the security deposit and first month's rent, or at least postpone them. It would be perfect. "A new place? Awesome." I took a step towards him.

He nodded enthusiastically. "Yes. And then this afternoon, I'm meeting with Sophia, and we're going to pick out paint colors for her room and new furniture and everything." He was practically giddy.

So the second bedroom was for his daughter. That made sense. He did say he got shared custody. And he'd told me his sister Yasmin asked him to move out.

I'd been so wrapped up in my own drama I'd forgotten he had a lot of his own drama these days. So, now was not the time for a big conversation about quantum throwdowns and such. He had more important things to focus on.

I smiled. "It sounds wonderful, Andro. Congratulations. I'm happy for you." I went back to my desk and sat down. "And if you need any help moving or painting or anything, I'm your girl."

"Thank you. I appreciate that." He glanced at his phone. "Well, I have to get to work."

Of course, he did. But…

"Because later I'm meeting with my new landlord. So, I'll catch you later?"

I nodded. "Sounds good." If I didn't tell him about the q-criminals, I might be putting him, and Sophia, in danger. That was not acceptable.

He started walking over to his office next door.

"Andro, wait," I said. "I need to warn you there are three quantum criminals causing havoc."

"Three!" he said. "That's a lot. Griffin?"

I nodded. "And it turns out Nancy's a bad guy. And … someone else, someone who's a strong q-lapser."

"Someone like Luke?"

"I'm afraid so."

He sank down on my desk. "Oh, no." After a few moments, he said, "What's the FBI doing? What are the cops doing? What's happening?"

"I don't know what the officials are doing," I said. "But Ryan and I and hopefully people like you are going to form our own task force to take them down."

"We don't have time for some committee." He stood. "What if my daughter is put in harm's way? We have to act!"

"I hear you," I said. "What do you want to do?"

"Let's do that home-in on thing we've done before."

I was afraid he'd say that. "Now. On our own?"

"Yes. There's no time to waste."

I was afraid he'd say that. "Yes. You're right."

"Come here," he said. "We hold hands and concentrate, right?"

"Right." I clasped his hand in mine, screwed my eyes shut, and concentrated. *We are where Luke and Griffin are. We are where Luke and Griffin are.*

Nothing happened.

"It's not working," he said. "Are you trying? Why isn't it working?"

"I don't know." It was very frustrating. Evidently, I wasn't a very good Quantum Cop, after all.

He stepped away. "Well, I have to go. Let me know if you figure anything out."

"I will," I said. "Be careful, Andro."

He nodded. "You too, Madison."

I didn't let myself wallow in worries. I drank and ate the rest of my lovely breakfast.

And then I popped all my boxes and suitcases into my office. Unfortunately, my office was so tiny even my small amount of worldly possessions filled it up.

I was just pondering how to take a shower when I heard a knock on my office door. "Madison?" It was Professor Chen.

"I still need to meet with you about your grants and advisees," he said. "And, unfortunately, Nancy's gone again. I don't know what's going on with my calendar."

Shoot. He didn't seem to realize Nancy was a quantum criminal and wasn't coming back.

But he was there yesterday. He should know what was going on. "Professor Chen, you were there yesterday. Nancy's not coming back. The police and the FBI are looking for her."

"I don't understand what happened yesterday." He paused. "Are you sure she's not coming back?"

"Pretty sure." Really sure. I nodded emphatically.

"But..." He trailed off and stood staring at me. Then he yawned.

"Do you want me to help you with the calendar software?"

"Yes." He turned and started walking down the hall. "And can you make some coffee?"

I hurried to catch up with him as he strode down the hall on his long legs. "Yeah."

As we walked down the stairs, he glanced at me and said, "I don't know what's going on with all those boxes, but you absolutely cannot live in your office. That's a firing offense."

Crap-city. Like I needed another one of those. "Yes, sir." Action item: find free place to live.

In the physics department office, I wrote down instructions on a piece of paper for his calendar software and gave it to him. I filled up the coffee maker and turned it on.

I figured I deserved to enjoy the fruits of my labor, so I looked around for a coffee cup. On Nancy's desk, I spied a Schrödinger's cat coffee cup. If I'd seen this before, I might have figured out much earlier that Nancy could q-lapse. Maybe I could have stopped her before she got into trouble. I shook my head. "For want of a cup, the coffee-drinker was lost."

Professor Chen said, "What?"

"Nothing. The coffee's almost ready."

I'd just poured myself a cup and sat down for a moment at Nancy's desk when my cell rang.

It was Ben. "Madison?"

"Hi, Ben. What's up?"

He laughed. "I'm here at work, at the station, and you would not believe the report that just came in over the radio."

Were those cops still there when I popped my boxes out of my room? "Oh, I'd probably believe it. What?"

"An old lady called 911 because a slutty thief murderer was going to kill her. When the officers arrived on the scene, the slut-slash-thief-slash-murderer disappeared in a puff of smoke. And then all her stuff disappeared, too." He guffawed.

His amusement was contagious. I chuckled, too. "I wish I could have seen her face when I disappeared."

He laughed. "The officers were freaked out, too. You should have heard them talking about some sneaky band of magicians."

"I tried to be nice, but the old lady was mean and grumpy. Hey, how'd you know it was me?"

"Well, I do know you're not a thief or a murderer..."

"Or a slut."

He didn't say anything.

"You better not be thinking I'm slutty!" But I couldn't help grinning.

"Of course not." I imagined him grinning from ear to ear. "But people and stuff disappearing is sort of a dead giveaway that you might be involved."

"I have a lease," I said, "sort of, and she just kicked me out."

"This is the place I helped you move into?"

"Yeah. Thanks again for helping me move, by the way." Hey. Ben had an empty spare bedroom.

"Where that girl Isabella died?" That sobered us both right up.

"Yeah. I guess I didn't want to live there anymore, anyway. Thanks for cleaning up, you-know, Isabella, too." I'd figured out belatedly that's why he'd wanted me to thank him the other night.

Maybe if I hinted around enough, Ben would offer me his spare room. "Now I've got a problem because I gave Isabella my last seven hundred dollars, and my lawyer says I'm out of luck in terms of the sublet since she died."

Ben whistled. "Seven hundred bucks? That's a chunk of change."

"Yeah, it is. A big old chunk."

"I thought professors made good money."

"I do okay, but I've had a lot of legal expenses lately. And I have a bunch of student loans that I've been paying. And credit card debt. Post-docs, my last job, don't make good money." So, I'm really poor. Get the hint, dude.

"Yeah, well, I hear that. Cops don't make good money, either."

"That surprises me. Your apartment is so nice." Should I mention that spare room? Too on-the-nose? "Thanks for letting me stay there last weekend."

"Do you need a place to stay?" he finally asked.

"Well, maybe," I said. "I wouldn't want to put anyone out. Of course, I'm not feeling a hundred percent right now because of that quantum duel I had yesterday."

"Quantum duel! Was that the thing that happened at the university? I didn't know you were involved in that."

"Yeah. I ended up in the hospital."

"I'm sorry to hear that," he said. "That settles it. You should come stay with me, at least for a little while."

"Gosh, if you're sure," I said. "That would really help me

out."

"I'm sure. I can help you move, too. Just tell me where and when."

I did. Then I hung up, very satisfied with myself.

Later that evening, I said, "Hear ye, hear ye," and slapped Ben's coffee table. Ow. I hurt my hand. "I call to order the first official meeting of the unofficial super-awesome quantum task force." We were all sitting in Ben's family room.

Nate said, "Super-awesome?"

Lisa just raised her eyebrows at me.

"I'm raising our morale."

Also in attendance were Ryan, Alyssa, and Ben. Andro was on speakerphone. Alyssa looked too scared to say anything.

Andro said, "Let's make this quick. I'm busy."

Ben looked from the phone to me and then back to the phone. What was he thinking?

"Yeah," Nick said. "Technically, Lisa and I aren't here." What was going on with the FBI? Had they abandoned the quantum task force? That was a discussion for another time.

"You're all here because you can q-lapse," I said.

Ryan pushed his glasses up his nose. "Or not."

"You're all here because you've been involved in the investigation, and/or you're one of the good guys!" I said.

Alyssa smiled.

Lisa summarized the quantum crimes of the last month, including the results of the two autopsies, so we were all on the same page.

Andro said, "Get to it."

"Yes, we need to strike while the iron's hot." Lisa turned to me. "So what can you tell us about your quantum throw-down yesterday? Any leads?"

"What?" Andro asked. "What throw-down?"

Ryan gave me a dirty look.

Alyssa gave me a dirty look.

Lisa shook her head.

"I'll fill you in later, Andro, if you want. I know you're busy with your daughter."

"Leads?" Lisa asked.

"Griffin was significantly injured," I said. "He was passed out so couldn't have q-lapsed to escape. And, actually..." I thought back over what Nancy had done. "I don't think Nancy knows how to travel via q-lapsing because she ran away from me and then looked surprised when she fuzzed out in the office."

"So, someone else was involved," Lisa said.

"We knew there was a third person," Ben said.

"Luke Bacalli," Nate said.

"Yes." I nodded. "It looks that way." I was still surprised he was back from the dead.

"So, Nancy's definitely involved?" Andro asked. "She's one of the bad guys?"

"Yes," I said. "I'm afraid so."

"That's a shame," Andro said.

"What was with that whole penis thing?" Ben asked.

"What penis thing?" Andro said in a stern voice.

Alyssa looked confused but interested, as well.

"I don't think that's the most pressing matter," I said.

"Yeah," Nate said.

Ben grinned. What was he thinking?

"Anyway," I said. "We should probably call area hospitals and urgent care places on the off chance that Nancy or Griffin showed up for treatment."

"I can do that." Ben raised his hand. Overeager much, dude?

"Good idea, Mad," Ryan said. "We'll make an investigator of you yet." He said that like it was a good thing.

"Did the student interviews yield anything?" Lisa asked.

I shook my head. "Only one of the kids had an alibi, and he was at the library."

"We got bupkis," Ryan said.

"Is that an official investigator term?" I asked.

"Yes," Ryan said.

"Actually," Lisa said, "how specific was his alibi?"

"Very," Nate said. "He got some library worker to confirm when he was there." He must have followed through with those interview notes we sent him.

Was that suspicious? "Who was it?" Lisa asked.

Nate accessed a document on his phone. "Arjun

Chatterjee."

"Maybe I should talk to him," Lisa said.

I shrugged. I found it hard to believe straight-and-narrow Arjun could be involved in criminal activity. "He'll be in class Monday morning." I'd texted the students that class was on for Monday.

She smiled her scary smile. "I think we can track him down before that."

"Do we have any other leads?" Alyssa asked.

We all looked at each other. I guessed that was a no.

"Last year, when you fought Luke and Griffin, didn't you follow them when they traveled elsewhere?" Lisa asked.

"Yeah, they, her and Andro, did," Ryan said.

"How did you do that?" Nate asked.

"I just followed Madison," Andro said.

How did I do it? "I'm not sure." I pondered for a few moments.

"Madison?" Lisa asked.

"Just a sec." It was on the tip of my brain. "It was instinct. I guess I noticed the maximum improbabilities and followed them."

"So, what?" Ben asked. "Like a disturbance in the space-time continuum?"

"Basically," I said, daring anyone to snicker. Surprisingly, since I sounded like an episode of *Star Trek*, they didn't.

"That could be a lead. Can you try that again?" Lisa asked.

"Sounds like a long shot," Nate said. "It's probably a waste of time."

Andro didn't say anything like, 'She can't do it anymore,' which I appreciated.

I looked around the room at the people I cared about. They were all depending on me.

"Madison?" Lisa asked.

Finally, I said, "Yes. I'm not sure I can do it, but I can try."

Chapter Thirty-Four

Friday night after the unofficial task force meeting, I slept in Ben's guest room, and it was totally uneventful. He didn't even bring me coffee in bed in the morning. Darn it.

Saturday morning, Lisa picked me up on the way to Arjun's apartment.

"Can we stop for coffee?" I asked.

She didn't even glance my way. "No."

Unfortunately, his apartment was empty when we got there.

"What college kid goes out early Saturday morning?" she asked.

I shook my head. "Not me." I paused. "Now, can we go for coffee?"

She just gave me one of her trademark intimidating looks and looked back at her phone.

I did recall Arjun's alibi was the library. "He might be at the library."

At the library, Lisa flashed her badge around and said she was looking for Arjun Chatterjee. No one claimed to know anything. But one guy jerked back and started looking nervous. He resembled Arjun.

"You," she said. "What's your name?"

"Dhruv Khan," he stammered.

She checked her phone some more. "Aren't you Arjun's cousin?" Arjun had a cousin that worked here? What did that mean for his alibi?

"What?" His voice squeaked. "How did you know that?"

How did she know that?

"I'm the FBI. Is Arjun here or not?"

"He's here." Before she could ask him where, he added, "In

the stacks. 3C."

"I know where it is," I said. The stacks were a great place to hide from students−not that I ever did that. I led her through the labyrinthine Norlin stacks.

She stormed through the cramped hallways and soon towered over Arjun's desk. "Arjun Chatterjee?"

"What?" he stammered, like his cousin. "Who are you? Professor Martin, what's this about?"

"This is Agent Baker," I said. "From the FBI."

"Yes, ma'am? Can I help you with something? I would be happy to help you with something. I am helpful." Wow, he was nervous.

Lisa hadn't moved. "We just want to ask you a couple of questions, Arjun."

"Okay."

Lisa looked at something on her phone. "So, you claim you've been studying at the library a lot lately."

"I am a student." Arjun bobbed his head up and down. "I study."

"We know your cousin Dhruv Khan is a work-study employee at the library," she said.

Arjun's eyes opened wide. "How?" He paused. "Second-cousin, but, yes, ma'am."

Lisa leaned forward. "Tell the truth, Arjun. Have you been at the library so much?"

Beads of sweat collected on Arjun's forehead and upper lip. "Yes, ma'am."

"Aw, Arjun," Lisa said. "I'm disappointed in you. I have a picture right here of you not at the library when you said you were at the library." Where'd she get the picture?

I felt my jaw drop. Prim and proper Arjun was a liar?

"Er..." A drop of sweat rolled down Arjun's forehead.

"You grew up in a wealthy family in India, didn't you?" Lisa asked.

"Yes, ma'am."

"Your father recently lost his job under some disgrace, didn't he? He lost all his money?"

Poor Arjun. I'm not sure I would have had the stomach for this interrogation. It was probably a good thing I wasn't officially a law enforcer.

Arjun's face turned towards the floor. "Yes, ma'am."

"Did he pay your tuition this semester?"

Arjun just shook his head no, as tears started rolling down his cheeks. I had to admit I felt sorry for him.

Lisa stood up. "Are you coming with me to FBI headquarters to tell me everything you've done?"

Arjun nodded, still silently crying. We escorted him out of the building.

As I walked back towards her car, she stopped. "Where are you going?"

"I thought I'd go back and help you interrogate him," I said.

"I appreciate your help in tracking him down, but I think you have something else to do."

Damn. I'd been hoping she'd forgotten. "Yes, ma'am." I'd promised to try to follow the improbabilities.

She turned back in the direction of her car. As Arjun shuffled in front of her, she asked, "What exactly is your visa status?"

Arjun looked miserable. I felt sorry for him--unless, of course, he was involved in murder.

In the physics department office a little later, I perched in Nancy's chair.

What had I promised last night? I'd look for disturbances in the space-time continuum? What had I been thinking? That sounded crazy.

Probably too much time had elapsed here in the office since the quantum duel, anyway. But we didn't have much else to go on, and everyone was counting on me.

I closed my eyes and concentrated.

What was improbable? What didn't belong?

The whole room seemed unsettled and weird.

I opened my eyes. I didn't know if the weirdness was my Spidey-sense or if I was a closeted neat-freak. Maybe I should pick up the rest of the furniture and debris off the floor. With Nancy gone, Chen hadn't managed to do it.

I sighed and got to work.

Once the place was more orderly and, okay, I admit it, I'd brewed and drank a big cup of coffee, I tried again.

I closed my eyes and concentrated.

Was there a little tingle here, in front of Nancy's desk? I stood up. Yes. I think there was something off in this spot. I tried to feel where it went. It went somewhere.

I concentrated on following weirdness. I concentrated on q-lapsing. *Follow the weirdness.*

And then, suddenly, I was cold.

I opened my eyes. I was back near the site of the disappearing mansion. What was so special about this spot, anyway?

The wind blew. Brrr. I shivered. I was freezing. My professorial jeans and t-shirt were not sufficient for the October wind.

I should try to follow the path of improbabilities some more before it went cold or colder. I shivered.

I closed my eyes. Okay, improbabilities, where are you? *Follow the weirdness.*

I tried to concentrate, but my shivering was getting in the way.

I thought I heard a laugh off in the distance. I opened my eyes.

Technically, the mansion site was over the next rise, in the little valley there. Could it possibly be back? No. The quantum criminals weren't that stupid, were they?

I heard what sounded like a laugh, and was that a splash?

I turned and crept up the small hill. I peeked over the top. Damn. The mansion was back. I couldn't believe it.

And was that Nancy cavorting in the pool? Naked?

Of course, if I was that curvy and voluptuous, maybe I'd spend more time naked, too.

"A peeper, huh? Do you like what you see?" a man behind me asked.

"I wasn't–" Everything went black.

Gradually, I came to. My head was killing me. Smacking the Quantum Cop on the head seemed unfair. I wasn't sure I could q-lapse, it hurt so much. Of course, that probably was their nefarious plan.

On the bright side, they hadn't actually killed me. Yet.

I was tied up and lying on a wet patio. It turns out being

tied up was very uncomfortable--how did those Shades-of-Gray people do it all the time? Besides that, the little rocks inset in the patio were digging into my skin, and I was wet.

At least the patio was warm. I may have been injured and uncomfortable and wet, but at least I wasn't cold. That was something, right? Things weren't totally dire. Yeah, I was fiddling on the deck of the Titanic.

"You took Professor Martin hostage?" Griffin's voice squeaked. He, and whoever he was talking to, seemed to be getting closer.

I quickly closed my eyes and tried to act unconscious.

"See! She's knocked out. She can't q-lapse if she's unconscious." The male voice was familiar, but I couldn't quite place it. "I've been using my quantum mojo to keep her knocked out."

Whoever this guy was, he didn't have as much quantum mojo as he thought.

"But that's crazy," Griffin said. "She's the Quantum Cop. She beat the hell out of me and Nancy the other day."

"Don't be such a pussy, Griffin." Who was he? Seeing him wouldn't necessarily tell me anything. The way he looked wasn't necessarily the way he truly looked.

Was the mystery guy Luke? I wanted to open my eyes and look, but I wanted them to think I was still unconscious. I didn't want them to hit me again. Look. Don't look. Look. Don't look.

By the time I finally decided to open my eyes, they had walked away. Dammit! From the splashing noises at the other end of the patio, they were all in the pool now.

My head was still killing me. I tried to q-lapse anyway. It didn't work. I couldn't concentrate.

Then I remembered something: surveillance! The FBI was supposed to put up surveillance. I was saved. All I had to do was wait for the cavalry.

Okay, cavalry, any time now.

Now was a good time for cavalry.

Time passed very, very slowly when you were waiting for the cavalry, trussed up like a pig, wet, and your head really, really hurt.

Why was it taking the FBI so long to rush in? If they'd been waiting to catch the quantum criminals doing something red-handed, surely kidnapping me qualified.

Then, I started wondering why they hadn't shown up earlier before I even got here. They should have rushed in when the mansion reappeared. Were the agents enjoying watching Nancy frolic in the all-together too much to bust in? No pun intended. She was the hottest woman I'd ever met, but still...

Something was not right.

Around the throbbing in my head, I tried to review what I knew about the surveillance here.

When Ben and I came here, he suggested the FBI set up surveillance. I agreed. I called Nate and suggested it. Nate said he was on it. But I hadn't seen any sign of surveillance before I'd been conked on the head.

And why hadn't the FBI thought of it themselves and set it up much earlier?

Something else had been nagging the back of my brain. Lisa said she wasn't informed when Griffin escaped. But what if someone else was? Someone should have been. That was the proper procedure, after all. If Lisa hadn't been informed, who would be informed? Her partner Nate?

Oh. My. God. I realized why that voice just now sounded familiar. It sounded like Nate. Could Nate be involved? Could he be a quantum criminal? When did he learn to q-lapse? He'd been to several of my FBI quantum mechanics classes. Could he have been faking when he said he couldn't do it?

Then I remembered something else about Nate. He was buddies with my cousin Ryan, and Ryan had said Nate was a theater major in college. Makeup! Theater majors knew all about makeup. Probably the quantum criminals were impersonating people using old-school theater makeup, prosthetics, and voice synthesizers. All they had to do was make someone like Nancy resemble someone else, one time to make the probability non-zero. Then, they could use quantum mechanics whenever they wanted to impersonate the person. It seemed at least a little less impossible than it had before.

Was Luke even involved? Maybe not. If Nate had been impersonating Luke, he was probably dead like I thought.

Nate was the quantum criminal mastermind.

And I was tied up as his hostage, totally at his mercy. The cavalry wasn't coming.

Chapter Thirty-Five

I was possibly concussed, lying on the pool deck of a magic disappearing-reappearing mansion, surrounded by villainous quantum criminals. No one knew where I was. No one even knew the mansion was back.

It was only a matter of time before the felons did something even more dastardly to me.

I tried to q-lapse to remove the ropes tying me up. No go. My head still hurt too much. It was like tiny little dwarfs were in my head mining with very sharp pickaxes.

First things first. I needed to get rid of this headache.

I needed drugs.

Sadly, there were no painkillers lying around on the pool deck.

Over by the pool, a cell phone rang. Nate answered it, but I couldn't hear what he had to say. Mumble, mumble.

I tried to q-lapse to give myself very good hearing.

Nate hung up, and then he said more loudly, "Damn it. I have to go into the office. Lisa brought in some kid Arjun."

Did I q-lapse, or was he just talking louder?

"Oh, don't go," Nancy said. "We're having so much fun."

"Why bother going in?" Griffin said.

"It's the perfect cover," Nate said. "And I can keep an eye on the investigation. They're never going to figure out I murdered those two physicists."

Neither Griffin nor Nancy seemed enthusiastic about that.

"While I'm gone, you guys keep an eye on Professor Fuck-up over there."

"I thought you said she'd stay out," Griffin said.

"She will," Nate said and then shut up. He must have left.

Nate had no idea I'd figured out what was going on. And if he hadn't been so cocky about his abilities, I'd still be in the dark, possibly literally. A rogue FBI agent was not good. Very not good. I had to get out of here and warn Lisa and everyone else.

"Griffin, now that it's just the two of us," Nancy said.

"Yeah?" Griffin said all hopefully like he thought she would ask him to have sex with her.

"Will you pop out and get me a drink? Pina colada? Frozen."

"We're supposed to watch Professor Martin, I mean, Professor..." He giggled. "Fuck-up." Grown men really shouldn't giggle.

"I'll watch her," Nancy said. "I want a drink. I promise I'll make it worth your while."

I couldn't see them, but I could imagine Griffin drooling over her. Was she still naked?

"Come on," she said in a sexy voice.

"Okay," he said. "Be right back." Presumably, he q-lapsed out.

I heard splashing.

I didn't have any time to waste. Nancy might help me.

I moaned.

All I heard was more splashing.

I moaned louder and added, "Ow! My head's killing me."

The splashing stopped. "Madison?"

"Help," I said. "Where am I? I think I'm dying."

I heard the watery sounds of someone getting out of the pool.

I moaned dramatically and fluttered my eyelids like I was having trouble opening them.

I heard the soft sounds of someone walking, dripping water, across the pool deck. "Madison?"

I opened my eyelids. "Oh, thank God. Nancy. Where am I? What happened? Oh no." I twisted around. "I'm tied up. What's going on?" I moaned. "My head really hurts. I think I need to go to the hospital. Call 911."

She wore her short red silk robe and had her hands on her hips. She was scowling. "You're not a very good actress," she finally said.

"I swear my head hurts," I said. "Can you please get me

some aspirin or something?"

She just scowled at me some more.

"Please, Nancy," I said. "I'm begging you." Was her expression softening there? I moaned gently as if I didn't have the energy to moan more loudly.

"I don't have to put up with your bullshit." A cell phone appeared in her hand.

I tried to q-lapse to make it go away. Nothing happened.

"Nate? I need to talk to you," she said. "But–" Now she scowled at the phone. "He hung up on me. He said he was busy."

I wasn't supposed to know Nate was involved, was I? "Nate, the FBI agent? Were you trying to get help?"

"Not exactly," she said slowly. "Are you still acting? I can't tell now." She sighed. "I guess the cat's out of the bag. Nate's involved."

"He hung up on you?" I said. "It sounds like he doesn't appreciate you."

Nancy was still staring at her phone. "You got that right."

"Are you sure you don't have an aspirin or something?"

She didn't answer me.

"Maybe you could help me up? It's all wet here, and the rocks are digging into me."

She glanced at me.

"Please. It's very uncomfortable, what with the restraints and all."

She shook her head.

"Oh, right," I said. "Nate must be the boss. He probably wouldn't want you to."

"I'm sure he wouldn't. But what does he know?" She walked a couple of steps, grabbed a chair, and slid it along the deck next to me. "Don't try anything funny." She leaned down and hoisted me up.

Ow. Everything hurt, but the headliner was my head. Mother f-er. I winced but didn't say anything.

"You're heavier than you look," she said as she settled me in the chair.

"Thank you for helping me up," I said, imbuing my voice with sincerity. "Maybe a drink of water? Maybe take off the restraints?"

She took a step back and put her hands on her hips again. "How stupid do you think I am?"

"I don't think you're stupid at all--and I would know, I'm a genius."

She opened her eyes wider, somehow conveying sarcasm. "Yeah, looks like it."

Good point. Maybe the genius thing was in doubt at this juncture. "Please. I promise I won't try to escape," I said. "And I've never lied or broken a promise to you. I could have hurt you the other day in the physics department office, and I didn't. I let you go. I did you a favor."

She didn't move to help me, but she didn't say no either.

"I thought we were friends, Nancy. I liked you."

"You did get me some sweats and get me released from FBI custody, which is more than I can say for Nate. I can't believe he just let all his colleagues ogle me."

"Men, can't live with 'em, can't disappear them without your boss getting cranky."

A little snort of laughter erupted from Nancy's mouth. "I'm sure Nate won't like it, but what the hell. Lean forward." She already seemed a little tipsy.

I did what she said and leaned, which did not help my headache at all.

She fumbled with the ropes but managed to get them off. "There."

I sat up and attempted to move my arms to my sides, but they were numb. I had to look down at them to see if anything was happening. They had moved to my side. I arranged my numb hands in my lap. "Thank you."

I wanted to pump her for information, but I didn't want her to think I was pumping her for information. "I did think Nate was nice." Until I found out how not-nice he was. Just now. "How'd you guys meet?"

Nancy pulled another chair over. "We met last year when he was investigating the quantum crimes."

"I have to ask. Did you know from the start it was Nate? Or did you think he was Barry at first?"

She looked down at the pool deck. "I thought he was Barry. I mean, I know Barry and I had broken up but when he came back from the dead, I was so happy to see him." She blinked her eyes.

Nate took advantage of her grief to get in her pants. He was even creepier than I thought, and I'd thought he was pretty creepy.

She lifted her head and stared at me. "So, all this is basically your fault."

I scrambled to think of something that wouldn't make her mad at me. "It's not so bad, is it? You have a super-power."

"Yeah." The ends of her mouth tilted down. "How's that working out for you?"

I forced a smile. "Not great." On the bright side, my head seemed to ache slightly less. On the dark side, my arms and hands were starting to get that pins-and-needles feeling.

"Aren't you guys rich, though? I thought Nate robbed a bank?" I was guessing Nate was the one who robbed it. And then he investigated the robbery. He did have a sweet setup. "How much money did he give you?"

"None yet." She crossed her arms. "He said he was keeping it safe."

"Oh. Uh, okay." I tried to say it in a way that indicated I thought that was bullshit.

She frowned. "Where the hell is that asshole Griffin?" She stood up and started pacing.

The air in front of her started to get fuzzy. I braced myself. If Nate was coming back, I was probably dead.

The form that solidified was rather rotund. It was Griffin, and he was holding a large frozen Pina colada and a plastic grocery sack with small bottles inside. When he saw me sitting in the chair, he shrieked, dropped everything, and disappeared again.

The Pina colada crashed onto the pool deck, glass breaking, spraying Nancy and me with icy coconutty pineappley beverage.

"Well, shit!" Nancy said and glared at me. "I wanted that drink. Now I'm all sticky. I'm going to take a shower. Don't move. No q-lapsing." She turned and started walking into the house.

I tried to dart towards the plastic bag, but I couldn't move quickly with my head still pounding. The bag top was open, and I could see it held a bunch of little black bottles of Extra

Strength 5-Hour Energy. Well, hallelujah. They might help with my headache. And they'd probably help with q-lapsing. As quick as I could with my pins-and-needles hands, I grabbed one and slammed it down. I slammed a second one down.

Now, I felt nauseated.

A fuzzy spot appeared and expanded.

I tried to q-lapse again. No go. Well, shit!

Was this it? I glanced around the pool deck. Was I dead?

And then it hit me: why was I just sitting here waiting?

Run away!

I got to my feet and ran as fast as I could. I ran across the deck, jumped off, and ran into the darkness. I ran through the scrub and up the little hill. My lungs burned. My head still ached. I was panting heavily.

When I got over the rise, I crouched down and peered towards the house, trying to quiet my breathing. Now I was wet and cold.

I smelled coconut. Oh, right, that was me. The wind blew. Brr.

Griffin was walking around the pool deck. He seemed much calmer than he'd been the last time I'd seen him--moments ago. "Nancy? Where'd you go? Why'd you take Professor Martin?"

She didn't answer him.

He went over to his bag and noticed two of his drinks were consumed. "Nancy?" I couldn't quite make it out, but I surmised he was making his confused face. "Nancy!"

Finally, Nancy walked out of the house, tying the belt of her red silk robe. "What? Where's my drink?"

Griffin pointed at the mess near his feet. "It's here. You saw me drop it. Sorry."

"Well, I expect you to go get me another one."

"But where's Professor Martin, I mean Professor Fuck-up?" he asked.

"I don't know. What did you do with her?" Nancy asked.

"What did I do with her? What did you do with her?" He paused and pointed at the empty bottles. "Did you drink my drinks?"

"No, I didn't drink your nasty drinks." She scoured the pool deck. "Fuck! She got away! She must have drunk your drinks and q-lapsed!"

"Oh, shit," Griffin said, and he said it like he was scared. Scared of me or scared of Nate?

"Yeah, oh, shit." Nancy sat down in a chair.

They stared at each other like they were the ones who were screwed instead of me. "It's Nate's fault," Nancy said. "He's the one who said she'd stay out and wouldn't be able to q-lapse."

"Yeah!" Griffin said. Then he added, "Somehow, I don't think he'll see it that way."

"I guess we have to call him," she said.

"Yeah," he said. "I guess we have to."

They looked at each other, neither one reaching for a phone.

Finally, Griffin reached into his pocket. "Fuck."

No doubt Nate would be here any second. He'd be able to q-lapse to do whatever he wanted.

And he had a gun.

The cold wind blew.

Chapter Thirty-Six

I hugged the ground, peeking over the rise of the little hill and shivering. Dead, spiky grass poked my stomach. The baddies, Griffin and Nancy, were still on the mansion's pool deck. How did they keep that pool deck so warm, anyway? Focus, Mad.

My head still hurt.

"Madison," a familiar male voice whispered near my ear.

I practically jumped into the exosphere. I did squeak in surprise, but luckily it was a pretty quiet squeak.

It was Andro. "Are you all right?" he asked.

My knight in shining armor "What are you doing here?" I asked him. "Not that I'm not super-glad to see you."

"I was worried. I called, and you didn't answer your cell. So I called Lisa, and she told me what you were trying."

I nodded, and my head pounded. I winced. "Yeah, I misplaced my phone."

"What's wrong?"

"Nate, FBI Agent Sawyer, hit me on the head. He's the quantum criminal mastermind. He killed Isabella and Barry." My voice caught.

"Oh, no. Agent Sawyer? That's hard to believe." He stared at me. "But more importantly, how hard did he hit you? Are you okay?"

I shook my head. Ow. Keep your head still, Madison. "I don't know. Pretty hard. I was unconscious. And I can't q-lapse."

Andro got his famous still-face expression. "I'm gonna kill him."

I tried to keep my head steady as I put my hand on his arm. "He's got a gun, he's trained to kill, and he can q-lapse."

"Shit." Andro sat back. "How are we going to stop him?"

"I don't know," I said. "How did you find me?"

"My super-power is apparently following you." He smiled gently. "I q-lapsed, trying to find you, and here I am."

I knew it wasn't very macho of me (I was supposed to be a real-life kick-ass heroine), but I was really glad he was here. "Can I ..." I wanted to ask for a hug, but it was stupid.

"Hug? Yes." He enveloped me in his arms. "Why do you smell like coconut?"

"Later," I said into his warm chest. I felt so much better. Everything might be okay, after all. My eyes might have overflowed a bit. After a few moments, I pushed him away. "We're not safe here. Is Nate back at the mansion yet?" I very stupidly hadn't been watching the pool deck.

"Yes." Andro's eyes were glued to the mansion.

Nate was back, and he was yelling and gesticulating at Griffin and Nancy. None of them looked happy.

And then the three of them and the mansion and the pool started to fuzz out, and they all disappeared. Crap. So much for catching them.

I suddenly felt like my bones were made of cooked spaghetti and collapsed.

"We can't fight him now," Andro said. "We lost him." He looked down at me. "I think it's for the best, for the moment. You don't seem like you could fight anyone. I'm taking you to the hospital."

"Wait. We have to warn Lisa and Ryan. Do you have your phone?"

"Of course," he said and handed it over.

I quickly dialed Lisa.

She answered right away.

"Lisa. It's Madison. It's life or death. Don't react."

Slowly she said, "Hi. We just started questioning Arjun."

"Are you alone? Is Nate Sawyer with you?"

"No," she said. "And no. He stepped out."

"Nate Sawyer is the bad guy. He's the quantum mastermind. He killed Barry and Isabella."

"N-"

"Don't say his name!"

"How sure are you about this?" she asked.

281

"One hundred percent. Infinity percent."

"Damn." She sounded choked up. I'd never heard her like that. "He's-"

"Don't say anything about him. He thinks the FBI doesn't have a clue about what he's up to."

"We don't," she said. "He..."

"Lisa!" I said.

She didn't say whatever she'd been about to say.

"He's armed," I said. "I hate to say it, but I think you have to shoot first and ask questions later. If you sneak up on him, you might get him. I don't think he can q-lapse if he's in a lot of pain. At least I can't."

"What do you mean a lot of pain? Are you all right?"

"Andro's with me."

"You-know-who's supposed to be in the building," she said. "I've got to go."

We hung up.

"Okay," he said. "Hospital now."

"No." I started to shake my head. Ow. Don't shake your head, Mad. "I have to warn Ryan."

Andro sighed.

I dialed Ryan's cell. "Ryan? It's Madison."

"Hi," he said.

"Your buddy FBI Agent Nate Sawyer is the bad guy, the quantum murderer. They're going after him now. And if you see Nate, God forbid, you don't know anything. You don't know he can q-lapse. You don't know he hurt people."

He was quiet for a few moments, probably battling with what to say. "I hear what you're saying. Bye." He hung up.

"Now, can I take you to the hospital?"

"Yes, please."

I woke up in a toothpaste-green room on a rolling metal bed (again). On the bright side, my head hurt a lot less (again).

Three men leaned over the bed staring at me: Andro, Ryan, and uniform-clad Ben.

Awkward.

"Did they get Nate?" I asked.

"Don't worry about that, Mad." Andro squeezed my hand.

"Just focus on getting better."

Both Ben and Ryan were looking at him like he was crazy. I guess law-enforcement types were all about justice.

"No," Ben said. "Agent Baker decided they needed to wait for you."

Andro frowned. "I said I would go. Madison's too hurt. She needs to rest and recover from what this asshole already did to her."

Ryan opened his mouth. He closed his mouth. Finally, he said, "I still can't believe Nate's behind all this."

"I saw him with my own eyes," I said.

"Yeah, I saw him, too," Andro said. "It was definitely him."

"But couldn't it have been someone impersonating him?" Ryan asked.

Lisa skidded into the room. "How is she? Is she ready to go?"

"Go? Where am I going?" I asked. My head felt decent. They must have given me some good meds. I might be able to q-lapse now.

"We're taking down the quantum mastermind." She smiled, but it was the scariest smile I'd ever seen, like the smile the angel of death might give you right before she reaped your soul.

"Couldn't someone be impersonating him?" Ryan asked again.

Lisa shook her head. "No. We very carefully searched his house while he was at work. We found a bunch of makeup, prosthetics, and voice synthesizers, and we found a lot of money, way more than from the one bank robbery we know about. It makes you wonder why he bothered robbing a bank. I guess he was trying to make us think Luke was back or frame Griffin?" It pretty much worked. We did wonder if Luke was back; at least I did.

"Well, shit." Ryan looked like he might cry.

"You searched his house?" Andro asked. "What if you tipped him off? He'll be even more dangerous if he knows we're coming."

"He doesn't know we searched his house," Lisa said.

"You don't know that for sure," Ben said.

"We're pretty sure," she said. "He's been under constant

surveillance since Madison called me. He hasn't done anything out of the ordinary. Plus, we picked up Nancy at her condo, and she's been cooperating."

"Nancy?" I asked. "Is she all right? What are you charging her with?"

"She seems fine," Lisa said. "A little shaken up by all this, but like I said, she's been helping us. That's how we managed to find the money hidden in Nate's house. She said he forced her to help him. I think her charges will be minimal."

I felt a little better. Maybe Nancy hadn't ruined her life, after all. "What about Griffin?"

"He escaped from prison," Ben said. "He deserves what's coming to him." All three of the law enforcers looked like they didn't care what happened to Griffin.

"Agents are looking for him," Lisa said. "So, are we going after Nate or what?"

"Yeah." I pushed the covers away and gingerly sat up. "Let's get him."

"You might want to get dressed first," Ryan said.

I was wearing one of those breathtakingly beautiful cotton hospital gowns--in front of both Andro and Ben. Ugh.

The unofficial quantum task force, as well as about twenty other FBI agents, were skulking down the hall towards Agent Nate Sawyer's office. In the bland office building, it was kind of surreal. We were all wearing bulletproof vests. Everyone except me and Andro were armed with guns and bullets and all kinds of other lethal weapons.

I was armed with dread. This was not going to end well for Nate. I hoped he'd just surrender.

Instead of guns, me and Andro had ampules of adrenaline. We were supposed to counter any quantum shenanigans Nate might stir up.

"Are you sure you're up for this?" he whispered in my ear.

His warm breath on my cheek made me feel tingly. Tingly was a good sign that I'd recovered from my head-bashing.

Lisa glared at us. I knew her glare meant, *Shut up.*

I nodded back at Andro.

Lisa whispered into her mic. "At the first sign of q-lapsing, blurriness or white mist, shoot. Go!"

The agents all rushed down the hall to Nate's office, with me and Andro bringing up the rear.

By the time we arrived at Nate's office, he was blurring. "No! Nate, don't! They'll shoot you!" My chest felt like it was being made into metamorphic rock. They were going to execute him.

By the time he'd even glanced my way, the bullets were flying.

Oh, poor Nate. The bullets slammed into him, pummeling his body mercilessly. He was dead in seconds. There was no way anyone could survive that.

I looked him in the eyes, and right before he crumpled onto the floor in a bloody mess, I'd swear he looked sad and scared.

The bullets stopped.

Everyone froze, examining the pile of flesh on the carpet for a few moments. It didn't even look like a person anymore.

I felt sick. If I hadn't figured out how to q-lapse, he wouldn't have figured out how to q-lapse, and none of this would have happened.

"Did you have to shoot him?" Ryan asked, voice full.

"Yes. He went for his gun, and he was q-lapsing." Lisa nodded. "Good job, team. Now, we just have to get Griffin. So far, we haven't been able to track him down. Madison, we'll be in touch with you and your team as soon as we find him. Be ready."

"He's probably long gone," Ben said.

"Yeah." I had a feeling things wouldn't end well for Griffin either. At this point, I hoped he was long gone.

"Come on, Ryan, Ben, Madison, let's go home," Andro said softly.

I couldn't feel good about a body riddled with bullets no matter what the circumstances.

Chapter Thirty-Seven

The drive back to Boulder was subdued, to say the least. No one said anything until we hit the city limits.

"I don't think that was right," I finally said. I felt bad about participating in it.

"He broke the law," Ben said, sitting in the front passenger seat.

"I hate to say it," Ryan said from next to me in the back seat, "but I don't know what else they could have done. Q-lapsers are almost impossible to catch and impossible to secure."

Andro's eyes met my eyes in the rearview mirror. He seemed sympathetic. I really didn't want to participate in a similar take-down on Griffin.

"Ryan," Andro said, "I'm dropping you first. Madison, you're next." We were traveling north on Broadway.

Ben glanced at me with an expression that said, *He doesn't know you moved in with me?*

"Uh, actually, Andro, I'm living with Ben now."

"What?" Andro's face stilled.

"I mean, I'm renting a room from him," I said. "We're roommates, er, apartment-mates."

"Yeah, no biggie," Ben said.

Ryan didn't bat an eye at this opportunity to give me grief. He must be even worse off, sadder than I thought.

We dropped Ryan off without further conversation. "Say hi to Sydney and Emily for me," I called after him. At least they could come home now.

He just nodded and mumbled, "Yeah."

Once we got rolling again, Andro asked, "Can you give me directions, Ben?"

"Yeah. It's on north Broadway, near the old hospital."

"Andro, let's stop for coffee near there," I said. "I want to talk."

We dropped Ben at his building and went across the street to a coffee shop.

After getting coffees, we sat at one of the tiny bistro tables.

"What's up?" he asked. "What are we doing here? If you want to apologize for not telling me you're living with Ben, it's okay. Recent events have put things in perspective. I'm okay with it. You need a place to live. I get it."

Apologize? I hadn't even thought of that. "You're okay with it?" Why wasn't he jealous? "You get it? Why don't you care that I'm living with a hot cop?"

"Hot cop?" He frowned. "Well, for one thing, I didn't know you thought he was a hot cop." He paused and took a sip of coffee.

I took a big gulp and burned my mouth. Ow.

Andro gathered himself. "I care about you, Madison. I may love you."

May? That's not what he said before.

He continued, "But we already discussed this. Right now, Sophia has to be my first priority. If you want to date Ben, I can't stop you."

We stared at each other. I struggled not to get swept into his mesmerizing blue eyes.

He reached across the table for my hand and squeezed it gently. I got that warm-all-over tingly feeling again.

He could stop me. All he'd have to do is ask me not to.

"Can we put a pin in this?" I said. "I wanted to talk to you about Griffin. I'm not sure we're doing the right thing," I said. "He's practically a kid. He's never been convicted of a crime."

He withdrew his hand. Darn. "That's because he's never been brought to trial."

"They had him sedated! He's not even allowed to live his life in prison."

"He could q-lapse away." He paused. "You're not thinking of letting him get away, are you? He's dangerous. Remember last year when he attacked us?"

"When we were parked, making out?" I smiled. That

was a nice memory, right up until we got attacked. "But if you recall, they all ended up running away when their attack was unsuccessful." I paused and took a breath. "I don't want to kill Griffin. I don't think it's right. No one should be judge, jury, and executioner. And I don't think it's right to keep him sedated in prison."

"What do you propose?"

"I propose we find Griffin and talk to him." I knew none of the FBI agents or cops would agree with my plan, but Andro might. He was a compassionate man. "We could warn him to stop q-lapsing and tell him to stay out of Colorado."

"But q-lapsing is very powerful. Look what happened to Nate," he said. "It's hard to resist doing it."

"We resist doing it. Mostly."

"That's because it hurts," he said.

"Griffin had an aneurysm," I said. "He knows it hurts. He almost killed himself q-lapsing."

He threw up his hands. "All right. You convinced me. It's worth a try."

I felt a smile break out on my face. "Thank you, Andro. You won't regret it."

"There's a flaw in your plan. How can you track him down when the FBI can't? They checked his address. They checked his past addresses. They checked his girlfriend's address. As Ben said, he's probably long gone."

"Before he was taken into custody, he'd been living here for the last four years. All his friends are here in town, including his girlfriend. I had an idea," I said. "You know how I sublet a room from Isabella. Well, there was no record of that." Hence I lost my rent money. "This is a college town; there's subletting all over the place. What if his girlfriend is subletting? She's probably trying to keep a low profile." Especially if she'd been involved in quantum shenanigans last year.

"Okay," he said. "I'll follow your lead."

To make a long story short, we beat the bushes among the geeks on campus and got a lead on where Griffin's girlfriend might be living.

"Is this his girlfriend's place?" Andro asked.

"Supposedly. I hope it is. It's our best lead." Briefly, I considered our options and decided knocking would be the least intimidating. Knock. Knock.

A smiling co-ed answered the door. "Hello." I thought I recognized her as Griffin's girlfriend. Her smile drained away. "Shit." She turned back towards someone in the apartment. "They found you."

The white mist in the middle of the room coalesced into a rotund young Asian-American man.

I took a step forward. "Before you do anything, Griffin, we just want to talk."

"Really?" he asked.

I took another step forward, and Andro followed me.

"Yes," Andro said. "We're here to talk, Griffin."

Griffin looked like he wanted to believe Andro. Come to think of it, they knew each other before all this started. Griffin had been Andro's student.

"So, talk," Griffin said.

"The FBI took down Nate Sawyer," I said.

"Thank God." Griffin sank on the sofa. "That guy scared the shit out of me. What happened?"

"They shot him," Andro said.

"A lot," I said.

"Oh, no." Griffin blanched. "Are you here to shoot me?"

I held up my hands. "No. We're not here to shoot you."

Griffin started crying. "I don't want to go back to prison. They kept me drugged up. They fed me through a tube. Please, don't make me go back there. Please."

Andro met my eyes. "We don't want to send you back."

"The FBI does want to take you into custody, but we don't," I said.

"Please," Griffin said. "I'll do anything."

"We're glad to hear that," I said. "If you promise to stop q-lapsing and leave Colorado and never come back, we'll let you go."

"Stop q-lapsing?" he asked. "Forever?"

"Yes," I said. "When you q-lapse, I can detect it. So, basically, q-lapsing can lead me to you."

He looked like he wanted to argue, but his girl sat down

next to him. "We just found each other again. We could go to California," she said. "Together. We don't need that weird quantum stuff. Come on, Griff, let's go. Let's go together."

"All right." Griffin blew out a breath. "I agree. I won't q-lapse. I'll leave Colorado."

"I'm going to check up on you," I said. "If you cause any trouble, I'll have to revisit our agreement."

"All right," Griffin said, nodding. "I said, all right."

We talked logistics a few more minutes, and then Andro and I left.

The whole thing had been surprisingly quick and low-key. Overall, it was much, much better than helping the FBI mow someone down in a hail of bullets.

Phew. I unclenched. Did this mean all the quantum criminals were contained? Was the quantum craziness over?

In the hall, Andro said, "I think that was the right thing to do, but I hope we don't regret it. I hope he doesn't commit any more quantum crimes."

"I agree," I said, feeling myself relax. "But freedom is a pretty good incentive."

"And love," he said with a slight smile.

I met his eyes and matched his smile. "Yes, it is." My heart did a little backflip.

"Can you come over to my new place for dinner later?" he asked. "We need to talk some more."

I didn't want to talk with him. I wanted to do other things with him. Plus, I usually ended up more confused than ever after we talked. I sighed. "Well, I am curious about your new place. Sure. What can I bring?"

"Just your unique self." What did that mean?

Back at Ben's place, he was doing research on his computer.

"Well, shoot," he said, pushing his chair back from his desk. "I can't find this Griffin guy either."

"Huh. He's a slippery fellow," I said. "Last year, he lived on some private tropical island for a while, so he could be anywhere. Why are you looking? I thought the FBI was doing that."

"You know I want to work for the bureau someday," he said. "I'm trying to help."

"You already helped them when we took down Nate, remember?" With difficulty, I suppressed my shudder.

"True," he said. "Hey, Agent Baker said an Arjun Chatterjee robbed the Apple Store."

Oh, Arjun. I was disappointed. And sad.

"If I could just figure out who robbed those two sororities, I'd be on my way to being a quantum crime expert. Plus, those sorority girls would be happy with me. One of the girls thought the perp might be a fraternity guy, but how many hundreds of those are there around here?"

It hit me. I was sure my earlier hypothesis was correct. "I bet it was my students Drew and Brandon."

"What?" Ben asked. "How do you know?"

"They're hard-core fraternity guys," I said. "And who's more obsessed with sorority girls than fraternity guys?"

"That makes sense," he said.

"They're in my class, so they know about quantum mechanics. I'd thought someone was impersonating them one day because they did their homework. But what if it was just them? We called them after they disappeared, and they answered their cells, but that doesn't prove anything." It didn't prove anything. I'd been stupid.

"This is a great lead," Ben said. "Thanks, Madison!"

Now, what would happen to Drew and Brandon? "Wait a minute, Ben. Does a panty raid rate cops and the FBI, and who knows what?"

"If it was them, they broke the law. Trespassing."

"But they didn't really take anything."

"They took the girls' sense of safety and security."

I couldn't believe I was arguing with him. Young women did deserve to feel safe and secure. "That's true, but I'm worried what the FBI will do. Look at what they did to Nate."

"Yeah. That was intense." He rubbed his chin. "How about if me and a few of the other guys offer to keep a close eye on the sororities to make them feel safe again."

That sounded like a win-win all around. "I think the girls would appreciate that." The cops would definitely appreciate it.

He stood up and got a Coke from the fridge. "So, what's going on with you and Andro, anyway?"

"We're dating." My heart felt a little flip-floppy again.

"Is it exclusive?"

"Uh..."

"That means no." He grinned. "What's going on with you and me?"

"Nothing." Why did I feel disappointed?

"So, we're totally platonic?" His grin was gone.

"Yep."

"And you don't care if I bring women home and hook up with them?" Did he look sad? What did that mean? Why did I care?

Ugh. "Nope. That's part of being roommates. Go for it. Hook as you please."

He laughed a little. "That makes it sound like I'm a hooker."

"Huh. I guess that's where the phrase came from." Who knew?

"So, do you think it's over?" he asked. "All this quantum stuff?"

I didn't know. "I don't know." Too many people had died or been hurt. "I hope so."

"Me too." He shook his head as he strolled out of the kitchen back to his computer.

For my part, I went to take a shower and get ready for my evening.

I was very nervous as I stood outside Andro's door that night, with a six-pack of *Negra Modelo* and a large bouquet of flowers. I knocked.

"Come in," he said. "It's open."

I opened the door.

Standing on the other side was Andro and a beautiful little girl with his amazing blue eyes.

"Madison, I'd like you to meet my daughter, Sophia."

She giggled.

Wow. She was adorable. I was so glad Andro trusted me enough to introduce me to her.

I carefully knelt in front of her. "Sophia, it is a real honor to meet you."

QUANTUM MURDER

She smiled at me.
My eyes filled as I smiled back.

Science Fact: Interpretations of Quantum Mechanics

Interpretations of quantum mechanics (QM) fall within the realm of the philosophy of physics. They are a conceptual way to relate QM mathematics and concepts with QM observations and the physical meanings of these observations. There are three main types of interpretations: collapse theories, Many Worlds theories, and hidden variables.

The Copenhagen Interpretation, a collapse theory, is the most popular interpretation of QM. In this interpretation, QM predicts the probabilities for different outcomes of pre-specified observations. During the act of observation, the wavefunction describing the system collapses to one option. If there's no observation, there's no collapse, and none of the options ever become more or less likely. All the collapse theories work similarly, with only the cause of the collapse being different. For example, in objective collapse theories, the collapse occurs randomly, with observers playing no special role.

The Many Worlds Interpretation is the second-most popular interpretation. It posits that rather than a wavefunction collapse and a resulting single outcome, all possible options come to pass, creating an infinity of worlds. An individual human experiences only one outcome because he/she exists in only one of these infinite worlds.

Hidden variable interpretations are less popular than collapse and Many Worlds interpretations. But an elegant hidden variable interpretation is John G. Cramer's transactional interpretation of quantum mechanics. This interpretation describes quantum interactions in terms of a standing wave formed by both forward-in-time and backward-in-time waves. Recall a standing wave, which can also be called a stationary wave, is a wave in which each point of the wave has an associated constant amplitude. Thus, in the transactional interpretation, the source and the receiver both emit physically real retarded and advanced waves that cancel each other out. Thus, the wavefunction collapse doesn't happen at any specific time; rather, it occurs atemporally along the whole transaction. Notice here the emission, and absorption processes are time-symmetric.

For more information and details about these and other topics, check out the Physics Is Fun website: www.physicsisfun.net

Thank you for reading *Quantum Murder*. I hope you enjoyed it!

- For more info about me or my work, please go to my author website, http://www.lesleylsmith.com/. Sometimes, I post links for free fiction downloads!
- Please check out the Physics Is Fun website www.physicsisfun.net for lots of information about fun physics topics.
- Reviews help other readers find books. I appreciate any and all reviews.
- A sneak peek of my new novel *Kat Cubed* follows.

–Lesley L. Smith

Kat Cubed
Chapter One: Universe 1: Kat, April 25, 2100, 7:00 am

Sitting alone in the greenhouse Kat Garcia asked, "Where are you, Pa?" The scavenger team was way overdue. She strained her eyes, looking southeast towards Denver in the moments before dawn. Everything looked gray: gray buildings, gray dead trees, gray dead grass. The gray clouds overhead didn't help.

Did something move over there next to that ruined building? She stood and stared. No, it was just a dead bush shifting in the wind. She sat back down again. The top of the old physics building had the best sightlines in town, but even up here, she couldn't catch a glimpse of the missing team. Nervous, she plucked a sprig of baby spinach from the garden bed next to her and popped it in her mouth.

She needed Pa. He was the only family she had left. Ma was missing. Her sister Emma was dead. "Come home to me, Pa. Come on."

"Kat?" her best friend Pablo said from the stairwell.

She jumped. "Hi, buddy. What's up?"

"Who're you talking to?" He made his way through the plants and came and sat next to her.

"Nobody." She sighed. "Myself." That wasn't too crazy, was it? She touched Ma's locket. Ma had given it to her for safekeeping until she came back. That was months ago. Where was she?

"Any sign of the scavenger team?" he asked.

"Nope."

"They'll be okay," he said, patting her shoulder. "Your pa and the rest of the team are experienced scavengers." He was sweet.

Kat pointed at the first hint of light on the horizon. "But the sun's coming up."

"They know to take cover during the day. They know we're counting on them."

She glanced at Pablo's face. He seemed so sure. Maybe he was right. She hoped he was right. "What do you think'll happen if they never come back?"

"I don't know." He exhaled. "We'll cherish our memories of them."

Suddenly she had to blink back tears.

"And I guess we'll figure something out, like we always do. We'll survive." He rested his hand on her back. "The group might elect you to be the new leader."

That was another thing to worry about if Pa didn't come back. "I'm only twenty. I can't lead the group."

"I think you can." His faith was touching.

"So, what's happening downstairs?" she asked. "Is Fei any better?" A sick baby was the worst.

"No." His gaze dipped to the floor. "Her fever's up."

"And we don't have any medicine." She scanned the edge of campus again. No sign of the missing team. "Did they try wet cloths to bring down her fever?"

"Yeah. But we're getting low on water."

"Not good."

"No," he said. "Not good."

Light blossomed over the horizon, illuminating everything in its path. The old university buildings were shades of pink and tan and red. All the vegetation was a dead crunchy brown except a narrow strip of green along the creek in the distance.

Kat knew some of that green stuff was willow. She also knew willow was a natural fever reducer. "What if we went over to the creek and got some medicine for Fei?"

"What? Now?" His voice squeaked a bit. "It's after sunrise. We can't go outside."

She pointed up at the sky. "It's pretty cloudy." She lowered her voice. "Do you think Fei will last another day?"

"No." His whole body slumped.

"Come on, Pablo. We can do it. It'll be an adventure.

Please come with me and help."

He glanced at her. "You're going whether I agree or not, aren't you?"

"Yes." She smiled in what she hoped was a charming way. "Come on; you know you want to help baby Fei. Wouldn't it feel great to save someone? Wouldn't it feel great to have a win for once?" She was ready for something good to happen. She was sick of losing all the time: losing faith, losing hope, losing people. "Come on."

He blew out a big gust of air. "You know I have trouble resisting you, Kat."

Oh, she knew. She was his best friend, after all. She grinned.

Down in the basement, the group didn't even bat an eye at Kat and Pablo going out after sunrise to get willow bark for Fei. Of course, Fei's parents, Bao and Chang, were beside themselves with worry, so they weren't going to object. But Kat thought someone would say, *Oh, it's too dangerous. You can't do it.* or *Wow, how heroic, Kat.* But no one did.

They geared up as quickly as they could. The danger was the sun. They wore lightweight loose cotton clothing and big hats. Pablo carried a thermometer with an alarm. They'd seen people die of heatstroke, and it wasn't pretty.

On the bright side, there were some old underground maintenance tunnels to the creek--which was one of the reasons they were living in the physics building. The tunnels were about seven feet wide and seven feet tall with a concrete floor and cinderblock walls, so they tramped to the creek in comfort.

Once they hiked about a quarter-mile, Pablo asked, "How'd your ma know about willow bark?"

"Ma's ma knew about herbal medicine and taught her some stuff. And, then, after Emma..." Kat swallowed. "After we lost Emma, Ma studied even more. She consulted every herbalist and doctor we met, and she had a bunch of books. She swore she'd never let anyone else die on her watch."

Ma was her hero. Was she still alive? Kat didn't see how she could be. She'd been gone too long. She wouldn't leave them alone so long if she'd had anything to say about it. Her eyes started to fill.

"Kat?"

She exhaled. She was on a mission, a mission to save a baby. Ma would approve.

"You miss them, huh?"

"Yes." She glanced over at him. "I know you miss your family, too." Pablo'd lost track of his parents during the Water Wars. He had no idea if they were alive or dead. And there was no way to find out.

"*Sí,*" he said.

They walked in silence for a few minutes.

"So, tell me about Emma," he said. "What was she like?"

Ma's locket held a picture of Emma. She resisted the urge to open it and look at the image yet again. "She wasn't much like me."

"She sounds great." Pablo grinned at her, trying to lighten the mood.

"She was very wise and nice and nurturing."

"You're right. Nothing like you." Kat knew he was joking.

"She was a lot like Ma. But in some ways, she wasn't; for example, she taught me about boys."

"Ooh. What did she teach you?"

"Let's see; she said boys like food and compliments." When she looked at Pablo, he was still grinning. "Who taught you about boys?"

"I'm self-taught. What can I say? I'm a genius?"

"What about your friend, Jake?"

"Jake? He was straight, but a real *hermano*." He sighed. "I miss him." Jake was another person he'd lost.

"What was he like?" she asked.

"He loved weather, of all things," Pablo said. "He could even predict it sometimes. Like when we'd get a windy spell, he'd say *A front's moving in.* And he'd be right. And he had a great sense of humor. We played so many tricks on his older brother Jason."

The tunnel brightened as they neared the end. The temperature was already rising.

They turned off their flashlights and set them down in the

tunnel.

"I want to hear about those tricks at some point," she said as they emerged. Even near sunrise, the heat pummeled them.

The scents of dried plants and dust made Kat sneeze.

"Gaia bless you," he said, squinting and looking up. "Still cloudy."

"Let's hurry," she said, pointing in the direction of the creek. "Can you check if there's any water running?" They usually went to the old reservoir to get water, but there might be some here since the plants were still alive.

"Yes, ma'am." He saluted.

Kat grinned as she jogged to the willows. They looked great–still green and alive. She got a small pocketknife out of her bag and started stripping bark off the closest tree. Sweat gathered on her back and face.

Pablo ran up, putting an empty bottle back in his bag. "Bad news. No water that I could see." He got out his own knife.

"It must be underground? I hope so, anyway. I hope these trees don't die." Even though it was cloudy, it was still plenty light outside. She couldn't even remember the last time she'd been outside during the day. A drop of sweat rolled into her eye.

He started stripping bark.

"Don't take too much from any one tree." She wiped her forehead.

"Yes, ma'am." They stripped bark. "It's kind of weird being outside during the day, huh?"

She shot him a look. Wow, his thoughts were similar to hers. "Yeah."

"Do you think things will ever go back to the way they used to be?"

"What way is that?" Before Emma died? Before Ma disappeared? Before Pablo's family disappeared?

Before Pa didn't come back?

"You know, when we lived during the day and slept at night," he said. "When we didn't have to worry so much about surviving. When we lived regular lives."

301

Even with all this cloudiness, Kat was getting h-o-t. She felt another bead of sweat slide down her back. "Do you even remember that? I mean, Ma and Pa told me we lived up in an actual town in the mountains when I was a little girl, but I hardly remember it." Thinking about everything that had been lost was too depressing. They didn't really even have a civilization anymore.

"I remember some stuff," he said. "We also lived up in the mountains. I went to school with Jake and his brother. My ma was a wonderful cook."

Kat held up a finger. "So, Emma was right. Boys do like food."

The clouds shifted, and the rays of sunlight pierced them like daggers. She knew the sun was deadly, but it seemed so cheerful.

The temperature alarm went off.

Pablo shoved a handful of bark in his bag and grabbed the thermometer. "We need to go back now."

She shoved some more bark into her own bag. She didn't want to have to come back here for a good long time. She stepped towards another tree.

"Now, Kat," he said, face grim. "I'm not kidding. It's getting dangerously hot out here."

She brought him along for a reason. She knew he'd keep them safe. "Okay."

Back in the tunnels, they picked up their flashlights and started walking back to the physics building.

Trying to lighten the mood again, she said, "Tell me about those tricks you and Jake used to play."

But he just sighed and said, "I'm not up for it, Kat."

At their encampment in the basement, most folks had gone to bed by the time they got back. Kat showed Bao and Chang how to make the fever-reducing tea out of the willow bark.

After a long night's work in the greenhouse, not to mention the stress of the creek mission, she was practically asleep before her head hit the pillow.

Kat was awakened by a scream. A strange bluish light

filled the lab. She'd never seen
anything like it. It came from a freaky window floating in mid-air! She carefully picked her way through the bedrolls to the strange window.

Pablo appeared at her side. "Gaia." He joined her in staring at the thing.

She whispered, "Gaia." As she peered inside, two people, a man and a woman, moved closer. She could almost make them out.

They moved closer yet.

Then, Pablo whispered, "Jake."

Kat's heart caught in her throat, and her fingers reached for her locket. "Emma?"

www.ingramcontent.com/pod-product-compliance
Lightning Source LLC
Chambersburg PA
CBHW071127200626
46817CB00018B/2363

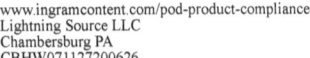